God's Arm

A Novel About Jesus The Man

William Anderson

Morning Star Press
2990 Hardman Ct.
Atlanta, Ga., 30305
404-233-6553

ISBN 0-9665914-0-2
Library of Congress Catalog Card Number: 98-091720

Printed and bound in the United States of America
First Edition

First Published in 1998

Cover Design by Iscah Rampersad

For Mother,
who now knows first hand
of the truth
and the light and the way

"*And to whom is the arm of the Lord revealed? For he shall grow up before him as a tender plant, and as a root out of dry ground: he hath no form nor comeliness; and when we shall see him, there is no beauty that we should desire him. He is despised and rejected of men; a man of great sorrows, and acquainted with grief: and we hid as it were our faces from him; he was despised, and we esteemed him not.*"

Isaiah 53

CHAPTER 1

The screams carried almost to the edge of town.

The fishermen far from the docks and the city easily heard the prayers and pleadings, and then the piercing scream of anguish rolling to them like something unfurling: that tunneled, distant, echoing way that sound arrives on quiet water, distinct from the swooshing of a flung net, or the rude abruptness of oar against hull. This was a scream wound in words, but words hard to separate because they were rolling over one another in agony: clear in their pain, but confusing in their message.

Eli Ben Yohanin, Jewish zealot, bandit, murderer, man of God, was being crucified. Only a handful of friends, mostly family, were there as witnesses. Over the years Eli had led several hundred farmers and orchard men in ambushes against Jews they saw as defiling the Laws, and against any solitary Roman soldier they found along the highways. But now, in his final hour, those who had been inspired by his words and bravery had melted away in fear of being hanged alive on a tree alongside their leader. Some stood back in the thickness of the olive trees and cedars growing behind the place of the cross. They wept over their own cowardice, ripping at their clothing and pounding their chests in grief. But the might of the Romans was terrifying in its swiftness and brutality against any who would defy its laws. So his friends laid back, ashamed behind the twisted trunks of the trees, skulking like shadows in the gathering dusk of the late afternoon.

While his mother wept, falling heavily upon the ground, heaving in wails and washed in a flow of tears, four Roman soldiers grappled with Eli's struggling body. He had been brutally scourged and was weakened from loss of blood, so they quickly tied his lower legs to the beam cut out of an acacia tree, and tied his wrists to the crossbeam bolted across it. Eli drifted in and out of consciousness. His back and loins had been ripped open with a whip of twelve leather lashes. At the end of each lash, a dull-bronze ball was held by leather strips. Pieces of skin glistened where the strips wrapped over the balls. His back had been flayed open, but he was bleeding even more profusely from the inside of his legs at his groin where larger veins had been opened.

First, two nails were driven through two small blocks of wood so that Eli could not tear his feet off them. The nail point was placed against his left ankle first. The officer nodded his head at the four soldiers to hold Eli tightly; then he quickly slammed a heavy mallet against the nail, driving it, smashing and splintering through the ankle bones and ripping tendons and rupturing nerves, muscle, and veins. They knew he would impulsively try to wrench free at the next strike, so the move was quick and it drove the nail through the ankle and into the beam. The officer tightened his shoulder and threw his back into the third blow, which embedded the nail securely in the wood.

To mask the pain, Eli attempted to yell a prayer as he saw the officer again raise the mallet. "Holy Father, I come to…," but the second nail sent a pain that caught the words in a scream that rolled them into a wail and sent them again out over the water and toward the town of Capernaum a mile to the East. Eli swooned when the searing pain shot up his right leg from the blow of the second nail into his ankle. He was now straddling the thick beam with his ankles nailed on its sides. Dark blood, almost like oil, welled out of both wounds and the skin blackened around the nails. They would leave his arms stretched and tied to the cross beam. The rope would hold his body weight better than nails through the wrists, and it was easier to remove him by rope. Six of the soldiers grasped the cross, waited for their officer to bark an order, then lifted it and dropped it with a thud into a hole they had dug that morning.

The fishermen heard the screams no more. The moans and soft tearful prayers of the slow dying Jew were now only for his prostrate mother and his four sons who were pounding their chests and ripping at their clothing in anguish. Twelve guards stood at attention around the cross. Eli's feet were only slightly off the ground in order to make it easier to remove his body when he died.

"Anybody want to bet on this one?" the officer barely turned his face to the guards as he cautiously eyed Eli's wailing, thrashing sons.

A muscular soldier answered, "He won't make it to morning, to the first hour."

This started a round of wagering among the guards as to when Eli Ben Yohanin would breathe his last. Roman soldiers would pass no opportunity to wager, especially when confronted with the task of spending the afternoon and night guarding a dying and despised enemy.

"I've got to go into town and get the circulars up," the officer said as he moved away from the soldiers and started down the lakeshore road toward town.

As he left, the muscular guard sneered, "Don't waste the papyrus. These zealots read only their own laws. Announcing the death of one of their bandits has ten more wanting to ambush one of us."

The place of crosses was enough outside the seaside town of Capernaum that the smell of any bodies left hanging after death would not reach the city's limits. Also, the village magistrate had requested that no screams be heard by anyone coming or going from the small public bath. It was a place for relaxation and business, and a place where no one wanted to be bothered with the shrieking of Jewish bandits.

The last lingering light of day saw the family move away in a symphony of wails. Eli's mother was carried on a blanket litter, her shrieks punctuating the dusk with the high-pitched cry of a snared animal. Her sons rode the wave of her pain with their own cries, curses, and pleas that the Holy Father deliver them all from the Angels of Darkness called Romans.

Night sifted in under the olive tree grove that stood behind Eli's cross. The temperature dropped, and he shook uncontrollably. Because Jews considered public nakedness a disgrace and an insult to their Lord, the guard had stripped him naked. Blood clotted over the lashes, except several so deeply dug, that they lay open to the white bone beneath. The wounds, where the nails had been driven in, continued to pulse blood out in tiny rivulets. Eli attempted to pull himself up to relieve the excruciating pain. His breathing was becoming labored because of the extension of his arms. It was the path to death. Slow asphyxiation: a drowning in one's own fluids. For some the ordeal took three days.

The night had revealed itself in a canopy of stars and a crescent moon. No one traveled at night. Robbers skulked the roads, lurkers with curved knives; predators who cared not for one's religion or nation. When the clear clumping of a donkey's hooves broke the quiet, the guards stopped their gambling game. Looking away from the dancing flames of their campfire, they saw a child-sized figure heavily robed and leaning so far forward on the donkey that they assumed whoever it was had fallen asleep. A hood covered the head, completely shadowing the face. The guards quickly dismissed the passing figure as nothing to be concerned about and returned to their wagering. Eli was alone some yards away. With his arms bound up and outward on the cross beam, Eli could now take only shallow breaths. The pain at the point of the nails was searing. He alternately attempted to relieve the pressure by pulling up on his arms, but that was short-lived, and when he stopped pulling, the pressure of his body went knifing back into his ankles. He fainted repeatedly.

He prayed constantly when conscious, which started to annoy the soldiers. "You want to break his legs?" one asked. "Can't do it," another answered. The decree was that he was to die slowly. He had murdered a local Jewish patriarch, called a scoffer and lawless, who owed a Roman of equestrian rank a lot of money. Eli proclaimed himself a Jew dedicated to driving the Romans out of Israel and to punishing Jews who left the faith. His group had robbed and killed many in their vain attempt to stir the Jewish people to an uprising. Eli would be an example. It was hoped he would survive two or three days gasping for air, screaming in pain for all those passing by to see and hear and become sick at their stomach and to tremble in absolute terror that it could be them up there if they angered the Romans.

So the guards had carried their coals a distance away from the moans. The hooded rider nodded in their direction. They ignored his salutation and stoked the fire, and didn't see or hear as Eli's fifteen-year-old son pulled a spear from under his cloak, slowed the donkey in front of the cross, and flung the spear with all his might into the torn and blood-caked chest of his father.

Eli, seeing his son raise the spear, smiled and whispered, "Thank you for taking me from this cross."

He never felt the spear point as it pierced his heart and stopped its struggling beat. The donkey quickened its pace, and the boy jammed his hand against his mouth to muffle his cries of sorrow. The guards wrapped themselves against the growing chill, and Eli, with a sigh as soft as the settling evening, sank in death onto the nails.

CHAPTER 2

Sea gulls hung as though pinned to the air, pulled with unseen strings by the ship; chalk-white beggars on the wing awaiting a tossed scrap. But scraps had been stowed as The Apollo was packed and prepared for landing.

The magnificence that King Herod had wished to portray, the glory he had seen as Rome, shimmered like a distant promise out over the unruffled sea to the approaching ship.

With little wind, the captain was having to work his sails to capture a pulse in the languid sea air. The ship barely glided over the watery blue plane stretching to the nearing shore. The white stone finish of the new harbor city of Caesarea Maritima beckoned across the calm distance, first by the flames atop its lighthouse that snarled and flickered in the spring afternoon, and then by three enormous statues towering like extended arms from both sides of the harbor's entrance. The upper stories of the enormous palace, the amphitheater, and the columned temples all glowed in alabaster-white from the fawning sunlight. It was an unforgettable sight for the cargo ships sailing the Great Sea between Egypt, Rome, and Athens, especially in an early evening like this, all enriched by the angle of the settling sun.

"We sail on fires," the slight, fine-faced Roman mused.

The sun was spilling its late light out over the waters in a jeweled array.

"You should have been Greek," his muscular friend murmured as he too looked back toward the settling sun and its offering

Caesarea, named after Caesar Augustus, was a marvel of engineering and construction in the god-forsaken desolation of the north Palestinian coast; a featureless sand and scrub area where the sea made a seamless merger with the shallow shore.

Herod, King of Judea, a brutal and brilliant schemer and dreamer, created one of the great harbors of the eastern world by devising new construction technologies that required innovation and monumental taxation and labor. So badly was a harbor needed here that it became an overnight success. It was a perfect midpoint, a crossroads between the spice and silks of India, the horses and peppers of Arabia, and the grains of Egypt. The buying power of Rome drove the enterprise. Rome lacked the agricultural base to supply the growing unemployed hoards streaming into it. Egypt, especially, had become the essential source for the breads cooked in Italian ovens; the grains given freely by the Emperor to keep the destitute thousands from further disrupting the life of the empire's governing center.

"The gods are smiling on us, Cassius," Julian Lycanius said as he settled into a folded bit of mast while they gazed over the open waters toward the approaching harbor. "There are moments like this that I want to reach out and capture in my hand, to release on another day, to see all over again." He turned his head toward his reclining friend, "Which god do you think favors us with this beauty?"

Cassius Orelius had put on his best tunic of linen, rubbed ointments over his skin and carefully combed his brown hair forward, dousing it with perfumes.

"Do you refer to this beauty?" Cassius smiled as he stared at himself in a bronze mirror. "This tan would be the envy of any god," he boasted. He had taken advantage of the voyage down from Rome to brown over his pale skin.

Taking a small glass bottle from a bag, he quickly turned it up, took a mouthful and began to swirl it around in his mouth. "What is it about the urine from Spain that is so special?" he asked as he spit the yellowish liquid over the bow. Smacking his mouth, he said, "Now I await the lips of the most beautiful this land offers. They will get no angry breath from these Roman lips."

"Hah," Julian laughed. "It will take more than the sweet smell of Spanish urine to attract even these barbarians to a face a god would run from. Even the 'She Wolves' in Pompeii would not take your money."

"She Wolf? Do I know the meaning?"

Julian laughed, "That's what we call the women of the brothel. When they have finished with a customer, they stand on the sidewalk and howl to announce they are available. And they are cheap; only two jars of bad wine."

"And what if you fathered a child…would you leave it at the city gate exposed?"

"I have no need of such places, but those who wish no child wrap their parts in animal intestine," Julian answered.

Cassius made a mock kick at his oldest friend and kidded, "In Rome we don't need brothels or intestines. We have our slaves whether willing or not." He waved his hand toward the approaching city. "But you…what will you do? We meet the two most beautiful, the two richest women of the city, and what will my poor artist friend

6

do? He will say, 'Wait! Before we bed, allow me to draw you for my next fresco!'"

Cassius adjusted a gold armlet on his right forearm. "You are not a lover; you're a brush man, a painter, the son of a senator; one who would dishonor his father by working with his hands. Why you are no better than a working man!" He chided.

Julian's lips turned up at the edges in a contented smile. "Why do I agree to sail the seas with one so vulgar? Be kind to me or I will have a god take your words to the ear of your father-in-law. His sword would render you quickly incapable of bedding a dog, much less a beauty. But we will see who is the first, my friend. The women do love my paintings, you know. They see me as tender as a loving god. You're just another rutting brute." He looked up mischievously.

Born the son of one of Rome's wealthiest lenders and apartment owners, Cassius knew the importance of status and of presentation. He had been a classmate of Julian's in schools in Italy and Greece. Both had been tutored in their homes by the same traveling Greek teachers. And they had belonged to the same gymnasium and found the same philosophers to their liking, but Cassius was traveling to this land, called both Palestine and Judea, not for the pleasures he could wring out of study, but for the money he could secure for himself through commercial ventures.

Returning to Julian's original question, Cassius responded, "My two young children would say we owe this moment to the Egyptian god Isis. Her ceremonies with processions, music, and tossed flowers are a delight to them. My wife would also choose this goddess. Anna talks often of Isis' purity, and of her devotion to finding her murdered husband, Osiris, and bringing him back to life."

He paused staring at his hands and admired their muscular thickness. "Having an afterlife is important to my dear wife. But that notion rarely crosses my mind, nor the minds of my more reasoned friends. We have agreed that this life, this moment, is all we have. After that…. the long sleep of eternity. My wife does not want to die and be dead." He spoke in a detached way, seemingly not bothered at all by the thought.

Cassius studied his face in the mirror. Every feature was an event. His head was not large, but his nose was bold and slightly bent at the middle. His eyes were heavily browed and brooding, and his lips were spread wide in a sensual thickness. He felt that his face compared favorably to many of the classical statues in his family's gardens. He wondered if a statue would ever be made in his honor. At least life size or larger would be preferable.

Cassius propped his left foot on a water jug wedged in the ship's bow. The breeze brushed his face like a soft hand. His eyes narrowed against the moving air and the hard light of the setting sun. They were tacking to the south across the sun's beam in order to enter the harbor from a northern angle with the wind at their backs. He felt a slight spray, a mist, rise from the cut of the bow. The ship rode heavily weighted down with Italian marble purchased by a new city official for the rebuilt town of Sepphoris.

Julian stared at the wet oak planking of the ship's deck. "My father said I do not know how to enjoy leisure. He said I bore too easily. He even shouted at me before we sailed and said I should have been the son of a dye maker or coppersmith where I could labor like a scavenging dog. I told him I agreed with Seneca that even though I am a man born to the leisure class, I need something to conquer."

Cassius looked at Julian affectionately, "I remember when I first met you, Julian. You were quoting Aristotle's 'The Sense of Wonder', and you still seek discovery. But my world is more of reasoning like the Stoics. I prefer Pythagoras and Plato; my love of commerce fits nicely into their belief in numbers and reasoning as the essence of our universe. God is in the numbers. As Plato said, 'Mathematics will draw the soul toward truth'. But I must say I agree with what our friend Seneca said when we heard him speak on Reason. He thinks Reason would be God's name if there were only one god. To perfect my reasoning is to come close to the gods. Perhaps I would even become a god," he half-laughed at the thought.

Cassius had taken a small vial of scented oil from a pocket and spread its dark thickness over his face. He liked the slight sheen it gave his pale skin. "Mine are Mercury, the god of commerce, and Money, the god of the deal." He then said dismissively, "Religion is a way for the state to control the masses. It's all about festivals and banquets. Entertain them and they will love you."

Julian nodded approvingly as he sketched his friend. Julian admired Cassius' tall figure and the mock heroic stance he could take, shifting his weight to one hip and holding his muscular arms slightly away from the body so the blood seemed to bring a fullness, a marbled roundness, to their form. Drawing had been a compulsion since Julian was a child. His father had wanted him to move quickly through his military duties, gaining honor and status there, then

8

come back to Pompeii and join in the family warehouse business along the docks. But after serving in Spain, Julian went back to study and apprentice under the flourishing reputation of the landscape wall-painter Studius, who had elevated the art of wall painting to a bold new level. Before giving up on his son as a dreamer and an artist for the rich, Julian's father told him to tour some of the provinces, to study their philosophies and the wonders of the eastern areas, and to come home and at least take some part in the family's growing real estate empire. The father promised it would result in a greater life of leisure and idleness; the goal of every self-respecting Roman. No Roman elite worked with their hands, and though the work of artists was admired, the fact that their creations required manual labor was seen as contemptible.

Julian had been invited to do a series of small sketches for the Emperor Tiberius at his villa on Capri. While there, Julian and the other apprentices and various guests had to endure endless pointless questions with which the eccentric Emperor bored his dinner company. 'Who were the ancestors of Pan?' was a favorite, and other obscure minutia on the gods. Julian took leave of Tiberius and his growing derangement after a month, saying he had sprained his wrist in a fall while admiring the villa's fish farm. The brief work had earned him a complimentary letter from the Emperor, thanking Julian for the short, but much admired art he had created.

"Rome is right," Cassius said, as he gazed toward the gleam of Caesarea.

"You mean, my friend, that only Rome, or someone trying to curry favor with Rome, could have built a harbor so beautiful. But I heard that the harbor at Alexandria is the greatest of all sights," Julian said.

"Well, we all must admit that we have slavishly copied the designs of the Greeks, but still, even a conniving desert rat like Herod can rise to greatness by emulating the grandeur that we added to the Greek designs." Cassius wrapped his cloak over his chest. The air was chilling, as a sudden wind clapped the flagging sails and swelled them into ushers carrying the ship forward in a lurch.

"I would please to disagree with you, honored Cassius," a short, expensively dressed man suddenly appeared on the deck next to them. The perfume in his gray, thinning hair survived the ocean wind to wrap his presence in expensive smells.

"Ah, the notable Marcus Tullius, we have seen little of you on this voyage. Welcome to the deck and a beautiful sunset." Cassius

9

responded to the ancient figure wrapped in a thick cotton cloak. His long face was the color of time; a cloud-pale, an ancient map streeted with blue veins, crevassed and creased as though each of life's events had chiseled its own signature. His skin was stretched to the thinness of mist.

"Voyages and my stomach do not agree. I have emptied more of myself into these cursed waters than I knew I was made of." His voice retained the gravelly, authoritarian vestiges of a man of rank, but was filtered through his bout with seasickness and eighty years of life.

"Forgive me, Cassius, but I overheard your description of Herod, and I do not mean to debate your opinion, but I was a part of his circle and I saw him as a man of infinite complexities. A rat, I must admit, was a part of that mosaic."

Julian gathered his robe and stood to show respect for this elder; a man who was known in all of the better circles of Rome for a costly arch he paid for on the Capitoline Hill. Marcus was also a major arbitrator between the Jewish ruling class in Jerusalem and the court of the Emperor. All sides trusted him. It was said he knew more about the inner workings of both the Sanhedrin and the Roman Senate than any man in Judea. He was returning from Rome after meeting a group of investors who wanted better ties to the big Jewish grain exporting companies in the port city of Alexandria, Egypt. The High Priest in Jerusalem had also given him several complaints about Pontius Pilate, but that was normal, and the complaints were not urgent. The priests still seethed over Pilate's appropriating much of the treasury of the Temple to build an aqueduct and reservoir. It showed his deep disregard for those he ruled.

"You told us as we left Italia that you owned much land here. Was that payment for service to Herod?" Julian asked. It was common for military officers and soldiers to be paid off in land in the countries in which they served.

"Yes. I was sent to Palestine by the Emperor Octavian in the springtime now many seasons ago. He had named Herod king and wanted someone he trusted to serve as his ears inside Herod's circle. I was only seventeen, but had assisted my father in the Senate and knew the workings of Rome well. I was sent as an advisor for Herod's water projects, so that he would not know my real purposes. My father had overseen much of the aqueduct and sewer construction in Rome.

He looked away from the men and toward the setting sun. His eyes recaptured another place.

"That August we were all shocked by the suicides of Antony and Cleopatra. Herod had supported Antony and knew Cleopatra well. He was depressed for months. I found myself coming close to him. I was taken by the grandness of his plans for converting Judea into a modern state with all of the architecture and engineering of Rome. I designed and oversaw his major water projects. Perhaps you will visit Solomon's Pools and the cisterns and aqueducts at Machaerus." His pride reflected through his drawn visage.

"So you see Herod as a visionary, a giant on this little stage?" Julian queried.

"As a Roman I see him as one who took a land of peasants and turned it into a modern state loyal to Rome. He knew the power in architecture. Everything we built was built on a grand scale as a symbol to show the power of both Herod and the state. Even after seeing the grandeur of Rome, you will be impressed by the Temple he built in Jerusalem. As a man, however, I saw him as one of dangerous personal appetites and a ruthlessness that sent many Jews to their graves. By killing off much of the Jewish leadership and installing his own friends in the Sanhedrin, he set up a conflict that agonizes Palestine to this day."

"Why is that?" asked Julian with a growing fascination.

"The priests who rule the Jews are supposed to be of a certain lineage, but Herod installed his own priests, so that many of the nation deeply resent their own leaders. And, as leaders will do, many have enriched themselves and the over-taxed peasants resent that also. Many say that Herod the Jew defiled his own religion."

Julian noticed Marcus's face abandon the conversation as he appeared to be in sudden discomfort. "I must say, honored one, you look as though the seasickness has returned."

"My stomach says I must again feed the fish," Marcus growled as he caught his throat and hobbled toward the other side of the boat to vomit.

Ignoring the old man's nearby wretchings, Julian mused, "We are an inspiration to ourselves, but I'm not so sure what we always bring to those we have conquered."

"Peace, security, the greatest set of laws the world has known, engineering, discipline, and," Cassius threw his head back and yelled with a pretentious joy, "and the most wonderful baths."

Julian yelled, "Captain, does this city have baths? We demand a warm bath, a hot bath, and a cold bath! We want mosaics, and cake sellers, and flutists, and a grand palaestra to work out on, or else turn this rat-infested vessel around!" They both shook in laughter.

"No baths, no docking!" they chanted in unison.

The Captain, a friend of Cassius' family, left the wheel and stood above the men. "Quiet your tongues. Old Herod left you the finest baths on the coast. Perhaps you will even find some young Arabians, a red-skinned Egyptian, or an olive-skinned Syrian who will do more than smile at your handsome Roman faces."

Julian grinned, "You mean they allow women in with the men?"

"Only to pull arm hairs," he mocked at them.

"Pull arm hairs!" Cassius complained, "Is that all they will pull?"

They all laughed, sensing the excitement of landing the boat and having arrived safely from a sea route that claimed almost as many as it allowed to finish their voyages.

Two small boats were being rowed out to act as a tow into the north end of the harbor. No one was allowed to come in under their own sail. The Captain left to guide the throwing of a rope to the oarsmen, and to work the rudder.

The two travelers stood, stretching their lean frames, and told their slaves to gather the belongings. The entrance to the harbor was before them, and the splendor of Caesarea now presented itself under a full sunset. As the small ship entered, they craned their necks and looked skyward at the massive statues towering to unprecedented heights over the harbor entrance.

"I am continually proud to be a Roman," Cassius boasted at the achievement of art and construction that went into the statues.

"You mean you admire Roman engineering and Greek design," Julian corrected. "But these towers truly are splendid in their size."

The Captain yelled to them, "The big statue there is called Drusion after Augustus' stepson. And, see, over there to the left outside the city wall is the amphitheater."

All of their eyes filled with the wonders of this white-stoned salute to the ego of Herod, the engineering advances of Rome, and the inspiring architecture of Greece.

As they passed into the still harbor waters, it was easy to see how Herod had created this sheltered area. He had extended out from the shore great encircling arms in the form of a broad-topped stone sea wall.

12

"By the gods it must have been rough anchoring along these coasts with no protected harbors," the Captain noted. "The winds would forever blow you to shore."

Cassius nodded and shuddered, "I can't imagine sailing all the way from the Tiber to the Nile without a decent bath or cafe. Praise the vision of Herod for creating this masterpiece against such a blank canvas."

Julian looked at his friend and chided him, "Yes, yes, I do believe an artist stirs beneath this man of numbers. The next thing I know, you will be borrowing my colors, insisting I allow you to work on my next fresco."

"Leave me my hot baths, a good night of theater, an evening with important friends, and a deal where I outsmart a seller: these are the true arts; the arts of pleasure, the art of profit-making," Cassius glowed in the certitude of his philosophy of life.

They were slowly pulled by the straining oarsmen into the glassy surface of the harbor. Sailing boats of all sizes and descriptions sat in the stilled water as if they were beached — sails folded, anchors lowered, weathered, gray-brown hulls with black tar waterproofing smeared and oozing from between their boards. Each vessel was its own story of daring and of profits sought as they plied the broad sea with each in its own splendid and dangerous isolation. Few passengers left any shore's safety to embark on a voyage across the void without first adorning themselves with amulets and other items to appease the gods. Few left the home shore without looking long at their waving loved ones, capturing that moment as though it might be their last well wish.

The wharf turned into a crowd of hoisters and loaders, and customs people and captains checking off each wine-filled amphora, each box and bottle, sacks of grains, animals and birds, and all the other effects of the civilizations of that world. Records were well kept. Shouts and orders, straining groans, side conversations, and laughter all gave the wharf area the feeling of a great bazaar, filled with the smells and objects of countries and craftsmen both near and far. Greek, Aramaic, Berber, Arabic, Thracian; they all came together in a symphony of diverse languages at this grand crossroads.

"Shall we try to see the procurator Pilate tonight?" Julian asked.

"The morning may be best. It will be well into dinner time before we can get situated. I hope that my lawyer Paulius has someone waiting for us," Cassius said as he strained from the ship's railing to see among the crowd on the dock someone who might be an emissary of his friend. "We will be staying at his villa. I have a letter from my father, explaining that I am here to look for business opportunities, and there are several villas for which you've been hired to do murals." Cassius then checked his baggage to make sure he knew the location of the letter.

It was custom and decorum to present oneself to the city officials, all of whom could be essential in a new world, albeit a Roman world, but one also filled with strange tongues and constant danger outside the city's limits.

"What do you know of this Pontius Pilate?" Julian inquired.

"The usual story of these province rulers; a military man, a political appointee who got the position because that royal court manipulator, Sejanus, whom Tiberius fawns over, is a friend of Pilate's wife. What Tiberius doesn't know is that Sejanus conspires against him, and if Sejanus ever goes, Pilate would go with him.

"Herod's son Archelaus was the first ruler over this land, but was a little over-eager in establishing his authority after his father died. He crucified so many Jews that their leaders traveled to Rome and appealed to Tiberius to throw out the despot. The Emperor agreed the crucifixion of a thousand Jews was a little too much, and wanting to avoid further unrest, he just made Judea, the area around Jerusalem, a full Roman province. This created a position to which Pilate was appointed. But the Jews were allowed to continue ruling their people from Jerusalem as long as they kept the peace. So what was the first thing this bumbler Pilate did? As Marcus just said, he robbed their treasury so he can build an aqueduct. Oh, yes, to show the Jews that they were under the rule of Rome, he put banners with the Emperor's face on them in the Jews' temple." Cassius chuckled, "The Jews went straight to Tiberius again, stomping and screaming, which upset the very emotional Emperor. So Pilate now walks on thin ground. My father says the High Priest in Jerusalem is a shrewd balancer. He knows Pilate must acquiesce on certain matters important to the Jews' laws, or they will appeal to the Emperor. It is interesting that the Jews are allowed to make their own coins."

"Their own coins? What's wrong with ours?" Julian asked.

"Oh, their religion forbids them to have images of people, animals …on anything."

"No images of a man's likeness? Why, I've never heard of such foolishness," Julian said with the annoyance of an artist detecting censorship.

"I understand their God commanded that they not worship any other image, and they take that to mean pictures of people cannot be drawn on anything," Cassius explained.

"How boring!" The artist's blood in Julian began to rise. "Perhaps I could draw their God. What does he look like?"

Cassius took his sandals off and began pulling on a pair of short boots. "He doesn't look like anything. He's invisible."

There was a pause and both men starting laughing hysterically. "They worship a god they can't even make a statue to, can't see, can't imagine?" Julian cried out through his laughter. "The Jews will make for some wonderful stories when we return home."

Cassius continued his thoughts. "So there is a careful balance between the Jewish leadership and our Pilate. Neither wants the people stirred up. I honestly don't know why anyone would want these administrative positions over such barbaric people."

"For the money," Julian sniffed.

"Oh, Pilate's gotten all their money; now he spends his days here in Herod's palace. I hear he only goes down to Jerusalem during the religious holidays, and then he travels with a small army for protection."

"Well, I suppose these lower class provinces deserve what they get," Julian observed with a bored tone.

"I possibly could have had a small country to lord over, but I prefer to earn my money through the excitement of maneuvering, of anticipating. Commerce is a grand game, Julian, but your love is the arts and philosophies, so you might find it hard to understand my passion for ownership and lending. You know you must end this fascination with drawing. It is an embarrassment to your father."

Cassius motioned for his slave, a small German man of thirty with a light complexion and blondish hair, to remove the hooded paenula cloak now draped over him and put the finer embroidered and colorful abolla around his shoulders. He wanted to look his best if he were to meet the procurator. Even though Pilate was a generally undistinguished Roman governing a relatively small area of this sliver of the empire, presentation was everything.

The ship carefully slid across the harbor waters. Several men stood by to grab the ship's ropes. The Captain was letting the ship drift

15

now, allowing the towing boats to ease it against the heavy beams of the wharf. Shouted orders to pull this way and that punctuated the maneuvering.

Cassius looked to see Marcus now being attended by several slaves in preparation to disembark. "Though Herod was a friend of Caesar's, I know his father was at one time a floor sweeper in some temple. Desert riffraff," Cassius sneered.

Julian asked his two slaves, both in their teens and from Gaul, to cinch up the baggage with his brushes, colors and papyri in it. They responded quickly. Both had had great difficulty on the voyage from Italy. Having never sailed, the slaves saw the passage as one of fearful danger. They had heard of the sudden storms on The Great Sea, and of the many ships that set out and never returned. They were eager to step off onto land.

Cassius spoke as they waited, "Another strange thing about the Jews' god is that they live in fear of him."

"They fear their god? This most boring of all gods who will not allow himself to be pictured?" The great mixture of Roman, Greek and Egyptian gods that were worshiped throughout the Mediterranean area offered solace and answers, but few of them demanded to be feared. Why would anyone want a god they are afraid of? Julian wondered. How insulting to the god and demeaning to the worshiper! Julian's expression showed he considered this one god idea the most foolish thing he could think of.

"You might ask the Jews about this whose land I'm taking," Cassius said. "Part of my purpose here is to take over a large area of land owned by a rural to whom my father loaned money when he visited last year. Our banker here says the man had a bad year with his crops and may not be able to pay either the interest or any of the principle. I may have our lawyers take over the land. It could be a nice start for me. Father said it is near the new city Herod's son Antipas has just finished called Tiberias, named for our now wheezing Emperor who loves young Greek boys."

Julian elbowed him in the ribs and smiled devilishly, "Ah, but you are bold out on the open sea. If I were you, I would fear that old Tiberius has bribed the gods to carry your words back to him."

"I have tried bribing the gods, to no ends." Cassius said with some annoyance as he carefully ran a brass comb through his hair in a final act of preparation for landing.

16

Cassius wrapped a robe over his shoulders and squinted at the setting sun as he reflected on it as a haven or a gateway for the other world. "The invisible live among us, I'm sure, but I get little out of them. I do believe in one supreme god somewhere, possibly in a world behind the sun, but all of the others…they may be imagined, or they may be real, but I have never once gotten any of them to answer a request I have made. I have begged, cajoled, even threatened not to make a gift at their temples if they did not grant my requests, but to no avail."

The boat nudged the harbor siding with a soft bump. The two men stood idly, awaiting placement of the wooden planks that would allow them to walk off the boat.

"I find my mind more concerned with acquisitions," Cassius continued. " I believe when we come to our end, we come to our end. Nothing will be there to greet us. It will be by our military and civil service and what we leave our children that we are remembered. It will be by how we honored the state. Lay me on a high hill over a vineyard or next to my apartments, and if there is any truth to a later life, I can enjoy eternity watching my grapes and dreaming of my profits."

They watched as their slaves gathered up their luggage near the ship's side as they observed the city before them and the sparkling clarity of the evening.

"I am glad to be out of the filth of poor Rome," Julian observed. "The Tiber is now a sewer from the congestion of humanity that crowds downtown. The poor fill the streets, looking for a handout. I fear we have ruined a generation by just giving them their ration of grain. Why should they work when the Emperor feeds them for free! I know of a wonderful old villa in the hills outside Pompeii. I can look forever at the majesty of Mt. Vesuvius. I think when we return I will make an offer."

They all disembarked amid the Captain's shouts to his crew to be careful with the long, odd-shaped clay jugs of wine they were unloading. He cursed one old man who seemed unable to get his land legs and called him a damned hull roach and a suspect for having allowed one jug to crack just so the wine could be drunk while they were at sea.

A thin, very tanned young man approached them with an obvious shyness. He wore a tunic with a tassled blue border and of a weave that indicated he was of some means.

"Sirs?" He asked from a noticeable distance.

With the authority of a Roman addressing a local, Cassius barked, "Are you addressing us?"

"Perhaps, honored one. I seek those who would be friends of Paulius Thadius."

"Friends!" Cassius fairly shouted. He was in a good mood and was overacting in his exuberance. "Friends of a man who would clasp the arm of Tiberius in greeting while he took coins from his royal pocket." He looked smilingly at Julian.

The boy did not know how to react and his eyes darted across both men.

Cassius realized he was playing to a confused audience in the boy, so he answered that yes, they were indeed his friends.

The boy nodded and said, "I am Jonas, an apprentice in the house of Paulius. I have come to direct you there."

Cassius spoke out of the side of his mouth to Julian, "You might know a lawyer would have an emissary here who was on time and spoke Greek, not the gibberish of the countryside. If only we could find slaves so organized."

"He was hoping you would arrive before dark so that you could dine with him," the boy said, still having not moved from his original spot.

"Well, we are here and are starved for something a ship's rat has not chewed on. But, while there is still light, I wish to pay my respects to the fort's commander. Could you direct me there first?" Then remembering, he asked, "Oh, how will we transport our baggage?"

"I have brought a donkey. I will take you to the fort, then return and direct your slaves in loading your baggage onto the donkey I've tied by the warehouse over there."

"With skills like those you have, you should have been a Roman, young man," Cassius prattled on.

Julian noticed a slight frown pass over the young man's eyes at the mention of the word, 'Roman'. "What is your ancestry, boy?" Julian asked.

"I am an Israelite. My father is a merchant here and wished me to learn more of money. He asked the honorable Paulius if he would allow me to be an aide for a while. He graciously agreed to do so."

Cassius laughed knowingly, "He agreed to because your father would pull his denari from the hands of one Paulius if he didn't, but that's alright. We must have some of the locals doing well." He waved his hand at the boy in a diffident way as though he, nor his father, were of much consequence.

They walked away from their ship and its fulminating Captain. The dock area was populated with statues featuring Herod's family. But the whole area was centered on a magnificent temple to the late Emperor Augustus, and to Roma, the goddess of Rome. It stood at the head of the harbor, framing the entire sea front in an undeniable exclamation, a defining statement of power. Its thick columned marble majesty dominated the interior of the harbor and the wharf area. The statue to Augustus was truly enormous and could be seen beyond the harbor and out to sea. To its right was a large plaza for public gatherings.

"I never cease to marvel at the beauty of a Greek design done right." Julian had pulled a charcoal pencil out and was quickly sketching the outline of the temple.

Cassius laughed, placing his hand on Julian's drawing arm. "My friend, you will exhaust your supply of papyrus if you start drawing every building we come to between here and Alexandria. Record some of it in your mind, or we'll have to buy a caravan of donkeys to carry it all!"

A thin man wearing outlandish brightly colored robes in ragged strips, stood above them on the temple steps. They noticed he was talking and gesturing with great animation to one of the huge columns. When the man saw them staring at him, he moved quickly down the steps and approached them. A sagging bag hung from one shoulder, and he used a cane.

"Most honored of all Romans," he spoke as though making an announcement, almost in a braggadocio fashion. "I will take all of your coins and for them I will give you the wisdom of the ages." He stuck his hand out, almost touching Cassius' chest. He smiled broadly and seemed quite pleased with his demand.

"You are no doubt a cynic," Julian observed.

"And proudly so," the man declared. "Do not hesitate. Everything you have belongs to me because everything belongs to the gods, and I am a friend of the gods."

Cassius smiled benevolently and said softly. "You are right, cynic, I would give you a gift from the gods that you will never forget." With a punch thrown so quickly the cynic couldn't react, bone cracked, gums and lips were ripped, teeth flew across the steps, and the man was propelled backwards to the ground unconscious.

Cassius shook his fist and kissed it as though to shake off the pain of having broken the man's jaw. "Damned philosophers! I thought we left all of them in Rome."

Julian ignored the sprawled and bleeding figure, made several more sketches and said with pleasure, "Ah, but that is why I am here: to record, to study, to take back the wonders that we see. I've always hated just listening to the stories of our friends who go on these great adventures. If I could only see on paper what they describe."

"They will be able to see the beauty I discover. I'll show them the mortgages I hold, the list of loans I have made, and the titles to the lands I have taken over." Cassius' voice fairly roared with the humor he found in his remark. He was glad to be on land.

As they crossed the broad, stone-surfaced plaza, they passed a man rolling a note into a thin lead sheet. He stood next to a small well, said a few words, then dropped it into the well. Cassius remarked dryly, "I see you can send a curse upon your enemies here also. I must say I find comfort in going to the ends of the earth and still finding little touches of home. We export our culture quite well."

"Amazing how easily culture spreads when introduced at the tip of a sword," Julian responded critically.

Their papers gave them easy access to the fort's commanding officer, a legate, a round-faced man of middle age, a veteran of the wars in Gaul, and a disciplinarian who ran his command in a traditional Roman, by-the-rules, way. Although he was short and thick in his frame, there was a typical superior Roman air about him that made him appear taller. He carried his head high from its squat setting on a bullish neck, and his chin protruded in a look of arrogance. They all exchanged their names and clasped arms in greeting.

"Most notable Plutoneus, it is our honor to express the good wishes of our fathers," Cassius said as he bowed slightly as they were shown into the general's offices.

The legate tilted his head toward the young men. "And I extend my welcome to this great city. Cassius, I know your father from the wars in Gaul. He was a brilliant tactician. We endured some very hard weather there against barbarians I never want to see again."

"My father has spoken often of your leadership. He too was glad to return to our homeland." As Cassius spoke, he felt his back straighten, knowing he was being appraised by the general for his bearing. He allowed his right hand, draped in the stella, to hang out in a certain carelessness that made a subtle statement about how he felt superior in social rank to the general.

"And Julian, your father, I heard had achieved equestrian rank in Pompeii. I hear he is now their Chief Magistrate."

"Perhaps you also heard Father had contributed to refurbishing the old baths at Pompeii. It cost more than I would dare mention. But he knew public service would not come cheap."

The legate smiled as much to the boys as to himself. Rome's finest, he thought. The product of the best Greek tutors and of monied families. It made him long for his villa in downtown Rome and for the company of his own sons, now at a local gymnasium run by Greek scholars.

"Well, you've come at a good time. Tomorrow there will be a small circus and a chariot race at the Hippodrome, and I believe there are some actors in town at the theater," the legate said.

"Very good," Cassius responded. "I'm not aware of a holiday. Who's putting the circus on?"

"As you know, last year Tiberius forbade citizens from financing circuses, but special permission was given to the family of Flavius, one of our city leaders. They were granted the right to honor the memory of their father by entertaining the citizens."

"You mean his son wishes to hold office," Cassius shrewdly noted, "and wishes to keep the family name in high favor. That or he wants the status his father enjoyed. So he parades a few lions, has a boxing contest, a footrace, and we all drink wine and praise the great and dead Flavius...and vote for his son."

Plutoneus chuckled, "Ah, vanity. Thy name is a circus."

He then ordered an aid to pour them wine, while motioning for his visitors to sit on one of several cushioned stools around a shelf-like table that extended from a wall. "What brings you to our sun-swept part of the empire?" he asked both of them.

Cassius was careful not to respond too quickly, taking a sip of his drink from a copper goblet. "In one word — profits."

"But of course," the legate smiled. "What would one expect from the son of such a great land owner and lender?"

"I look to gain some land here — the owners have been slow in paying my father — and to increase the holdings of my family. But I don't want to risk our money on such as wheat; a crop that I must go hire a lot of workers for, or buy seed and put up with the weather. I'll probably rent it out to the previous owners. My real interest will be in apartments, perhaps in Jerusalem. I hear it is quite crowded. Any opportunities to which you could direct me would be accepted with great appreciation."

Plutoneus said admiringly, "You have the soul of a businessman, Cassius. Do you wish to make Palestine your home, or will you direct your affairs from Pompeii or Rome?" Plutoneus downed his drink, and an aide quickly poured more.

"Oh, I will hire someone to manage here, but I am considering buying a villa, and living here some of the year. It could make for nice trips by my friends. They could get a good suntan; maybe do some hunting in the hills, or just enjoy the vineyards. But I don't know this part of the empire well, and I am a little troubled by the Jews. I understand some are murderers and bandits of the worse sort, killing even their own people if they stray from this one god they worship."

The general stood and walked with great stiffness back and forth over a rug lying in front of his chair. He had suffered a slashing sword wound years ago across his back, and prolonged sitting caused the muscles to tighten.

"Ah, the Jews, the Jews," Plutoneus mused. "What a strange group. They debate endlessly over their laws, which the Emperor has allowed them to have as long as it keeps them quiet. They have a Pharisee group that is a kind of fraternity. They wrote their own interpretation of what they call the Law. The ones we deal with are the Sadducees, who are the governing group out of the Temple. Then they have many who are no more than scoundrels, highway men who live in hiding in the caves and forests. And I have recently heard of an ascetic, fanatically clean group that lives in the desert somewhere near Jericho. Actually I think these Jews are so split that they present no military threat to us right now."

He looked at them, made a mock grimace and said, "The baths are so magnificent here, and the theater is filled with such great mimes and singers. Frankly, I fear my men grow a little soft. We could use a fight, but get only small bands of brigands which we gladly hang alive on trees."

They all laughed at the difficulty of maintaining an empire over people so obviously beneath the Romans.

"And what of you, Julian? I would almost say that you have an eye for art."

Julian blushed at having been caught staring at what appeared to have been a hole in the man's forehead. "I'll sunbathe on the beaches here and let Cassius support me." He paused while they chuckled at his professed decadence.

"You wonder about this, I know. I see you study the forms of my face as would an artist." Plutoneus pointed at the scar. "I was about to run my sword through an enemy once, and he shouted a curse at me to live forever in pain. When I arrived here my head started aching so badly that I could hardly stand. An Egyptian doctor was called. He drilled a hole to release what he said were evil spirits brought on by the dying man's curse. Disgusting fluids ran out, but the aches left, and I recommend his drill if your head is captured by a curse from an enemy."

Julian nodded, pleased with the story. "Actually, I am here to study the philosophies and architecture. I have also been hired to paint murals in several villas: one here and one in Sepphoris. I will then travel down to Alexandria for more study. My father hates my working with my hands, so I too will soon enter the world of profits."

"And what kind of murals will you be doing?" Plutoneus asked.

"I was fortunate enough to study under Secures."

"Oh, good...good. Then you will be doing the new landscapes." Plutoneus had been interested in poetry and art as a young man, but when in military service, he found a lust for adventure and a path to power that the philosophies could not provide.

Both Cassius and Julian were impressed that the reputation of the inventor of a bold new way to paint the walls of the wealthy was known not only in this barbaric part of the empire, but by a career military man.

Plutoneus chuckled, "Don't look for any clients among the Jews. They get hysterical if they see the painting of a face."

"Yes, we discussed that absurdity," Julian shook his head. "What does their art consist of? Surely they have some appreciation of beauty."

"I've seen no example of their art. They are a barren group to me. Frankly, I avoid them except to deal with some of their ruling class which lives much as we do. A few of them do know the beauty of profit, and they're damned good at it. Their homes are graced with beautiful frescoes. Paintings of faces don't bother their upper class."

Julian finished his second glass of wine and could feel its glow slowing his thoughts; what a pleasant way to end a boring sea voyage, in the easy conviviality of peers. In the upper classes it was considered rude to put on airs with an equal, but not to one of lesser rank.

23

Cassius felt as though courtesy demanded they take their leave, even though he could tell the general was enjoying this break from his routine. "You have been most gracious, legate. May your genius (divine double) protect you. We hoped to see the Perfect Pilate in the morning and pay our respects. I will tell him of our pleasant stay with you."

Plutoneus didn't respond to the mention of Pilate, in fact, his face seemed to go a little cold at the name. "If you are traveling to the Sepphoris area, you might need a guard. The roads can be very dangerous. The province of Galilee is known as a hideout for bandits and murderers. It is even looked down upon for the different way the people there speak their own language." He smiled, "The most barbaric of the barbarians, you might say. It's even said that if you must spend the night in an inn there, make your will out the night before."

They laughed and Cassius said he would appreciate a small guard detail, especially since he might be forcing a family off their land.

Plutoneus reached in a drawer and pulling out two medallions said, "Allow me to present you with medals commemorating your arrival in our city. We need good Romans such as you in this part of the empire, and I wish to honor your presence among us." He handed the dull, silver colored medallions to the pleased men.

Both bowed and thanked him profusely, turning them in their hands as they did. On one side was a bearded man with a dolphin tail, and on the other side the harbor entrance was portrayed with its statues. The letters KA were next to a picture of a sailing vessel entering the harbor. The letters were abbreviations for Caesarea.

Gathering up their cloaks, they said they would probably accept his offer for a guard as they moved outside the city. They thanked the legate again and left.

Emerging from the fort, they walked back out and across the broad plaza area to the temple fronting the harbor. An unrestrained sun begin spilling like a fiery egg onto the ocean's horizon. Strips of clouds hurtled outward like flaming plumes; last heralds of the fading day. A soft, orange light painted the harbor area. Ships were stilled inside the harbor as the business of the great port was succumbing to the quietness of dusk. Shadowing was hard along column edges. The red accent lines of the buildings, the shine of the marble and white stone were all drawn into their ultimate brilliance by the angular, hard cast of sunset. Both men drank in the moment. They looked forward to discovering this strange land, and motioned for the boy and their slaves standing next to a heavily loaded donkey, to come and lead them to the villa of their host.

The palace plaza that stood above the waterfront was as spectacular as any architecture the two travelers had ever seen. A long pool area had been dug out of a promontory that fronted the sea. It was a broad, open area of marble flooring, which contained statues to various deities and featured the splendid palace, where the procurator Pilate spent most of his time, though his offices were supposed to be in Jerusalem. Everything was of white stone, marble, stucco, and painted plaster. It was obviously an area of thought and planning and all in harmony. It became an evening feast for the eyes as the travellers walked slowly across it in awed silence and toward the streets and buildings of the city proper.

The boy led them down narrow, side-walked, flat-stone paved streets, unusual for most Palestinian towns, where the streets were often little more than foot-pressed dirt. Two snarling dogs scavenged along the edges of a building to their front, prompting a thick-set man to appear out of a door and chase them, barking as they retreated, down an alley.

Cassius responded approvingly, "Now this is a well-run city. Those mongrels would be allowed to wander our poor Rome's avenues in abandon. I saw one devour an infant abandoned by its parents just before we left on this trip. Repulsive, but you might say the dogs keep the streets cleaned."

"I would say," Julian observed, "that Herod swore he would never be caught in another cluttered street of Rome when he designed this city."

"Don't remind me," Cassius agreed sardonically. "To move in Rome at any time has become like entering a raging river. I hate that now about our city. And to sleep at night is impossible with all the freight carriers coming in, clattering over the stones." He shrugged his shoulders in dismay at the thought.

They passed by markets now closed for the evening, four-story apartment buildings, and a host of special shops and cafes before entering an area of large homes. The streets were named after the craftsmen that tended to work and live together: Weaver Street, Tailor Street, The Street of Jewelers, and so on. Above their roofs and to the east of the city they could see the top rows of the theater.

"Boy?" asked Cassius. "Is that not the theater?" And he pointed.

"Master Paulius likes being close to the sounds and laughter," Jonas answered. "There will be actors there tomorrow night. I believe he wants you to attend."

"Ah, an oasis of civilization in the land of goat herders," Cassius said, unable to resist his impression of this land he had heard from his father.

"Oh, it is far more than that, sir," Jonas suddenly became animated. "This is a place, small though it is, that is rich in ideas."

"Ideas!" Cassius stopped and guffawed. "Write that one down, Julian, for laughs in Pompeii. We come to this sorry strip of sand inhabited by goat herders and grape pickers, thinking we will be bored beyond tears, only to discover that we have arrived in a land of great thinkers!"

Jonas was confused about Cassius' reaction and blushed.

"And just what ideas greater than those from Rome have these great thinkers thought?" Cassius asked loudly. He stood with his hands on his hips, his maroon robe hanging off his broad shoulders in a defiant and authoritative stance. His head was held back and his strong chin jutted outward.

The boy was intimidated by the posturing image of the empire and said with some timidity and in a softer voice, "Our country has for generations been a crossroads where the feet of the nations pass. They bring the thoughts and ways of the world even beyond India and from lands few have seen south of Egypt. They have come through here for centuries as traders and as conquerors, and still they come with foods and animals we have never seen and ideas we have never thought of."

Julian beamed, "I like our guide. He is a watcher at the gate, a learner. Perhaps I will do a sketch of you to show my Roman friends that reason does reign even in the empire's darkest outposts."

Jonas drew away as though touched by a hot iron. "No! That would not do," he protested.

Cassius mocked, "Do you see yourself so ugly that you would break Julian's brushes?"

"It would be a human image and against the commands of the Law." The boy was obviously filled with fear and concern.

"The Law?" Cassius harrumphed. "I know of no Roman law that says we can't draw."

"The Law of Moses. It is one of our Commandments not to draw one's picture. It would be seen as creating an image before Him."

"Oh, so you're a Jew," Julian seemed pleased. "We were talking about your strange God who is so evil he wants to be feared. Say, you should go to the baths with us tomorrow. You and I can discuss your God and His philosophy."

The boy held up his hands and shook his head. "Oh, I couldn't do that. Exercise is done without clothes on there. We do not find that acceptable."

Cassius threw his head back and laughed, "Of course, we exercise without clothes on," he bellowed. "Who would ever run and lift and play ball in their clothes?"

"Tell us," Cassius commanded, 'what does your god offer to you for obeying him?"

Jonas answered quietly, "He offers us a place in His Kingdom."

"Oh! And in which part of the empire is this kingdom located?" Cassius scoffed.

"Right here in Israel," Jonas assured them.

Julian jabbed him, "The boy did say this was a place of new ideas."

"He should have said it was a place of idiots," Cassius scoffed. He motioned for them to move along as though the conversation had become too ridiculous to continue.

But Julian remained curious about this idea of one god. "Tell me, boy, what does this demanding god offer in return for giving up all other gods?"

Jonas answered with a youthful exuberance, "Oh, he offers a kingdom."

Julian looked puzzled. "And in which part of our empire would that kingdom be?"

Jonas' eyes searched around as though seeking the answer. "I, I believe it will be right here."

"Enough, enough!" Cassius grabbed Julian's arm and nudged him along and away from the conversation. "There's food to eat and wine to drink which we will find far more real than this imaginary kingdom."

The villa of Paulius was a sprawling one-story series of rooms centered around openings off two courtyards. Clay tiles covered the roof with an overlapping dull orange that gave a colorful accent against the white plaster exterior. The main house was walled and had to be entered through a thick wooden gate that opened into a carefully landscaped yard. A life-sized statue of Venus stood to the left of the gate. Her hair had been painted blond, and gold bracelets hung from

27

her arms. The god of happy endings, Bonus Eventus, stood across the small yard. The area was centered by a small pond with enormous gold fish lazily moving in the tepid water. Seven foot wooden columns, painted white, bordered the yard's edges with rushes of spring vines eagerly winding around their lengths. It was all beautifully planted.

They were met at the door by a small Syrian porter, an older refined man who spoke Greek, but in a lyrical, overly-enunciated way. "Welcome to Villa Sophia, masters."

They stepped into a beautifully adorned atrium greeting area. From the front door, there was a view straight down a large, high-ceilinged hall and out into a peristyle courtyard. It was a typical long, one-story Roman villa. Off the atrium and the courtyard were the many rooms of the home. The light of the atrium and the courtyard created a scene of hard light edged by heavy shadowing. To their left was a small terra-cotta statue called The Weary Herakles. It was a copy of the famous original done by the Greek sculptor Lysippos hundreds of years before. To their left was a life-sized marble statue of the nude Apollo. He stood relaxed, looking eerie in the perfection of the carving. Wall fountains, paintings, and gold edged moldings all spoke of the immense wealth of the owner. Intricate mosaics adorned the floors of the front hall in tiny painted stones, showing actors in the masks of satyrs and one wearing a goat's head mask. They were performing a play. The men admired the floor and then looked at one another and smiled at the obvious cost a mosaic of this detail demanded.

Cassius laughed, and whispered to Julian, "Father said Paulius has named his home after his wife, a ravishing young Greek whom, it is said, our aging lawyer cannot satisfy."

"Do I hear the voices of rich young rulers?" A boisterous voice shouted from a room off to one side of the entrance area. A thick-set man in his fifties in a red bordered toga appeared. He was heavily robed in a finely-weaved toga. His hair was a strange mixture of gray and red, obviously dyed, and combed forward. His face was fleshy, his thick nose was reddened with tiny blood vessels at its tip and his eyes were ringed with evidence of a life spent to its fullest. He had a generous mouth which spread easily against his heavy cheeks. Both forearms had bracelets and three of his fingers displayed rings. He came toward his guests quickly and eagerly, in a way that was powerful in its energy.

"You must be Cassius!" Paulius exclaimed in admiration as he extended his hand to embrace Cassius' arm. "I see your father in every feature."

Cassius smiled and felt a sense of pride in being compared to his successful and doting father. "That I am," he beamed.

Paulius gave him a hug, slapping his shoulders, then stepped back and looked approvingly at Julian. "And this must be the famous artist who did such fine work for our Emperor."

They clasped one another's arms. Julian smiled broadly; he immediately liked this effusive man and his gregarious way of greeting.

"And where did you work for Tiberius?" Paulius inquired.

"Most recently at the Villa Jovis on Capri. It sits on a high precipice over the sea and allows him the seclusion he favors. I found it magnificent, but I worried how it removed the Emperor from his empire and those that scheme to take it over."

Paulius could see the slaves and baggage trailing out his front door into the garden and instructed the porter to bring it all inside to their assigned rooms. They were led into a large room to their left. It had one high glass paned window, but like most rooms of the era was softly lit by several lamps; one an exquisite gold leaf statue of a boy from whose outstretched hands, lamps flared. The floor was tiled with colored mosaics of exotic birds and flora. On a wall to the left was a fresco of a lake scene. The furnishings consisted of several tables on three legs or on a pedestal, benches, and two divans. Though sparse, the furnishings were elegant and obviously very expensive with gold and jeweled inlays. The wall to the left held an inset marble statue honoring Tiberius. Columns went down two sides of the large room. Made of brick, they were covered in plaster and varnish which gave them a glossy look. The room opened by a double door out onto the courtyard. Incense burned in a corner heavily scenting the room. As the party stepped into the room and the slaves and the porter busied themselves with bringing the numerous bags inside, Jonas came forward and asked, "May I take my leave now, Honored One?"

"Your usual good work, Jonas. Tell your father a quiet night, and I will see you in the morning." Paulius smiled at the boy, who then nodded and walked out into the evening.

"I like him," Julian said. "What is his work with you?"

Paulius circled his left arm under Julian's and, ignoring his question, gently guided him across the room to a seating area. "Let's visit for a moment, and then we will dine. You must be weary from the trip. Tonight we can catch up, and tomorrow we will have fun and perhaps give a small banquet with some friends from the baths tomorrow night. I have a talented cook that will serve in a bronze form what may look like a fish, but is pork. Disguising food is a game for relieving the boredom the elite must sometimes endure," he smiled wearily.

A servant, a woman of some bearing, narrow-faced and sad looking with a long, hooked nose and a small-boned frame, came out of the kitchen area with a set of gold goblets with jewel insets. Wine had already been poured in them.

Cassius, responding to the opulence of the goblets, remarked, "Now I know where all my father's fees are going." Pointing his finger at Paulius, he kidded, "You, my good lawyer. Very nice," he said as he turned the goblet in his hand while reveling in its design and admiring its inlaid stones.

"Oh, I got it for hardly a coin," Paulius said. "In Rome this would go for a fortune. Many of the goods from Arabia and India pass through here on the way to Athens and Rome. I get to bargain and choose before all my friends do," he laughed. "There are advantages to living on the edge of the empire, even if it is part wilderness and inhabited by the ignorant."

"I hope to take advantage of that fact," Cassius said as he stood up from the cushioned bench where he sat. "Let us toast the edge of the empire and the fortunes it holds for us. And, of course, our great Emperor, for granting us the privilege of getting filthy rich under his rule."

They all laughed heartily at that and raised their goblets in a salute.

"So to answer your question about Jonas, Julian," their host remembered, "his father is one of the wealthiest men in our city. He is very well-connected with the Jewish ruling body, the Sanhedrin, in the courts at Jerusalem. He knows when a Jewish landowner is behind in his taxes or loan payments, and he informs me. For a fee, I am able to find men of money who wish to move on the property and either loan more money to pay off the existing loan, or offer a cheap price to buy it."

"How did the Jew make his money?" Cassius inquired.

"He got his start with Herod before the king died some thirty years ago. Since Herod killed off the old Sanhedrin court and appointed his own, this Jew became well connected through contacts he had with the new court. Along with several Romans, a rich Syrian from

Damascus, and some Egyptian connections, he has money in warehouses, holds many farming and forest properties, a small fleet of ships and, of course, apartments. He is also the banker for the Jews in this area and collects their taxes to the Temple. Each man over twenty must pay a tribute every year. He collects it and takes a commission. I do his legal work, and get in some of his deals. And, I am most happy to have his son apprentice with me, which keeps my association with the father strong."

Cassius chuckled in glee, "Ah, Paulius you will be my guide. Let others call on the gods for help, I will call on Paulius."

"Oh, I like that. I have now achieved the status of a god. Perhaps you will hire Julian to design a temple in my honor."

Joining in the fun, Julian exclaimed, "Only if I can also demand that this wine will be served at your temple. This is truly delicious, especially after the rat's urine, called wine, we endured on the ship."

"Some of the vineyards are quite good here, and I especially like the fruits. In the spring, one can hardly walk in some parts of the Galilee area without slipping on fallen pomegranates, figs, and dates; in fact, this is date wine from the groves at a place called Jericho."

"An interesting name," Julian observed. "Should I see this place?"

"Well, the Galilean ruler, Antipas, has maintained his father's magnificent palace near there. Jericho is a beautiful and very old oasis near the Dead Sea, which is a stink hole filled with salt. But Jericho is a retreat for many of the wealthy in the winter and may be worth a visit. It would be two days down and back from Jerusalem. The land is wretched, with its barrenness. I would surely take a military escort. Brigands live in the caves near the highway. There's such riffraff that travel our roads, you never know. Be sure to bring me back some balsam if you go. It is called the balm of gilead, has a fragrant scent, and is good for headaches."

An attractive servant appeared with a tray filled with various fruits and bread. She pulled a long, short-legged table in front of the three and laid the platter on it. She looked at Julian, and as his eyes idly turned toward her face, he noticed her eyes darting away, and when she turned to walk to the kitchen, he noticed the shapeliness of her legs. He kept watching her movements until she disappeared through the door.

"Where is your server from?" Julian asked nonchalantly.

"Oh, she is a slave I bought while in Egypt last year. Her family, it is said, had been prominent in Alexandria, but the whole lot of them were jailed in a dispute with a Roman legate over property rights, and because her father threatened to call down hordes of desert nomads on the city. Her given name is Esna, and I allowed her to keep it. She's quite smart for an Egyptian; she already knew some Greek and now speaks it well. A little sullen, I think, but she does her duties here with a certain, should I say, intelligence about her."

Before they ate, he had the servants jab at the air all around the food with pins.

Paulius said in bored explanation, "I have had stomach problems and believe it to be spirits who live above my food. The stabs keep them away long enough for me to eat without their entering my mouth."

He then became animated, sitting up on the divan and saying, "Oh, you must include Alexandria in your travels. It is the one necessary stop for those who would educate themselves. I brought back a large quantity of their cotton for myself. It is unmatched for softness. Most of our clothing here is made of it, and, of course, I made a little profit off of what was left. And the library there, of course, is a wonder of the world."

"Yes, I plan to go there from here," said Julian. "Perhaps I will ask the girl what attractions I should see."

"She's not a tour guide," Cassius grumbled. "She's a grape server."

Paulius concurred to acknowledge the difference between Romans and those they enslaved, regardless of the slave's previous life. "A smart grape server. A dependable and oddly attractive grape server. But no more than a grape server."

"Your floor mosaic is wonderful," Julian said, looking at the complex display of tiny tiles, each painted separately and laid out like an enormous puzzle.

"As you can see, it is of a grand hunt we went on in a remote land south of Egypt. It was like a paradise of wild animals, some of which I had seen in the circus here, others I doubt any Roman had laid eyes on; all very exciting and dangerous. The river was filled with enormous snakes, crocodiles, hippopotamus, trumpeting elephants, and the air was clouded with the largest white birds. The people were savages living in grass huts, very black of skin and fearful of us. I believe it is a place of the gods, or at least a place where they go and rest from the weary work of dealing with us." Paulius beamed with satisfaction.

"Does your Jew friend have any properties near Sepphoris?" Cassius inquired. "I understand that it and Tiberias are two wonders of the interior of this country, and cities where there may be a need for apartments."

Paulius rubbed his chin and answered, "He does have a five-story building on the outskirts of Sepphoris. If he calls the town Zippori, it means bird on a hill, or some such in their Hebrew. Anyway, my friend is having work done on the building. Tomorrow, on the way to the baths, we could stop by his villa and ask if he would consider selling it. He's a wily one, I can tell you. He balances his strict religion and his desire to become wealthy better than anyone I've seen. Nathan Ben Issaih is his Hebrew name. I keep trying to get him to take a Roman name. It would help him more in business."

Several servants appeared with enormous silver trays colorfully arrayed with various foods: charred lamb cooked on a brazier, yogurt, nuts and fruits, and mugs of beer. They would eat from plates that were imported redware; glossy, dull red, beautiful and very costly. Squeezed juices were served in glasses tinted blue with cobalt dust.

"I trust a light meal will please you tonight," Paulius almost apologized. "We need to save room for tomorrow evening's banquet."

"This is perfect," Julian responded. "I must admit I am weary from the voyage, and sleeping on a still bed is my desire. In fact, standing still while relieving myself makes me happy after weeks of wetting my own legs as I tried to aim my water on a rocking vessel."

Paulius had quickly jammed a large piece of meat in his mouth, and with food hanging from his lips, he mumbled appreciatively. "Can't stand the damned ships. Wish that I could fly. We need a god that will accede to our need for flight."

Suddenly, the door was pushed open so hard that it slammed against the wall. Standing in its frame was a woman of extraordinary beauty. Her hair was a striking blond, almost white. She had a round face, unusually fair and smooth skinned. Her lips were thick, pouty, and accented in red lipstick. Her eyes were a dreamy gray and lidded in a sensual, cat-like sullenness. She stood next to a muscular young man who grinned sheepishly. His arms were badly scarred and his nose appeared to have been broken at one time, being slightly off center. He appeared to be of German descent with a full head of greased down red hair.

Paulius was at first startled, with meat and bread crammed simultaneously in his mouth. He chewed rapidly, gulping down chunks with a loud swallow, and finally spoke in a feigned attempt at joy, "Ah, Sophia, my wife. Just in time for some cake."

33

"Cake?" she purred. "That's not what I had in mind. Is that what you had in mind, Leo?" She smiled seductively at the man next to her. "I, uh, thought it best to escort your wife home, honored one. The streets, you know, are not for the beautiful at night."

Paulius squinted from his reclining position on the couch. "And in what campaign did you receive those wounds? It looks to have been a terrible fight," he said referring to the man's scarred arms.

The burly young man looked at Sophia, their faces almost touching, as they stood close within the tight doorway. They both laughed, and he answered, "I was in some campaigns in Macedonia. Very bloody business. I forgot my arms weren't shields."

Paulius sat up and squinted through his bloodshot eyes. "Say, you have a familiar face. I have seen you recently, but…perhaps at the baths."

"Not the baths. I've only recently been brought to, uh, come to this city."

"You might say he may not be long for this world," Sophia teased.

"I'm afraid your wife is fatalistic. She sees death's kiss riding on every moment."

"Oh, save me the poetry," she scolded her escort and pretended to push him out into the hall. Turning to Paulius, Sophia said, "I'll see this young man to the garden gate and thank him for his generosity in providing me with protection."

Cassius and Julian were left with their mouths slightly ajar, and looked at their friend who seemed somewhat embarrassed over the scene as he reached for a mug of beer.

"My wife comes from an independent line," he apologized. You surely know Senator Appius. Well, this is his youngest daughter. I met her while hunting lions in Syria two years ago. Her family had brought their own caravan filled with party-goers on an extended hunting trip. Appius kindly invited me along as I had helped him on some legal matters. We were in the brush armed to the teeth with spears and swords and stout slaves, when all of a sudden, she popped up in front of me and said, 'meow.' Well, I just roared. I could not believe such beauty existed, or that she could be interested in an aging old frog like me," he laughed heartily.

Julian could hear Sophia giggling from the atrium area, then she reappeared and her lipstick was smeared and her flow of hair once so carefully held in broaches, now hung in some disarray. She walked in and kicked her shoes across the floor, touched Julian, then Cassius, on the shoulder with a delicate brush of the finger, before walking over and kissing Paulius on the top of his head.

"Oh," she complained. "My lips grow cold when I kiss such a snowy top," she teased about his graying hair.

Paulius took her hand and kissed it, leaving grease on her hand from the lamb on his lips. She gently rubbed the back of her hand across his forehead in a kidding, but contemptuous, motion of disrespect. It was common for Romans to commit such acts of social abuse, and the powerful regularly exercised such behaviors over those they saw as weaker. Generally only men engaged in such rudeness, and never a wife in front of other men.

"My love, let me introduce you to our visitors," Paulius said, as he sat back and motioned to the two men. He was forced to ignore her flagrant behavior.

She turned and walked toward the rear of the room and the door that led out to the courtyard. "Not tonight, dear Paulius, I fear I am too weary from the evening. I would want to be fresh for such handsome men." She disappeared into the flickering torch light of the interior yard.

"I think your wife is a goddess, my friend," Cassius interjected, partially to save Paulius from feeling like he had to sputter out some apology for his wife. "Such beauty is rare."

"Well, my beloved first wife died during the birth of our second child, and I myself almost died in grief. I wonder if the gods are giving me a life of misery by awarding me Sophia, or is she truly, as you say, a goddess that pleases and spites me?"

"They do that, you know," Julian said. "The stoics say the gods are all evil, and they have us around just for their own pleasure. She is as beautiful as a goddess, no doubt. Perhaps I could put her in a wall fresco for you. If I captured her in a painting, you might gain some control over her."

"I like that very much!" Paulius exclaimed. "If by drawing her image I have a power over her, then we will know that she is a goddess. If she continues to be so frisky and independent, I will know that she is just the hopelessly spoiled daughter of one of Rome's wealthiest men. Woe, knowing the haughty as I do, as I am, I should have known better than to marry a Senator's daughter"

Cassius belched loudly, and said in a weary voice, "Well, the hour is not late, but the muses are filling my mind with dreams. The food was excellent, and I am honored to be your guest. Could a servant gather my boots so that I might retire for the evening?"

"Oh, how rude of me for keeping you up," Paulius said as he pulled his stout frame up off the divan and straightened his robe. The servants here will show you to your rooms. There is a chill about tonight, so cover your bed well."

He guided them toward the courtyard, and, lightly slapping each man on the shoulder, bade them good night as they walked across the courtyard and into their separate rooms. The Egyptian girl led Julian. He could see in the flickering torch light that the courtyard was even more carefully landscaped and rich with statuary than the front garden entrance.

She pushed a door open, and they entered a spartan room with a bed and two small three-legged tables. On both tables were oil lamps. A large porcelain wash basin sat on the table that was under the one window in the room. The window was closed by two shutters that could be swung open. The tables had glass inlaid tops, and the bedstead and frame were of polished cedar with ornate carvings of gazelles cut into the wood. Floor to ceiling frescoes covered every wall. A tiled mosaic of fish leaping from the sea graced the center of the floor. The room was spare and small, but elegant.

Esna was tall for an Egyptian, Julian thought. Her legs were long, her hands rather large, and her face narrow. Her eyes were dark brown pools floating under even darker brows against a reddish brown complexion.

She avoided looking at Julian and busied herself with placing towels next to the water basin and blankets on the feather-stuffed mattress.

Julian took from his luggage a pouch filled with a toothpaste made of ground bone and shell, crushed rose petals and honey.

"What does Esna mean in your language?"

She continued her work and answered in a soft voice, "It is a village of tombs where my father thought many of our ancestors stayed."

"Why would they live in a village of tombs?"

"They were buried there."

Julian stood from his crouched over position. "I don't understand, they were buried there, but they live there?" he asked in some confusion.

Esna turned toward him as she unfolded a blanket, "Our culture believes that our dead live among us and guide our daily lives along with the gods. Death and the afterlife rule our lives in many ways. So to be named after that place where the ancients live is an honor."

"Your master said that you came from a prominent family in Alexandria." Julian wanted to know more of this slave.

Her eyes dropped and she paused before responding. "My father owned a very large field of grain grown for the Romans. He angered the Roman legate, a man consumed by greed. My father owned land near Lake Mareotis outside of Alexandria. It is a place of special holiness for a reclusive group called the Therapeutal. They reject worldly goods and have a reverence for life that my father found especially appealing. My father believed in our gods, but he was very interested in other meanings to this life and had become attracted to this group and enjoyed going out on the seventh day when they allowed outsiders to come and hear their teachings."

"Is your father still alive?" Julian asked.

"I pray so. But he was jailed by the legate when he refused to sell the lake land and swore to defend it against the Romans. I was also taken and sold," her voice cracked. She turned away.

Julian felt the urge to go to her, but she was a slave, regardless of her former position. He forced his mind to other desires. "I am very interested in visiting Egypt. I have heard much of the great library at Alexandria with the writings of the ancient philosophers and teachers. I will need a guide, someone who knows the city." He paused, "I might ask Paulius if he will loan you to me for that purpose."

She turned, joyful tears filling her eyes, "Oh, master, would you do that? I have read in the library of which you speak. It is true that all the great thinkers of the civilized world have their thoughts and writings there. I have heard the teachers of the city and know many of them because of my father's interest in learning. I could show you the wonders of that great land, the magnificent plazas and gardens, the pointed tombs that touch the sky, the temples…"

He laughed in a mild protest, "Let's not talk of it anymore. I have much to study here first before going further. It's just a thought."

"Yes," she whispered, as tears streaked her high cheek bones, "a wonderful thought. May your dreams take you to a place of calm." She bowed and pulled the door gently behind her.

Julian stood for a moment in a rush of feelings. He had never taken notice of a slave girl before, and certainly not an Egyptian, whom the Romans thought to be dull and lazy people. But Esna…he turned the name in his mind as though it were a song. Removing his stockings and garter belt, he lay in the soft bed. As his mind wandered, he half-dreamed that the feathers upon which he lay had formed into wings that were taking him and the long-legged slave girl soaring out over the blue of the Great Sea and down toward the mysterious land where the dead still lived and ruled the living.

CHAPTER 3

He was dreaming again. His eyes would widen, blank and unsee-ing, his mouth drift loose in a detached hang, his ears tuned inward to no sound other than the vaporous voices of his mind. Drifting over metaphors and similes, working words like his mother weaved; a thread here, a turn, a twist there and the disconnected words became a small story. It was the smooth wood of the shelf that held his atten-tion.

It felt like flesh and was as pale as the skin of a shorn sheep. He stared at the curving grain lines, and thought of the beach at Caesarea and of how the grain lines looked like waves, frozen just as they lapped the shore. A round, brown knot reminded him of the dark, empty inside of a tall, clay jar. He pictured the shelving's flat surface as the family field at the base of the hill on which his village of Nazareth was located. Jesus absent-mindedly rubbed his hands over the shelf he had just pegged into place. As he ran his fingers along the underside, the sharp, pointed pain of a splinter piercing his finger brought him with a yelp back into the large room in which he worked. Jerking his hand away from the wood, he could easily see the splinter sticking like a tiny spear out of the skin. He attempted to pull it out with his teeth, wincing at the intensity of the pain as it resist-ed his repeated attempts. After a studied placing of two of his finger-nails, he pinched the splinter and eased it out. A drop of blood bub-bled out and sat in the fine dust on his finger. He mashed the blood and spread it out over his finger until it was a brownish smudge, dif-ficult to distinguish from the olive complexion of his skin.

Jesus has been hired to come up from Nazareth to work on the house of assembly in Capernaum. The assembly was a part of the large, black basalt stone home of Joel Ben Nazar, a relatively well off fish exporter. Because it was the largest home in the small seaside vil-lage of Capernaum, the Nazars had for years opened one side of it to the village Jews for use as their Sabbath house of prayer and scripture readings, and as the court house for the town. Joel was also a lay preacher of the Pharisee fraternity, the priests who occasionally tend-ed to the countryside populace, as opposed to the formal Sadducee priesthood who served from the magnificent Temple in Jerusalem. Joel prided himself on his knowledge of the five Books of Moses and the interpretations his group had contributed over the generations. Many of the local Jews thought that he, like many scribes and lawyers, was too arrogant and condescending in his displays of intolerance for those without formal training in the readings. In truth, most of the Pharisee fraternity felt the Galileans were an ignorant, generally illiterate lot, quick to fight and rebellious by nature. Joel defined himself by his own version of the Laws and preferred the company of priests over peasants. He thought that the Pharisees held Judaism together. His was a world of words and defense of God's intent in those words.

The Nazar family lived on one side of the long structure. They had allowed the left side of the house to be enlarged over the years until it was now big enough to accommodate a gathering of sixty of the faithful. The local officer of the Roman garrison had given money to refurbish the building out of sympathy for the Jews and as an act of diplomacy to keep the locals calm. The room was also used twice a week to hold court and do the city's general business. It was an honored Roman tradition for city leaders to donate to buildings for the city. Joel's elder son was in charge of planning and starting the meetings, and of designating readers when the room was used as an assembly for worship. Thin columns went down both sides of the room. Benches lined the walls. A raised platform with steps on either end centered the room. Rising from it was an altar and an ark. On a nearby table lay a brass fire pan and small hand shovel for the incense rituals. Next to this were a ram's horn, a candelabrum, and a palm branch. A partition with lattice work at one end of the room segregated the women from the men.

Jesus had been hired to chisel more niches out of the thick walls to hold a growing library of papyrus and leather scrolls that would be stored for the few who could read, but very few were literate in Hebrew in the Galilean villages. Literacy was a power the religious leaders had and held over the populace.

A growing revulsion against the instillment of the Greek and Roman cultures into their lives had pulled many of the Galilean Jews closer together in their faith, and they felt the need to reaffirm it on a more regular and formal basis. They had no great Temple in Galilee, no center such as The Temple Mount of Jerusalem where one could offer sacrifices and attend festivals, so if a village's Jews wanted to worship, they gathered in the town's largest home. The idea of a formal meeting place for the Sabbath in the Galilee area had caught on first over at the new port of Caesarea, then all over and all at once.

"So saith the Book, 'Old men dream dreams, but young men see visions.'" Joel's deep voice announced his entry into the large stone room, his arms filled with scrolls and pages crudely bound with linen strings. Each had a tag attached to its end, bearing the name of the person who had made the copy. They came from the copiers in the Community at Qumran.

Joel was middle-aged and of little humor; an arid man, gregarious and ebullient only when strolling the marketplace like a celebrity. Although not a fully-qualified Pharisee, he was nevertheless of that fraternity, as his father had been. There was an air of distrust about his bushy-eyed gaze, as he professed his knowledge and parried to all who would give challenge. Pity the souls who stepped over the tight bounds of the rules of the Sabbath, or brushed against a tomb while walking, or was not scrupulously observant of cleanliness in every facet of their lives according to Joel's interpretations. He was quick to forbid them from entering the synagogue on the Sabbath as a punishment, and scorned them to their face. As a large property owner, he was also on the three-man court that sat on the city court that met twice a week in the room in which they now stood.

Jesus looked up. His hair was carefully combed and trimmed just above his shoulders. A mild perfume wafted from his hair as was the custom. He parted it in the middle. It was a shade lighter than that of the Jews who lived to the south around Jerusalem. As he looked up to Joel, the fullness of his hair swung away from his face like a slow departing wave. Joel could not tell if his face looked so intent because of the harshness of the light, or if he were upset about something.

"Many hide from the light," Jesus said. "And when in it, all they can see is themselves." He continued staring at the contrasting light and shadows. His voice carried easily across the wide room, though he seemed to be speaking with little energy.

Joel, who thought carefully about the meaning of any slightly obtuse statement, paused and responded, "Unfortunately, there is pleasure in the darkness."

Joel let the scrolls slide onto the shelf Jesus had built. He turned toward the long, lean, relaxed figure of the carpenter and thought of Jesus' father Joseph, a devout and pious Jew, whom Joel had known, though not socially. He remembered Joseph because of his almost perfect scriptural memory and his unusual understanding of the Hebrew language. Aramaic had replaced Hebrew as the common language years earlier, so Hebrew was often now the sole province of the religious leaders. It was unusual that a carpenter could also read Hebrew. More of the young man's mother was in his face, but what a strange face, Joel thought. So many emotions rode its smoothness, such unusual twists and turns. He thought this was either the ugliest man in the village, or the most compelling.

"You and your father had an enviable building business. Did you allow it to go away?" Joel was ever curious as to the income of people. He was also curious as to why one who had built columns in Bethsaida and houses in Sepphoris would be doing this minor repair work.

A faint crease measured its way over Jesus' face. He knew Joel's mind to be a purse filled with coins of information about all with whom he came in contact. He disbursed his knowledge in snippets of gossip, innuendo, and whispered secrets. And from each who leaned close to hear his betrayals, Joel would expect a later favor.

"I have been moving away from the world," Jesus answered.

"Then how will your poor mother live?" Joel pried.

"Do you believe, Teacher," Jesus ignored the question, "that we are in the image of The Father? That we actually look as He looks? That He is all of us and we are Him?"

Joel scowled, "Why even ask such a question! No one can know The Holy One's face. It would be an insult even to imagine that one so perfect could look like a blemished human."

"Do you believe that man can be perfect?" Jesus asked.

"What is perfect?" Joel responded warily. Why would a common worker ask such a deeply philosophical question?

Jesus looked up, a little surprised that the question had been asked, "Perfect is as The Holy One is perfect."

Joel pushed down a scroll on the shelf so that its wooden ends made a decided and emphatic statement of his exasperation with the implications of Jesus' remarks.

"Then of course not," he answered abruptly. "To even ask that question is dangerously close to saying man could be The Holiest, blessed be He, and I myself have thrown the first stone at men who made that claim. The Holiest One knows we are weak in the flesh. That is why He gives us other ways of staying in His good stead. We are the chosen, and therefore special. Our life is to journey toward perfection, not to achieve it. To say we could achieve it would be blasphemy. It is the journey by which we are judged as a people. So declared the Lord in Isaiah, 'My thoughts are not your thoughts, nei-

42

ther are your ways my ways.' And as He said to Job, 'Where wast thou when I laid the foundations of the earth?' We can barely understand the powers of The Maker; we don't even know what 'perfect' is."

Jesus bit on one side of his bottom lip in contemplation. He refused to acknowledge Joel's rebuttal. "Perhaps we ask too little of ourselves. It would be worthwhile to see just how close a man could come to the Perfection of The Holy One. And then, by this example, would not others follow? And then would not Israel be restored to its favored place?"

Joel sniffed self-righteously, "Jesus, you speak as a wood worker who has kept his nose too close to his wood. If you look up, you will see that many of us are examples of those who spend every day attempting to come close to the Likeness." He ran his hand over a wrinkle in his robe, as if to show how he even tried to be perfect in his dress.

"But Teacher, what if a man did come closer to being perfect than any other man ever had; should our people follow that man as their example?" Jesus persisted.

The lay priest was clearly not pleased that he was being questioned by what he considered little more than an itinerant laborer. Then he stopped himself and thought that at least this was a poor, ignorant rural who was trying to learn more of the faith.

"That man would be the Messiah," he answered patiently, feeling he was doing a good deed for the day by being so generous with his time with one so hopelessly naive. "Until then, Jesus, you should look to those of us who are your religious leaders. We know the way. Any others, I would say, are charlatans asking for a stoning, or they are possessed by the devil. It would be very difficult for a worker such as yourself, to walk a perfect way unto the Holiest One. I would say it takes more schooling than you have had to even know how to make the walk." He smiled beatifically, "I mean no disrespect, of course," and tipped his head in a false measure of respect.

"Little Isaiah, you know Jesus, don't you?" Joel asked his son, who had been sitting off to one side writing Jesus' remarks on a flattened deer skin. His desk contained a small jar for his ink and one for water. The strict Jewish laws required him to clean the quill in water each time he wrote YHWH, the Hebrew word for God. He was a teenager singled out for his small stature even by his parents. He was very bright and inquisitive, and was the best at signs (writing) in the village. So perfect were his letters, that people would marvel on the

Sabbath at his writings. However, he was also rebellious and gave his father headaches with loud and impertinent remarks about whatever entered his mind. And he voiced fiery opinions about the Roman occupation and dreamed often of leading an army against them.

The guerrilla movement, though small in Galilee, was known by all and supported with food and safe houses by the rurals. It held great attraction for young men in the daring exploits of its part-time warriors. Little Isaiah's father was always upbraiding him for drawing battle plans on their precious papyrus and animal skins instead of making copies of the scriptures.

"I spoke to him in words. He spoke to me in song," the boy smiled.

"Song," repeated the ever suspicious Joel, though he acted only mildly interested. "He sings instead of speaking?"

"I thought Jesus was only a builder, but he is far more. He tested me in Hebrew on the words of the prophets while he was working." Little Isaiah chuckled. "But his questions were much too difficult for me. I'm glad he doesn't teach in the School of Books!" He held up a piece of leather with Aramaic writing. "He speaks in stories, and his words are different...like singings."

Joel's head jerked around toward his son, his eyes glaring as he hissed the word, "Different!" Then he caught himself, dropped his eyes back to his work like a snake stopping in mid-strike, deciding to recoil and take a different point of attack.

Joel felt a challenge to his authority at any remarks by a local, especially a village carpenter, who said he could read Hebrew. But Joel was too political to confront Jesus directly, so he would ascertain what this potentially blasphemous word 'different' meant in another way.

"I knew your father; he was a learned man who claimed lineage with David. He was very intent in his observance of the Torah, and I know he stressed its importance to you and taught you well. He confided in me once that your mother had been visited by an angel in a dream. The angel said that you would be playing a role in the salvation of our Nation. He believed for a time that it was no dream." Joel finished wrapping a scroll in protective linen. He then peered into a large box called 'of a secret' where donations were left for the village's orphans. It contained several little robes and blankets.

"I was saddened by Joseph's sudden death. I know it left your mother with a large family. I'm sure she has been served well by you and your skills in stone and wood. I know it most likely cut short your schooling. I didn't hear that you attended the Temple academy in Jerusalem."

Jesus knew that Joel was preparing to insinuate that, because Jesus had not gone beyond the local Nazareth school, he was unqualified to test anyone on the scriptures. It was the kind of easy arrogance of the learned that had angered Jesus for years.

"We have a good school for a small village," Jesus answered, forcing himself to sound positive as he felt his face flush with annoyance. "I learned Hebrew easily, a trait I must have received from my father. I have read the scriptures many times. I have a small group of friends that I debate with. I read to them," he smiled, "then we debate."

Joel couldn't stifle a smug snicker. He stood, legs apart, a hand on one hip, the other pointing a finger at Jesus. "Ah, hah," he said as though he had caught Jesus in a trap. "Reading is one thing. True understanding is far different and far more difficult. That requires attending the schools in the Holy City, being close to the Temple, and living for a period in the great shadow of the house of the Torah."

Jesus found himself rubbing one hand over the knuckles of the other in a growing tension, so he sat back, stretched his legs out and forced himself to smile at Joel, "Then this village is blessed to have one as learned as you. One, who, as you say, has lived in the shadow of the Temple and has great knowledge of the Laws."

Joel hitched his girdle up, thinking, as usual, that he had won the day. He changed the subject. "It is good that your mother moved here. Nazareth is blessed with fertile ground, but there seems to be little land left that is not owned and managed by outsiders. Here you can find work, and the fishing is good. There is no hunger. But I have seen little of you. Have you been doing work for Herod's son at Tiberias?"

Jesus almost laughed at the man's persistence in trying to humble him. The question was insulting and prying. Although many Jewish craftsman had earned good money working in the building of the nearby cities of Sepphoris and Tiberias, Jesus knew Joel was insinuating that he, Jesus, was willing to work with, and for, gentiles and pagans. Tiberias had been built on top of an old Jewish cemetery and was considered unclean by the very devout Jews. He marveled at Joel's ability to forever question one's true faith. It was the elder's nature and his weakness.

"My father and I worked at Bethsaida where I laid brick when I was young. I also learned to read Greek there. I worked at Sepphoris after his death, building houses for the wealthy who live on its northern slope. All land belongs to The Father, whether a pagan lives on it or a priest. Therefore, I easily work for all men."

To complete his growing picture of this strange builder, Joel asked who he debated with. "These friends you read to, would they be the ones with zeal, the ones who want war with the Romans?"

Jesus answered. "I speak with many people and some do show great zeal in their anger at the Romans. They want a rebellion as we had twenty years ago. I believe their anger is more about the paying of tributes to Rome and the insult that makes to The Holy One. They think paying tribute to the Emperor is a form of worship, especially when it must be made in Roman coins with the Emperor's face on each one. The way I see it, these already belong to the Emperor and it is no form of worship to return to him what is already his, so pay Caesar his due."

Jesus idly ran a finger over his bottom lip, feeling dryness along its edge. "Others of our people are so sad or mad in the head they cannot get through the day without crying. We suffer hurting hearts as well as hurting heads. We defy the promises of the prophets both as a Nation and as People. When I'm not working, I seek answers to these evils that weigh on our land. I am now looking for others who feel our people must come together under the love of The One. He comes, and we are not ready, each unto ourselves."

What a naive man, Joel thought. "Love?" he asked, soliciting no response. "We come together under fear of The Blessed One's power and His anger when we break His Commandments," he corrected Jesus. "There are many interpretations of the scriptures, differing even from village to village, and our people are severely split as to how to observe the Books. But all signs point to a Blessed One of wrath who will bring terrible punishment on us if we disobey Him. "

Although the scriptures were very exact in their depictions of God's word, there existed no one universally accepted interpretation of the five books. The Pharisee fraternity of lay priests had limited sway over the populace in Galilee with their thoughts on the Torah. Each of these lay priests (not called rabbi until later) could put their own spin on the interpretations of how to conduct one's daily life. So Israel became a land in endless debate over how to observe the laws of its God. Joel reveled in these discussions. He defined himself by the minutia he could bring forth from memory. In fact, he could not imagine a good Jew discussing much else, unless it was his crops or animals, or to complain about the wealthy Sanhedrin ruling body in Jerusalem, whom he thought to be impostors — not of the right line of priestly ancestors. Judaism was, in part, a culture of debate.

Jesus nodded, as much to himself as to the busy figure now putting scrolls and books in the Ark. "Isaiah says that The Father will send one who will suffer for our Nation, one who comes up as a root out of dry ground. Daniel says He will be both a suffering servant and son of The Father with the power to forgive sins. What say you about these prophecies?"

Joel was intrigued by this questioning, especially by one not widely known as a scholar.

Speaking with his usual self-assuredness, Joel answered, "Suffering is a part of our service. The Messiah will be divine. Why would He suffer? The true sufferers will be the non-believers. As The Holy One said, 'I will show wonders in the heavens and in the earth, blood and fire and pillars of smoke.' It will be a terrifying time for the unclean and the pagans. Just be comfortable, Jesus," he intoned in a fatherly way, "that you were born of Abraham's line and that you do good works, and you obey the prophets and The Holy's instructions. Blessed be His Name asks no more."

Jesus felt a tightening in the back of his neck at the smugness and defiant certitude with which Joel spoke. Seeing little point in arguing over interpretations, he sat with an obvious glumness. 'A root out of dry ground,' he thought as he imagined just who this most-waited-for Son of The Father would be and how He would arrive. Jesus felt that the message of this Son would have to be a new one, a dramatic departure from the way of life now led by the likes of Joel, whose Pharisee fraternity had become nothing more than dry ground.

Joel closed the sycamore wood lid on the Ark, "Oh, you may not have heard. One with zeal, Dan, was hung alive from a tree yesterday. They ran him down in the nearby hills. There is much talk of his family and followers taking revenge on the Romans, but I suspect they will continue their cause by shouting around the village well, and with an occasional ambush. They have the sentiments of all those who would like to see the Romans and the other dogs out of our land, but they don't yet have the support for a real war."

"The war is not with the outside; it is within," Jesus said as he looked up at Joel for the first time. His eyes had a burning look about them, reflecting a depth of conviction that made Joel suddenly look away out of a fear he could not fathom. There was an authoritativeness about Jesus, unusual in that his tone of voice had an elegance the educated Joel had never heard from a common laborer.

"First, Teacher, there must be a change of mind by our people. A change of mind that will allow true repentance; to truly see who The One is, for we live in a circle of gods. The idols of jewelry and fine clothing, of owning two donkeys instead of one, of offering cinnamon and other fine spices to a guest," he said, waving his arm in a broad sweep. "We surround our lives with materials that we would not give up even for The Father, while others worship their interpretation of the Books with a smugness that is its own idol."

Joel felt an instant revulsion at the implications of Jesus' revelations. Who was this man with wood shavings under his nails to come into this holy place and make such statements? Why was he calling The Holy One 'The Father?' It was much too intimate.

His eyes narrowed in anger as he asked with great suspicion, "And just what does 'change one's mind' about the scriptures mean? That..." The word hung in the air as though it were a knife point about to be thrust, "That is a very dangerous phrase, carpenter. You speak against tradition!" His eyes flared as his voice raised in pitch.

Jesus quickly realized he was being misunderstood. "No, no, not change one's mind over the scriptures, but open one's mind to the Word, so that a change of mind could take place."

Joel was thrown off by the answer, and, needing somewhere to direct his overflowing hostility, he turned and snapped at his son, "Work on your signs, boy. I have one who would purchase a scroll, so don't tarry!" The slight-framed boy sat on a stool and started copying while he listened.

Their conversation was interrupted by a large man in a finely stitched linen robe bordered with blue tassels and a high, white fold of cloth on his head; he burst through the door, dragging a ragged-looking man with disheveled hair behind him. The large man, Aaron, was another Pharisee who owned a large olive oil press and acres of orchards. He was a more advanced Pharisee, meaning he had had more intensive schooling. Aaron was also a member of the local court, and an even more scrupulous observer of the scriptures than Joel. Behind his back many called him 'camel knees' because he prayed so often and so publicly during the day. Pushing the man into the center of the room, Aaron announced, "Unclean!"

Joel demanded with all the authority his voice could muster, "How did you defy the scriptures, Lathan?"

Lathan was in his forties; slight of build in the best of times, he now looked emaciated. He was barefoot, and his tunic was tattered and soiled. He had lived on a nearby farm; he had been a familiar figure on court days and in the little market that sprang up around the town well.

"My wife is with child, and we have no food. I caught a hare and several lizards. We were forced to cook them, and as we were eating by the side of the road, Aaron walked by and saw us." Lathan hung his head in shame at the desperation that caused him to eat forbidden food.

Joel stuck his chest out as he tried to muster all the height and physical force he could to give more authority to his words. "As you well know, eating things that crawl on their bellies like lizards is forbidden by the Law, but exceptions are made if it would save the life of a pregnant woman. However, the Law does not excuse you, a healthy man capable of work and wages."

Lathan drew his skinny frame up, trying to assume some measure of pride. "I lost my farm in foreclosure. I hurt my back while plowing. I am now reduced to begging. I needed the food as badly as my wife."

"We all have hard times, Lathan, but that is the measure of our faith. Consider the testing of Job by The Holy One. Perhaps you are being tested, and I would say that today you gave in to the angels of darkness." Joel clinched his jaw in a facial statement of finality.

"I judge that you will remain unclean until after Passover," he commanded. "We will recommend this tomorrow at the meeting of the judges." Both of the men sat on the city court because of their age and money.

The bedraggled man's whole being appeared to slump downward as he turned to leave. Jesus walked to him, placed his hand on the bony frame of the man and said with cheer and great joy, "It is said: 'You are the fairest of the sons of men; grace is poured upon your lips.' Therefore, The Holy One, blessed be His Name, has blessed you forever."

Lathan looked startled. Tears welled in his eyes as Jesus reached down into his bags and pulled out dried fruit and flat bread with olives. He placed the food into the reluctant hands of the man.

Jesus gently lifted Lathan's arms in prayer, then lifted his own. Praying from Psalms, he sang softly, "O Father, who art on high, be merciful to Lathan, O Father, be merciful to Lathan, for in Thee his soul takes refuge. In the shadow of Thy wings he will take refuge till the storms of these hard times pass by. If it be Thy Will. Amen and amen." His voice was soft but with a resonance that carried like the hum of distant bees over the room.

"Who are you, Master? I do not know of you." Lathan asked with a mixture of awe and fear. "Are you a teacher or…"

"Oh, it's just Jesus from Nazareth," Joel blurted out in cynical dismissal. "He's a carpenter. He repairs plows and things." It continued to anger Joel that Jesus was saying 'Father.' It was so unheard of that he was speechless to address this apparent blasphemy.

"Well, he has repaired my heart," Lathan said solemnly as he stood. "You are more than a wood worker." He took the sack of food, cast a critical eye at the two priests and left.

Aaron cleared his throat for attention and attempted to bolster the prestige of his friend. "The Holiest One will be pleased with your judgment, Joel. I will spread your decision throughout the village."

Joel, not wanting Jesus' kindness to point out any compassionate shortcomings of a teacher, instructed Aaron, "Have Lathan come to my door, and I will provide him with some fresh breads and soup."

"You are known for your works, teacher," Aaron gushed, ignoring what Jesus had just done. "I will fetch the poor soul."

Joel raised his eyebrow with a look of boredom as Jesus stood silently. "Well, it looks as though you are awaiting a reward also," he said with some annoyance. He pulled a Jewish coin from his robe. Instead of handing it to Jesus, he laid it on a shelf with a obvious thud and an air of disdain before leaving for his adjoining house. "Your coin," he said, as he motioned for his son to follow him. He walked out, humming in a satisfied baritone voice.

Jesus shook his head at the contemptuousness, started not to take the coin, then remembered how it would help his mother. He gathered up his tools for the final bit of carving on the lintel above the outside door.

Joel walked into his living quarters, where his wife was pulling a tray of bread from a hot clay oven. "Which of us has sinned that we have such a rebellious child?"

His wife glanced at him as she picked up a clothes basket. "Perhaps it is not our sins, but that you are too hard on him." Her voice had a weariness about it.

Ignoring her response, he asked, "Did you see Mary's son Jesus in the assembly room today?"

"Jesus? Which Jesus? Which Mary?"

"Oh, you remember the family of Joseph the builder? The boy, well, man now, thinks he is a scholar!" Joel emphasized the word "scholar" with a laugh. "But he's just some village stonemason. How absurd!"

"Isn't everyone now either a scholar, a mystic, or a special messenger of the Almighty?" She said with some annoyance. She had little interest in the conversation and went outside to bring in some clothing she had left to dry.

Their son walked in reluctantly. "Papa, I would like to stay and play more word games with Jesus. He is no ordinary worker."

Joel glared, "I will not have you sitting at the feet of some low class plow maker who happens to have a good memory! I see his face, and I know his kind. I've heard he will drink wine at any table that invites him in. He has been seen in the company of many women, talking too freely with them; why, he's not even married, and he must be over thirty. That's the way of these traveling workers — no respect for the beauty of discipline. They're misfits, wanderers, dreamers, would-be philosophers. They roam our roads with their advice for anyone foolish enough to offer them a seat at their table. I remember this Jesus as a young man; he was a dreamer; one who thought too much. His mouth blows as the east wind…all dust and hot air."

Joel's anger rose even more, "And you said he told you of a different way to interpret the scriptures! The Law is all that holds our people together. Why, this man may be a blasphemer. 'Different' is a very dangerous word when connected with the Words. He could be filled with the angels of darkness, and you are to stay away from him."

Joel was leaning over the boy. He was a formidable father; a stout figure acknowledged as a deadly fighter twenty-five years earlier when the Jews had revolted against the cruelties of Herod's son, Archelaus.

Seeing his father work himself into a rage, Little Isaiah ignored him and walked back into the assembly area. Jesus did not see the small figure standing inside the room staring at him. The boy was fascinated by an easiness about the carpenter; Jesus was an adult with a childlike glee and an enthusiasm for playing word games with the boy and telling parables to see if he could understand them. Then Jesus would laugh heartily when Little Isaiah could not answer. But Jesus seemed to find his greatest joy in explaining to the boy what the parable meant. The intellectual nature of Little Isaiah made him want to

51

write in shorthand whatever Jesus had said, to later tease his friends with, in their own games of one-upmanship.

Jesus had overheard Joel's angry denunciation in the next room, and walked to the open window, raised his arms and extended his hands out. He appeared as a silhouette in the long rays of the setting sun.

"Oh, Eternal One, the Highest and the Holiest, sometimes I feel so close to you that I wish to call you Abba. I thank You for allowing me to honor Thy name by providing Lathan in his moment of need with food and some words of comfort. I ask that You bring peace to the heart of Joel as you have brought it to mine. I am thinking of You more and more, and my heart fills with a joy I have never known. I want to walk through the villages shouting of how our Nation must open its mind to your love, to a new covenant, and to Your coming, but I am a teacher only to a few close friends, and a mere builder who has no authority to most. Know that I will continue to speak of You and Your greatness to those who will listen. Blessed be Thy Name, Holy One. Amen and amen."

He watched as the evening began to gather like smoke, smudging features and forms in the village into a softening gray. Night was casting a veil on the clear, blue afternoon sky with a deepening purple. The afterglow stayed on like an echo reverberating in a lingering statement against the encroaching darkness. Jesus quickly reached into his tool pouch, and finding a small hammer and several chisels, stepped outside the main door of the assembly. He had a few final notches to make in a carving that he had drawn earlier in charcoal on the lintel over the door. He had carved a border of a twirling vine, and in the center he chipped the last pieces of wood that revealed a pot of manna and Aaron's rod. Finished, he stepped from the stool he had been standing on and looked at his work.

A short, dark skinned, and wrinkled little man with a wiry white beard approached. It was Levi the Elder, called that because he was the oldest man anyone knew in the entire Galilee area. He had been a teacher for decades, a scribe at the Temple in Jerusalem, and had been a part of Herod's circle of advisers at one time.

"Your work graces our assembly," his voice was small and high-pitched, almost like a child singing.

Jesus turned and looked down at the little figure dressed in several layers of draped clothing. He looked like a walking bundle of robes and mantels except for the clarity of his eyes focusing out from under a tangle of brows. Jesus thought he looked like an old, stumpy olive tree; a gnarl of a man.

"And peace to your house," Jesus answered and bowed slightly. "After this long day, I would agree with the saying, 'Better is the end of a thing than its beginning.'" He put his tools in a crumpled bag on the ground and smiled at the man. "I do think my talents are more for building yokes and plows than for being a carver."

"No, no, you use those gifts well. Most of us spend our brief time here never knowing what we are to do with our talents." He turned his cane in the pale, grainy dirt with a nervous energy that belied his age. "Someone said you were from Nazareth. That you were the son of a Joseph who claimed to be of David." The little man had an impish grin as he talked, as though humor circled every word, and he found amusement in the simplest question.

"Yes, our line does run back to the king, at least my father always told me so, although some of our relatives and others in the village said that being of the line was a claim that many make, and few can prove."

The man cackled and leaned hard with both hands on a cedar cane. "Oh, many want to be a king, or perhaps the next king, or even the Messiah. And to be any of these, it is felt they must be of the line. What do you think, builder? Would you care to be the Messiah?" He was teasing this stranger. It was his way of getting to know someone, to study their reaction to his probing humor.

Jesus cinched his tool bag, and the dull thud of the wooden tools made a muffled sound as he lifted the bag and slipped its strap over one shoulder. "I don't…" he paused, reflecting. "I don't know that we want an earthly king; we already have a heavenly king." He gave a dismissing laugh, "No, I would not be the carpenter who became a king."

Levi grinned; his face rippled in the looseness of its ancientness, and the remnants of his teeth protruded like little yellowed stumps. "Oh, a bold statement," he chirped, obviously enjoying the conversation. "But the sun has fallen and my vision falls with it. I am one of the many that walk through a mist. My eyes have looked too long at the sun's eye. I must be on my way if I am to find my house. Perhaps you would like to breakfast with me in the morrow? I do remember Joseph. I heard him speak at a place of assembly when you were a child. You are tall like he. But are you as holy? We could talk more of these things in the morning."

Jesus almost sagged with tiredness, but he was intrigued by the man and answered, "Tell me your name and where you live. I will be leaving for Sepphoris tomorrow, but I would enjoy your table."

"Levi the Elder," he squeaked, still grinning in his impish way. "I live on a slight rise over the water just beyond the docks. Ask any of the dock workers; they can point you toward the houses where the Methuselah crowd lives," he giggled. "A number of us live in connected houses. By adding all of our memories up, on rare occasions we collectively equal one sane mind."

As they talked, a group of men began talking loudly at the nearby city well. Voices swelled in the evening air. One young man suddenly began wailing and pounding his chest and shaking his finger at the others. Jesus walked to the edge of the group. He was slightly taller than the rest, the average height of the men being five foot six inches, so he could easily see the thin man who now had ripped part of his robe off.

"He did have the right to take the life of the compromiser!" he shouted. "A Jew that will join with the Romans in a business enterprise is no better than the dogs they lie with."

A man who had just joined the group asked what the Jew had done.

A broad-chested man wrapped in a dark robe answered with some authority, "He entered into a business to sell grain to a Roman, and somehow the Roman outsmarted him. Now his family stands to lose one of the best fields on the Jezreel Plain. Mark me," the man continued, "the whole family will all soon be found begging for handouts in Jerusalem because the father wanted to gain more wealth."

An older man in a bleached white robe with maroon stripes shook his head. "We all must deal with gentiles sometime. We have been taxed to death; one dry season is all that separates many of us now from charity. We need to increase our treasure when we can."

"But the Jew had the Roman in his home," the man's voice soared in a angry reasoning, and he began stamping his feet. "He allowed him and other gentile dogs to dine with him. So he wanted to make money; he didn't have to become unclean doing it. We can do business with the Romans, but we don't have to eat with them." The man, his shirt ripped and undergarments exposed, had scattered dust over his garment in his stamping. The dirt yielded its essence easily in puff-like clouds as fine as mist.

"But the one with zeal didn't have to kill one of our own people," a voice spoke out. "If he wants to kill anyone, let him kill the Romans."

"So be it," a harmony of voices among the gathering rose in agreement, more studied in their tone than angry.

"We need a leader who will stand against these pagans, both in our house and outside. And especially one who will stand for the Jews of Galilee and not those in Jerusalem who look down on us. I for one saw that leader in our friend who at this hour is stretched over a tree." The angry man began elbowing his way through the group, "You stay and moan over the loss of a betrayer; I go to join those who would defy the Romans." The gathering evening melted around his figure as he moved, still shouting, down the street and toward the road out to the crucifixion scene.

Another man, very dark complexioned and thin of build, said angrily, "He is right; we have turned into a nation of cowards. Where are the great Israelite armies of our ancestors? Where are the heroes who rose after the death of Herod? Only those with zeal are willing to give their lives for the faith! The rest of us fight only over how to interpret the scriptures. We fight for words, not for our nation."

Another answered piously, "But we are fighting for our nation when we debate The Holy One, blessed be His Name. The Word is the bond that makes us a nation. We honor The Holy One when we study His intent, and we strengthen our nation in doing so."

The older man asked angrily to no one specifically, "Have you seen a man hung alive on a tree? It is humiliating. The Books command that no Jew should ever die in that manner, yet the Romans stand ready to get out their nails with the least provocation. We can be true to The Holy One and still live. We must survive in this world, as pagan as it has become. We must be realistic if we are to survive. They surround us with their culture like a wave crashing against the Law. Our people give in to their language and their ways. It is a hard road for many to remain on. Their new city of Tiberias and the rebuilt Sepphoris stand like marble gods, pulling our weak with their theaters and baths and markets. The Romans do nothing better than we."

"They make better mortar," Jesus said impulsively.

He had edged into the crowd toward its center. He felt a sense of excitement, a compulsion to enter the discussion, but he hadn't meant to start out with a statement that so immediately stated his occupation.

55

There was a flurry of comment. No one thought they had heard the voice right. Mortar? What did he say?

"It is not those that can kill our bodies that we should worry about, but those that can kill both our bodies and our souls." Jesus felt like he was suddenly outside of his body and listening to his voice talk from a distance. He had never been a public speaker, and his eyes danced among the darkened forms for a reaction.

A hush fell over the group of thirty men. They stood in brown solemnity, their cloaks, shirts, sandals, and skin all of one family of hue: a pastel, soft tan brownness, a uniformity of sand coloring that covered homes, ground, clothing, skin, hair and eyes, that rendered their whole world as one of immense singularity of tone.

A nasal voice drifted up out of the gathering, "From where comes this wisdom?" They all peered for the source of Jesus' voice.

A clean-shaven man with short hair who smelled of fish, broke the silence with some irritation. "Stranger, would you ignore the evil visited on us by the Romans? We all know the one called I Am is coming soon, but I see no signs of it, and until then we must either live with this evil or overthrow it, and I see no Jewish armies. No, it is this world and these Romans we must worry over."

Jesus could feel the tension of the rebuttal and the muscles tightened along his neck. He had never spoken out on religious issues in any gathering of strangers before. In nearby Nazareth where some of his brothers and sisters kept the old family home, he had rarely asked to read at assembly, nor was he known for taking issue with the local elders on interpretations. Only a small circle of friends knew of his constant reading and his intense passion for discerning the intent of the old prophets. To them he spoke constantly of his thoughts. With his mother in Capernaum, Jesus had begun to live between the two villages. But few here knew him apart from the casual word that he was the one working on the assembly house masonry.

A man taller and much more muscular than Jesus spoke out, his voice an angry rumble. His hair was long and tangled and his skin darkened by the sun. There was an urgency about his voice, like one who would be impulsive and definitely prone to action.

"The Blessed One's coming will be heralded, and I have heard no heralds, and seen no signs of the Messiah. Until such times as I do, I say we go out to the tree where the beloved hangs, cut up the damned guards, and take down the one with zeal." The air seemed to continue reverberating after he stopped speaking.

Jesus felt a rush of words that he wanted to say, but he was anxious about what these men would say if he spoke his mind. Tempers flared easily at these village square debates, and death by stoning came quickly if one strayed too far away from the local understanding of politics.

"I ask if you would rather call up The Blessed One's anger or the anger of the new Babylonians we call Romans. So say the prophets — that it is not father, mother, brother or one's robes or land that matter. It is about our love for The Blessed One and our preparation for His coming. It is about all of us together and each of us alone." Jesus again waited with some anxiousness for a reaction.

Simon's deep voice roared out of the circle. "Whose words speak to us from the darkness? Who would speak against the family?"

"I am Jesus of Nazareth, from the House of Joseph," Jesus answered quietly. "I do not speak against the family. I speak for the family and for our villages. I say we will bring destruction on both if we put our souls into driving out either Antipas or the Romans. The Father will drive them out in His own time, but only if our nation gives its heart and soul to His Kingdom through renewal of our faith." His voice calmed, "The Kingdom will be for the little flock, not for men of violence."

An older grey-bearded man, in a robe that had been bleached so white it almost gave off light in the evening darkness, grumbled, "Better you hide that face or in the morn someone will put a stone in the middle of it. We care nothing for those who find no fault in Rome or its lackey Antipas. "

"Oh, I find great fault with the Romans," Jesus corrected. "They are one of the faces of the devil that stalks our land. They are the Babylonians of today, the Syrians, the Egyptians and all the others who have marched over this land. But how much of our efforts and our blood do we waste in chasing these dark angels, when the greater cause is our own hearts. What is within us is what we must bring out. That's the vineyard we need to work first. Then when we come together in our faith..."

He was interrupted by a gruff, but knowing man's voice, sounding as though he had heard a grain of truth. "Perhaps he has something. We are too split over our faith. We must be of one mind to form a rebellion, and what better way to come together than under the banner of The Holy One, blessed be He?"

Another voice floated out of the shadows, this one cynical. "Easy to say, friend. You get two Jews to agree on anything, and you have the largest army you will ever raise."

This was met with nods and derisive laughter.

Little Isaiah stood unseen among the robes, writing Jesus' words in shorthand in the fading light, until his mother's call sent him scurrying inside. He had been writing on the same leather strip that he had used earlier when recording Jesus' unusual phrases. It was difficult to stand and write while balancing an ink bottle between his arm and side. He rolled the leather up and stuck it inside a pouch, now determined to follow the carpenter around Capernaum and record his words. It was partly rebelliousness against his stern father and partly an attraction toward Jesus that he could not explain.

The elder John, a respected old Pharisee, tried to bring a closure to the gathering. "We Jews live in a delicate balance with the Romans. While we all stand eager to strike hard against those who occupy our land, we lack sufficient agreement among our people to support a war. So you could say that The Holy One has not ordered that this be done. He has not told us the End Of Days is actually here. Though we look for a son of David to lead us and restore Israel to its rightful place among nations, no leader has come forward. I would join my brother Simon before the sun rises if it would be a part of a total war. But those Jews among us who want to drive the Romans out with their ambushes and banditry are but bees with small stingers. Until we get a sign that a Messiah or The Holy One Himself is coming with legions of angels, with heralds that stir our souls, I say The Holy One, blessed be He, is not ready. Let us give comfort to the man's widow tonight in her grief."

There was a general murmur of agreement, and the crowd seemed to split apart. Jesus felt his arm wrapped in a thick hand. He turned to see the burly man looking down through his swirls of black hair.

"I am Simon. I invite you to sup at my house." Not waiting for a response, he turned Jesus and led him down the street that hugged the shoreline. Capernaum was a modest fishing village of less than 2,000. Herod had constructed a post, or small fort, in the center of the town and stood on a rise looking out over the waters of Lake Gennesaret, as some still called it, or the Sea of Tiberias, as the ruler Antipas officially named it in honor of the Emperor. The town's main enterprise was its fishing and processing of the fish for shipment, and as a growing export center for the olives and fruit grown on the nearby plains. Most of its exports went north to the cities of Syria. Very little was exported to Jerusalem. In fact, except for Passover, Jerusalem and its influence seemed far away from the Galilee region.

They walked past the docks and their burning torches on poles that flared over the night so thieves would be hesitant to steal the netting and boats anchored there. Simon pointed to a skiff tied to the wharf. Nets draped heavily on hangers next to the small boat. Water had pooled beneath them as they drained off the day's efforts.

"We netted well today," Simon mused, almost to himself. "I caught one of the largest barbels I've ever snatched off the bottom. But we'll save that for broiling another night. Tonight my mother will fry us some nice musht." He smiled, "If she likes you, she might give you some of her special pickled sardines. But you may not meet my good wife. She has been ill and rests in her bed."

"You are generous to ask me," Jesus said. "We have, or I should say my mother has only recently moved here. We are busy sweeping out the dirt. It is a poorly built place, but there is a fig tree and a well-tended olive tree or two shading the place, and it has a good herb garden." Jesus had to lengthen his stride to keep up with the long, loping gait of the fisherman. He felt he was talking to himself as this Simon galloped ahead.

"Will you be going to Passover?" Jesus almost yelled.

Simon stopped and turned with a look of amazement on his face. "Now why would I do that? It's a three day walk to Jerusalem, a night or two there, then three days back. And all that to worship in a temple run by thieves dressed as high priests?"

Jesus knew well of the disdain many in Galilee felt for their faith's leaders in Jerusalem. Few went to all three of the major festivals there. But many, including Jesus, went to Passover every year. Galilee's Jews considered themselves separated by more than distance from the Jews around the Holy City. They were highly suspicious of the Jewish ruling body and its constant compromising with the Romans. And distance made their independence very easy.

The evening sky was as still and quiet as the sea's waters. Night weighed over Capernaum as they walked in and out of shadows cast by large torches the city had set along the main street that paralleled the sea.

So small was the village that they found themselves at the door to Simon's black basalt stone house within minutes of having left the gathering. The home was attached to several others, all around a shared courtyard, and all consisting of unfinished basalt and hand-made brick walls plastered in white that was streaked and splattered with dried mud where the plaster joined the ground. The courtyard had a shared oil press and clay oven for cooking bread. Dust clung to the plastered outside like a veiled coating, giving it a perpetual tan coloring. Each house had a flat roof for sleeping in the summer's heat and praying. On each roof was also a shed or an open upper room for guests to spend the night in without disturbing the host living below. Stairs climbed steeply up the outside of the house to the roof. Each home had a single window covered tightly by goat skin or wood slats that swung outward. It was feared that too many windows invited thieves. For that reason they were also cut high on the outside wall.

Simon's house was typical, though a little larger than the others. It was basically a large room for sleeping and eating, and a small cooking area that was a shallow pit in the floor. The place smelled, as did most homes, of fried foods, garlic and onions, smoke from the small fire, and a hint of human waste from the open sewer drains just outside the house. To counter this, small dishes with burning incense and dried herbs were placed throughout the main room. If nothing else, the home challenged the nose with a conflict of smells from chamber pots to the lingering smells of cooked foods.

The large room contained cushions and rugs, two tables, one on a pedestal, the other with three legs. Hand lamps proliferated, filled with oil and painting the room in soft pastels. Only the rugs had bright colors woven into them. The cooking hearth had a small flame heating a pan filled with slices of fish. Food was generally cooked outside in the courtyard oven shared by four families. Clay jars filled with foodstuffs lined the shelving along the walls.

Simon's size and deep voice filled the room, but he spoke lovingly to the tall, solid woman bent over the fire. His wife lay in bedding along one wall. They had been giving her goat's milk and barley porridge, and she now slept easily, oblivious to her husband's voice.

"Mother, this is one of Mary of Nazareth's sons, Jesus. He's come to share in our meal." Both men had slipped off their sandals as they entered and stood on the rugs that were spread out over a flagstone floor.

"Welcome. I have some fish, radishes, dried fruits and bread. I wish we had a better wine to offer you," the woman smiled broadly. She wore a small rolled bronze amulet around her neck. Though a Jew, she, like many others of the faith, had numbers, signs, and symbols imprinted on the thin sheet as magic to ward off fevers.

Jesus was struck by her gentleness and said worriedly. "Oh, I have come unexpectedly and placed a burden on you. I can come another time."

Simon's voice boomed as though they were a hundred feet apart, "Let me give you a proper welcome."

He then kissed Jesus abruptly and with gusto on each cheek, then, picking up a small jar beside the door, he sprinkled a rose smelling perfume over Jesus' head. Reaching down again he handed his guest a large bowl with water sloshing in it. Jesus quickly washed the dust from his feet.

"I want to hear your words." Simon said. "Our dinner table is never empty as long as there are fish in the sea. You will be our guest." And with that they sat on the thick rugs. Wooden and clay bowls with food were placed on the rug in front of them. They sat cross-legged and ate with their hands or by slurping any liquids. The clay plates and goblets were cleansed along with their hands.

"Tell me, what is life like in Nazareth?" Simon asked.

"Oh, the land will easily feed a family. But so much of the land has been taken over by a handful of owners. Families who have lived for generations on the land are suddenly cast out and told to come back as workers. I too have gotten little work from the new landowners. There was work for all while Antipas rebuilt Zippori (Sepphoris) and then built Tiberias. There's even little work still being done at The Temple. This has left many skilled craftsman wandering the roads. There is more work up this way," Jesus said.

"You know where our taxes and first crops have gone!" Simon almost yelled. "Into Tiberias! Antipas has built a damned monument to glorify Rome. Every fish we bring onto the dock is taxed. Why, we have to smuggle some of our catch in after dark."

Jesus nodded with a discernible sadness. "Lying about what you make on your loom and what you catch in the sea has become a part of our culture. Keeping possessions has become more important than keeping one's faith."

Simon dragged a piece of bread across a dish filled with clear, thick olive oil, letting the oil soak into the porous bread. "Well, I say the answer is to bring our people together in an army, just like the Maccabeans did years ago. We need a leader who will drive the angels of darkness out of our land. We need a rebellion like we had after the death of Herod."

He looked intensely through his bushy brows at the long figure of Jesus. "So what is your trade? I thought you were a teacher when I heard your words at the well. It was the way you spoke that made me want to learn more. But your dress is that of a builder."

Jesus sat and crossed his legs, straightening his back as he did. He was taken with the burly bravado and intenseness of the big man reclining before him. He was attracted to men of passion, but not fools.

"I build a lot of scaffolding for brickmasons, though I make and lay brick and set stone walls. But I like wood, its textures and colors, more than stone." Then he laughed heartily, "but sometimes the wood works on me."

He held up the reddened finger in which the splinter had stuck, and showed a nail that was discolored from having been jammed between some stones he was laying.

"I admire the ability of carpenters to see the form of a plow or a building before it's built and to make things good that are broken. I have no talent beyond flinging my nets," the burly man mumbled as he heartily ate his food. "My brother always puts me first on the rope to pull the seine in." He laughed heartily, "That's what I am, not a fisherman, but a rope puller."

"Oh, I don't know," Rachel, his mother, interjected. "I'd say you have many talents." She stood from her cooking and counted on her fingers in a sarcastic way. "Let's see, there is cursing. There is fighting. There is snoring until the animals want to run from their shed. Then there is eating as much as five men, and…" she paused as though this were a serious recitation, "there is drinking a vineyard of wine daily."

Simon and Jesus both laughed heartily.

"Only my mother can say these things," Simon roared in his normal speaking tone, " I would feed anyone else as bait to the fish!"

He took a bite of the oil soaked bread and some of it ran out over his black beard. There was a clumsiness about him, but there was also a boyish appeal.

Jesus picked up the previous conversation, "I learned about wood and stone from my father. We worked on many buildings over in Bethsaida when I was young. Papa had me learn to read and write some Greek there. He said this would help me. He said my gift from

The Holy was not to be in working stone or wood. He taught me much of the scriptures, and he taught me the honor of work. Any work, but especially the work of the mind."

Jesus grinned and held up both hands, which were long fingered and thick around the wrist. "Looking at these tools of my trade and how badly bruised and bloodied they are, I would say my Papa was right. But in our world, the mind puts little food on the table. It is the back."

Rachel liked his self-deprecating humor and the relaxed way he talked. She felt she had known him before; he fit so quickly and easily into the flow of their conversation.

Jesus took a drink of wine from a clay goblet. "I was building a shelf in the assembly house today when I came out and heard the people speaking of the one nailed to a tree. I knew of him. He has helped many people, but his hatred for the Romans overcame the love that should fill his heart. I fear that kind of hatred will bring the Romans down like a hammer on us."

Simon shifted his weight and thanked his mother as she placed a plate before them with cucumbers, barley porridge and raisins on it. His interest in their conversation seemed to heighten, almost into an eagerness. "That's why I was interested in you coming to our home. I have not heard one speak the words you did, and I wanted to hear more. You speak with authority, though I am uncertain who it is from. I didn't know if I was listening to one who would lead a revolution, or one who would give a different interpretation of the Torah. We live for that time when the One King will come with his hosts of armed angels and drive these sons of dogs into the sea. If you wish to lead a fight, you will find many willing to join."

Jesus felt a hesitation; he had spoken impulsively to the group at the well. "The…" He paused, "The prophets, as I have been reading them, say that the Kingdom is our only concern. As evil as the Romans are, we cannot be distracted from our purpose here, and that is to glorify The Father."

"So you don't think The One's purpose is to destroy the Romans and restore Israel to a leader among nations?" There was a touch of anger and accusation in Simon's voice.

"I do believe that He wants to restore Israel, but He is more concerned with us individually and how close we can come to His perfection. Will our nation be saved with an army? The words of The Psalms of Solomon say The Father will raise up a king from David's line who will neither rely on horse and rider and bow, nor will he collect gold and silver for war, but he will strike the earth with the word of his mouth forever."

Simon took a long appraisal of Jesus. There was a gentleness about his eyes, but his mouth was a confluence, like clashing currents of varying emotions: a full grin one minute, a disturbing sadness another, then a soft, almost effeminate smile, loving and understanding. The rough-edged Simon was as much fascinated by the complexity of this man as he was by his words. He was also disturbed, and confused that Jesus kept referring to The Father. It sounded too familiar; too personal.

"So you also see a Messiah, but he won't head an army of angels, and he's going to talk the Romans into leaving. Hah!" he said in disbelief.

"I also believe that we are all in the image of The Father. That He is within each of us and that when we look upon one another, we see His image." Jesus let the sentence hang as though waiting for a response.

"Hah!" Simon roared. "I hope He doesn't have my face, or I'll find another god to worship!"

They all laughed heartily and didn't hear the door open.

"Brother!" Simon looked up as a much smaller man entered the room. His hair was short and reddish brown, and not combed with the neatness with which Jesus wore his. Jesus smiled at the direct, rugged way of these fishermen and noticed how deeply life on the lake had etched their faces. There was great character in their lines that mapped their life on the plane of water over which they rode and flung nets and cursed and caught the winds.

"Andrew, this is Jesus, a builder from Nazareth. He will be living in our village off and on." The men kissed each other's cheeks, and Andrew sat as his mother served a baked mushti fish on the same plate the fruit had rested upon. She put bread on the plate and poured olive oil across it.

Simon's voice boomed with a kinetic excitement as he looked at Jesus while speaking to Andrew. "Jesus is well read in the prophets and is saying things I have not heard. I'm not sure of his words, but they are of great interest to me. Sit, sup with us and listen," he invited.

Simon took a great bite of bread as he talked so his words were slightly garbled. He ate with the same relish as he talked—hurriedly.

He pounced on words, throwing them out like projectiles with a startling and riveting force.

"We're good Jews. If we do good works and observe the Laws, we will be at the side of the Ancient of Days when He comes to restore the greatness of Israel," Simon asserted.

Jesus ate quietly for a moment. "I have studied much of Isaiah, Ezekiel and Daniel. I hear in their sayings that a messenger is coming to show the way directly to the Kingdom. We will not need to depend on the priests and scribes to tell us how to enter the Kingdom. We will not need all of their interpretations of the Law. We will not need to waste our animals as sacrifices to the Temple, or even pay our meager denari in taxes. We can each speak directly to the One as Moses did. And I am thinking more and more that it is a simple thing He asks. It is obedience to Him. It is to follow only Him. It is to simply love Him and Him alone. I say that it is all very simple. I say, forget new Babylonians that come from Italia. It is the children of the Nation preparing ourselves for the Coming that is important.We have exiled ourselves in our own land, and it is an exile brought on by our own wickedness. We are surrounded by gods of our own making. I even wonder if we can live in a land as rich as Galilee and be true in our faith. I wonder if we all should not move back out to the wilderness where our world is stripped of all of its distractions."

They gasped audibly. Simon put his plate on the rug. Andrew felt his body move slightly away from Jesus. Their mother pushed back against a shelf as though the words rode on some frightful, howling wind. "You say?" She gasped. "But do the prophets say this?"

Simon almost whispered, his face had a frightened look. "I am glad it is late and no ears are around other than our own. These are words we have not heard. I hear you say we attack our own Temple and throw out our own leaders. This is new. It's, it's very dangerous."

"I say nothing that has not been said before," Jesus said matter of factly. "Isaiah, in speaking of the servant, spoke of our faith as it is today when he said, 'He sees many things but does not observe them; his ears are open, but he does not hear.' The way to the father has always been among us in the Laws, but few see or hear anymore. We are too bound up in following our self-appointed priests and worrying over the Romans. The Father's breath is all about us, but we do not feel its power. He speaks to us directly. We are all priests. We do not require that others connect us to His love. But it is to His love we must go and go quickly for He is truly coming."

65

Simon's face contorted and twisted as though he were in pain, and the words burst from him in an attempt to understand what he had just heard, "You're not a carpenter! Who are you? No stone mason could utter such words. Where did you learn these things?"

Jesus almost blushed at the strong reactions. He raised his hand in protest, "No, no, I am only a man who works with his hands. I have never spoken in the place of assembly. My father taught me Hebrew and the Law when I was young. I have read the Word all my life."

Jesus paused, reflecting, then said, "As I have grown older, I have thought on these things more. I ask, have the Pharisees not placed walls between us and The Holy One with their endless interpretations? Have the Sadducees not taken our sacrificial animals and taxes to enrich themselves more than to make the way straight to the Kingdom? Do they not compromise the Word as they try to appease the Romans? I see our shepherds getting richer and most of the lambs getting poorer. I wonder if they have not turned their backs on the Kingdom. I ask myself these things."

Andrew spoke. His voice was more tenor, and it rang in the small room with a high-pitched tone tinged by fear. "Are you not afraid you will defy the interpretations, the very Laws themselves? Don't you speak outside tradition? Should we not worry that the one called I Am will be angered? Should we not rid our house of you, or else our house be cursed?" Words, thoughts, worries, and fears all flew from Andrew's mouth. He started to stand, thinking he might bolt from the room.

Jesus looked at Andrew with a frightening intensity. Emotions ran over his face and through his voice that were both passionate and almost angry, but no one in the small room felt he was mad. They watched his face as much as they heard his words, and the two were a powerful combination.

But then the velocity of his force changed in an instant and Jesus held his right hand with the fingers raised toward Andrew like a calming wand. Andrew felt he could not move in any direction. He was terrified of what sounded like blasphemy, but he was also caught by the look of this stranger in his home and the uniqueness of what he was saying. He was confused, awed, frightened, and immobilized by Jesus' sheer audacity in confronting the Temple.

Jesus then spoke with a calmness that drew the brothers and their mother into his voice. "In Isaiah, the Word says that a foundation of stone, a tested stone, a precious cornerstone, is being laid in Israel for those who see Him as their foundation. That doesn't say that a stone is being laid around the tangle of interpretations and sacrifices. It says to me that the stone is being laid for those who see our Lord as their foundation."

Simon cocked his fleshy face at an angle. His eyes darted over Jesus as though he were viewing some strange geography. He asked in disbelief, "So you say, you think, you ask…that," and then he could not form exactly how he interpreted Jesus' words, and his voice just stopped.

Andrew, who had moved to the door, cautiously said, "I have heard of one called John the Baptizer who is speaking near Jericho. He speaks of the world's ending and the glory of heaven coming soon. Perhaps you should go and hear his words and see what you think."

Jesus had not spoken these thoughts to anyone outside his small circle of friends, and he was emboldened by the fishermen's reactions. He felt a swell within him, as though the words were a wave, and their inherent power was lifting him to say more of these ideas he had been developing.

Jesus nodded, "I have heard he speaks from the wilderness, that he feels the prophets spoke of our time, that these are the days that they spoke of when they said the Kingdom was coming. He speaks on the eastern bank of the Jordan, baptizes in the river, then sends those who have repented onto the western bank, thus symbolizing our ancestors crossing into the promised land."

Jesus thought for a moment, then said, "He is about being reborn in the Spirit. I do want to go and hear him, but Jericho is some distance, and my mother is in need now of my work." Mary's admonitions about the work she needed done at her new home pushed the talk of God away from his mind.

As though a spell that had been broken, the fisherman suddenly remembered the work of the next day and Simon offered, "We must do this again soon, but it may be best if we not speak of this sup until we learn more from you. Although I must tell you, as wise as your words are, I doubt they are all truth. The Law has been carefully studied and interpreted for centuries by men smarter than the three of us. You may be unaware of what your words say. They speak against the Temple and its priests by saying we can ignore both and enter heaven by going directly to our Lord. You speak of this love. Do you mean the love as one would have for a child, or a wife, or a friend? We are to fear The Most Holy, but love? You do not speak of rising against the pagans, and many of us want that." He spoke with a threatening tone, "We want that almost more than life"

There was such a repressed violence about this large man, that the room almost quieted with the reverberations of his sudden anger. Then Simon looked at Jesus and instructed, "I would ask that you think more on these things and teach us again when you return. See if the prophets still speak to you in this strange way."

They all stood. Jesus cinched a cord tightly around his waist.

Andrew spoke up as he handed Jesus his long woolen robe. "I'm not sure I understand, nor do I know by what authority you speak of these things. But I, too, find myself wanting to hear more. But do not say to anyone that we should ignore the Romans."

"Are you here for a while?" Simon asked.

"No, I have work near Sepphoris," Jesus answered.

"Herod built that city to the glory of his pagan world." Simon scowled and arched his eyebrow disapprovingly at Jesus. "Only the richest Jews live there. So what if its beauty is unsurpassed; what is beauty if it is built on the pain of others? Antipas is a brigand no better than the thieves along our roads. His taxes have caused many of the chosen to give up their property."

"I have seen some of the Greek plays in the small theater there and built several shops," Jesus admitted to them with some caution.

"Plays!?" The brothers asked in unison and with incredulity. "The theater is a place of Roman politics. Why would a Jew go there?"

A strict Jew would not think of attending a play in the theater at Sepphoris or the more elaborate one at Tiberias, and Jesus felt some caution in responding; however, he felt he must stand by his convictions that gentiles were not to be avoided, but to be taught of God's existence in an attempt to save them.

He answered with an obvious enjoyment in discussing the theater, "The Greek plays are mirrors of the heathens that write them, but the hypocrites (actors) are worthy of watching. How they draw the emotions of the audience with their pretending is both entertaining and a lesson. I study them and how the audience reacts."

The brothers found this man perplexing and confusing, but bold in his thoughts and apparently fearless of the opinion of others. He was obviously on a new kind of mission that separated him from the traditional Jewish faith, although it seemed based on that faith. There was a titillation, an excitement, about what Jesus said. It was fresh with a simple purpose and promise, though they could not grasp its fullness.

Jesus changed the subject, "Tomorrow I will be working for a wealthy Jew who owns apartments in Sepphoris." He smiled, "My mother will be pleased that I will be paid in coin and not in dried fish or fruit." His voice filled with humor so that his words spilled out as a talking laugh, "I often have to work harder to bring my earnings home than I do to earn them."

Andrew laughed in a giggling, boyish contrast to the deep, tumbling laugh of his brother, "I can see you being paid in chickens or goats or other animals, and having to carry and lead all of these creatures, squawking and kicking, over miles of road! Especially with the thieves that roam our countryside. Why you might be robbed of a chicken!" He joked in laughter.

Simon spoke, barely stifling a chuckle, "We give our work a free boat ride. It is from the sea into the frying pan."

Jesus smiled at Simon's remark, and, responding to Andrew, said, "The devil roams our land in many guises. I suppose I look as though I've already been robbed in my carpenter's clothes. A thief might say, "All that man has is his chickens. Let's forget him!"

"You're never too poor to be robbed on these roads, or run over by a horse as the Romans thunder by with their shining helmets and stubby little swords." Simon's anger rumbled out in punctuated words that hit the air like fists.

"Tell me again, Jesus," Simon continued, "how it is that you speak with such feeling and knowledge on our faith, yet you see no harm in spreading our faith to the gentiles? We, not those dogs, are The Chosen."

"You limit the power of The Father when you say that," Jesus disagreed. He had thought long over the reach of God, and that if He was the Great Creator and a loving God, then His love must be unconditional and endless and universal in its scope, or else He would be no more than a tribal and fickle God, who was only interested in the Israelites and who found pleasure in using the remainder of the human race as pin pricks to jab, harass, and subjugate the hapless Jews. Jesus found the heart of God to be breathtaking in its scope.

He answered Simon with great self-assuredness, "The door to heaven is open to all who will knock. The gentiles can never knock if they are never told. While He has favored the Israelites, He is the shepherd over all of the nations' sheep. Would He not want us to go out to all the nations, praising His name to them? To do otherwise is to say that His love is limited. I interpret the Books to say it is without limit."

The men's eyes darted over the face and figure of Jesus, then to one another. Their brows furrowed, their mouths crooked and twisted nervously, as they ruminated over Jesus' words.

Suddenly Andrew blurted out, "Oh, I see. You believe we could conquer the Romans through our faith." Then he stopped as though that line of thinking made no sense as he understood the world. "But the Assyrians, Babylonians, Greeks — all were past conquerors, and our faith changed none of them. Only the children of the Twelve Tribes know our Lord. Others would make our people slaves."

Jesus asked, "What if The Holy One sent a messenger who told you that The One wanted more from you than good works, more than chasing Romans, more than going to the Temple three times a year. What if this messenger told you that you, Andrew, had to make your own peace with Him and then go out to all the nations and spread His Word?"

Simon's baritone voice rattled the room, "Well, of course, we would put away our knives and go out onto the roads. But we have seen no such command. The Books say we are the Chosen above all others. We are separate and better in The Holy One's eyes than other peoples. We have no need to bring them into our faith. And we have seen no such messenger, though all the Israelites speak of one coming."

Jesus felt a surge of conviction that swept him up and made him want to say, 'I may be that one — don't ask me why I believe this, but I feel it in all of its terrifying wonder.' But the words would not come. Although with each conversation he was becoming more certain in his message, he would just as quickly withdraw within himself; the sudden feelings of inadequacy shook his frame and sent his mind running for a change in the conversation. The thought was just too stunning to speak.

He breathed deeply, putting a finality on the discussion. "The history of our people has been one of debate. It must be a gift of The Holy One, or His way of being entertained by our endless arguments." Jesus laughed, "It is no wonder that we consider ourselves sheep; that must be what we sound like to Him." Jesus impulsively bleated like a lamb, which broke the tension, and all three started bleating and laughing as he gathered his robe and moved out the door.

"Seek us out at the docks when you return," Andrew said cheerfully. "We will remember your name and this evening. And I would be interested in your thoughts on this baptizer if you have the chance to go down there and listen to him."

"When the weather warms," Jesus said. He bleated and laughed again as he disappeared into the night, "And when my mother has all the chickens that I can chase back to her from Zippori," he yelled back out of the dark.

The chill of the late winter air caused him to hurriedly slip into his boots and drape the heavy robe about his shoulders. It was a clear night, with a full moon casting its softness over the small town in a candlelight brightness that allowed him to easily negotiate the dirt streets that led away from the waterfront house and back to his mother's home.

Mary had her sleeping gown on when Jesus pushed open the wooden door that he had built and framed. She was of average height, of a thin frame and weighed less than the average woman in her forty-ninth year. She stood very erect, but there was a distinct gentleness, a loving quality about her. Her hair was losing its deep brown to a rain of streaks of gray. Her face was full, the cheeks tapering down to a small chin. Wrinkles spread from her eyes and mouth in a testimony both to the hard life she had led since her husband's death and to an unremorseful sun that marked the skin of all who worked the land. They had never been totally impoverished. Her husband's architectural and building work had given them a modest, comfortable life, and her many children had worked their small farm well. Since his death, most of their land had been sold, and some lost in unpaid loans in the land grabs by Antipas to be given to the wealthy and powerful. Two of her sons worked in the remaining vineyards and fields that belonged to them on the outskirts of Nazareth. Jesus, being the first born, had inherited most of the land. But he had deeded it to his mother.

Jesus had continued his father's work, but many of the large construction projects started by Herod, and now his son Antipas, were winding down, and craftsmen walked the land by the hundreds looking for work. At the same time, Jesus had become far more interested in his faith. He had always read; he was the only child of Joseph's that could read Hebrew, and he spoke more about his faith than her other children. But four years ago, in his thirtieth year, it became obvious to all who knew him that a transformation was taking place in his life. It was a seeping infiltration of his mind by the true meaning, the true fulfillment of the Torah. The more he read, and he usually did it alone, the more he begin to see new meanings to the prophecies that the local priest and the Temple priests, or the schools, were not saying. He had always been known for his storytelling abilities, and for a streak of rebelliousness.

At first, he kept all of this to himself, then he began discussing his interpretations with a close group of male friends around his home. He found it exciting. He thought of himself as a warrior of the old prophets; a warrior of words preparing to battle with his own religious leaders and their passion for wealth and authority. He would speak aloud on the plain below Nazareth, posturing and pacing like an actor. But few saw the real intensity of this passion, until now, until recently, when he had found the urge to speak his thoughts: to issue them out gingerly, with timorousness, shy extensions of his ideas, to see what the reaction would be.

Jesus was very close to his mother. He felt she lived God's Word in her easy smile, the gentle way she spoke, the sharing she would do for anyone who came hungry to their door. She easily touched all who came in contact with her with her unconditional love. Mary told her children there was holiness in helping those with less, and Jesus, she thought, of all her children, had taken this message to heart. He had filled their house with every stray animal that whimpered at their door. He had cried easily even as a teenager when when he saw lepers or the crippled being abused. He had been teased as a child and as a teenager for how easily he came to tears over another's pain. He seemed to always seek out those that others shunned. Mary had worried over the way he would take the misfortune so close to his heart. Though his laugh was spontaneous and often, sadness came quickly, and, as a mother, she didn't want her son overburdened with hurt.

As she approached fifty, Mary told her boys that she felt the need to be closer to old friends and family and so was moving to Capernaum, the small, but busy sea town. Two of her daughters, now married, already lived there where their husbands were involved in exporting fish to the north.

There was a gracefulness about her. Her lips were full, her mouth was not wide but expressive, and she saw much of herself in her first born Jesus. She had seen something special in him ever since his birth, when she and Joseph were just starting out and were, like many married teenagers, quite poor and struggling.

"Where have you been? I was worried because you left your work at the assembly long ago and no one seemed to know where you were," she said as she unrolled a feathered pad for sleeping.

The room had one oil lamp flickering its glow and casting deep shadows against the meager furnishings of the room. Jesus picked up a clay hand lamp from a table that rested on a stone pedestal and brought it to the other side of the room where he too began preparing his bedding. "I supped with two fishermen. Their mother knows of you. You must meet these men. I liked their company very much."

She touched her son on the shoulder and kidded, "If I know you, you will have table talk with everyone in Capernaum before the month is out. Few can get a supper invitation as well as you."

They left one small lamp flickering all night. It was the custom. She saw his broad smile in the softness of its glow that enfolded them. "It is not just by bread that we live, mother."

He heard the humor in her voice as she lay down, "Nor is it by wine and visiting; it is also by children and grandchildren." The room was that empty quiet, that full nothingness where heartbeats slow and minds drift lazily as though carried on a languorous and wingless flight. Her voice sneaked across the void, "I wish you would find a good woman, son. You are thirty-five years and one of the few of our faith that has not taken a wife."

It had become a ritual: Mary prodding Jesus in the quiet moments before sleep for her oldest child to give her grandchildren, to carry on the family name, to keep their part of the line of David alive.

"Between my work and my reading, there seems too little time, as I've said," he spoke with the impatience of having had this same conversation over and over.

There was a pause and Mary rebutted in a voice now as weary over the subject as was he. "Temple priests work and read. Scribes and lawyers work and read the scriptures and so do our teachers, and they all find time for a wife. You're a builder, son, not a scribe or a priest. You have only rarely read scriptures in the meeting houses." She paused, then, "Your father would have been proud of your interest in the Torah. He used to say that you were the proverbial well-plastered cistern...not a single drop of scripture escaped from you. He filled your childhood with The Holy, but he would also have wanted his first son to honor the family name by carrying it on.

"Family is the rock of our nation, son. Very, very few go without…" She stopped as she saw him turn on his side away from her and say, "We'll see, mother." He simply wanted the conversation to end.

Jesus had some time ago silently committed himself to celibacy. It had been after several years of torment of trying to come to terms with a growing sense that he was meant for more than a life in stone and wood, but he couldn't fathom his direction, and in the process of that groping, he had begun to read and pray throughout the day and to wonder. He now wanted to see if he could return to the first man, before Eve, when there was only Adam there at the supreme moment of creation, fresh with the touch of his Maker. He wanted to approach a God-like state of perfection where there was no place or need for sexes or sexuality. He was seeking, he knew, a near impossible state for a human—one that he struggled with in all of his humanity.

Mary sighed into the silence, "Good night, Jesus." Her voice traveled the space as gentle as a smoke plume barely pushing itself against the air. She loved him dearly, but worried that he had not found himself. Joseph had told her that he was a special child, that he was of the line of David, and that perhaps he could even be God's messenger. The prophets did say a branch from the vine of David would come one day. "Perhaps," Joseph had said to the child as he held it high over his head, "Perhaps, it will be you, Jesus." Joseph and Mary had talked often of their special child and of the intense dream they both had had of an angel announcing Jesus' birth, but the poverty of their lives and the struggle to survive had pushed away thoughts of royalty and of saviors. She drifted into sleep not thinking of the future of her son. He was a carpenter, a stone mason, a wonderful and kind man, but perhaps not a messenger. Her last thoughts as she drifted away were of her dead husband and how greatly she missed him.

CHAPTER 4

Jesus opened one eye. He had awakened to the sound of a cock clawing at the dawn with its rasping call. The room was dark with edges of light angling under the door and through the cracks in the window shutter. His blanket smelled of fish and onions and garlic from his mother's supper. He could hear the two small lambs stirring in the hay inthe adjacent room where animals were kept on cold nights. Mary was breathing deeply, and he dressed quietly trying not to awaken her, but when he picked up his tool bags, the shifting wood inside startled her awake. Her bed was a wooden platform covered in a grass-stuffed mat and softened with heavy blankets.

"I was dreaming," she apologized in a soft voice.

"I'm sorry I woke you," her son said.

"No, I need to be about. Let me fix you some breakfast."

"I met a man last evening who invited me to come by his house before I left town. I will eat with him." Jesus folded several pair of stockings, a shirt, and robe in a goat skin carrying bag.

"What man?"

"He said his name was Levi the Elder."

Mary lit a lamp, and the room took on a fuzzy lighting. A stray coal had trailed a smoke plume during the night, and it clung fog-like to the ceiling. She unlatched the single window and pushed it open briefly to reveal the clear sky of an emerging day. The early spring morning was too cool to leave the window open and after inhaling a few refreshing breaths, she latched it back.

"Oh, I remember Levi. He came to our house in Nazareth several times to visit your father. He was very learned and seemed to enjoy discussing the finer points of the Books with Joseph."

"Your father would be pleased that you are again reading the Law, but I worry a little when you say you might want to visit at Qumran." She walked over and kissed his cheek, chiding him as he opened the door, "More importantly than visiting a desolate place like Qumran, you might visit a home where the wealthy father needs a good wood worker, and the daughter likes old carpenters with broken finger-nails."

They both laughed as he stepped out into the light breaking over the eastern hills of the lake. The mornings would be warming quicker now with the budding months well under way.

Jesus passed the small garrison stationed in the port town. It was here only because Capernaum sat on the border of the next province making the village a major tax collection point. Two sentries stood with slouching disinterest next to the large stone building that housed the post. None of the passing villagers honored the soldiers with so much as a nod.

As Jesus rounded a corner of the building, he smiled at a helmeted sentry huddled in a long woolen robe against the early air. The sentry nodded back, noting the tool bag Jesus carried over one shoulder.

"Are you a wood worker?" he asked in Greek, more out of boredom than interest.

Jesus stopped and looked into his eyes. He was a young man, of pale skin and round face — typically Roman. "Yes, wood and stone and some carving," Jesus answered in rough Greek. The sentry seemed lonely for conversation, and Jesus asked, "Have you been in our land long?"

"A month."

"Have you found joy here?"

"Joy!" the soldier suddenly became energized in disbelief. "Joy in a land of barbarians? Joy where the people dream of putting a knife in your back? Where there is no circus, no theater, no bath? There will be joy only when I return to the vessel that brought me here."

"Well, enjoy the fish and the fruit. It is good here."

The young man leaned against his spear. "I like the wine better," he said.

"So do I," Jesus grinned back. "May the day be good to you." He bade goodbye.

"The day will be very good when I leave here."

Jesus nodded, adjusted the weight of his bags, and walked around the garrison over the flat-stoned pavement of the main street. It was a short distance down toward the docks and the harbor now filled with the sounds of men stirring about the wooden world of boats and oars.

As he moved away from the basalt blocks of the garrison's main building, two husky men with netting over their shoulders caught up with him. The shorter one, a swarthy man in his twenties asked, "And what were you discussing with the pagan?"

Seeing the anger in their faces, Jesus answered, "A garden of Eden."

They looked at one another, then peered at Jesus as though he were crazy. "That murderer knows nothing of the Garden."

"He knows the sweetness of the grape. He enjoys the fruits that the Holy One has provided us with."

"He eats the fruits of our land that he and his kind have taken by force, by slaughter. He knows nothing of who provided them," A shorter man with a hood over part of his head said with a hissing denial. "Why would you speak to him of the Garden?"

"Is a lamp to be brought in to be put under a bushel or under the bed?" Jesus asked, then answered. "The light should be placed on a table to allow all in the house to see."

"Who are you that speaks in riddles?" the man with the hood demanded.

"Who would you say I am?" Jesus asked.

"I would say either that you are a fool, or that the devil sits on your tongue."

"I am one who would teach even pagans about the Light and the Way."

"You are a Jew who teaches those who would crush our people. There are those who would put a knife into one such as you," the burly man threatened.

"Even the smallest of seeds can grow into the greatest of shrubs, but they must be sown and allowed to sprout into the light."

The men were angered, and one jabbed his finger at Jesus, who stood calmly before them. He felt an inner peace, like a shield, as the men leaned their angry faces close to his. He could smell wine on the breath of one and onions on the other. They appeared to be on the verge of striking him, but he purposefully allowed the joy he felt that clear morning to fill him, and it was reflected in the easy way he stood and the relaxed way his face answered their anger.

"You defy our laws and customs with this crazy talk. You have been told; in this village you don't speak with pagans! Or you will have no tongue with which to speak!" Slightly confused by the way Jesus simply stared back at them, they became intimidated, thinking he may be mad or even a devil, so, with a few added obscenities, they walked away jabbering to themselves, waving their arms in exasperation. The streets, they concluded, were filled with the crazy.

Jesus saw Simon and Andrew together with two other men hoisting their sails, trying to catch what little breeze played about on the waterfront. Seeing they would have to row out, all four began straining at the oars, and their dull bumping against the sides of the vessel joined the general clatter of conversation, and the thuds of clay and wood containers being heaved about as the day of the sea port began. He didn't need to ask directions. A small group of dwellings, all square in shape and browned in mud or blackish in their basalt siding, sat joined by an alley running down the middle. Because the Torah prevented Jews from much activity outside their home on the Sabbath, small wooden arches connected the houses. Many Jews said that since the houses were connected, all the houses were really one house and this enabled families to visit one another on the Sabbath. It was one of many small ways that those who lived by the intricate interpretations of God's Word survived the stultifying strictness of those interpretations.

The houses sat on a slight rise that looked out over the water, and several white-headed elders sat silently on a bench watching the water as it turned from morning gray to a more decided blue. Several gulls drew looping circles searching the water for fish ripples.

"Praise the Light," he greeted as he approached them. "His Word lives in the beauty of this sea."

They turned in a creaking way and smiled. A woman, spindly of leg, hunched in her back, and gnarled in her hands like a tree root, answered, "Give thanks to His Name, for He is good."

"I'm looking for the door of Levi the Elder."

"There," one pointed to a house bunched with others. Its door was irregular within the thick walls and in need of repair as the planking was badly weathered. Goat skin stretched tightly over its one high window.

Jesus knocked on the door, clattering it loosely against its frame. He subconsciously began appraising how it could be fixed, when the door scraped open against a rock flooring. Levi the Elder stood in all of his miniature grandeur in the light. He had a single robe on, like a large night shirt, and he busied his bent fingers with tying a cord around his waist. Levi waved his hand in a bare movement for Jesus to come in.

"Peace be unto your house," Jesus said in the customary greeting before entering. He removed his sandals and left them on a mat next to the door.

"Praise The Name, and welcome," Levi said and waddled in the stiffness of his age over to a depression at one side of the room where a small fire burned. A young girl with a two-handled clay water jug was emptying its contents in a larger brass pot.

78

Levi thanked her and she left. He asked Jesus if he would fill two silver goblets with the water. "Why is it that our mind grows stronger as our body grows weaker?" Levi asked rhetorically. "I have trouble pouring my own water now and emptying the same water from my bed pot." He sat next to the fire on a cushioned bench.

"I am preparing some locust for myself, just like an old beggar," Levi cackled as he plucked the heads, the front legs, and the skinny part of the back legs off the large insects. He would boil them in salty water then sprinkle nutmeg over their cooked remains. They had a crunchy, decidedly shrimp-like taste.

Bending his head over and raising both hands, he said a short prayer. He washed off the clay plates and two beautifully carved silver goblets, then offered Jesus a plate with figs, dates, a small piece of dried fish, and some bread with oils to dip it in.

"The goblets are from one of the palaces of Herod the Great," Levi said. "Herod and I actually toasted one another with these very goblets. The chests around the wall contain other memories I brought from those days when Herod was transforming our nation into his own image. It was at once exciting and terrifying. The making of an empire is a wave of great exhilaration for those riding it, and, I suppose, crushing for those underneath its force. I tried to save as much of our religion and as many of our priests as I could. I held several positions within his court before he died." He appraised Jesus' age, "About the time you were born I would say."

Jesus nodded as he dipped his bread in the oil. "I was born just before his death. My family briefly fled to Egypt, fearing the violence of his last days. His life affected our people like few others since King David. We still suffer Herod's life, and now that of his sons."

One corner of Levi's mouth went up in a wry, knowing smile, "And what is your understanding of Herod?"

"A man who would be both a Roman king and a Jew. These are difficult to be at once. Herod was always a king first."

Levi chuckled, "I've not heard that. But I would agree. He knew power; he was its servant, and had no problem killing many of the lambs of the Lord, or murdering our Temple priests. He even killed his own wife. Yet he had a desperate hunger to be known as a Jew."

"Many have that hunger, Elder; many believe just because they are born a Jew and called a Jew, that the way to the Kingdom is theirs," Jesus said.

They were now both reclining on a dusty and faded rug in the center of the room. The room was set in the half-light of weak oil lamps. Levi had not yet removed the window covering. The space was a convergence of odors, not all pleasant. The young girl had not emptied all of the contents of Levi's chamber pot, and onions and garlic stalked about. A small bronze incense shovel with coals was producing a reed-thin straight column of cinnamon smoke in a futile attempt to obfuscate the foul odor clinging to the air. But their noses were at home with the pungency of the impoverished.

A shelf to one side was filled with linen-covered scrolls and string-bound books. Each scroll had a tag attached to its wooden handle with the name of the writer. A work table sat next to the bench with several hand-held oil lamps and a papyrus sheet laid flat by two glass ink bottles. Writing sticks were scattered over the area. Rolls of papyrus stood in one corner and wooden chests and goat skin bags lined the walls of the room.

Levi noticed Jesus looking at the array. "My life is now reduced to my reminiscences. Perhaps someone will want to read about our times, and they may dig up my writings in these old chests," he cackled in bemusement. "But pity the poor scholar that would attempt to decipher my hand. I have written all of this in Greek. It will forever be the dominate tongue, I fear. Any future reader will, however, find a revelation about the history of our people. There are many documents there from Herod's court, along with short hand notes I took of many of his worst and his finest moments. Should I include your words in my history, carpenter?" Levi teased. "If I am moved by your words, I must warn you I will write them. Learning from the wise is my passion. The greatest day of my life was when I walked into the rotunda of the library at Alexandria. I went there after the death of Herod, to see if there are truths greater than those told in the Books of Moses."

Another tap on the door interrupted their conversation. Levi motioned for Jesus to see who it was, and he stood and opened the door. Standing in the light was a thin, older man and a middle-aged man wearing fine blue bordered robes, and a large turban, with gold bracelets on his right forearm. The older man had a deep scar down his chin and deep-set, fierce looking eyes, giving him a physically intimidating appearance. Both looked fleetingly at Jesus, nodded, and entered the little room. Heavy perfume drifted from them.

"Ah, Alphaeus," Levi exclaimed joyfully and they hugged. "And Matthew, you too are welcomed." He did not hug the elegantly dressed man, but clasped his arms.

"Here, here, you two must meet my new friend, Jesus of Nazareth, the son of the departed Joseph." Levi scurried around the two men and waved a tiny hand at the silhouetted figure of Jesus still standing in the light of the door. It was an impressive, straight figure, haloed against the morning. He closed the door, revealing a gentle, smiling face. Both men were struck by the clarity of his dark brown eyes and the unusual configuration of his face; compelling and interesting. They acknowledged one another with kisses on the cheek.

Levi stood between them. "Jesus is from the line of David. His father Joseph was a tecton (builder). He did work at Bethsaida before his death. Perhaps you knew Joseph's father, Jacob, another builder." Levi grabbed one of Jesus' hands, holding it up in view. "Looks more like the side of a steer than a hand," he observed in his good-natured way at the over-sized hand.

The little man then turned toward his friends and, smiling his toothless, impish grin said, "Jesus, this is my old friend, Alphaeus, who stops by on occasion to see if I am still alive, and this, Levi-Mattya, a good Jew, even though," he poked the man jokingly with his short cane, "he is the chief tax collector at the border crossing."

Jesus beamed, "Alphaeus! It is my honor to meet such a famous warrior. We spoke of you as boys, and of the rebellion you led against Herod's son." Jesus laughed, "I can remember waving my little wooden sword in childish battles with my friends as a boy, acting as though I were you."

Levi said proudly, "I thank The Blessed One for allowing these heroes to live long lives so that you younger men can be inspired by their willingness to die to save our faith. Where the slain lay there stood Alphaeus."

Jesus felt humbled before this legendary fighter. One of Herod's sons, Archelaus, had been appointed upon his father's death to rule over the province of Judea — the Jerusalem area. He had so abused his authority that the Jews had revolted. It turned into a massacre with thousands of them being crucified. The memories of that resistance had become a part of the Jewish culture, and one of which Jesus was well aware.

Jesus looked at Matthew. "So you are also from the tribe of Levites and you prefer your Hebrew name. That speaks more about your faith than does your profession."

Levi-Mattya had a firm voice, and a well-tended beard and moustache, both thick and black. "I am only called Mattya by my father and his old friends. As the tax collector, I am known simply as Matthew, or most probably," he chuckled knowingly, "the dog, the thief, the traitor, and who knows what."

"Caesar must have his due," Jesus responded in a subtle approval of what Matthew did for a living. "His coins are not ours anyway. They have the Emperor's face on them, so they must belong to him."

"It is understanding of you to say that," Alphaeus nodded. "As you know, Mattya means 'gift of God' and to us, he is that. The people could do far worse. Mattya is an honest tax official. Others take the post to steal the people blind. He is is an honest man in a despised profession."

"Let us not speak of money, but of the wisdom of our elders," Alphaeus suggested. "Levi, I have brought some date wine from Jericho so that we might liven your heart and bring joy to your brain." He pulled a small glass decanter from a hiding place under his robe and handed it to the delighted Levi.

Levi held it up as though it were gold. He squeaked, "Jericho wine! I've had none since my days in Herod's court. We will all savor it." He hurriedly searched through a trunk for more goblets. He also fumbled around for pieces of bread and handed them out. The new guests had already removed their sandals and were settling onto an expansive rug.

"I met Jesus last evening at the house of assembly where he was doing some work. We spoke briefly. I was impressed with his words and invited him to breakfast. We were just discussing old Herod and kings in general.

"Herod was at once the most brutal and the most politically brilliant man I ever met," Levi continued to say, as his nubby teeth bit into a flattened piece of bread. "He ruled because Rome allowed it, because Herod provided the Emperor with a loyal supporter who had his own army and didn't cost the empire anything. He wanted to be admired in the court of the Emperor and in the Roman Senate, but he wanted to be accepted by Jews as a Jew."

Jesus shifted his weight. "Most kings owe their allegiance first to themselves and to holding on to their throne. A Jew must look to only one King, and one Kingdom."

"But what of Solomon and David? They were great kings. And what of the prophets saying a Messiah will come to us, a new king, from the line of David?" Alphaeus questioned.

"They were leaders for their time, but Isaiah says the Will of The Father will appear in the form of a servant who will bear our griefs, who will suffer, yet will not cry out. He says the Word shall prosper in this servant's hand."

Alphaeus nodded in thought, his face an array of rivulets like tiny streams coursing his skin in the drainage of age. There was not a smooth spot of skin left, except on the end of his large, long nose. There seemed to be some Arabian apects to his appearance, but in the past in this land of nomads and travelers the distinct cultures had intermingled, creating a new look that blended the variations of them all.

"Yes, I know the scripture well," Matthew stirred as he sipped the expensive wine. "It does speak of one who is acquainted with grief, a man of sorrows. That could describe any of the children of Israel. We wear sadness everyday, as our lands and treasury are taken. We live our lives at the whim of Herod's sons and that thief Pilate."

"All that you have said is true," Jesus said. "But you speak of material poverty, the sorrow of losing one's possessions. I believe we have lost much more than that."

Levi peered from his sunken sockets out over the jutting cheek bones now so prominent as the fleshiness of his face had eroded. He poked at a shallow pit that served as the cooking place. Small flames emerged at his prompting.

"What loss do you speak of?"

Jesus ran his hand through his thick hair, pushing it away from his face so that it fell behind his head. Levi studied his face and thought of the passage Jesus had just been referring to in Isaiah, 'He had no form nor comeliness that we should look at him, and no beauty that we should desire him.' Jesus face was not handsome in a conventional sense, but unusual, difficult to assess, and even riveting in its form and turn. Yes, Levi thought, there was a beauty there that transcended handsomeness. There was a mystical way about his eyes, and his voice had a strange hypnotic effect about it.

"It is a poverty of the spirit. We concern ourselves with Romans and their evils against us. We worry over the rich who would lend us money to pay our taxes, over our neighbor who might have a larger family tomb, over those with more colors in their robes, more fragrances in their hair, more sheep than we, a larger olive press; but I hear few cry out over how far we move away from the Light when our eyes see only the gods of ownership."

Levi's small face scrunched up in disagreement, "Oh, we argue daily over the spirit. The Pharisees believe in an afterlife and interpreting the five books. The Sadducees accept neither an afterlife nor angels and believe the five books of Moses are to be taken as they read. The Community of the Poor believe we are all wrong, that they have the straight way to the Kingdom with their celibacy, cleanliness and isolation. They prepare for a fiery and terrifying coming of The End of Days. They expect to be soldiers alongside the One. Others argue for the Judaism of Herod the father. Those with zeal live to war against all pagans. They live to stab their curved knives into the hearts of Romans. No, much of our life as a people is spent debating every day for the soul of the children of Israel. We are a religion split and in endless discussion about who is right. Is the Messiah coming? When? Do we give interpretation to the Laws or not? And this debate is one of our great strengths." He waited for Jesus to respond.

Jesus drew the tart juices from a pomegranate and picked the drained seeds from his mouth. "Some of those of whom you speak are ravenous wolves in sheep's clothing who would set themselves up as the sole keepers of the gate to The Father, but they demand that you pay them money and sacrifice your animals before they will allow you through their gate. Others are hypocrites, actors, pretenders who are more interested in being bowed to in the marketplace. They seek a religion that feels good, that is the smooth way. They see The Father's commands as an invitation to interpret and debate. No, the debates of which you speak are more for the perceived power that being right earns, than for the sake of the glorification of heaven."

"There is a fire in you about these things. Some could see it as the devil at work, others as a new and important teacher who interprets the prophets in ways that others don't," Matthew said as he felt himself being strangely stirred by this man's intensity, and at the same time by the simplicity and the elegance of his arguments. "But you challenge the establishment with which many are comfortable."

"I am starting to believe that the coming of the Kingdom is near, and that the prophecies are about to be fulfilled while we worry about the foolish. I believe that the time is urgent; I feel it," Jesus said as he clutched his robe in a tight fist to emphasize that point. "But not all see what I see, and fewer hear what I hear."

"Then who is right?" Alphaeus asked, anticipating no answer. "Perhaps few hear as you do because you hear nothing but your own untrained mind, or could it even be the devil that talks to you? Others read the scriptures also, and they find a meaning different from yours. They will say, 'Well, who are you to say these things that we don't agree with?' It will be the reading of a mere wood worker from an obscure village not even indicated on maps against the chorus of voices of the learned and the Temple leaders, whom everyone looks to as true teachers. You never even attended the Temple school. You've not been a scribe or lawyer. You, whom no one ever heard of, runs the risk of being seen as a devil, not a savior." He was carefully studying Jesus' reaction, testing him with a harsh appraisal while trying to discover just who this man might be. No one wanted to close their mind to the possibility that even an unknown could be a special messenger.

Trying to understand Jesus' theme, Alphaeus asked, "Can you sum up your message?"

Without hesitation and with an infectious joy, Jesus answered, "So He said, to love the Lord thy God before all else, with all your heart and soul." Jesus sat in the quiet of the room for a moment, and then, with words delivered so softly that the the men unconsciously leaned forward to capture them, "It is about love," he summarized.

The phrase was not allowed to hang for long. "Love, huh? That's too simple for the priests," the Elder leaned back and mused. He chuckled almost to himself, "Perhaps so simple no one will understand it."

"By whose authority will you ask the people to accept your teaching? Who was your teacher?" Matthew queried.

"By the Word of the Lord of Israel as communicated through the scriptures, and…" Jesus ran his hand across his beard in a nervous contemplation and hesitation as he sought to form a final answer and find the courage to say what he truly felt. He then looked directly at Matthew. "And as The Father speaks the scriptures to me."

"The Father speaks to all of us through the scriptures, but again, builder," Alphaeus asked, "who are you if you are asked to speak at an assembly on the Sabbath? Who are you to speak ideas that disagree with the readings of those honored for their knowledge — ideas that actually attack those leaders? You almost sound as though you would go outside the Torah, outside our religious leaders. Our nation was built upon and is held together by the Torah. If you say the Lord tells you directly, that could be very dangerous. Would you say you are a new prophet, a new teacher, or one who would start a new faith? Who would you say you are?"

All three men were chewing slowly on their bread and staring intently and suspiciously, but with great interest, at this stranger.

Jesus's voice was alluring. It easily ran the range of emotions, going from loving and tender to a sadness that was contemplative and searching. "You do not hear me. I say The Father speaks directly to me. His breath is my breath and my words are His words. I have found all of this to be at once terrifying and profoundly moving. I'm filled with the Word. I want to tell it to everyone I meet, but half the people I speak to want to stone me. I have come to accept that if I am not willing to suffer and to be a servant, I am not worthy of the Kingdom. If I am not willing to die for my beliefs, I cannot claim them."

The Elder raised his eyebrows, "Thousands have died for their beliefs, but few have said they spoke directly to the One. When I saw you working at the house of assembly, I did not think of you as one to whom He would be speaking directly. You do not wear the robes of a rabbi. You wear the rough clothing of a...a rural worker."

Jesus' voice took on an edge and an air of frustration. "Should I put on costly robes? Must I have bracelets, a phylactery strapped to my forehead, and a high hat? Must I talk about what fine schools I attended? No! I believe we are all priests, made in The Father's image. We all have the right to speak the words He breathes through us. This notion of having to be formally trained before being believable has created a caste of priests who wish to protect their position, controlling the people by claiming that they alone can read Hebrew, and they alone know how to interpret the Books. I speak of freedom for each man to come directly to the Heavenly Father. It is not enough to be of Abraham's loins, or just to do good works, or to be seen running to the synagogue on the Sabbath. How false it looks for us to half-run to worship on the Sabbath, as though this eagerness to enter the house of worship will blind our Father to our sins." His voice filled the room with a certainty that was very passionate, but its hard edge was softened by the sincerity of the expressiveness of Jesus' motioning hands, the almost elegant way he stood, and the roaming punctuations his eyes, mouth, and brows gave in support of every word. It was a finely tuned and orchestrated combination of word and movement.

Levi maneuvered his small frame off the thick wool cushion as he stood and seemed to try and straighten his humped-over body. "So you think that The Holiest One speaks to you directly?"

Jesus looked away, thinking of what Levi had asked, and realized how harsh and inflammatory his words sounded to some, and how quickly those who saw evil spirits everywhere could brand his words as those of the devil or a blasphemer.

Jesus looked at Levi's tiny form and spoke with the intent of someone who is trying out a statement for its effect, experimenting, not entirely with confidence, but with the force of his voice, trying to sound certain. "Yes, Elder. He speaks to me in the fields, on the roads, in my prayers, and in my readings. He speaks to my heart and fills it to the point that I must empty its contents into the hearts of others."

Levi took a thin, pointed stick and picked at his teeth in thought. He found himself enthralled by Jesus and the way he spoke. He felt that the presence of the Spirit had entered his little home, but still there was an uncertainty that kept him at a distance; the roads were filled with so-called messengers from God.

"Have you thought of putting down your tools and teaching?" Levi queried.

Jesus gazed at the window in reflection, then looked back at Levi, "More and more I do, but that is difficult to do when there is work to be done."

Levi sat on a stool in front of the shelves. "Then you, like those you criticize, are more concerned with this world than you are with the next."

Jesus nodded in some sadness, "I, too, find the devil at every turn. The more I read the scriptures, and the more I am stirred to move toward their commands, the more reasons I find not to do so. You are right, I am no better than those I criticize."

"What of your wife? What does she say of this?" Matthew asked.

"I have chosen not to take a wife," Jesus answered with a discernible reluctance. Celibacy was unusual in a culture that valued big families.

"Do you not lay with women at all?" Matthew persisted.

A candle on a table to Jesus' right cast a glow over that side of his face, while the other side was more shadowed. It gave him a dramatic look. "I decided some years ago that I would attempt to become as close to the One, the Perfect, as I could. The One has no need for the pleasures of the bed. To have a wife or seek out the bed of women is to distract my eye and my heart from the One. His is perfect love that transcends the bed. I would like to be as much like The Father as a human can be. In some way that is to be not man or woman, but as one with…with the Spirit."

The men cleared their throats and shifted in the seats. The conversation was getting uncomfortable if this man was saying he would be like God, or God-like.

Alphaeus, with one eyebrow raised in concern, asked, "You are not saying you would be God, I hope. That would have you dead by my own hand, I should warn you."

Jesus shook his head, "Not The Father, but like The Father. Some find they can make that journey with a wife. I wish to see just how close I can come to Him, and I believe I cannot come as close as I now wish if I take a wife. The Father is my family. All of man is my family. I have no need to create another family."

Levi toddled over and placed his hand on Jesus' shoulder. "I would say that you are moving very close to the Eternal's great Commandment to love Him with all your heart and soul and mind. It is always our desires that are the most difficult to control. We hear the laughter of the table. We see the beauty of a woman. We smell the fragrance of perfumes and feel the smoothness of silk, but the Eternal remains away from our view. He is all around us, but nowhere to be seen. We can see Satan easily. He resides in all things pleasant to the touch and the taste. We see the angels of darkness in all of life's pleasures, we hear them in the murmurs of a seductive woman. And I also see many of our people giving in to the temptations of the Romans. They are washing over little Galilee like an invisible sea. One day we will awaken and we will have drowned in their Greek language and their ways of commerce. It seeps into the mind of a man, and he hardly knows it is there. Such are the ways of Satan. We badly need a leader who will show us the way, who will bring us out of this spiritual wilderness. We need another Moses."

Jesus trembled, his eyes cloudy with tears, and looked up in agony at the little man. It was hard to tell if he was responding to what Levi had just said, or lost in his own thoughts. The three men were touched by this stranger's easy display of emotions.

"This desire to live the Word is filling me, Elder, with a joy I can barely contain. But I am also swept by a crushing sadness for our people. Yes, Satan stalks our land in many disguises, and he has succeeded in turning many away from The Holiest. I want to rush about the streets and yell that I have the answer, that it is all so very simple. But when I speak, I am laughed at for having no schooling or training. The hostility against one who would speak differently than the priests is deadly."

"You are as close to the Truth as anyone I have talked to in years. But what you speak of is, as you say, dangerous talk. I have been a part of the Temple court. I know many priests and scribes, and they are like old wineskins that cannot accept new wine, like old garments onto which you would not sew new cloth. Your ideas would not take with them, and they would be confused and angered. I suspect that many would even have you stoned to death. You would be a threat to their comfortable lives."

"I know," Jesus said with great gravity.

"I was one of them," Levi added. "I sought high positions with the evil that was Herod. I was highly respected in Jerusalem. I have owned many robes, many sheep, and much land...but as I await the calling of the Eternal, as I come closer to the end of my days, I see great truth in what you have said. Few realize, as you do, where our true poverty lies."

Jesus seemed relieved and encouraged. He stood looking very singular, very straight and alone and, looking at the three, asked, "Will you pray with me for the path I should take?"

They held their hands up and prayed in the growing light of the morning, separately, then, moved by the emotion of the moment, their voices swelled in various chants and pleadings, rising in an orchestra of separate notes but in a unison of conviction that rang out to the connecting houses and down the shoreline. Jesus wept as he sang out for strength and certainty, filling the room with the pain and joy of one on a voyage to a uncertain shore; a nearly blind man seeking a distant light. Soon their voices descended into the murmurings of the spent; they were so moved by the experience that they clasped hands in a transcending brotherhood.

Jesus thanked his little host for the food and the other two men for the comfort of their prayer. He picked up his baggage and pushed the door open.

"You are being moved by The Holy, Jesus, but you will need to remove all other things of this world from your thoughts. And you must know that the closer you come to The Holy, the further you will move from some of His children," Levi said from his doorway.

"You might find, as you did today, a son who wanted to follow you with a father who would stone you. It could be a mission of love that ends in tragedy, and you must be prepared for that. You also must worry about being crucified. The Romans are wary of one who would unite the Jews. To them you are not about religion, you are about politics."

Jesus felt doubt sweeping over him, and a chilling feeling of doom. Standing in front of the old priest, he trembled with a terrible loneliness. To walk among the orchards of Galilee and discuss to himself these thoughts was a joyful exercise, but to voice his feelings and see the reactions of Simon and Andrew, and hear the warnings of this man who would know, caused him to grasp his tool bag as though it were a child's comforter.

"I am still a builder. Many ask for my work," Jesus said, trying to sound cheerful. In fact, he found solace in his work and the way it allowed him to escape from this agonizing realization.

Matthew stepped forward to say, "It is a call that you hear, but not to wood and stone. Perhaps you will touch the hearts of our people. Perhaps what you say is right. It is surely a kind message in a very cruel world. I am a hated publican, yet you have prayed with me. Your love transcends the anger of most. Call on me when you have your answer." They all waved goodbye as Jesus strode away toward the big Roman road, called the Via Maria, that led west out of Capernaum.

"I think I should go back and write down some of this man's sayings. I want to study them to see if he calls for rebellion against the Romans, or a new kind of Judaism," Matthew said. "Perhaps some day we will want to remember his sayings."

The place of crucifixion outside Capernaum was called The Place of Hanging. This was the term, not crucifixion, that was commonly used, since victims were seen as hanging from the beams cut from a tree. As Jesus approached the spot, a mile outside of town, he could see the family wrapping their loved one in linen. He stopped at a cart where the beams lay disassembled. Dried blood was all over the end of the beam to which the feet had been nailed. Large nails with skin attached to them lay next to the beams. Several soldiers who had spent the night there were gathering up their belongings. They were being cursed at by an officer for allowing their victim to be speared while they weren't paying attention.

"We had careful instructions that this murderer was to hang for several days," the irate officer barked at them. "Were you asleep?!" he yelled.

A short soldier, whose helmet seemed too large for his small head, begged, "Sir, we were here only a few feet away all night. A few travelers passed, but we heard nothing until this morning. As the sun rose, his mother came out and screamed he had been killed. We looked over and…well, there was a short spear sticking out of him."

The officer slapped the soldier across his cheeks, sending his ill-fitting helmet clattering across the ground. "And I suppose he had the spear hiding up his end, so when you idiots weren't looking he pulled it out and stabbed himself!"

The three men stood stiffly at attention, but with their eyes cast to the ground. "You will wish you had gone to the grave with the murderer before the legate is through with you. Now get the tree back to the garrison."

The roadside traffic moving past the scene was heavy, as people were on their way to work or to other villages, and the soldiers did not notice Jesus as he stood next to the cart. It had no railing, and he touched the bloodied end of the cross where the ankles had been nailed. The horror of the cross sent shivers through him. It was the ultimate pain and humiliation a Jew could suffer. He wondered what it must be like, his thoughts becoming dark and foreboding, as he imagined the excruciating pain of the great nails slamming through the wrist, and the two days of gasping and gurgling as the body drowned in its own liquids.

Shaking his head as if to fling away the thoughts, Jesus looked up to see the officer walk over to the horse that pulled the cart. He felt disgust wash over his mind at the utter callousness of the Roman. His teeth clenched and his eyes narrowed as he gave way to an anger steeped in generations of Jewish suffering. Seeing Jesus staring at him, the officer hesitated for a moment, tempted to walk over and slap the Jew with the broad side of his sword. Instead, the officer muttered a curse and mounted his horse. He jammed his heels into the animal's sides, and the cart lurched away with such force that one of the nails rolled off into the dirt. As the guards marched away toward Capernaum, Jesus picked up the nail and walked over to the distraught family as they finished wrapping the body. The mother wailed in a high, song-like pitch and had to be restrained from throwing herself over her son's brutalized form.

Jesus handed the nail to a man who stood consoling the mother. "Keep this in remembrance of the courage of this man. No one of us can show our love for The Holy One more than to give our life in His name."

The man stood, his eyes swollen from crying, and numbly took the nail, looking at it and feeling its heaviness. He mumbled, "Bless your house," put the nail in his cloak, and stared at the stranger, not knowing what to make of him. "Are you a teacher? You don't wear the robes of a teacher," the man observed.

"No, just a servant." Jesus smiled.

"Oh, a slave," the man uttered with disappointment. He quickly turned his back on Jesus and returned to consoling his mother.

Barley was well up in the dark, fertile fields. From the shoreline of the sea the land quickly rolled into swells and then into rounded hills. The hills looked over many plains and small valleys. The road through the countryside was hard-packed, but yielded its dust easily when walked over and made a crunching sound as the leather of Jesus's sandals pressed against its granular surface. The roads could be slippery because of their tiny pebbles, and ankles were easily twisted, especially if one walked along the road's edge or went down an incline. Many of the roads were lined with low stone walls made from the stones that were dug up and pushed aside when the roads were cleared.

As Jesus approached the new city of Tiberias, he passed roadside statues to various gods, often tiny enclaves dug into the side of a hill. Each was its own self-contained miniature temple, often complete with a so-called priest, eager to accept an offering and hear whatever request one wished to make. The road was paved with flat stones and filled with foot traffic, wagons, and carts of every description. A caravan of camels from Damascus came plodding by with great bundles of spices and silks strapped in goat skin wrappings along their sides. A traveling troupe of athletes that had just performed in Tiberias met Jesus as they headed for the theater at Sepphoris. They were followed by a troupe of actors, one of whom wore a mask with a grotesque snarl and continually ran up and tried to scare the wits out of walking travelers, as his fellow actors laughed uproariously. A juggler stood next to a small spring seeking donations for his skills. Close by, a farmer had set up a stall and was selling fruit. His wife had cookies and cakes in several open baskets. Jesus passed a small group in the shade of an enormous, twisted olive tree. They listened intently to an astrologer predict their lives by the stars in return for a small fee or some food. The last mile leading into Galilee's capital was a fascinating bazaar of desperate men, schemers, survivors, and those who would save a man's soul, for a small price, of course.

It was after noon, and the few tools Jesus carried were pulling heavily on his shoulders. He stopped by a broad field being plowed by two men. One of their plows was pulled by a drooping donkey, thin in the haunch and ragged with its shedding winter coat; the other plow was pulled by a cow.

Jesus rested the bags on the edge of the field and pulled out a goat skin, from which he took a sip of water, and from inside his clothing bag he pulled some dried apricots and bread, and he said a short prayer. The two men stopped their plowing and sat under a tall cedar tree nearby. As he watched them start to have their own lunch, he got up and walked over. He saw them offer a short prayer and knew they were Jews.

"Praise The Father, and good day," he said as he approached them.

They looked up with some weariness from their work. Their hair clung to their heads, wet with the sweat of their efforts in controlling the wooden plows as they had lurched and reeled through the soil. One man noticed a dead sparrow lying where they had sat; grabbing a lifeless wing, he pitched it off to one side.

"A good day?" growled a short, small-framed man. "Easy for you to say, traveler."

"The Father has blessed you with rich soil," Jesus smiled as he sat near them and chewed on the fleshy skin of an apricot.

"The Father has blessed the new owner with rich soil. He has blessed us with a strong back to work what once was ours," the taller of the two answered as he chewed on a stringy, dried piece of meat.

"Over there," the short man leaned around and pointed toward the end of the long field. There was a rider on a large brown horse coming slowly toward them. "Over there is the pagan who owns this rich dirt you speak of. And trotting next to him is the Jewish traitor hired to oversee our farm." The rider sat very erect, accompanied by a stocky man struggling to walk and keep up with the horse.

"You say you once owned this land; did you sell it?" Jesus asked.

"By The Eternal Spirit, if only we had done so when we had the chance," the shorter man said wistfully. "This land has been in our family since before the Maccabeans. But several years ago the gentile there on the horse, one Crispinius Teritinius, offered to loan us money if we would plant more olive and fig trees and grow more barley. He said the new cities of Tiberias and Sepphoris would be good markets for our foods. We got greedy for the new Roman money. We saw all the people moving into Galilee. We saw the wealth of the new cities, and we wanted a part of it. So we worked hard and grew more foods, and Crispinius took it and stored, saying that he was waiting for the prices to go up." The man took a long drink of thinned wine from a soiled goat skin container. Some of the pale purple wine ran down his bearded chin.

"While he waited, we ran out of money, and he had a bailiff come one night with papers in Greek, which we cannot read, that we had stupidly signed. They said that we had agreed to pay Crispinius interest even though he had not paid us for the produce he was storing. That night we were thrown out in the road and told we would be welcomed back as tenants."

The other man remarked with scorn. "The Roman doesn't know our soil. He tells us to throw seed on that rocky ground there and in the path here. Seed won't grow on bad earth."

Jesus sat silently with them for a moment thinking on the comment. The men periodically peered back over their shoulder at the rider who was heading toward them at a plodding pace.

"So say the prophets, that we are soon to see the Word come among us and that the son of man (the Israelites or humanity) will gain a freedom they have not known since the days of David," Jesus said, as he sat cross-legged across from the men in the shade of the tree. "We will be freed from our land, for it is not an earthly kingdom to which we go."

"Are you a teacher?" the taller man asked.

Jesus hesitated, not wanting to tell them that he was a carpenter, but he did. "No, I am a builder by trade."

The taller man scoffed, "I think you've been reading too many knots in your wood. The only one of authority, and that's questionable, who speaks of a coming is that baptizer down at Bathabara along the Jordan. And everyone knows heaven will be here on this land. You're not well read in the scriptures if you don't know our land will be restored, and our ancestors will come to life and live among us here. Blessed Be His Name will be our king forever."

"I hear the Baptizer speaks of a new covenant where each of us asks forgiveness in his own heart," Jesus ignored the man's criticism. "I agree, and I also say that a man's life does not consist of the abundance of his possessions. He who lays up treasure for himself is not rich in The Father's eyes."

The taller man jumped up excitedly, "You say! Who are you to say?" He grabbed a pouch that carried his food and drink , almost fell over himself running away from Jesus, and stopped to stand defensively behind his plow. The rider and his panting follower arrived at the tree at that time, looking puzzled as to what was going on. The rider was dressed in a tunic of fine weave. His hair was dyed blond and combed forward in the Roman style, but he had the swarthy coloring and pronounced features of a Syrian. His fingers were circled with rings, and he wore an amulet to the god Apollo around his neck. He spoke to them in fluent formal Greek, which the sweating man accompanying him translated into Aramaic.

"What is the meaning of this meeting during the work time?" He demanded in a contemptuous voice. The words were dutifully translated.

The taller man shouted, "There is a devil under our tree who, with no authority, would predict the End of Days; who would say our land means nothing."

"We have no time for philosophers who would amuse our workers," Crispinius said with great authority in his voice. He reached to a strap on the saddle to touch a short, silver handled sword.

Jesus calmly nodded his head, picked up his belongings and said with great calmness to all four men, "O men of little faith. Don't seek what you are to eat and to drink, or be of anxious mind. The Father provides food for the birds, doesn't he? Surely he cares more for you. Seek His Kingdom, and these things shall be yours as well."

The Roman scoffed and, pointing to the dead sparrow, threatened, "There's one sparrow your god didn't care for, and that's what you two will look like if you don't return to work."

In a voice that was at once soft yet carrying, Jesus answered, "The Father cares for all living things, but none of us can stand before him until we pass from this life. And that step before His final judgment is what we must prepare for."

The Jew translated, and the rider spurred his horse menacingly toward Jesus. He unsheathed his sword and held it next to his side, ordering, "On the road with you, philosopher, or you will have no legs to stand upon before your god or anyone else!"

Jesus stood his ground and raised his right hand slowly with his fingers extended in a half wave. He felt power surging in him and was confident that he could confront the end of a Roman sword. It was a growing courage that he knew he would have to have. It was evident in the near-violent reactions he was getting as he spoke his heart. His mind moved easily into a prayer of thanks for God giving him the fortitude to defy the power of the Roman, while at the same time he thought of what it would be like if this angry landowner actually charged at him and ran him through. Jesus was fortified by seeing how a firm but peaceful response to an angry man could so confuse him that he would back away.

Crispinius was struck by the unusual features and the voice of this strange man. For some reason he couldn't bring himself to spur his horse further. He became afraid that the man was a devil and that he was trying to trap him into coming closer. He turned his horse suddenly, sending the tenant scrambling out of the way, galloped over to the hapless taller man, and began cursing the man's ancestors and threatening to run him off if he and his brother did not go back to the plow.

The shorter man, who had been standing close to the tree during all of this, whispered, "You teach in a way that I like. If you come this way again, stop by our fields. I would like to hear more." And he scurried out into the rich brown dirt that was clodded, tumbled, and turned from the plowing. Jesus shook his head at the fear the men exhibited for the new owner and wondered as he walked away how he might weave the everyday lives of the countryside into short, symbolic stories — parables — that would allow his thoughts to be better understood, but only if the listeners dug into the story, used their minds and really wanted to hear his message. It seemed the more direct he was in speaking, the angrier many people's reactions were. As he grew in developing and voicing his feelings, there was an accompanying fear, a growing realization that he could easily be killed by any number of people. The need to conceal his truths in a layered message was becoming more and more apparent. Those who had no interest in what he said would simply be amused by an entertaining short story. Those who would listen would take the time to search and think, and in doing so, truly understand and learn.

Nazareth was fifteen miles west of Tiberias, a gleaming city of white stone and polished marble that Herod's son, Antipas, had built on the shore of Galilee's sea, which he had proclaimed the Sea of Tiberias. A fee was charged to enter its gates, so Jesus avoided it and turned on a westward path as he entered its outskirts.

The roads west toward Nazareth remained heavy with throngs of people. Most trudged along on foot, some rode donkeys or oxen, and the wealthy were noted by their horses or carriages. Jesus stopped three miles outside of Nazareth at Kefar Kenna. Like most towns of the northern Galilee area, its small box-like houses washed up the side of a long, sloping, grassy hillside. Other hills rode away from it in swells, long since stripped of much of their rich forests. Galilee was the garden spot of Palestine, punctuated by groves of cedar, pine, oak, sycamore, olive and fig trees, with fields lush with wheat and vegetables. This was a time of planting, and of tending the green shoots already emerging in the early spring. The fields were alive with the figures of farmers on this warm, clear day.

Jesus stopped at the rock-ringed spring that gave the tiny village of Kefar Kenna its water. He had been walking most of the day, and his shoulders ached from the weight of his tools and bags. He would spend the night at his home in Nazareth before walking the four miles over to Sepphoris tomorrow.

"Jesus," a woman's voice called from behind, "is that you?"

He turned and was surprised to see Rebekah, the daughter of Simeon, the local Pharisee. Jesus had known her since she was a child, when his family visited relatives in Kenna. He had not seen her in some years, and now she was stunning in her beauty. Her head was covered in a tall hat tinged in purple, a sign of wealth because of the costly dye. Her brown eyes were wide apart and almond-shaped with thick brows. Her hair was combed back from her full forehead in a bun, with strands left to hang down in ringlets under the hat. Gold dust sparkled in her hair, giving it an auburn coloring. Perfumes scented the air around her, both from her hair and from little amulets hanging from a waist-length necklace. Her nose was long and straight ,with a small ring hanging from the side of one nostril. Her lips were colored with orange lipstick. Her mouth was large, with the bottom lip especially full. Rings circled her fingers, and large bracelets sparkled from her wrists. She wore slippers encrusted with gems. Ankle rings with tiny bells jingled when she walked. Jesus remembered her as a thin, awkward girl who laughed easily, whose father was a poor man: a local, part time teacher who made his money through working a vegetable field up the slope behind the village. Obviously, their fortunes had grown.

Jesus ran his fingers through his hair in a self-conscious attempt to present himself as more than a dust-covered, sweating traveler. "Rebekah," he smiled, his mind searching for things he could say to her. "Surely, the hills sing for joy at such beauty as yours."

She laughed heartily, "Yes, it is you. I remember when I was a child and how I thought that if you had lived in the days of the prophets, you could have written the book of Psalms or the Song of Solomon. You used to read me scriptures about fields and animals and add your own thoughts. Your words were pictures. I thought you a word painter." She looked at him, reflecting, and with the glow of memories, both of his entertaining ways and of a girlish love she had had for him. "I still remember," she repeated awkwardly, embarrassed by a surge of feelings for this boy turned man.

He took a small cup from his baggage and leaned over the spring wall into the cool, dark waters, and, lifting the cup, held it up to her in a salute before drinking it all in one turn.

He joked about himself, "Ah, those were the times when I followed my father around carrying his hammer."

"And now?" she asked. Her eyes had a dark blaze to them that was playful and enticing, though unintentional. He grinned at her, caught in her energy and joy.

Looking at the obvious wealth she possessed, he paused for a moment to wonder how she would react if he said he was an artisan, one of the lowest positions in Palestinian society. But Jesus was more. He was not just a simple local carpenter. Most people possessed carpentry skills on their own. It was a very self-sufficient village society. His keen mind had made him much in demand as an architect and manager on the rebuilding of nearby Sepphoris. It was a world where the power of the Roman coin was taking hold and opening new opportunities for Jews willing to move to the cities and enter into business. Jesus had resisted developing his business further because of his intense and growing interest in his faith.

"I have honored my father and the talents he passed along to me. It allows me to work outside where I can see The Holy One alive in the fields. Unfortunately," he held his fingers up for her to see, "I collect more splinters and broken fingers than I do shekels." They both grinned at his hands, and at the blackened blood behind two of his nails which he had hit with a wooden mallet while cutting stone.

"And who would your husband be?" Jesus asked, certain that a woman of this beauty in her early twenties would be married.

She had an infectious giggle that spilled into her voice. "Me? I think I have become one of my father's possessions. Suitors come to our door bringing herds of sheep and every other beast to show him of their success, but he takes his walking stick to them and yells that they are not fit to pick his olives, let alone take the hand of his daughter." She acted like she was pouting, "I guess I'll be a wrinkled old fig taking care of my old father."

"And what of your family? Who is your wife?" she asked.

Jesus shook his head, saying he had none. He then grinned and said in a self-deprecating way, "I couldn't ask a woman to endure a husband who preferred sitting on hilltops daydreaming during the day and debating the Word at a different dinner table every evening."

She laughed knowingly, "Ah, you are still a poet and entertainer." Her heart quickened as she found herself drawn into the intensity of his eyes. His bottom lip was full, his mouth not especially wide, but it spread easily in an appealing way when he smiled, pushing his cheeks out and seeming to engulf his whole face. It was a wonderful, endlessly spreading, unaffected grin. His skin was smooth and a light olive against the red tinged brown of his hair and thick black brows. She remembered thinking how ugly she thought he was when they were younger, though she liked the way he made her laugh and the way he described things. He talked differently from other young men; in a disarming, familiar way he overcame her low opinion of his appearance. Now he seemed more serious; his face had matured to a handsomeness that was not of the traditional sort, but of a compelling nature. His eyes were more passionate and absorbed when he talked. His whole demeanor was somehow captivating now.

"Oh, I'm just an old donkey," Jesus finally responded to her query. "I don't pull a plow yet, but if carpentry doesn't get better, I might ask your father if I can hitch myself up to a plow in one of his fields."

She laughed, then asked, "Would you bray, and sometimes just sit down and refuse to plow?" She found herself easily slipping into the fantasies they had created years before.

"Oh, that I would, and I would kick the evil one out of any field hands that made me plow more than one row a day."

His humor brought back fond memories of the times when their families knew each other and would visit during festivals and at the markets of both towns. Nazareth and Kenna were so close together that the Jews of both villages were like an extended family in their faith, friendships, and hardships, which made for common bonds.

She persisted, "But you never took a wife?"

He looked at her directly and admitted, though still with a suggestion of shyness, "No, I have been growing in my faith, trying to understand the truths that are in the Word. It has come to occupy all of my time outside of work. I doubt that I could seek The Father and have a wife at the same time."

She could feel her emotions as she contemplated his words, and found a growing thirst for knowledge, any and every bit of information she could gain from him. "So, did you study to be a teacher or a priest in the Temple? Did you attend the Temple school there? Who was your teacher?"

"My teachers are at the table, in the fields, and on the winds, but not inside the Temple. We did not have the money for that. I do feel a growing need to voice my thoughts, to speak of the prophets as I am coming to understand them. My thoughts would not be welcomed by those who run the Temple. Soon, however, I may ask to read and teach at the houses of assembly in Galilee. Maybe others will see the intentions of The Father as I now do."

"If you can read Hebrew, then you are well schooled, and I hope to hear you read some day."

His mind seemed to suddenly slip from her, and he stared at the cup in his hand, preoccupied. She looked at a young girl who had come with her who was busy filling a clay water jug as they talked.

"This is my cousin," she said, nodding toward the girl. "My father and I are just visiting. We moved over to Sepphoris years ago. My father now ships his crop to the markets there and owns some land in the area."

Jesus felt surprise at hearing that her father, a strict interpreter of the Laws, was living in a gentile city and obviously trading with gentiles. He remembered the family as being very poor.

"Is he...is he still a Pharisee?"

"Oh, sometimes he will conduct a service, but he realizes that we must survive in this world, and the Roman influence grows stronger.

He deals directly with gentiles, but has a Syrian Jew who takes our crop and sells it. We lived in Jerusalem for a while, where my father worked in the Temple while trying to keep our farm here, but the trip back and forth became too much, and some of the Jews in Sepphoris said that if he would expand his farm, they would set up a market in the city. You may have noticed how fast our area here is growing. The roads are almost too crowded to travel on some days."

Jesus found himself torn between his attraction toward this beautiful woman and the disappointment he felt at hearing of another of the faith joining in the pursuit of wealth.

"My family would gain great pleasure in seeing you again and hearing of your family." The girl had the clay water jug balanced on her head and stood impatiently next to them. "Walk me to our old house and say hello. My father would be pleased to see you. We've not seen your family since we moved to Jerusalem."

Jesus hesitated then agreed to, and they walked up the slight incline of the village's main street. "Are you able to keep your faith amid the temptations of Sepphoris?" Jesus asked as they walked.

She looked surprised, "Of course. I believe we are stronger in our faith than ever." She laughed, "You won't find us at the baths. We stay very close to the scriptures, though we are among the gentiles. We must live in this world," she justified.

Jesus squinted against the brightness of the day. "I have worked there and attended the Greek plays. I enjoy their comedies, the way they look into the hearts of men, and the way the hypocrites (actors) affect the audience. But beyond that, it is a city built by the forces of darkness. Its ideas are polluting the people of Galilee with images of money and pagan gods." He was trying to apologize for questioning her faith when he too had moved among the pagans, watching with great interest and some delight at their use of words and portrayals of the human condition.

She seemed a little flustered, but finally answered, "The Pharisees have always felt that The Holy One gave us the right to interpret the scriptures. It allows us to survive and adjust to changing times. My father remains strict in his observation of the Torah, but he is able to prosper more by trading his crops in the city, and he is able to help more of the growing poor among us with that wealth. Many come to our door for food, and none are turned away. We are better able to help the poor because of our wealth."

"The Father gives us talents that may result in treasures, and it is where we put our treasure that our souls are found." Jesus didn't want to be drawn into a debate with this woman whom he suddenly found so beautiful and appealing. He softened his voice in order to avoid sounding overbearing.

She smiled and almost skipped in her natural exuberance, "Then The One will be pleased with where my father's soul is. We help many people."

Jesus was as taken with Rebekah's energy and independence as he had been when he knew her years ago. There was and had always been a breezy way about her, a freedom from constraint, a sense of adventure, a rare boldness, and an inadvertent sultriness.

The old house was a two-story, stone and mud-brick place with stairs going up the outside to the flat roof and its upper room which was a covered open-sided shed for guests. Trees shaded the entrance and a small vegetable and herb garden was fenced to one side. Two horses with extravagant saddles and bridles stood swishing their tails near the front door.

Jesus grinned at her as they stopped next to the horses, "I remember when your family had one old skin and bones steer. You rode it and plowed with it. Now…", he ran his hand over the neck of one of the large brown mares, "now you ride well, and own two at that."

She rubbed the nose of her horse. "Isn't she beautiful? I love to ride her across an open field. I find joy in the wind on my face." She looked up dreamily at Jesus, and for a moment they simply stared at one another. His heart began to go out to her, and he reveled in the feeling of romance, an emotion he had denied himself for years.

"My daughter!" It was the deep, gravelly voice of Simeon. He stood in the doorway of the home, filling its frame with his robust girth, almost sparkling in his very white turban and robes. Blue broadly bordered his sleeves and the end of his clothing. His boots were a rich leather, and silver bracelets climbed both arms. His beard was thick, curly, and a fading brown, now heavily streaked in gray. He had an almost overwhelming energy about him.

"And who would this stranger be, that seeks to groom my horse?" He referred to Jesus, who dropped his hand from the horse's neck.

"He is a donkey in the guise of a carpenter," Rebekah teased.

"If he is a donkey, then he is a familiar one." He studied Jesus's face from the few feet between the door and the horses.

"He is from the house of Joseph; it is Jesus from Nazareth," Rebekah answered cheerily.

Simeon stepped from the door and walked close to Jesus, appraising him, and then he announced with a loud chuckle, "Well, it is either my old friend Joseph or his younger version," and grabbed Jesus by both shoulders in a gregarious welcome.

"I didn't recognize you with the beard, and you've grown taller than your father."

Jesus grinned and said, "It is good to see you also, Simeon. The Holy One has blessed your house with fortune and your eyes with a lily of the field." He nodded his head toward Rebekah.

"Yes, now I remember my young Jesus. You are the one Rebekah thought so ugly to the eye, but perhaps a secret writer of the Song of Solomon."

Rebekah blushed and slapped at her father's round shoulder. "I did not say he was ugly," she protested, then quickly smiling, she complimented, "I did say he had a voice of music and poetry."

"It is good to see you, friend," Jesus said. "My father spoke often of his fondness for you."

Simeon looked with regret, "I was sorry to hear of his passing some time back. Joseph was as knowledgeable as any scribe or lawyer about the Law. His home was always open to passing teachers. It was known among travelers as a place for table talk. I ate there several times myself as a young Pharisee. We discussed our nation and its favored place and the pains we now endure under the Romans. He always felt that you were here on a special mission, though he would not say where this belief came from." Simeon laughed and put his hand on Jesus' shoulder with affection. "Do you remember just before you became a man, you spoke on the steps of the Temple?"

Jesus grinned and awkwardly nodded.

"You asked your father if you could speak on the schooling he had given you. You practiced your understandings with your brothers until they begged you to preach to the family donkey. Joseph promised that he would find you a place where you could speak. It was at Passover; the crowds were great, and he found a little corner at the steps leading into the Temple. We pushed a few people back, forming a circle." He laughed again, obviously relishing the memories, "And you were like a young prophet, telling all who would listen of your knowledge. I must say, I was impressed, and Joseph was so proud he talked about it for years."

Rebekah joined in teasing, "I heard they left you there, thinking you were following them. They told you it was time to go and thought you followed them. They were days out of the Holy City before realizing you were still on those steps teaching." Her voice was filled with merriment, and Jesus laughed out loud at his being such a troublesome child.

"And how is Mary?" Simeon inquired.

"She is well. She is now in Capernaum where members of her family live. I have remained in Nazareth where several of my brothers and sisters still live. I will sleep there tonight."

A man caught their attention as he appeared from around the side of the house with two small children. They were obviously quite poor, judging from their dress, and very thin. The man pushed the two boys back and stepped forward with a certain disdain, almost a resentment in his voice, "May the Holiest One continue to give this house blessing, master."

Simeon responded quickly and eagerly, "The One Whose Name We Do Not Speak, but with a presence everywhere, has blessed my pocket with a special gift for you, shepherd, and for your lambs." He handed the man a coin drawn from a pocket in his breeches, and the man turned without thanks and hurried the boys, in their soiled clothing, bare feet and tangled hair, away from the house. Simeon did not acknowledge what he had done; it was expected, and, turning to Jesus he said, "Well, come in and enjoy some cookies. They're pistachio and almond with a touch of cinnamon. Delicious." Simeon led them both to the door where they slipped out of their sandals and entered the well-lit room in their stocking feet.

The room was furnished with several marble benches covered by cushions colorfully stitched in Arabian designs. Costly glass bottles, clay jars, and pots sat on various shelves along the walls and a large bed was in the center of the room. It was used as both a couch and as a bed to sleep upon. Jesus was introduced to Simeon's family members who were relaxing with cookies, honey-fried nuts, and a sweet pudding called Ashurey.

Jesus accepted a cookie. It was not often that he tasted cinnamon, as it was brought in from Arabia and was very expensive.

"You know how the Arabs control the cinnamon market, don't you?" Simeon asked Jesus.

"In the marketplace, cinnamon is said to come from a nesting material made by giant birds that live high on cliffs where no man can go. It falls from their nests and the Arabs pick it up," Jesus related.

Simeon smiled mischievously. He whispered at Jesus so the family members, all talking loudly, couldn't hear. "An Arab who I have been trading with told me, over some very strong wine, that the cinnamon comes by boat from a land so far away only The Holy One could find it — a place even beyond India. But the Arabs' main source of treasure is their control of the spices, so they have to make up those tales to protect themselves. Very wise, huh?" Simeon seemed pleased with his understanding of this well-kept secret.

Seeming to ignore Simeon's revelation, Jesus asked, "Master, please satisfy a question I have as I observe you; do you believe that your wealth will help you find a straighter way to the Kingdom, or has gaining your treasure made you poorer in spirit? Will it be as difficult for you to enter the Kingdom as it is to enter the Eye of the Needle Gate while riding a camel?" He raised his hand and said quickly, "Do not be offended; I ask only to learn."

Simeon's short legs dangled from the side of the bed. It was heavily pillowed, and a large white wool blanket with a brown olive branch border spread decorously over the bed.

"Oh, I like that comparison, and no offense is taken. In fact, I often ask myself that question since my crops are now a part of the gentile marketplace. Where I once walked, I now ride a horse. I even have a carriage. For the midday meal, I used to eat no more than dried beans and onions on bread. Now I have poached fish with capers. My horses dress better than the poor Jew I just gave a coin to. Yes," he looked very intently, "As a Pharisee, I think often of how my talents have turned into treasure and how the pursuit of the treasure is now an idol. I take comfort, however, in knowing that the more I make, the more I can give."

"My father gives much," Rebekah spoke up proudly, but with some defensiveness in her voice. "You saw the poor outside. This goes on daily. And without gratitude as I know you saw. They bless our home only to take my father's coins, and once given, they scurry away as though offended. I feel we keep them from working by giving them a reason not to work." Her face flushed slightly in anger.

Simeon looked in rebuke toward his daughter. "Never say those words again, daughter," he admonished sharply. "It is in service to man that we serve The Holy One. It is our duty and privilege."

"There will always be the poor," Jesus said, "but I believe it is not by possessions that we will be judged, for he who lays up treasure for himself, who thinks of himself as first, will be judged as poor and last, and many who are said to be poor will be found to be wealthy when they stand before Judgment. It must be so if we are to fulfill the words of the ancients."

"I didn't know you attended the schools in Jerusalem," Simeon said, surprised at the seriousness and knowledge of a man he remembered as being more fun loving than philosophical as a youth.

"No, after my beloved father died, my schooling ended. But I have read much, and I say that we must move beyond the words of our leaders and more toward the revelations of Isaiah, Daniel, and Elijah."

"You say?" Simeon peered from his bushy gray brows at Jesus who sat across from him on a bench. It had struck him that Jesus had not started or ended by saying the traditional, 'It is said,' or 'As the prophets say,' and it was blasphemous for anyone to make such statements as though they themselves were directly quoting God.

"It is in the scriptures for all to hear," Jesus answered quietly. "I only repeat the words of the prophets. But I do feel their words are about to be fulfilled."

This oblique answer seemed to appease Simeon's concerns. He asked,

"Do you have an interest in doing more work in this area? I could use help on my farm, especially from one who knows the fitting of woods and stone, and who is moved by The Holiest One as you are."

"Father does need help," Rebekah agreed eagerly. "There is much work here, and we have a small house away from the main house that would suit you well."

Simeon gazed appreciatively at his daughter. He had been too strict on the men who had come for her hand, and now, in the fullness of her beauty, it was time he let her go, not to a man who sought the family's wealth, but to one who walked in the Word and sought only the riches of the soul.

Simeon slid off the bed and reached for an engraved bronze pitcher. He poured juice out of it into a cup and handed it to Jesus.

"The cookies were good," Jesus thanked him. Drinking the juice he said, "I beg your forgiveness, but the hour grows late and I must make Nazareth before dark. May I have my sandals, please?"

Rebekah paused; a look of disappointment swept her face, and then she reluctantly walked out on the doorstep and retrieved his dusty sandals. She touched them tenderly, looked back in the house at the broad-shouldered Jesus, forced a smile on her face and entered, chatting again about how he must come soon and see the farm.

"I will be working outside of Zippori on an apartment building, and I may travel down to Jericho to hear the prophet who speaks of the End of Days."

"Oh, that is John the Baptizer. He is the talk here. His kind of talk frightens me," Rebekah frowned.

"Who is the owner of the apartments?" Simeon inquired, seeming more interested in commerce than preachers.

"Uh," Jesus had heard the name only once. "I learned of the work after a man came through Nazareth saying they were looking for carpenters. I think the owner is a Jew from Caesarea named Nathan."

Simeon's ebullient countenance dropped enough for Jesus to notice. "Nathan was a follower of Herod's, and is a Jew who travels with the haughty. He cares not if one is a gentile, a worshiper of Isis, Dionysus, or any other god. He is well connected with the Romans at the port, the Syrians and Greeks at Zippori and, I believe, has been to banquets that Herod Antipas has given. I deal with the gentiles only when I must, but Nathan is comfortable with them in every way. It has made him quite wealthy."

"My father and I worked at Bethsaida. I have worked on building the colonnade on the Cardo (Sepphoris' main street). If we keep our eye on The Father we can easily live in a world of different faiths. It isn't what comes from the outside that spoils our heart." Jesus spoke with great self assurance and it showed.

Slipping into his sandals, he said to Rebekah, "The Holy Father has graced our land with much beauty, but none that reflects His joy as do you."

A faint cry came from her lips like the distant bleating of a lamb, so faint that it was like her last breath, and as Jesus passed by into the front yard she almost wished it was. He stopped at the horses, looking back at her in the late afternoon light; she shimmered like a mirage against the tan coloring of the walls of the house in the stark, white woolen robe she wore. Her eyes reached out to him in a plea that froze him momentarily. He found himself wanting to go back to her.

107

"You must remember us when you finish your work. We are much in need of your talents at the farm!" she called to him in a poorly disguised plea.

He wanted to go back to her and spend the rest of the evening with good wine and table talk. He wanted to take her in his arms in all of her suppleness. He wanted to gaze at the singular perfection of her face and tell her stories that made her giggle and laugh in waves in an unbridled joy. But he stopped short and pushed himself to deny the desires of his body and his heart. It was almost all he could do to say, "My work may only now be starting." And, regaining his will, Jesus raised his hand, smiled, and forced himself to head back down the sloping main street toward the road to Nazareth. His heart ached as he walked, and he wondered aloud if he could not know this pure love for both God and a woman. Why did he turn from her? Why did he feel he had to forsake all of this earth to become one with God? Had the calling become so obsessive and compelling that he had to wrack his emotions in constant denial of all that was dear to him on this earth?

She stood for a moment watching his tall figure and wondered what he meant by his statement. She went back inside. Her father walked over and clasped her arm. He saw the great sadness on her face and knew that Jesus had touched her as no man had been able to.

"Now how could that ugly old man in his thirties bring such sadness to your face, the face that has attracted every man from Caesarea to Jerusalem?" His voice was jovial and kidding, but they shielded the concern he felt for her obvious dejection.

Her eyes darted up in a sharp rebuke, "How could you say I thought he was ugly in front of him? No wonder he has gone." She pouted and turned away from him.

In a soothing fatherly tone he said, "My daughter, I would break the Laws before I would bring sadness to you. Jesus is a man of great mirth, and I only laughed with him." He kidded, "You must admit though, it is an interesting face."

"It is a face like our land…rugged, rich, lonely, carefree, and dangerous; both easy and difficult to travel over." She stared out the open door, talking as much to herself as to her father. Her heart ached at the thought of not seeing him again for years.

"He is a man of little means, daughter," Simeon warned.

She looked at her father and pleaded "But you have means, father. You could help him. He could be a part of our family."

"I think Jesus has slipped beyond those bounds. I believe there is a holiness upon his shoulders now that fills his heart so that there is no room left for another. I would be surprised if he were to work in wood much longer."

She removed the linen hat from her head and pulled the pins and broach from the bun that held her thick, dark hair together. It collapsed in a cascade about her shoulders.

"He is moving closer to the faith, daughter. He speaks easily from the scriptures with a great knowledge. He cares nothing for wealth, for my wealth, unlike every other young man who bays like the street dogs at my door. I don't know if they want your hand or my hand outs," he grumbled.

She tried to cheer herself up, walking back to the door to see if she could see him once again. She placed her hand on the door and gazed into the distance. With a false cheerfulness, she said to no one, "Oh, he'll come by the farm soon. He'll come soon."

CHAPTER 5

They were up early and arguing.

"If I find out the man is a gladiator, I will put you on the next grain boat to Rome!" Paulius' shouts muffled through the rooms like deep, distant thunderclaps. It was still dark before the cock's crowing, but they were up and yelling, and Julian was pulled from a dream about a god who had stolen all of his inks so he could only draw by scratching. He was more annoyed at what the dream had meant than the hard voices.

"Would someone of my rank stoop to the level of a gladiator?" Sophia asked indignantly.

"Oh, I know the fantasy of the high born women of this city. We men don't just sit at the baths having our hairs plucked. The men there speak of late night meetings of wives, of the wagging tongues who describe in lurid detail the anatomies of the gladiators they prize. I have seen that muscle boy you had the gall to bring to my door," Paulius answered.

"Probably in the houses of the whores that sit across the street from the baths," she snapped in rebuttal.

"Paulius needs no whores," he sneered. "Neither does he need a wife who acts like one."

A door slammed, and Julian could hear a pot shatter against a wall. He assumed Sophia had thrown it in a final act of defiance.

Paulius, the mild, gracious host was known throughout the city as a banker and lawyer who was a terror to cross. He was one of the city's most powerful men, connected to all levels, accomplished in part because of several shadowy characters who he paid to listen in on conversations at the baths, read through documents left on desks at night, and to follow wives and husbands to find out with whom they may be having affairs. He knew well the pulse of Caesarea, and he parceled out this information in discreet packets where it suited his purposes.

Julian lay in the feathered softness of his bed thinking of his wife and two small children. He would write them a short letter saying he had arrived safely and fill its borders with sketches of some of the different skiffs, tubs, and sailing vessels he had seen in the harbor. His trip would take him away for three months. Over his wife's protests, he traveled to fill his head with fresh ideas for wall paintings for his clients. It would be good for business. It was essential to the artist to get out of the masses crowding Rome, the same old jutting Italian hills, with their familiar animals and flora. Palestine and Egypt were new territories for his fertile mind. He would come back with stacks of reference drawings to enliven the villas of the rich. The Roman rich were not adventurous or creative in their decor, but they did relish a wall painting that showed beasts and landscapes different enough to give their home a slight edge over a neighbor's.

There was a tap on Julian's door. It was Cassius. "Julian?" he whispered.

"Come in. I'm awake; by thunder, I might add."

Cassius stood in the door wearing a new tunic and sandals. His form was shadowy in the first seeping of morning through the door from the courtyard. He stepped inside the room and sat on a stool while cinching up his sandals and rubbing his face.

"It appears in this strange land that cocks are not required for awakening. One simply engages their wife in a shouting match to chase away the gods that carry us into sleep." He observed sardonically.

Julian could feel the cold air of the room on his arm that lay outside the covers and rested on his chest. He hated to take that first plunge out from under the warmth of the blankets.

"I thought that the man looked suspicious last night — a little too much of a rogue; there was a swarthiness about him. His arms, though, did look like the battered remains of close-in fighting. Perhaps it was done in battle, but I have seen too many gladiators with those same forearm marks."

"I must admit, to my surprise, that one so powerful as Paulius would disrupt the household, yea, the entire neighborhood in accusing his wife of indiscretions with the lower class. Is that not rather lower class in itself?." Cassius was of the upper ranks of Roman society where the rules of the culture were carefully observed and those who would break those rules were instantly publicly ostracized.

"My friend, it is everywhere that our great culture declines even as we remain the world's most powerful empire. I observe it and I write of it and am probably an unwitting part of it," Julian said with some remorse.

"Still, we do not rejoice in having the powerful revealed as no more perfect than a rural. There seems to be no self-denial to our passions," Cassius said.

"Being haughty is what we are all about. You must admit to enjoy being carried to the baths by a large retinue."

Cassius jerked the covers off his complaining friend, "You know me too well. Let's see what morning food awaits us."

Julian fairly jumped out of the bed and rummaged over his baggage for a toga. Finding it folded, he spread the long wrap out and started putting it around his body at his left shoulder, then diagonally across the back and under the right arm. The toga was the badge of Roman citizenship and rank. He found two finger rings he had left on a table, and an engraved arm band from his wife. To ward off the lingering morning chill, he slipped on a pallium, a cloak that clings to the shoulders.

He stepped out into the sudden brightness of the day. The sky above the courtyard was a deep and clear blue. The sun remained low, but sharded the sides of the courtyard in dazzling light streaks that found their way through the buildings of the city.

The garden was a meticulous salute to order and design. With a statue to Dionysus, the god of wine, at its center, and several statues to Augustus, Tiberius, and two apparent Egyptian gods Julian did not recognize. The gardens in the yard were filled with small shrubs and pruned trees, with some early flowers heralding the spring. An herb garden and some vegetables grew to one side. Columns circled the yard walls, and a trellis held vines along one wall.

"Ah, you're up. No leisurely lounging for you young warriors," Paulius bellowed as his two guests entered the main room. He was sitting at a table covered in documents.

"I was just going over the legal papers for your foreclosure on the farm of the Jew, Cassius. It is past due. You do have every right to take the property. It was a shrewd loan your father made. When I advised him to do it, I knew the Jew had suffered several bad years and was at a disadvantage. Oh, forgive my waking you this morning, but I was vexed throughout the night over the rudeness of Sophia, and I wished to straighten the matter out with her before the day started." Paulius was full of energy, a characteristic for which he was well known.

"That kind of beauty," Cassius remarked as he sat on a cushioned bench, "surrounds itself with all manner of gods. They fight over who shall guide her. It must be difficult on Sophia to deal with these furies."

"Well said, well said." Paulius was pleased that his guest had led him out of the embarrassment of his temper tantrum.

Several servants appeared, including the Egyptian woman. They carried silver trays with various nuts and fruits, and an egg salad made of parsley, onions and covered in oil.

"The eggs are from wild fowl that we keep just outside the city," Paulius bragged. "They are smaller than chicken eggs, but a rare taste I thought you might enjoy."

"You honor us to the extreme," Julian said gratefully. "To come off even a well-heeled sailing ship after several weeks, and to be accommodated in such style as you provide, will be a part of the delightful story we tell of our trip upon our return."

"If my name is to be spoken among the equestrian rank of Rome and Pompeii, then I must try harder," he said. "This morning we go to visit the Jew called Nathan, to ask about his apartments in Sepphoris. There is to be a small circus here, as we discussed, and a race at the hippodrome; we might stop in, then go over to the baths where I can introduce you around. I have bearers to carry each one of us to the door of the baths, so you will be pleased with your entrance. I can assure it will be noticed and appreciated. In fact, I'll have you announced as we arrive. Tonight we will have a small banquet, the size depending on whom I favor with an invitation."

"Your kindness knows no end, Paulius. My father will look forward to entertaining you when you return to the homeland. He has built a nice villa very near Mt. Vesuvius. The view of its white top and occasional smoke plumes against the sky is a true picture," Julian praised him as he bit into a boiled egg.

Cassius chewed on shallots and munched on sweet millet balls flavored with dates and apricots. "I would like to push on to Sepphoris, perhaps tomorrow, before we go to the farm of the Jew. I will need a bailiff to go out to serve the papers and an escort from the legate."

"Whatever assistance you require, it will be done." Paulius talked with a mouthful of food. Juices ran over his fingers and on to his expensive robe. A servant was quick to blot the spots with a damp cloth. Paulius pushed the man away with the swipe of an arm as though he were a nuisance. Julian nodded hello to Esna. She managed a shy, quick dip of her head, but seemed more concerned with not angering her master.

The door to the courtyard opened and a older black woman stepped in and announced, "Master, your wife will enter now."

The men turned to watch the regal entrance of Sophia. She was stunning in an ankle length cotton robe with purple dyes along the bottom. A gold, jeweled pin held it at the waist. Her blond hair was pulled back tight from her face, then allowed to fall in carefully curled ringlets over her neck. Her lips were auburn colored with lipstick and her cheeks powdered in rouge.

Her demeanor had changed completely from the night before. She was apologetic, servile, asking what she could bring in from the kitchen, picking up bits of food they had allowed to fall on the mosaic tiles. She placed a hand on her husband's drooping shoulder and wished him well for the day. She said she would be overseeing the planting of an early garden, but first would be going over to the baths for the women's morning massage before the men came in for their exclusive time after midday.

Cassius allowed his mind to wander over what she would look like reclining nude in the baths, until Paulius stood and said it was time for them to have the bearers bring up the litters.

"Let's start at the public toilets before we go to Nathan's. It will be a good introductory place. We usually get a good turnout there in the mornings."

Sophia kissed her husband on the cheek and quietly apologized again. He seemed pleased that his power over his house had been restored, and asked that she make all preparations for a banquet of twelve for the evening. She seemed delighted by the prospects of a dinner party and disappeared into the kitchen.

Julian looked at Cassius and shrugged. A strange woman — mysterious, deceptive, and typical of the spoiled younger high-born. She would not have been allowed such impetuousness had she and Paulius been living in Rome, but out in the distant provinces a beauty such as she could flout her worst traits.

Cassius put on an abolla, a beautifully-stitched cloak, and Julian put his pallium back on. They walked out the front and admired the garden and a pond with bloated gold and yellow fish. Small statues to various gods graced the corners, and they walked between two tall, thin cedar trees and out a heavy gate to the street. Villas sat in the morning light up and down the road, all white against the sun, all carefully sheltered with trimmed and sculptured trees and shrubs. The closer a person lived to the center of the city, the higher their rank. It was a side street that had been paved in flat stones so the residents did not have to track mud into their homes when it rained. As a gift to the city, a wealthy neighbor, to show off his civic responsibilities, paid for the stones to be placed. It was expected that he would run for a city office and the paving would be to his favor.

There is a new stone at the end of the street," Paulius remarked. "Pilate paid for repair work and dedicated the repairs to Tiberius. How meager an attempt to ingratiate," he sniffed.

"A little bit of Pompeii," Julian cooed with nostalgia at the orderly, well kept streets.

"Can you imagine what manner of hovel, what mud-dripping huts would sit on this ground had we not come to bring civilization here?" Cassius said with disdain.

Two of the inside servants led the litter bearers around from the stables at the back. Each litter was carried by four men.

"The man has more slaves than my father had an army," Cassius observed sarcastically and with some appreciation.

"Oh, half of them are probably borrowed," Julian laughed.

Paulius came through the gate in all his finery. His hands were weighted with rings and his head topped with a capitium. He wore slippers encrusted with jewels and gold stitching.

"Hold your heads high," Paulius commanded his bearers as he motioned for them to lower the narrow litters the three men would recline upon. With a heave, each man was lifted, and the entourage went off toward the center of town a short distance away.

Public toilets were surprisingly open; a carry-over from Rome, where men gathered to relieve themselves along ornately carved marble latrines. It became a social place for conversations with little regard to what one of the parties may be doing.

"Ah, Victor," Paulius shouted with his normal enthusiasm as they came up on the latrines which had the appearance of a fountain with seats around its circle. With indoor plumbing in only the richest homes, the public latrines provided a sanitary way to carry off waste through its underground sewage system.

Terentius, a short, stocky, pale-faced man in his thirties, was sitting on one of the latrines as the three approached. He smiled broadly, revealing yellowed and missing teeth, but the jewelry on his arms and fingers spoke of his position in the city.

"Master Paulius, my favorite deal maker," he returned. "You bring a parade with you today," he kidded in the ways of those who know one another, and with a familiarity that infuriated the more pious Jews.

"All the way from Rome, sons of the Senator Orelius and the great magistrate of Pompeii, Lycanius. I do not parade with riffraff," Paulius bragged.

The bearers stopped at the latrines, lowered the party to the ground and watched as all three relieved themselves.

"Terentius owns part of the harbor. If you, Cassius, want to ship any of your grains or dried fruits out of here, I will introduce you to the man who will store it while you await a vessel." And almost under his breath he said, "For a small fee, of course."

They all laughed, and Terentius, who finished his business and stood adjusting his tunic said, "Not half the fee that Paulius will charge you for legal work."

"Do you have land here?" the short Roman inquired of Cassius.

"I will shortly. I'm foreclosing on an estate owned by a Jew a day's ride from here, out toward Sepphoris. I hear the land is quite fertile, and there are profits to be made."

"Hire you some strong men," Terentius warned. "The rurals will steal your crops and knife you if you try and stop them. There is much banditry out there."

They were interrupted by a tiny man with a ragged, wool, sleeveless cloak on. "May the gods bless all who use these latrines," he said to them in a raspy voice. He fell to his knees and began scrapping up loose dirt and throwing it over himself in an act of servitude.

"Oh, infernal gods, can't a man relieve himself of his water without you sending a dust ball to beggar us!" Paulius cursed. He motioned to one of his bearers who pushed the man away so hard that the man went sprawling out over the pavement. Paulius walked over and kicked him hard in his side as he screamed and went skittering away, half crawling, half running.

"Am I back in Rome?" Cassius asked in disgust. "The begging there has gotten so bad, all of the best people are moving to villages outside of town. We're sick of those who crouch."

"Power attracts the worthless as well as the powerful," Terentius bemoaned. "The rurals swell our cities with their whining. We have created a populace of the lazy, because we give them handouts to keep them quiet. Circuses and bread, as the Emperor has said. I won't even go to the Colosseum in Rome. Drunks and those with their hand out spend their days waiting for the free wine and food given at the games. It has ruined them and the hoards they breed."

Paulius, ever cheery and energetic, broke in, "Well, friend, I want to show my guests the sights, so if you will excuse us, we might have a bite at the cafe over there before journeying on."

Terentius seemed eager to ask Paulius something; his face showed a certain tension as the litter bearers prepared to leave. "Ah, my banker, have you heard of any good banquets tonight?"

Paulius turned his head toward Julian and grinned broadly, acknowledging that it was not he who had been the first to ask for a dinner invitation. In the upper ranks of Roman society, there was a constant game being played as to who would be invited to the evening meal. It was a source of immense embarrassment to eat alone, and much of the day's activities was spent in trying to finagle an invitation.

"Well, I'm considering a small, private dinner, and you will be the first to be asked, of course. Enjoy the day!" Paulius concluded and motioned for his bearers to move on.

The cafe was called The Augustan, and its menu was normally a light fare of pancakes, raw vegetables, cakes and puddings. But today they featured heart of lamb and a syrupy wine mixed with water. Heads turned as Paulius' party approached. It was located on the first floor of a three-story building along the main avenue; an area of cafes and clothing shops where the rich roamed and ran their bejeweled fingers over ivories from Africa, bags of pepper from India, and finely-woven cotton cloths from Arabia. The main city baths were just down the street, which was called Lucius Street after a wealthy city father who had paid for repair work on the street and its drains.

"Oh, you're too, too haughty, Paulius," a high pitched voice came from the crowd seated in the cafe. It was Appius Sextus, the head of the weavers association in Caesarea. He had made money in wool and controlled some of the cotton imports from Egypt and Arabia. He was known to have arrived penniless from Italy where his family had several vineyards known for producing a low grade wine.

"Someone calls your name," Julian noted.

"Oh, these public cafes," Paulius moaned. "They've even got weavers coming here. He's made some money, but has donated none for any public works, and I even hear that he works with his hands in some of his weaving shops." They were seated at a table near the front door so all could see them.

Appius was a foppish dresser. His hair was obviously a dyed red and a poor job at that. He had used his curling iron too much, and

117

his hair had an affected curl, again too obvious. Rings covered his fingers. As he approached their table, he was too obsequious. "Paulius, the metro's most honored lawyer, we've not seen you along the street lately."

Paulius turned a cold eye up at Appius and said with little humor, "I've been too busy at my leisure." And then carefully examining Appius' tunic, Paulius reached up and pulled off an imaginary piece of wool.

"Would that be a stray piece of wool from your loom?"

Appius swung his chin down to see as Paulius flicked his finger, as though he had touched something nasty. Smiling with great diffidence, "You're getting too close to the looms, my friend. You really should leave the common work to the common man."

The man blushed and said with obvious false bravado, "Oh, but, of course I do. Any lint collected by me came during a transaction I'm sure. We're having a great year, by the way. Perhaps your wife would wish to come and view some of the smaller threads we are sewing with."

Paulius looked with a delicious glee at his two companions. "She wouldn't leave with," as he pretended to pick lint off Appius' tunic again, "wool balls on her robe, would she?"

Cassius and Julian chuckled as they toyed with a plate of small pancakes a waiter had delivered. Appius knew he was being handled for the amusement of friends, but he also knew that Paulius was an essential connection into the upper ranks of the city's society, so he endured, even persisted, in trying to get a dinner invitation.

"Today, I'm skipping the second meal. Makes for a big appetite for the banquet this evening. I'll be showing some new cotton that feels almost like silk. We just got it in from a secret source in Arabia who brought it from India. I have never seen cotton of this quality. Knowing the standards Sophia holds…" Paulius raised his eyebrow and rolled his eyes at his friends in a mockery of Appius presuming to know anything of his wife's tastes. "I could bring them to your home tonight, if you wish."

Paulius had become bored with Appius' attempts to get an invitation but did admire his technique of showing cloths. He waved his fingers in a dismissal, "Alright, alright, weaver, if we dine tonight, you will be on the list. But bring the cloth." Appius grinned broadly and bowed repeatedly as he retreated.

"By the gods, is being in the upper class really worth the sniveling, groveling, scheming riffraff forever trying to wheedle a seat at your table! The man has no ancestors of note, attended no gymnasium of distinction, and slurs his speech. No training in rhetoric even! He thinks he can wear a broad crimson strip on his robe and he is suddenly of rank." Paulius snorted and waved his hand in dismissal.

Paulius, still irritated, scoffed, "If he shows at my door I will have the doorman take his cloth and tell him our tables are already filled. Unless, of course, he wants to eat with the servants."

Cassius grinned, knowing the cruel nature of Roman social hierarchy offered, "Oh, let him in and we can serve him cheap wine and uncooked food. It will be great merriment."

Julian smiled and relaxed in the sun as it peered through the wood shutters of the cafe window. The moment felt good. "Being a man of the brush has its own problems," he whined. " I am asked to banquets because they want to use me as a name they can brag about to their friends. They want to say, 'Oh, Julian has done frescoes at the summer villa of the Emperor, and is about to do one for us.' But they have no respect for me because I work with my hands. Even though my father could buy all of them, and my talent surpasses any idea they will ever put forth. Thank all of you, good spirits," he waved at the ceiling, "for giving me a rich father and a talented eye."

"Well, some of us are born to the brush, and some to the hunt," Cassius said with a mouth full of pancake. "I am the lion and my prey is the coin. How I attack and defeat those who would deprive me of the coin will make me richer than my father perhaps. And, as you say, good Paulius, those who would best me at commerce already follow me like flies in Rome, but, alas, it is the price of profits, and a price I am willing to pay."

"Speaking of profits, let's go and meet the Jew and see if his apartments are to be in your future," Paulius concluded the meal of the sixth hour (there would be a snack in the afternoon, and then a long dinner at the ninth hour), and they walked out into the warming day.

Down a broad avenue and out near the hippodrome was the street where the upper class Jewish community lived. Caesarea, like all Roman cities, was subdivided among peoples of some commonality: various trades lived together, religious groups congregated by neighborhood, and the various classes had their own area. Those such as dye makers, whose business gave off offensive odors, had to live on the edge of the city or outside its gates.

119

Nathan had a home that looked very much like the home of Paulius, with a garden entrance, sculptured trees and shrubs, a fountain in the center, but no statues or animal figures carved into any of the benches or the lintel over the door. Nor did slaves meet them at the door, but only paid servants. The inside of the home was simple but tasteful, with a variety of pottery Nathan had collected, and beautifully embroidered rugs and cushions on two long divans, exquisitely sewn in flower designs. There was a receiving area which led into a large room with an atrium ceiling. Polished columns formed a portico there and off this room led many small rooms including the office of Nathan. The house was in a horseshoe shape with a back garden between the two wings. An oil press and large oven were at the back of the house.

A servant met them at the gate; his son Jonas greeted them at the door. "My father awaits your distinguished company," he bowed slightly.

Paulius blustered on in with his usual familiarity, "Where is the merchant prince? Tell him we have half the coins in the empire awaiting him."

A loud, high-pitched laugh emanated from the garden as the tall, caramel colored figure of Nathan briskly entered the room. He wore a tunic of white that stopped at his knees, with britches underneath and short boots. He had a long, hooked nose, thick brows and black eyes. His hair was curly and black with streaks of gray. His mouth was thin and broad. There was an exuberance about him and an energy. He obviously knew and liked Paulius by the way they grasped one another's arms and kidded easily. Three men carrying scrolls and looking of some import had been meeting with the powerful Nathan, seeking his willingness to join in a deal they proposed. Each had brought him a gift to, in effect, bribe his help. Gift giving was a normal business practice. They nodded at Paulius as they brushed by to leave.

"Did I hear the mention of coins? Are these the rich young rulers from the land of the Emperor?" he asked as he appraised the two.

"They're rich, because they know how to hold on to their coins when they enter the company of an old camel trader like you," Paulius said with a short laugh. "And where is that good Jewish wine? Does Yahweh not allow it at the midday?"

Nathan looked at Cassius and Julian and smiled, "Feel safe here, men. The One, the True, the Eternal has run all those dog-headed

Egyptian gods and those petulant and spoiled Greek and Roman gods out of this house. Feel safe from their indignities for once."

It was a reflection of the closeness Nathan and Paulius felt for one another, that they could engage in such camaraderie about this delicate subject. But poking fun and ridiculing was a part of Paulius' style that endeared him to most, but angered some.

After introductions, Julian inquired, "I would like some time to ask you more about your religion. I am traveling the area in search of truths, but the strangest story I have heard so far is of your one god, who has no name, nor face that he wants portrayed. An invisible god is both absurd to my rationale mind, but also intimidating. He could be so powerful that even his presence would overwhelm mortals."

Nathan motioned for them to sit and spoke as they crossed the room. "You speak right. Yahweh is one of many names we have for Him, and He is so all powerful that we could not bear to actually see His face."

"You'll have plenty of time to learn of this and other mysteries of our area," Paulius interrupted. "Oh, by the way, Julian is a master at frescoes, and you two might also wish to talk of his doing some work on your walls, that of course respects the limitations that your religion demands."

Nathan nodded as he eyed the group behind a constant smile, observing their mannerisms and body language; he was a continual study of human nature. "Herod thought the children of Israel were too limited in their art."

"You mean boring," Paulius chuckled.

"Alright, boring, so he attempted to rebuild our land in all the grandeur of Rome and Athens, and damned near bankrupted our people in doing so. We paid a high price for art!"

Cassius had little interest in hearing of politics and interjected, "I understand that you have an apartment building near Sepphoris. I am here to buy property and that could include apartments. Have you considered selling yours?"

"Ah, the deal maker works his magic," Nathan shrewdly observed. "Do I see the honored lawyer here trying to help a young Roman get his start?"

Paulius shrugged innocently.

"Well, I've not thought of it, but I am about to put money into the one there, and it might be a good time for me to offer it as it is. In fact, I think some workers are already there doing some necessary repairs. I've had it for some time, and the tenants who have lived like the rats they are, have left it in some disrepair. But it is a good location, and if managed right, there would be profits."

"Who lives there now?" Cassius asked.

"A Syrian and his family occupy the bottom floor. He wanted the indoor sewage I had installed. He makes his coins through a warehouse that stores grains coming in from Galilee and does quite well. As the floors rise, the place sounds like the Tower of Babel with Indian traders, Roman merchants, Greeks, and a former gladiator that lifts weights and drops them on the floor. He almost killed a tenant below when the weight crashed through one morning. There are a few Jews there who are minor merchants and stall owners." He extended his arms in a show of resignation, "But if it sounds like Babel, at least I own the Tower and as long as the babblers pay their rent…"

Jonas, who had been standing near the front door, walked quietly behind his father, leaned to his ear and whispered something. Nathan nodded, muttered something back, reached in a pocket and handed the boy a small leather pouch.

"As I said, at least they pay their rent, though they tear the place up, as you will find all tenants do. Jonas just spoke to me of a poor Jew outside looking for help. It is our religion that demands that we help our poor, but they seem to be coming in ever increasing droves." He sat forward, looking annoyed. "In helping, and I know we must do it gladly, I feel we are hurting some."

Julian grimaced, "The poor? You, yourself give money to the poor? That is the job of the officials of the city, not of the people."

"The children of Israel are commanded by our Law, the Books of Moses, that we make our Lord pleased through our good works. And I, of course, would not dare raise the anger of the Righteous One. We give at synagogue to orphans, we pay to the Temple, we pay for our schools, we pay…" he rolled his eyes. "It goes on and on, but we do it for the glory of our Lord."

"I continue to be surprised about this god and his demands, and I do not intend to offend you, but giving your own personal fortune to the rabble…I cannot see the reasoning behind that." Julian twisted for a more comfortable position on the heavy cushion on which he sat.

"No offense to you," Nathan smiled patiently, "but we consider ourselves a chosen people; The Holiest, The One who rules over all gods, has made covenant with us and because we are chosen by Him, we will be rewarded by Him, but only if we obey His Laws."

Paulius felt Julian was pressing Nathan too hard; he did not want a possible deal to become lost because of a discussion of what any god had said or did not say. He had seen Nathan and other Jews erupt in anger if challenged too strongly.

"Well, you are fortunate, Nathan to have a God who has singled out the Jew," Cassius laughed, "I wish one of ours would single me out for a year of leisure."

Nathan picked up the opportunity to move toward business and nodded emphatically, "Paulius, if you left your business, the entire city of Caesarea would shut down."

"You are too kind, my friend. I just push papyrus between people; mine is not a great talent."

Cassius laughed, "Neither is being humble a great talent of yours. These mere papers you speak of are the oil that lights much of the commerce of the city."

"Even newcomers recognize your influence and give little sympathy to your high-priced whining," Nathan kidded. "Now, when do you wish to look at the apartments?"

"Tomorrow, we will head into the countryside to foreclose on a large farm that owes my father interest. Perhaps we could also go by your apartments as a part of our trip."

Nathan rubbed his beard in thought. "That is soon, but I will make arrangements to meet you there in two days. It will be good experience for my son; I'll bring him along."

Jonas had gone to the front door. Outside at the gate stood an overweight man in dirty robes and bare feet. He whispered loud enough for Jonas to hear him across the garden. "Would you tell the powerful Nathan that Es-ram stands at his gate and would be honored to speak with him. Perhaps you will permit Es-ram to enter."

Jonas didn't answer, but walked across the garden and handed several coins to the man who fell to his knees and prayed in thanks. Jonas walked back into the house seemingly unmoved by what had been a rather routine act of charity. Julian had watched them through a window and shook his head at the absurdity of helping people who would simply show up at the door with their hand out.

Paulius, seeing that his work was done and that a deal was in the making, stood and straightened his tunic. "I'm sure you heard the Flavius family is having a few races and a little circus at the hippodrome and amphitheater. Would you honor us with your presence?" He asked Nathan.

Nathan stood, a splendid figure, thin in the face, strong cheekbones; he looked a mixture of Arabian and Jew. "I anger too many of my Sadducee brethren now with my dealings with those of other beliefs. To go and watch the races or the gladiators would be an offense they could not stand in Jerusalem, and I must stay aware of my position with the governing body."

"Forgive me," Julian inquired, "but I am traveling to learn, and your religion is one I have never encountered. Does your faith look with disfavor on you for associating with those who do not accept your faith?"

Paulius felt his neck tighten. He cared little for these conversations about the Jewish faith; a belief that seemed devoid of all reasoning. He also knew how inflamed discussions could become, and his job was to bring together those who would seek wealth. Even level-headed Jews like Nathan had a limit to how much and how deep they would go in discussing their god to those they considered infidels.

"It depends on which sect or fraternity of our faith you subscribe to," Nathan said as he ushered them toward the large, thick oak paneling of his front door. It was carved intricately in olive branches with ivory inlays.

"My family was a part of King Herod's reign. He believed that doing business with gentiles and pagans, or with anyone, was right. The Land is ruled by the Sanhedrin, our Jewish ruling body in Jerusalem. They deal daily with the Romans, and I praise Yahweh that they do, because it allows us to keep some control over our lives."

Jonas opened the door and the noon light flooded in.

"But those who criticize me are the Pharisee fraternity, and those zealots who want to overthrow the Romans through force. The Pharisees believe it makes a Jew unclean to associate with pagans. They are very critical of those like me who move freely in both the world of Israelites and the world of pagans. They feel I cannot do both."

Julian nodded as they stood at the door. "This land is more complex than any I know of in the empire. There is such disagreement here among the original people, and that is combined with all the other peoples and religions that come and go here."

"We are a crossroads," Nathan said with a slight sadness, "and the land gets trampled at a crossroads."

"Well, enough of all this, my friend," Paulius interjected, becoming impatient with Julian's endless curiosity. "We have races and circuses to see and baths to relax in…here at the crossroads," he tried to joke.

Cassius said to Nathan, "Then we will meet at Sepphoris soon, and I wish you safe passage."

They all said their goodbyes, and the three reclined on their litters and were carried toward the hippodrome several blocks away. The streets were filled with people of every description, from beggars (those who crouch), to richly appointed merchants, Pharisees with their multi-colored robes, to hawkers sitting against building fronts and yelling about their wares. The streets had sidewalks on either side, and most shops had awnings over their front. The display of wealth of Paulius' entourage drew loud shouts for rare spices and ivories; one man had several monkeys in cages he was selling, along with finely-carved silver and gold rings and bracelets. A multitude of weavers offered all manner of tunics, cloaks, and robes. Carts and carriages, donkeys and camels, and an occasional Roman on a horse all jammed the streets in a grand disorder, with no dividing lines. Everyone was mashed in a general moving, careening, jostling mass of humanity. The litters were stalled several times and had to maneuver over and around people and stalls of produce that stuck out into the street.

Caesarea Maritima was typical of any Roman city: a commercial center, a trading port where all the world's goods flowed into and out of, a rampant collection of the exotic and the mundane, a turgid river of the sinister, the schemers, the elite, the impoverished, searchers, philosophers, entertainers, soldiers, pale-skinned Macedonians, black Nubians, reddish-colored Egyptians, caramel-colored Arabians, Goths, Syrians, and Indians. A chorus of humanity all jostled for their dreams on the streets of Caesarea.

They came to a corner which was tight with people, obviously peering at two men who stood on boxes which elevated them slightly above the crowd. One man was grappling with the mouth of the other, who waved joyously to the crowd, even though he was apparently having a tooth extracted.

"Ah, we have one who pulls teeth," Paulius observed. "He appears to be doing so without causing pain to his friend."

And amid a roar of approval from the crowd, a tooth was suddenly jerked from the man's mouth, while the man who had lost the tooth stood and smiled broadly to show it had been painless.

Cassius said sarcastically, "I've seen that scheme before in Rome. The jackal pulling the tooth had put it in his friend's mouth earlier, and he's only pretending to pull it. People are so afraid of the pain of the tooth puller, that they will fall for any liar. The way they really get the evil spirit out is to heat a drill red hot and bore a hole. I've never seen one smile after that."

As they eased along the edge of the crowd, the tooth puller held up several earthen jars and said it was urine breath sweetener from Spain, well-aged and guaranteed to cure bad breath.

Cassius scoffed, "Urine from Spain!" He scoffed. I'll wager you the tooth puller relieved himself in the jars this morning."

"We used that when I was in Spain before we would go on leave," Paulius admitted. "I was told after a night of laying with several women that my breath would kill a mouse at fifty leagues. I didn't know if the bad breath was because of the urine, the women I had kissed, or some god angry because I had failed to pay him homage." He laughed heartily.

As they turned onto an avenue of columns and headed toward the hippodrome, the crowds became too thick for the bearers, so the three were let down and led by Paulius; they began to elbow their way through a section of beggars and obviously poor street merchants.

"Damned rurals," cursed Paulius. "They were too stupid to keep their farms, so they come to the city looking for handouts. There's nothing they like better than a funeral-inspired free chariot race and circus. But they do know that that the funeral is being put on for only one reason; to gain public favor for the Maximus family."

The hippodrome was a stadium centered by an enormous circular dirt track. On one side of the track a large obelisk and three conical columns of red granite towered. On this side the track was longer than the other and banked against the wall. There, a mighty red granite quadrangular stone had been placed called a 'horse frightener'. It was felt that the sun flashing off the rock would appear to be fire and scare the horses as they raced into the curve, making them go faster. The three finally made their way into the arena and took their seats on marbled benches. It was a beautiful structure of pink and white marble and white limestone with statues to various gods and emperors gracing the upper edges.

Horns blew, and the family of the deceased Flavius Maximus entered and gathered at a roped-off section with portraits of Tiberius on poles surrounding their seats. The crowd which packed the seats,

126

applauded and yelped. Many were now drinking heavily from goat skin containers. The horns blew again, and four wooden chariots dusted the track as they jerked out of an opening underneath the stands and began circling as the crowd cheered and began wagering what few coins they might hold.

Each chariot was pulled by one horse and driven by men without shirts, but wearing shorts, red capes, and high boots. Each man held a long whip. They guided their horses up to a flag and stood anxiously while the son of Flavius stood and yelled out what an honor it was to be giving this day to the memory of his father, and how he hoped the people would long remember the name 'Maximus'. He then motioned to the trumpeters to blow, announcing the start of the race, and waved to an official down on the track to start the chariots.

A white flag was waved and the four chariots lurched off, hurtling dirt and clouds of dust from behind their churning wheels. They came to the first turn where the red stone loomed and one horse shied into another, causing its chariot to skid sideways and flip, throwing the driver out onto the track and under the hooves and wheels of the chariot behind him. This chariot rode up and over the body, but not before a hoof caught the downed driver squarely against the forehead, sending blood and brain tissue exploding out of the back of his head. The chariot rode up and over his face, crushing it and leaving him splayed out over the track and almost obscured by the dirt and dust that the careening wheels had kicked up. Two men jumped onto the track and grabbing his arms dragged the lifeless figure over to the wall and unceremoniously dumped him there as the chariots came sliding around the far curve in a storm of hooves and cracking whips.

The crowd roared its approval and held their drinks to the sky in a salute to the early bloodshed.

Cassius yelled against the din of noise, "The son of this Maximus has my vote already! What a pleasing way to start the day!"

Julian was quietly sketching a grove of trees that stood on a slope outside the track and the nearby waters of the sea that was easily seen from their seats. He was indifferent to the race, but looked up from his sketches long enough to watch the bloody death of the rider. They sat through the end of the first race, and Paulius suggested they walk down to the amphitheater and see if the circus had started. He did not want to get caught in the drunken crowds that would be filing out of the hippodrome.

127

Food vendors awaited the throng outside. They had set up on the ground outside the hippodrome, offering wine, nuts, breads, dried fruits, dried and heavily salted fish chunks, garlic bolls, honey cakes, and cookies. Some had also spread blankets with all manner of jewelry. With the bearers following, the three walked with the disdain of Romans who know their rank and want others to know it also. They moved in a slow, diffident glide, heads held slightly high and making little eye contact. They were like perusers, casual appraisers, seeing little value in anyone other than a fellow Roman.

"We call this the market of thieves," Paulius announced as they walked past the line of beseeching merchants, and headed toward the circus several blocks away.

"They steal from your home at night, then come to the streets and sell it back to you in the day. We should just take all that the bastards have and distribute it among our friends who owned it anyway."

"One of my dreams is to catch a thief breaking into my home," Cassius said and gritted his teeth. "I keep several sharpened swords by my bed at my villa in Rome, just waiting for the dogs to try and come while I sleep."

"Thank the gods for the state," Julian signed. "Without its discipline, no dignified person could inhabit an inch of the earth."

The amphitheater was a beautiful, white marble structure shaped like a horseshoe with the western end the stage, backed by a view of the sea. Statues graced its entrance and its heights, and several small temples to the gods stood just outside the arching marbled entrance. There was a grace to its symmetry, and all the nostalgia for home came rushing back to Cassius and Julian as they walked under the high entrance.

"Ah, the circus," Cassius reminisced. "I can travel the world and still find the glories of my homeland. This Herod fellow was quite the student of our culture. I find it hard to believe he was also a Jew."

Paulius smiled knowingly, "Well, there are Jews and then there are Jews. Herod had his cake and ate it too. He forced the Jews to respect him, or his power, by getting a license from the Emperor to run Judea as he would as long as he kept the peace. Tell an Emperor you'll run a quiet country and pay him taxes as well, and you've just made yourself king."

"He was a superb builder," Julian admired. "And on such a stupendous scale for such an insignificant part of the empire. I'm surprised there is a coin left in all of Palestine."

They climbed the stone stairs to a good seat. "Actually not too insignificant," Paulius corrected. "After military service and practicing the law all over Italia, I saw my profession overrun and thought I could set myself up away from the predators around Rome. I went to Alexandria and found instant chance for wealth in wheat trading, and from there I came to this place, found few of my talents and thought I would position myself between Rome, Damascus and Egypt."

Cassius laughed, "So you would be king of the lawyers along a trade route?"

Paulius nodded, "Why not? Herod had built a little Rome surrounded by excellent vineyards, beautiful women from all over the civilized world passing through with boring husbands, and more money moving around than the Roman treasury."

"I like that kind of thinking!" Cassius exclaimed as they sat on the marble rows softened by cushions that the bearers had brought up and placed. "I just hope it allows you plenty of time for leisure."

"By the gods!" Paulius, sounding stunned, rose suddenly; his gaze transfixed on a group of gladiators limbering up at the far end of the dirt floor of the amphitheater. "Uh…order yourself some food and wine. I will be back shortly. Excuse me." And he hurried down the steps, his light cotton toga flowing behind like an obedient cloud.

Cassius and Julian looked at one another and shrugged. In the middle of the dirt floor several animals were being paraded around: a small elephant, a crocodile snapping and hissing between two men with poles, a baby rhino, several antelope tied on rolling platforms, and a large male lion in a cage. At the end of their little parade were several men who appeared to be pygmies. They had bows and arrows with them and waved to the half-filled stadium. The spectators seemed indifferent to the whole thing. They had seen African animals before, and began hissing impatiently. Many were drinking in the growing heat of the sun and seemed ready for more excitement.

The parade was followed by music and acrobatics, performed simultaneously. While this went on, the races finished at the hippodrome and that crowd began filtering in; all were well into their wine and still buzzing about wages won and lost, and the near decapitation of the chariot driver. The sponsoring family entered amidst a few blaring horns, but none noticed Paulius as he passed by them and went into a door that led down to a large number of rooms underneath the stands that formed the basement beneath the floor of the arena.

Torches flickered and smoked along the walls, giving light to an otherwise dark series of halls and holding areas. The place smelled of animal and human waste. A feeble attempt had been made to absorb both with some straw on the dirt flooring. Thick wooden gates, instead of doors sealed off the various areas. It all had the feel of a stable or a jail, as the rooms served a wide menagerie of animals, gladiators, and performers. It was a dungeon world of the hopeless, the helpless, and the hopeful in the case of the performers. They aspired to have coins thrown to them, or to be invited to perform in the villa of a rich man who might be watching. The better performers, however, would be at the outdoor theater on the other end of Caesarea. To be performing for a funeral-inspired circus was to be hardly paid, but it was a place to start.

The animals were coming in off the arena floor down the broad hallway as Paulius strode along it, brushing startled attendants aside. He walked up the ramp leading to the outside and stood in its harsh light, looking intently across the dirt arena to a group of gladiators exercising and slinging their various weapons in mock combat with unseen foes. Each practiced on his own. There were twelve of them. They were almost naked, except for strips of cloth tied around their groin area. Their bodies glistened in sweat, not from the heat of the day but from the tension of that place and that moment.

"Son of a jackal!" Paulius cursed. It was Leo, the man who had escorted his wife. Anger seized him as he looked around for the official who ran the amphitheater. "Pannius!" He yelled at a short, plump Greek standing just to his left. The man was fidgeting with some papyrus written instructions on how the circus should flow. He knew Paulius well by his reputation, but they had met only once at a public banquet. Paulius would never have such a minor official in his home.

Pannius turned his head slowly toward the call of his name, but once recognizing who it was, almost ran to see why one of such high rank would be calling him.

"Distinguished Paulius, what an honor and a surprise to see you here," he stammered obsequiously.

Ignoring his greeting, Paulius grabbed him by one arm and jerked him back into the half light of the tunnel. "The gladiator Leo...do you know him?" He asked threateningly.

The little man broke out in a sweat, his eyes darting to the brilliant light of the arena as though searching for Leo. "I, I do know of one.

He's a Macedonian, a thief caught invading the home of a Roman official in Athens. He's the best fighter of the bunch." He nodded his bald head as though pleased with his immediate answer.

"I have an opportunity for you to keep your job and possibly your life, my friend," Paulius said as he smiled and continued to squeeze the man's arm like an exclamation mark at the end of his words. "I wish to honor the death of Flavius by making this a memorable event. I fear it is going rather slowly now and the crowd is displeased."

Pannius looked scared. "Going badly? Oh, my apologies, but, but I was paid only a limited amount to put this on and…"

Paulius removed his grip and placed his hand on the man's shoulder in a sudden show of paternalism. "Oh, of course, your reputation is an honor to this arena, and I would personally not want it to be damaged by a single event."

"May the gods give you even more wealth for this kindness," he groveled.

Paulius leaned into the man's frightened face as though telling him a confidence. "One of our city's most powerful men told me this Leo broke into his home, which I don't understand, because these criminals are supposed to be locked up here. Something very valuable was taken, and the man asked that I make sure this thief Leo not be allowed to disrupt the life of a city leader again."

Pannius was sweating profusely, and Paulius could feel him shaking under his hand still draped heavily over the top of Pannius' shoulder. "How do you propose that be done, and what could I possibly do about it?"

"If this scoundrel Leo survives his first fight, let the lion loose on him." Paulius squeezed with a vise-like grip that sent a nerve shattering pain through the manager's shoulder.

He began to sputter in confusion, "But…the…but we are not to allow animals and men in the same arena. The Emperor decreed this circus be allowed only as a favor to the Maximus family, and it was to be done according to…"

Paulius relinquished his grip and stood erect as though at attention when the Emperor was mentioned. He spoke reverentially. "Of course, I know that, and I would never ask you to go against your instructions by the Maximus family. But I am only trying to help you out of the escape of Leo which I know you had nothing to do with, but for which you will be blamed for and possibly flogged."

Pannius' eyes bugged out against a face swollen from too much wine and perpetual eating. "Flogged? Escaped?"

"Yes, the fact that this Leo escaped while being held in this place for which you are the manager could make it appear you were careless. You would be terrified if I told you who the man was that had asked me to come to you. He is of violent temper. Why, I saw him kick the teeth out of a poor defenseless street beggar yesterday, because his foot itched and he needed something to scratch it against."

Pannius was sweating profusely and breathing rapidly. He was terrified that he would blurt out how Leo had indeed been allowed to leave.

"Since I am here to help you out of a serious situation, you must be honest with me. I am the most honored lawyer in Caesarea, and I can help you if my client wants you flogged, or perhaps even worse."

"Anything you wish to know," Pannius said panicked. He knew too well the power of the city's elite.

"I was told by a source that you were approached by a woman of high bearing who asked that you allow Leo to escape," he lied, wanting to see if Sophia had indeed come seeking the gladiator.

Pannius drew back, shocked that Paulius knew. He swallowed hard and answered in a whining voice, "I do not know her identity, but a woman of great bearing, a tall, blond-haired woman did come in the dimness of my room here and offered me more coins than I have ever seen if the gladiator Leo would be freed for the night. She said she would be responsible. She said it was to be a surprise for a group of friends she was entertaining."

Paulius' pulse quickened with anger, but his face remained calm and understanding, "Would you recognize her?"

"No, no," his eyes contorted in fear and his face appeared pasty in color. "The lamps were low on oil in my room, and she had a veil over her face." He looked down in obedience, "I do not know the wives of those of high rank."

Paulius looked with great seriousness, "Pannius, for this you could be flogged thirty-six times, and you would never be the same man again. Have you ever seen the blood that flows from a lashing? But I can save you. I want to save you because of your honesty with me. But I also want to protect you from the anger of your client, the Maximus family. Get one of the slaves that work here to loosen the rope on the lion's cage, then prod the lion so that it lunges at the cage door. It will run out into the arena as Leo celebrates his victory, assuming he has one, and we will see just how great a gladiator this thief is. This way you have nothing to do with it; in fact, I suggest that you be serving wine to the Maximus family when this occurs. You can, of course, have the slave killed so he will be able to say nothing. The lion somehow got out on its own."

Paulius could see urine running down from under the terrified man's toga and across his bare feet. Bowing slavishly he quickly agreed to the plan. Paulius slipped him several coins, squeezed the shoulder again which shot a sharp pain across it, and slipped back through the half-light of the tunnel past the lion which had been parked against a wall and out through the door that led him back to his seat.

He picked up some cookies from a vendor and handed them to his friends who sat enjoying the music below. "My apologies, please," Paulius said as he sat. "An important client waved me to come and meet several Indian traders he wants to set up a new exporting business with."

"Business over pleasure," Cassius nodded, accepting his excuse. They had conjectured for a moment about where he had suddenly gone to, but then forgot it as they lazed in the sun.

With a blast of brass horns the gladiators were announced. Each was armed with a different weapon, and two had no weapons but were expected to kill with their bare hands. None of the twelve looked particularly muscular or menacing, except Leo. He was tall and broad shouldered with bulging arms and long, swept-back hair. Several women seated in front of the three begin tittering and kidding one another over which of the gladiators they would prefer bedding with. All chose Leo, as the fighters paraded around the arena looking uncertain and scared. Leo waved a short, thick sword above his head and got the crowd cheering for blood. Suddenly he whacked a tall, thin black man in front of him with the flat of his weapon, causing the man to jump forward, crashing into a heavy-set, balding German in front of him. Leo threw his head back laughing in contempt while the others crouched and held their weapons up as though they were about to be attacked. The crowd roared, "Blood!, blood!"

The arena manager stopped the little procession and could be seen giving the men instructions on who was to fight and when. Ten of them walked over against a wall, leaving Leo and a stout Egyptian facing one another. Both had only the briefest of cloths, wrapped like small towels and pinned with a brooch. The amphitheater was small enough so that the audience was close to the floor of the arena and could get a good view of the men's faces, though they still were of some distance.

Julian and Cassius looked at one another as they thought they recognized Leo, but were initially reluctant to say anything for fear of embarrassing their host. But Cassius couldn't resist the chance to gain some measure of advantage over the powerful lawyer.

"That one there looks very familiar," Cassius observed in a scrutinizing way.

"All Greeks look alike to me. You've seen his face in a hundred of them," Paulius was quick to chuckle nervously.

"No, I'll think of it in a while. Maybe I'll go down after he wins and take a closer look." Cassius had no intention of frontally embarrassing Paulius, but the subtle threat of recognizing that Sophia had indeed brought home a gladiator—the lowest of life, and a supreme insult to a man of rank—was enough for Cassius to know that he had penetrated the social armor of this proud man and could use that advantage if he wanted.

"Well, there will be little time for speaking with scoundrels," Paulius objected. "We have the delights of the baths to attend and in Caesarea they hold many pleasures," he said with a subtle leer.

Cassius detected the slightest bit of vulnerability in the play of the lawyer's corpulent face, and he knew he had gained the advantage on one of the city's most powerful men There would be no need to further push this game. He knew that he had now secured a favorable fee and any assistance he would ever need from one of the most powerful men in the whole of Palestine. The trip was already a success.

The Egyptian had a three-pronged spear and knife. Leo had only the short, flat sword. The stout man crouched, holding both weapons far in front of himself as though their length would keep the athletic opponent at arm's length. Leo turned his back and pranced about circling the man who looked terrified. Suddenly Leo leaned over showing his buttocks to the man. This enraged the Egyptian who rushed at Leo's exposed rear end. Leo could see him coming as he looked head upside down through his legs. As the man lunged with the spear, Leo rolled to one side causing the man to sprawl out on his stomach in the dirt.

Leo was on him with a catlike grace and a ferocity that was almost shocking. Straddling the back of the hapless Egyptian he first stabbed his arms, then cut off an ear which he flung to the crowd, before stabbing the screaming and bleeding man up and down his back, but not fatally.

The crowd screamed for more, standing and yelling almost deliriously. Julian looked over at the Maximus family who was smiling broadly at the enjoyment of the crowd.

Leo stood and pranced with his chin jutted, his chest swelled in a shameless display of his masculinity. He walked a prancing circle around the man who lay screaming in pain, his face covered in matted blood and dirt. Leo grabbed one of his arms and turned him over on his back, putting a foot on the man's chest. He held his sword high to the audience asking for their opinion; should he go ahead and kill the man? There was no hesitation—they all turned their thumbs down.

The man attempted to rise on one elbow and begged for his life in a tongue Leo could not hear above the incessant chanting for death from the stands. He reached down and picked up the Egyptian's weapons and, one by one, stuck them in the hapless figure. The spear went into his navel, the knife into his throat, and Leo, with a dramatic high arching swing plunged his own sword into the gasping man's heart. It was very brutal and very bloody.

The reaction was wild. The crowd yelped, jumped up and down, slapped one another in delight, and in drunken revelry performed mimics of the final plunge into the heart. The Maximus family hugged one another in relief that this costly circus had worked and their name would be remembered with favor at the next election.

Suddenly the lion bolted out of a tunnel and into the arena. It seemed confused; its enormous head held high as though it was trying to locate where it was through a smell or a sighting. It ran this way, then that, pausing, staring, sniffing, and then it saw Leo.

For a moment the crowd hushed, as though rendered speechless. There was a mixture of horror and interest. There had been no contests between a man and a beast in the arena, and it was not a part of the emperor's agreement with the Maximus family to allow them to hold the circus. The family, an entourage of seven, all looked at one another in shock. But before anyone could react, the lion spotted Leo across the arena, strutting along the wall holding his sword high in victory. The crowd yelled at him and pointed at the lion now down in a crouch and inching toward the tall figure. Leo turned his head to see the enormous animal break from his crouch and charge at full speed across the dirt. The last memory of life the Greek had was of the dirt being kicked up by the lion's claws, slow motion sprays of brown flying backwards and the ruffle of wind coursing through the shaggy mane as the animal bore down and into his terrified figure. Leo made a vain attempt to raise his sword in defense, but the impact of the seven hundred pound animal sent the splendid body of the gladiator slamming against the stone wall where the lion mauled him, biting into his face and neck. Guards ran from the sides with spears and poked at the animal, running it back into its tunnel and cage. Leo lay dead of a broken neck. Blood ran from his torn face and ripped chest, a dark, thick stream of life coursing into the soft tan earth of the arena floor. The whole event was over almost before it started.

Several thousand stood in disbelief. Some were too stunned to speak; they had enjoyed the blood and the violence of human combatants, but to see a lion kill a man in a land where lions still roamed along the edges was a frightening reminder to many of what could happen to them. Besides, they had admired the showmanship and good looks of the Greek. Others were thrilled by the exhibition and chatted demonstrably over this rare sight.

"They'll need a good lawyer," Paulius said. "Excuse me for a moment," and he moved down a few rows and over to the roped off section where the Maximus family was huddled in worried conversation.

"I'll wager Leo will not be seen at the door of Paulius again," Cassius slyly grinned.

"I'll wager someone has a pocketful of coins for removing the latch on the lion's cage," responded Julian. He then sniffed, "Well, it was the Roman thing to do. Leo was only a thief and a braggart by the way he strutted the arena. I suspect he angered one of the gods who gave approval to the whole business."

"Speaking of business," Cassius nodded toward the Maximus family. Paulius was patting them on the back, hugging one of the daughters and putting his hand on the shoulder of the son.

"A good lawyer is always at the scene of need."

"Or of money," Julian noted.

CHAPTER 6

Nazareth was a village of less than 500. Its small, square mud and stone homes rolled up a long incline that faced south over the Plain of Esdraelon, east to Mount Tabor and west to Mount Carmel. The hills rolled like soft ocean swells, treeless except for clumps of planted cedar and olive trees. It was a very fertile land with early plants greening the fields.

The air was chilled when Jesus rose from his pallet and reached for a long cotton shirt. He put on a fresh tallith, a small undergarment of purplish blue-dyed cotton with four tassles. Then he pulled on stockings, sandals of camel hide, and a short tunic as was the common dress of artisans and laborers.

The house of Joseph, son of Jacob, sat halfway up the gentle slope upon which Nazareth was built and was joined to three other single story stone houses that all centered around a common courtyard area. Stairs ran up one side of the house so that the flat roof could be accessed and slept on in the summer. A rickety shelter, open on all sides and called the upper room, stood on a corner of the roof for guests. In the courtyard was a large oven and a oil press that all four families shared. The home was basically one large room with a closet sized room along one wall where Joseph and Mary slept. Food was cooked in a depression in the floor, and the floors were of flat fieldstones found nearby. Dirt was between the stones creating a constant need to sweep. Shelving along the walls contained an array of foods, utensils, herbs and household implements. Clay was the medium for pots and jars. There was one window, and it was high as were all windows of the time to keep out thieves.

Joseph's old workshop was a separate room off the side of the house connected by a small door. Jesus stood and stretched to shake the sleep from his body. As he did, he paused to look longingly at the room's benches and the tools still hanging from the stone walls. They were his father's, kept as sacred reminders of the tall man whose evening table criticisms of the Temple rulers had shaped much of Jesus' early thinking.

He had overslept, and he was late in leaving for his work near the hill on which Sepphoris was built. It was an hour's walk away.

His brother James, shorter and of a darker complexion like that of their father, called him to eat. From a small fire in the floor James had cooked corn along with several eggs.

"My brother cooks better than he tills the soil," Jesus kidded as James stopped cooking to pray over the food.

James scoffed, "You move a few stones around and shave some wood and you call that work. Why, that brow has probably never known sweat!"

They smiled and cleansed their hands along with the cup and dish from which they would eat. At the end of a short prayer, Jesus said, "I've fixed the plow and the yoke. The wood was old on both. I think the yoke may have been used by our father."

"I am glad that one in the family continued his trade," James said as he scooped cooked onions over the bread. "Labor in the soil remains good though much is now owned by a few. So many of the farms have been lost. Too many of the people of Nazareth have moved to Tiberias trying to open a shop, or the most desperate go to Jerusalem and take handouts from wealthy Jews. Already the rich among us live in villas at Zippori." He laughed cynically, "I've even thought of working over at Kefar Hananyeh and making cooking bowls." It was a nearby pottery center supplying many of the various bowls and jars for area villages.

Jesus smiled at the frustration of trying to survive off a land as generous as the Galilee. "Repairing tools has not kept my mother in the ways my father kept her. There was more work for carpenters then. Now the landowners have their own carpenters, and the roads are filled with excellent craftsman since Herod's big building projects are nearing their end," Jesus noted.

"So you will go near the rich Jew's and the pagan's city and do columns for their streets and frames and windows for their homes." James concluded. "Best put on some linen robes, or they may not let you in town."

Jesus knew well of how he looked of poverty and low status. But his outgoing personality had always made him agreeable and desired company around evening tables even in the rich quarters of Sepphoris."When I work around gentiles, I speak of the faith to them. I tell them what I hear the Books to say. I invite them to visit the Temple."

James looked up suddenly from his eating. His eyes flared as he spoke. "You heard the Books say? When did you start hearing things others have not? Did our priest tell you that the Jews were now to start going to the Temple and invite gentile dogs and pagans? At the Temple last year, did one of the Sadducees tell you this? I know the

Community of Bathers out in the wilderness never said such a thing. You want a knife in your back, my brother? Then tell one of those with zeal that you find no fault in preaching to Romans."

Jesus ate his bread and sipped on goat's milk for a moment, collecting his thoughts. He was a little hurt and disturbed at his brother's sudden anger over a simple interpretation he had made. But they had argued repeatedly over the years about the leaders of the faith. James, three years younger than Jesus, worried that his brother had drifted too far from the strict rulings of the Temple leaders. James' strict adherence to the priesthood at the Temple was not shared by most in the Galilee area.

"Do you not believe that The Holy One created all people?" Jesus persisted. "If He did not, then what other god did? He also created those who oppress us, and those from India and Egypt and beyond. He is the All Knowing. He did not just create the children of Israel, and is not unaware of where the rest of mankind came from. His Knowledge reigns over all. If the gentiles can hear the Word, The Father would have them hear it. As I do my work, I have tried to show this light to those I see in darkness."

James stood and put his clay plate down hard on a bench. "I don't know many teaching carpenters," James said sarcastically. "I worry very much about just what spirits are speaking to you, brother. The next thing we hear you will be eating with tax collectors and lepers. Do not bring shame on this house, I tell you, with these strange hearings."

Jesus would not be quieted as he tried to convince his brother. "It is said in the Books, 'Because you did not serve the Word with joyfulness and gladness of heart, therefore you shall serve your enemies whom The One will send against you.' We serve the Pharisees and the Sadducees with their colorful robes and their interpretations. And we serve the angels of darkness who have come in the form of the Romans. We do not serve the One in joy; we now serve the rich of our people and the Emperor in sadness."

James leaned forward looking warily at his older brother. "Jesus, you have been arguing your versions of the Laws for years with any ear that would listen, but you have never said such things about the Temple as this."

He paused, his demeanor became more loving and James said in a laughing voice. "I remember as a child you would climb the old olive tree outside and think you were hiding among its branches from us and would quote the prophets as though you were from heaven. We called you the Olive Prophet. That was funny then and harmless, but this now...just where have you been to hear, as you say, such things?"

Jesus could see his brother's angry doubting and felt he owed him an explanation. "Brother, I have spent my life with my hands, but I have prayed long and read much and debated often with my friends and with you. These things have brought some truths that do not require one to attend the schools, or be a scholar. I am over thirty years, and during that time I have seen our people grow in their anguish, whether it's arguing over what is the truth in our faith, or how we can drive the evil ones out. Our leaders live in great wealth and spend their days wanting to own more and more property. There is great suffering, great injustice, especially by the destitute and the forgotten. The words of the old prophets are about the meek and humble, and I see no one serving their needs."

James put his plate down, again with an obvious emphasis, on the floor. Wiping his mouth with his forearm he said with great steadiness, "You have been too long in the wine, brother. This kind of talk from one of no more authority than you will get a stone against your head and bring disgrace on our father's house. You have no teacher who you can say taught you these words. I know our father didn't."

James quickly saw how his words hurt his brother and reached out from his cushion and grasped Jesus' arm. " I agree with you that many of our people live in great suffering. But there will always be poor among us and a Messiah is coming to right the wrongs, and I agree that it may be soon. But that day will come in a mighty blast and an army of angels. You need not worry yourself about predicting this coming or try to spread some interpretation that you alone see. The Blessed One will take care of that when He sends the Messiah."

Touching Jesus on the shoulder, he cautioned, "Take care with what you say, my brother. Leave the teaching to those who know such things. We are but tillers of the soil and stone men. It is to those schooled better than we, not to those with sore backs and dirt under their nails that our people look. The Temple leaders are not perfect, but they are the great protectors of our faith."

Jesus watched in silence and disappointment as James dragged the repaired plow into the yard and secured it to the back of an old cow. He then returned, hoisted the heavier yoke on his shoulder and said rather quietly, "You will pass Jacob's house on the road to Zippori. Stop and tell him of our talk. He is not as friendly to the Temple as am I. See what he tells you about this wish to teach." Jesus, depressed over his brother's rejection, prepared some food by slicing an onion on buttered bread, poured some almonds out of a jar, along with dates and figs, wrapped it all in a thin cotton cloth and stuffed it into a shoulder bag.

James' wife and children were already out working the nearby fields, and Jesus stood in the emptiness of the main room of the stone house, looked through to his father's old carpentry shop, and longed for the strength his death had taken away. He raised his arms and prayed, asking that if it pleased God, to fill his heart with the joy and the certitude Joseph had shown. He asked for inner peace to stop the surges of unfathomable sadness that he was periodically left with, a sadness almost debilitating and paralyzing in its severity. He prayed for an understanding of this anguish, but felt no relief. "Why, Father, do I suddenly feel the need to speak to others of my thoughts? Why, when even my own brother thinks me a fool? Are you guiding me Father, or am I possessed of a devil who would have me say these things? Why do I go from great joy to a sadness that leaves me almost unable to move. Only when I rush to a hilltop and speak to You do I feel whole again." When he had finished, his mind wandered, and he thought of the beauty of Rebekah, and he wished she were there to comfort him with her laughter. He had never felt so alone in his own house.

Gathering his plumb line, adaz, set square, and hammer, Jesus put them in his goat skin tool bag and stood, looking about the modest home in which he had been raised. Something seemed almost foreign about his home now; a place of the past with his father dead and his mother living miles away, and a brother angry and accusing. Memories filled his mind. He stepped out the door, reached over and touched the gnarled, twisting olive tree standing against the house, and remembered how he had climbed in it and up onto the flat-topped, mud-covered roof of the one story dwelling. He remembered how he and his friends would scramble up the outside stairs and hide under the thatched "upper room" on top so their mothers couldn't find them. He left the small house with great reluctance; a sense that he was now for the first time in his life moving away from the familiar shore of Nazareth and sailing to his own compass, though at that moment he knew not the direction it pointed.

It was court day in Nazareth. Held each Tuesday and Thursday, the village's meeting house attracted the city council who judged disputes, and it attracted farmers in the immediate area to come and do a little trading. Most in Nazareth were fairly self-sufficient, still minor trading with goods, not money, was a constant activity.

The street leading to the back of the village was paved down the middle in badly worn, flat field stones. Lightly colored, gritty dirt bordered the stones in a perpetual rising dust from the slightest breeze or foot traffic. The stone, brick, and mud homes had rugs laid out at their front doors on the ground, where the owners attempted to sell their wares. Early foods were displayed in wooden bins. A few birds were laid out still feathered, their eyes gray-lidded in death. There were potter's shops, weavers, a salt merchant, a smith with his seething little furnace to one side of his home, a hairdresser who was also a perfumer—as so many doused their hair and beards in perfumes—a mouse catcher, a pawn broker, and Jesus' childhood friend Philip who sold knives from a cabinet. From shelves built over the cabinet hung an array of knives: curved scythes, daggers, carving and cutting knives. To anyone passing, these merchants attempted to enter into conversation. Philip was Jesus' age, but looked older with his hair receding and streaked with early gray. He had a fierceness about his eyes, a lurking anger that was as quick as his laugh. He was sharpening a knife when he saw Jesus walking up the hill.

"Ah, it looks as though the carpenter has work, so heavily laden is he with his tools. Could it be a member of the Sanhedrin has asked you to help build a new villa?" Philip kidded.

Jesus stopped before the knife stand. Philip was one of a group of men who had grown up together in Nazareth. Most had remained in the area; many, poorer than their fathers, had been scraping by as tenant farmers, artisans like Jesus, or beseeching would-be merchants with a shelf full of homemade knives. Some had drifted away to one of the cities; they were rarely seen again, except at funerals. But those who had stayed had remained very committed to their faith, and this had taken a turn toward anger and a deepening resentment toward the Roman occupation and the ruling Sanhedrin. It was rumored that Philip's knives had found their way into the backs of several prominent Jews suspected of dealing with gentiles in a flagrant way. He was one of explosive disposition.

"Your time would be better spent sharpening your understanding of the scriptures than putting an edge to a knife," Jesus chided his old friend.

"Hah!" Philip scoffed and grinned, "What would a plow maker know of the prophets?"

"I may not know much of the prophets, but I do know how to call the devil's name when I miss a peg and hit my thumb."

They both laughed in the easy camaraderie of old friends. Philip continued to banter with him, though his question had a real curiosity about it. "I've seen you in the fields behind the cemetery reading. You're not going to turn into a scholar on us are you? The roads are filled with scribes and lawyers and teachers as it is. Someone's got to stay and work."

Jesus' demeanor changed; his eyes took on a more somber look as he answered, "There is a time for all of us to realize why The Father has placed us here. It has been a slow sun rising for me, but the light has entered my life as never before. My thoughts are filled with little else but the words of the prophets and their meanings. It is taking over my life, my friend, in a way that is both joyful and as awful as a night-storm can be to a child."

Philip put down a carving knife he had been sharpening and thought he saw the eyes of Jesus filling with tears, but the early sun was bright, and they were both squinting against its glare.

"I remember when we all went to Passover at the Temple as children, and you startled everyone with your knowledge of the scriptures. We all thought you would be a priest or a teacher of some kind. Your father talked often of an angel that visited your mother before your birth who said that you would be special." Philip grabbed Jesus' arm and twisted it as he kidded, "But we both know you are only special at dreaming in the day, at wandering across the fields, and at jabbering to yourself." Philip laughed in a short, loud burst. "You're special at table talk, that's your gift. And it didn't take an angel for all to see that!"

Jesus laughed heartily, grabbing Philip's thumb and twisting it until they both banged into the cabinet, knocking down some of the the knives. "Hey, dreamer, don't knock down my business!" He yelled in mock anger as he sorted out the knives now in disarray. Then he said seriously, "Perhaps The Holy One is telling you it is your time again, as he guided you at the Temple."

"This sense of something wrong and something about to happen is stirring within many in Galilee," Jesus said as he leaned against the side of the house. "There is much talk of how our nation has strayed and of how the End of Days may be at hand. I see a great anticipation everywhere."

"Ah, the talk of a Messiah is on everyone's lips. I do wonder often what he will look like; will there be a fiery cloud, great winds and heralds? Will He look like us, or be on wings? It could be terrifying."

Jesus lowered his head covering to shield the sun. "I compare today like the exodus from Egypt and like the return from exile in Babylon. We need a new covenant with The Father, one that will again bring our nation out of the exile we find ourselves in now."

Philip picked up a knife and rubbed its wooden handle absentmindedly. "We can't do it without a Moses. The people won't just rise up on their own and resist. They are too split now over the Laws' interpretations, while others just sit depressed and hopeless over the might of the Romans and their taxes."

"You speak of a leader, Philip, but I worry," Jesus said, "over one who would bring an uprising."

"You worry!" Philip interjected. "That's what the prophets promise —a battle led by Yahweh and His angels and joined by us."

Jesus was silent for a moment as though collecting his thoughts, then he said slowly and with deliberation, "The Romans would crush us, but more importantly, we would be fighting the wrong enemy. The angels of darkness, the devils that lurk in our hearts, cause us to forget the commandments; these are the enemies of our people. This is where the fight must be waged; in each man's soul."

Philip leaned against his cabinet and rubbed his chin. "You say that we as a nation are as much in exile as were our ancestors in Egypt and Babylon. You say that we need a Messiah to lead us out, but if the Romans occupy our land, how else are we to restore our nation to the days of David but to drive them out?"

"Oh, no, I speak not of an exile of place, but an exile of the soul," Jesus answered. "We blame our troubles solely on the Romans, but I believe the way to remove the Romans is first to remove from our hearts the desire to have what the Romans have — their possessions and wealth. The answer is to love The Father with all our hearts and minds. Don't you see, beloved?" He was almost pleading for an understanding by this old friend. "We can be free of the Romans, never by defeating them in battle, but by joining our hearts as one with The Father."

Philip asked, "So you say the prophets tell us that we must seek peace within ourselves, not war with the occupiers?"

"We must as individuals save ourselves one at a time, then go out and serve His Glory, bringing all together in a community of the spirit. I believe that we are in the day of the fulfillment of the prophecies. It will demand that a new covenant be made."

Philip looked anxiously about, then gripped Jesus by the arm and pulled him inside the door next to his knife stand. They stood in the soft light of several hand lamps in the main room of Philip's house.

"Jesus," Philip was nervous and anxious acting, almost fearful. "We have had many discussions over the years about the prophets and about our priests, but you have never said these words. No where in the Book does it command that a new covenant be made. Are you speaking outside the Book? Who would you say you are?"

Jesus felt a rush of excitement at the discussion. It was important that he get the reaction from one he had known so long, had debated so many times, and one who he knew to be passionate, always fiery, about the faith.

"My brother, I think I would like to be perfect." The words hung with a ringing clarity in the air as though with form and substance; a phrase they could both observe and study. Jesus carefully watched for Philip's reaction.

Philip gave a short laugh, then asked, "Perfect? The streets of this land are filled with those who would be perfect. Some of these teachers smash their noses bloody running into buildings for fear their eyes will see a beautiful woman."

"No, I mean perfect as our Father. As perfect as the first man. More perfect than any man who ever lived. And in that perfection I might be an inspiration to others." He looked at the floor in a moment of anguish. "This is laughable to you and those I know, not for transgressions I have made, but because I am not known as a great scholar or teacher." He looked up intensely into Philip's eyes. "I am consumed by my love for The Father, and that love, if I am true to it, demands that I seek to be as the One I love."

His wiry frame seemed tense. Philip's eyes wandered to a long vein that ran down Jesus' bicep, adding to the muscular look of his arms. His whole body was filled with the power of this self-revelation. "We have forgotten the covenants of the ancients. Especially have some of our priests forgotten. They have placed themselves squarely between the Nation and The Father. The holy ground of the Temple is used more for selling sacrifices than it is for the glorification of the Kingdom. I do believe that the Kingdom is upon us now and is also unfolding in the future. And our people don't even know it. Oh, they speak loudly of the End of Days and of how a Messiah will save them, but I tell you they mistakenly believe they will be observers to God's war with the Prince of Evil. They are wrong. They must save them-selves first if they are to enter the door of heaven. I believe it will take someone to be an example of The Father to change our people."

Philip seemed shaken. He sat on a stool. His eyes wandered the room, searching for words as though they could be seen hanging in the soft light. His voice lowered in a reverence he had never shown his friend. "Jesus, you are one of my oldest friends, and I have always known you to be very learned for one who was not taught at the Temple. You read the scriptures better than any of us, and your arguments have proven you far wiser than anyone I have known. But these are powerful sayings, and if The Father is speaking through you, then you must think of leaving your tools and going out to teach. Could it be that you are that one to lead the way? If you are, you must be careful. Our priests could become very angry at what you say. Perhaps you need a group of us to be at your teachings to protect you."

At the suggestion that he simply give up his work and become a teacher, and even more, that he proclaim himself, Jesus the woodworker, as the nation's new leader, Jesus balked. His whole frame seemed to move back defensively. "But I would have no way to live, and I must tell you I am still studying the scriptures and praying to learn what The Father would have me do. You will be the first I give notice to if I do speak at the house of assembly here."

Jesus then relaxed and grinned, "I remember your fists well, as I hope you remember mine from our childhood. I may need your strong arms to protect me instead of throwing me to the ground as you once did."

Philip's face broke into a toothless grin. Many of his decayed teeth had been extracted by the local tooth puller. He put his arm around Jesus' shoulder. "You are showing great courage, and I want to stand with you if you decide to put your tools down." He reached under his cloak, pulled a short dagger out and handed it to Jesus, "You might need this."

Jesus quickly shook his head and pushed the knife away. "No, this is not the way. We must bring our people together not with the sword, but through the Word. If we are struck, we must turn the other shoulder. If they would stone us, we must be willing to give our lives for His love. His gift to us is this love and this forgiveness. It is our calling, our part of the covenant, to take those gifts and share them with our brothers."

"You have more courage then I, my friend. Know that if I stand with you, I will have a sharpened dagger under my cloak."

Jesus' eyes crinkled in a smile. "There will be no need for that. Tell our friends here of our conversation. I am interested in their thoughts and maybe in even having them travel with me, as you suggest, to help spread my message. One carpenter cannot change the Nation alone. It will take many disciples. Perhaps I will speak at assembly sometime and our friends could be there to listen." Jesus broke into a grin, and with some excitement, said, "Wouldn't that be good! A group of friends traveling in fellowship to call for a new covenant."

Philip kidded, "As long as the wine flowed along our path." But then his demeanor turned serious. "Some of our fraternity may go along for an evening or two, but few could drop their work and travel for long unless they believed you were starting a rebellion, or.." and he couldn't seem to finish his sentence.

"Or unless they believed in their heart that The Father had given me a special message. That I was more than their childhood friend, Jesus." Jesus finished Philip's thought for him.

"By the Almighty!" Philip exclaimed, "be careful about making that claim." His face then screwed up in a query, "I am unclear if you would lead a rebellion against the leaders of the Temple, offer a new interpretation of the Torah, or just demand a more disciplined life."

"Philip!" Jesus squeezed his friend's shoulder. "You know that I would never lead a revolt against our Temple, nor would I attempt to change the words of the prophets." Jesus sounded incredulous that Philip would even make such a suggestion.

Their conversation was abruptly interrupted by an impatient customer outside who was asking loudly how he could buy a knife if there was no one to wait on him.

"We will talk more, my friend. Until then, may The Holy One give you peace." Jesus put his hand on Philip's shoulder and pressed it in affection.

"May He give you protection," Philip laughed weakly.

As Jesus walked away, he passed the last few houses on the road out of town and each house had someone out front selling foods and wares, or tending a small garden, and each spoke to the man they had known for years. There were no strangers in the little village. It was a close-knit, very much Jewish place, but an inconsequential village not even drawn on the Roman maps of Galilee. Nazareth was almost a suburb of the old government administrative center of Sepphoris, and a five-hour walk from Galilee's new capital of Tiberias. The Herods had built both to establish the authority of Rome, honor the Emperors Augustus, then Tiberius, and to intimidate the local populace with the power of Rome. They hoped that two strategically located urban centers would forever alter the culture of the Galilean plains and hills, and for many Jews they did. It was architecture as intimidator. Sepphoris had become as much a city for wealthy Jews as it was for Romans. Their sprawling homes contained elaborate mosaics of faces and figures that many strict Jews shunned. But Galilee was a mixing pot, and Jews felt a certain comfort in dealing with all manner of people.

A shriek startled Jesus as he approached the Street of the Weavers. "Not my shuttle!" A woman screamed from the door of a small house to his left. Several priests were dragging a wooden weaving shuttle out on the street and breaking its various parts into splinters.

The woman fell distraught in the street, wailing and pleading as the men went back and forth from the dwelling bringing our wool, cloth and then food, which they threw in a pile and set afire.

"Why do you cry, sister?" Jesus asked as he leaned over the sobbing woman and touched her arm.

She looked up with tear swollen eyes and between sobs said, "The teachers say the wood of my shuttle came from a grove of trees that was too near one of the pagan's roadside temples. So it and all the cloth sewed on it is unclean. I was having it repaired by a man they say is a heathen, and because I left him alone in a room with food on the table, they throw the food out, saying it, too, is unclean. They put me out of business and starve me," she cried.

The three men stood around the woman as her livelihood went up in flames in the middle of the street. Arms clasped authoritatively against their chests, one spoke with great gravity for the gathered crowd to hear. "The Laws are clear. Heathens do not get close to our food, and we use no materials made unclean by being around the pagan idols. Hear this, and know the Law."

Jesus stood almost in their faces and responded angrily, "You worry over wood and wool. I heard you say nothing of the woman's heart. You should know her by her fruits. Does she gather grapes or thorns?"

The taller of the three scowled, "Jesus, your father would be shamed by these words. No man lived closer to the Law than did he. How dare you dishonor his name!"

Ignoring the accusation, Jesus angrily denounced them, "Why would you denounce the mote that is in this sister's eye, but not consider the beam that is in your own? You hypocrite! First cast out the beam that is your own eye."

The taller priest, who served the Nazareth area and knew Jesus, drew back in shock. "You would curse us for upholding the Laws?" he stammered in confusion and anger.

"Do you know this infidel?" the other two demanded. "He must be a pagan!"

The man seemed momentarily embarrassed, then apologized, "I knew his father. But I had no idea the son had turned out so evil. Obviously, Satan has entered his heart."

"Let's leave this spot at once," one of the men demanded. "Evil dwells here, and we will have no part of it." As they turned in obvious haste, their robes swirled out and their tall hats tottered.

Relatives of the woman tried to stamp out the flames and rushed to her side as she lay sobbing on the stone entrance to her house. Jesus was ignored in his attempts to console her. He turned and walked slowly away, slapping his thigh with the flat of his hand, angry now at himself because he had so easily been brought to anger with the rabbis. "Perfect!" He mumbled sarcastically at himself. "Hypocrite is what I am." He cursed at his weakness.

Stopping at the spring that provided water for the town, Jesus filled a goat skin bottle. As he stood on the rise at the top of the village, he could see distant snowcapped Mount Hermon to the north and the rounded summit of Mount Tabor just to the west. The rich farming lands of Galilee spread before the village. A small cactus had rooted next to the stones around the spring, and it scraped against his leg as he turned to leave. He jerked his leg away from the prick and saw a thin, red tear above his ankle. Reaching down he picked up some dirt and rubbed it over the scratch to clot any blood that might issue from it and walked off toward the family tombs that sat at the back of the village. Several were dug into the slope of the hill and had rounded stones rolled against their entrances. Others were more simple stone affairs, and all had been whitewashed so they were easy to see and no one would touch them and become unclean. He rubbed his finger along the rough edge of one, thinking it absurd to avoid the dead. He heard a moaning beyond the silence of the stones to his left and saw a woman in rags leaning against the wooden door of a tomb dug into the hill.

She sensed she was being watched and turned with a start. Her face was half-covered by a shawl, but she had clearly been crying, and her hair was disheveled. Her clothing was ragged, and she shrank back against the tomb door. Putting her hand over her top lip she shrieked, "Unclean! Unclean!" This was the warning lepers were made to yell at anyone approaching them.

"I, too, am becoming a leper," he calmingly said to her.

She wiped her cheeks and looked confused. "Then why do you walk freely here?"

The customs were very strict concerning lepers. It was unheard of for one of them to be found in a public place. Trying to look at ease at her shocking appearance, Jesus smiled and raised his right hand in a half wave. "I would ask the same. If you are unclean, why are you out in the city cemetery?" he asked.

The question brought tears again to her reddened eyes. "My dear mother has died. I have come to see her body, but the door is sealed, and she too will be dust before long." She then cried uncontrollably, wailing in a high-pitched keening sound.

Jesus stepped next to her and touched her shoulder. She recoiled against the tomb door. But as she looked into his eyes, she saw them misting in a joy she had not known in the years of her illness. His hand had a calming effect; it was warm and full. She felt it was almost imparting a strength, a reassurance, into her shaking body. This was an affection that even her own family had not shown in years. She pulled a cloth from her ragged cloak, wiped her eyes and nose, and looked at his silent gaze.

"Who are you? If you are a leper why are you here? Why are you dressed as a worker?"

"Who do you say that I am?" he asked rhetorically.

The shawl shadowed a scaly, pale complexion. She stammered, "I...I don't know, but you can't be a Jew."

"I am very much a Jew," he answered. "I believe in the Law, but I hear the Word speak to me, and it says that your soul is not at fault in your illness. The Father's love will guide you in these sad times and bring you eternal happiness in His Kingdom."

She looked astounded. "You asked who do I say you are. I say you look like a worker, but you speak as one of a good mind and of authority. Where are your fine robes and your rings?"

She could see anger draw the compassion from his eyes, and his mouth turn down slightly at the edges. "Does The Father say that his Word can come only through a robe?" His voice demanded. "We are all priests. We all can speak directly to Him and He to us, and you must not forget that."

"But I live in a land that scorns me," she sobbed.

"Then it is a world that scorns The Father. But I say to you," and the anger left his voice, his face brightened, and his eyes misted over again, "I love you, lamb, and you should know through my love that you are not alone in this world."

"By The Holy One!" she cried out, falling to her knees. "Are you from Him? How else could you say these things. No one loves a leper. Are you a healer too?"

Jesus seemed unprepared for the question. "Healer? Well...no, I," he regained his composure and filling flush with his genuine affection for this miserable woman said, "I am simply one who has a loving and forgiving Father, as do you, and I...just wanted you to know that." He seemed to be losing his focus about where he was going with the explanation of who he was.

They stared mute at one another for a moment, in a standoff over both being confused about who he was. The woman was filled with the power of his words, words she had not heard in years.

"Would you like to borrow my comb?" He had asked a question so bold for a Jew that she looked dumbstruck.

"Comb?" She stammered. "You would lend me your comb? You know lepers are not supposed to brush their hair." She unconsciously touched her hair with a sad look, as though that one place on the body all women considered a point of beauty, was now forever and cruelly denied to her.

"Your face is a flower that the Father graced this world with. There is no need to hide it under such a tangle." He grinned and reached in a pocket and pulled out a bronze comb.

Standing, she looked deep into Jesus' eyes and felt a sense of calm, and shyness, almost a girlish rush of shyness that was such a distant feeling, even though she was not yet in her thirtieth year. Blushing, she slowly removed the shawl and touched the tangled mess of her brown hair, took the comb and, still fixed on Jesus' gaze, proudly began trying to pull the comb through her hair. It was so tangled that it quickly became caught in the knots of neglect, and they both laughed loudly and freely.

Their companionship was shattered by screams behind them, "Unclean! Get away from our tomb. You have disgraced our tomb!"

They turned to see a family richly dressed in bleached white clothing with colored bands across the edges of their robes. The mother wore many gold bracelets, rings, and necklaces.

The leper's face dropped in horror. Her hand came to her mouth in a spontaneous and futile attempt to cover the boils on her cheeks. She fumbled with the shawl, throwing it overhead, and dashed the comb on the ground.

The father, a portly, black-bearded man, yelled at the leper, "You shame our family standing next to the tomb of our ancestors!" And looking at Jesus in his rough workman's clothing, he shouted, "And you must be a devil!"

Jesus reacted angrily, "Your heart is as the night, and when the Kingdom comes, you and your kind will not be seen by The Father who is angered by those who care so little for the helpless."

The man was so angered he tore at his outer robe and stamped the ground. His wife began wailing in agony at this whole sudden, unexpected, and now mortifying scene. They had traveled up from Jerusalem to visit the grave site of an ancestor, only to be shocked at the sight of a diseased one, an outcast, and this impertinent man who stood in defiance of the Law.

The leper regained her composure and said to Jesus rather calmly, "They are right. I must leave and go back into the hills, but you have given me a joy that I have not known in years. My heart is filled with a gladness that lifts me and makes me realize that the Eternal has not forgotten me. Whoever you are, I praise you." She turned, touched the door of her mother's tomb, and ran off among the chalky white of the tombs until she disappeared among their limestone containers.

"Are you a devil?" the man shrieked at Jesus who was now standing alone.

Jesus stooped and retrieved his comb. It was filled with her hair. He did not bother to remove the hair, but instead ran the comb defiantly through his own hair.

"He is not a Jew, but a pagan," the man's son said, looking up at his father who had ripped part of his robe.

The anger subsided in Jesus and he said, "I am the son of man, as are you. I am a priest as are you, and I would not abolish any part of the Law. I would say to you that everyone who is angry with his brother shall be liable to judgment, and I now turn the cheek of friendship toward you, and I rejoice in The Father's love for you."

The woman wailed again, crying in a voice now weakening, "All the way from Jerusalem, and we find a devil on the hallowed ground of my ancestors' remains!" She collapsed in sobs at her husband's feet.

"Not a devil, only a lamb of the Shepherd. One who would love you as The Father does." Jesus sighed, drew his bags higher on his shoulder, raised his right hand in a kind of goodbye and left the cemetery to the sobs of the woman. Her flustered husband yelled at the retreating Jesus, "We will tell our priests at the Temple! I knew we would find devils in Galilee. Damned mixed breeds! Friends of gentiles!" His insults rang against the heavy stillness of the air. Jesus whistled softly and felt good as he found his way out of the cemetery. 'Chased out of my own village,' he muttered to himself, smiling at the irony of it.

It is a meandering road that leads the four miles to Sepphoris, a road that follows the lazy curvature of the melted hills. Flat cactus prickles along its course in thick gregarious bunches. The plant's interior is fruity, and it was preparing to bud. Lilies of the Field were already out, and spring was breathing its warmth into the earth. Galilee is fertile ground and grows a multitude of crops. Most of the traffic Jesus encountered travelled toward Nazareth; villagers bringing back goods they had traded items for. A mile outside Nazareth, at the sixth hour (noon), the road passed by a large corn and wheat farm with well-pruned olive orchards. A small thatched-top booth elevated on spindly wooden legs leaned precariously in the middle of the twisted trees. It was barely above the height of the trees and used for watching over and guarding the harvest from thieves, and also for yelling at birds that would pick the fruit of the trees standing nearby. Jesus could see through the grove a tall, well-proportioned older woman standing in front of the little tower with her hands on her hips. His baggage was weighing heavily on his shoulders, and he was thirsty so he stopped, let his bags drop to the ground, and walked through several rows of trees to the woman.

"May The Father keep your tower from falling," he greeted.

Her face was weathered, but retained much of the beauty of her youth. She stood very straight. There was a pride about her bearing.

153

Her hair was covered by a small, white scarf, which accentuated the tan on her rather pale complexion. He could smell the perfume in her hair. It was sweet and added to the pleasantness of her appearance.

She looked at Jesus, her hands still on her hips. "It will take The Father and a good carpenter to keep this booth from crumbling."

Jesus took his head covering off. "Is your husband not good with the hammer?"

"My husband rests in yonder tomb." She pointed toward a tomb dug into a rise behind the home. A stone facing with small columns on either side of the entrance suggested that this was a Jewish family of some means.

"I'm sorry," Jesus lamented.

"While he awaits the coming Messiah, I have to manage the farm," she grinned to reveal a beautiful set of teeth. "Now isn't that just like a man—he rests; I work."

Jesus laughed. He was attracted to her humor in the face of grief.

"So that you do not think badly of all men, widow, I will lay hammer to your booth, if you will reward me a few fruit from your trees."

She raised an eyebrow in mock seriousness. "Your wages are cheap, woodworker. Does that speak of the quality of your work? Would the fruit be worth more than the work?"

"A sound tree cannot bear evil fruit. I have opened my heart to Our Lord and from His goodness all that I can do, I do in His name. That doesn't mean that all I do is good, but it means that I try."

She studied this stranger from the road. There were so many out now who would take advantage of a widow, who would steal from her house in the daylight, and at night would strip her gardens and orchids of their fruit. A woman had to be wary, but this was no common traveling worker. He was much too intelligent; his face spoke of too much honesty and openness.

"I agree to your demands," she held a finger up to him, looking serious, but only kidding, "No fruit until the work is done."

Judaism was a contradictory culture where women were not considered first class citizens in many ways, but in others they were. It was a common saying that 'women are of a light mind.' This was the reason given for not allowing them the schooling boys had. But at a time when death by accident and disease was common, many farms were run by widows.

The widow had an excellent toolshed, and Jesus found all he needed to shore up a rotted post and right the leaning platform. It took an hour, and he was sweating at the end. The widow had gone about churning milk in a goat skin as she watched this energetic man go quickly about his work. When he had finished, he walked to the side of the house where she sat on a stool next to a large cistern for catching rain water.

"Now your sons can climb up with no fear of falling into the trees," he announced as he wiped his brow with a cloth.

"I have decided to raise your wages," she teased. "You do good work, and I wish to reward you with a meal. Won't you come in and join me?"

"Thank you, widow. I tire of my onions and bread. I would like that."

"I have cabbage with mint, garlic soup and some sesame wafers. Will that satisfy a carpenter's stomach?" she asked as they entered the four room house. A mosaic of geometric patterns decorated the main room's floor, which meant this was a woman whose husband had done well. She also had several beautifully carved bronze bowls, and the mats and rugs spoke of some modest wealth in their color and craftsmanship. It was decidedly better than the home Jesus had left in Nazareth.

They washed according to the Law and prayed, then helped themselves to the food.

"Surely you have sons to help."

"Only one is here, and he is out in the fields. My other son took his inheritance and went to Tiberias where I hear he has squandered it all." Tears welled in her eyes. "But if he would only return I would run to him and give him his father's ring and robe. I would forgive him if only he came back."

Her thoughts returned, "We do better than many. The Father has blessed our house, but it is hard with all the tithes and taxes we must pay."

"Tithing your crops is hurting you?" Jesus asked.

She looked a little reluctant to complain to this stranger, so she said, "Oh, it is my duty, of course. We follow the Law very strictly, but we pay taxes for the Temple and the poor; a part of our crop is taken to Jerusalem for the holy feast, a free-will part for the priests, a tithe for the poor. Then we can't harvest the corners of our field so that passing poor can eat of it." She said quickly, "I do not complain, I simply say it makes us work very hard to feed ourselves and try and

155

sell some of the extra while observing our faith. And then Antipas demands his tribute as does the Emperor."

Jesus sipped his soup, tasting the strong garlic. "It is not just by bread that we live. But I would ask you, do you worry so much over the tithe that you neglect coming as close to the Word as is humanly possible?"

She seemed surprised; she was a little offended that a stranger would ask such a question. "Of course not, I…"

Jesus interrupted her, seeing that he had been too familiar in his question. "Forgive me, widow, I dare not offend you or question your faith. I guess I was speaking of our people in general. We worry over the demands of the priests so much that it is easy to forget how simple the path to the Kingdom is."

Her brow furrowed, and she put her spoon down. "Do you say the priests stand between the people and The Father?" Her words were measured and serious.

Jesus, having been rebuked and questioned by so many, paused, wondering if he should be cautious in his words. But he was impatient with what he saw as hypocrisy by his religion's leaders and the need for a new covenant. He was also growing in his confidence by the day; it was feeding on itself now so that he was openly expressing the feelings in his heart.

"Listen to your own words," Jesus put his plate down on the mat upon which he reclined. His face was relaxed, though his eyes had an intensity that stirred her in a way she could not describe. He continued, "Too many of the children of the Land think of where their treasure is and not where their heart is. They worry, as have I and as do you, over their robes; will they ever have one of fine linens and colored bands? They worry over their foods; will they ever have a drink of Jericho wine, be able to eat of a cow instead of fish and goat. They worry over their rugs and mats, even their dirt floors. Some would trade their soul for a mosaic floor such as you have. And all worry endlessly over obeying every"—he held his index finger very close to his thumb—"little interpretation that man has commanded from the Law."

She was swept up in his revelation; his utter and amazing frankness. It was both frightening and exhilarating. She felt her breath draw in, not knowing whether to demand that he get out or to keep listening. Her eyes automatically darted toward the windows and door to see if anyone was overhearing them or about to enter.

"You do not believe in the Laws?" she asked cautiously.

"My life is guided by the Laws and especially the words of the prophets," he said assuredly. "But I do not think the Laws are being fulfilled. I think our faith is being blinded by an evil that crept upon us over generations. It is an evil that says that men dressed in the self-importance of thick robes of expensive color can change the Laws until the true meaning, the very simple meaning, is lost. Our faith was never meant to be complicated."

Her plate fell from her lap and landed with a dull thump on a rug. Her mouth sagged as his words stirred mixed emotions in her mind.

"Who are you that would rebel against the Temple?" she demanded to know, gathering her composure long enough to say something, anything—afraid to let his words just hang in the air as though they would have some awful effect on the room. "Where are you from? Are you a new teacher? Are you a…"

Jesus shook his head and looked intently into her eyes. "I am not an evil spirit, as you wanted to ask; no, I am a simple stone and wood worker from Nazareth, the son of a builder; a man of great faith."

She seemed confused, "But how could one such as you know of these things? Could dare say such things? I know of no schools that teach this and no Sadducee or scribe that raises these questions."

Jesus felt this familiar moment; a frustration and disappointment that his interpretations of the scriptures were questioned because of who he was. The thought ran across his mind; should he be wearing robes that made him look more like a teacher, scribe, lawyer, or even a rabbi? Why was it that one had to 'look' like they could speak with authority before their words would be accepted?

He persisted. "I believe the Kingdom is being ushered in like…like a single lily in an empty field. This lily is strange because it stands alone, but as it drops its seeds, other lilies are soon seen, here, there, until the emptiness is filled with a flowering beauty."

She thought on what he had said, then, "So you also do not see The Eternal being heralded by hosts of angels in armament, coming amidst great noise and fire? You see a single messenger, a Messiah, telling a few at a time."

His face was aglow with an earnestness, a passionate appeal to his audience of one. "The prophets tell us in the books of Daniel and Isaiah that a servant will be sent to tell of The Father's Coming, not by armies of sworded angels. I look for that servant now. I read carefully from the prophets as to how to recognize this messenger. He will be announced by a new Elijah.

"And I believe that the Kingdom will not be of this earth, but of a heaven removed from here. The Father will reign, but not here so that we will not continue to live in our houses and work our fields. The road to that place is clear and direct and requires no more and no less than the giving of one's heart and soul. Heaven will be a loving land where the meek, the helpless, the poor, find a richness that the rich can never know. It will be a place which a woman will know, because heaven is like the care and love and unconditional forgiveness that a mother gives to her child. I have seen heaven in my mother's form; her touch, her wiping away my tears, her gentle kiss goodnight."

She sat stunned, unaware that the food on the plate she had dropped had spilled onto her sandal. She almost whispered, "This is, this is…dangerous talk, but I," she paused, her eyes again surveyed the room as though someone may have entered unnoticed, " but I am moved by what you say. You must be more than a man of wood." She looked carefully at him, pressing down her eyelids as though she may be missing some shred of light and understanding. His countenance was so complex, so mercurial, as calm as the gentlest sea, then fiery and demanding, then teary with compassion, before breaking into the most infectious smile. But what an unusual face; it was as plain and unnoticeable as any peasant or handsome beyond words in its arrangement. He was like every man in one man, she thought.

"Where do you go from here?" she asked.

"I go to build at an apartment building up the road."

"Why would you go and do that?"

He looked at her puzzled. "That's what I do. I am known to myself by my work."

"You would be measured by the strokes of your hammer?" she asked incredulously. "You who teach in this way? You should be known by how you teach, not by how hard you work."

"Teach? I do enjoy saying my mind, but I must eat. I am not a scribe; I am not fed by the Temple."

"But the Lord saith, '…every one that thirsts, come ye to the waters, and that hath no money; come ye, buy, and eat, yea, come, buy wine and milk without money and without price.' Isn't that what you are seeking — to come to the waters; the great love of our Lord?"

The words rang with an irrefutable clarity. Jesus clinched his teeth together in disgust at his self-doubts. She was right. If he were true to these thoughts of even attempting a perfect life, how could he continue spending most of his time worrying about earning money? 'Come to the waters,' danced in his mind like some joyous song, like a magical light suddenly turned on to reveal a great passion he had been groping to articulate and form. Tears welled in his eyes at the power of this simple revelation.

She was sitting on a plump cushion on a bench, and slid to her knees on the carpeting. She looked up at him in a worshipful way, and he was uncertain of how to act. "Master, you are a teacher who hears The Father in a way that few ever have. I will help you, and I know others in the area whom I will tell of you, and they will give you food and a place to rest."

Jesus blushed and stood. Joy ran through him like a mighty wave carrying him into an exhilaration, a pent-up emotion now loosed so that he felt freed for the first time in the years he had been agonizing over his faith, and the faith of the Jews of Galilee.

"You called me teacher," he said almost childlike in his pleasure.

"I call you master, not knowing anything about you. And I say that no man, no priest, nor my dearly beloved husband has ever spoken to me, a woman, with the knowledge of a woman as you have."

"The Father's love is open to all who will accept it. Those who have had less will have more in his Kingdom. Women will be honored in His house as easily as men."

She stood and with a fiery conviction and anticipation pleaded, "I will tell others of you. I will gather the farmers here, and we will listen to you. Please return and speak."

He swelled with the thrill of a gathering that would come just to hear him, but then he thought of how they would ask who he was and who had been his teacher—what schools he had attended, and what job he held at the Temple. He also thought of how the Pharisees in the area would react, and how he could easily be stoned if he angered them. No, there were too many unanswered questions still for him.

"You have touched my heart with your kind words, but I still have my work up the road. I...I...perhaps after that; yes, it would be good to speak maybe here in your home to a few friends." He was stammering, trying to deal with conflicting emotions.

"A few friends!" she almost shouted. "Speak to the countryside; go out into the fields. Start in your own village!"

He stepped back as though there were a repulsing force in her suggestions. Shaking his head, Jesus rebuked her, "In Nazareth? No, there I am just Jesus."

His face dropped in a disappointment he could not disguise at the name, 'Nazareth.' He appeared to be distracted for a moment. His eyes lost their softness, and he looked around in discomfort, ready to leave. "I have much walking to do before dark. May the Holy Light bless this house."

She gazed at him confidently. "The Light has blessed this house through the words of a stranger. I wish that you will remember me if you come this way again. You have now made me want to do something." She looked frustrated and cast her eyes around, searching for an answer, "But I don't know what now. Come back and tell me how differently I should now worship. I feel there is more to your message than you have spoken. Come back and tell me more."

"Just know that you can touch the Word directly," he said as he placed his hand on her shoulder, and she felt a warmth course through her. "It is all around you. Just knock and the door will open. Know that it is a mighty friendship that we are promised." With that he left her standing, exhausted in her emotions, but she ran to the door to look hard at him again, to follow his every move as he slipped the bags over his shoulder, ran his hand through his long hair to move it away from his forehead, and walked back onto the road and away. The widow watched with a yearning up the road until his figure disappeared around a curve. She then sat heavily on her door stoop and wept uncontrollably, because she felt a loneliness she had not felt since her husband's death at Jesus' sudden impact and his just as sudden departure. There was also a nagging sense of shame for having listened to his words; did they defy the Torah? Did they attack the Temple and its priests? But overriding this was a thrill at the uniqueness and simplicity of his message. It was a song to the heart.

As he disappeared in the distance, she sank with the realization that she didn't have the courage to tell her friends; she could never say it exactly and in the way that he had. She could not dare ask the local Pharisee what Jesus said; he might want to chase Jesus down. She wished that she knew how to write more than her name and a few words, because she would write his name and what he said. Instead she took a knife and went out and cut a notch in the wood he had hammered. She looked at the notch and thought of how he had entered her heart as decisively as the knife had entered the wood.

As Jesus approached Sepphoris, he began to see soldiers in their red capes at roadside guard stations—a show of force, a show of empire. The traffic increased dramatically as the little rural road, more a path, ran into the major Roman road up from Caesarea. Wagons of all sizes lined the road, packed with goods moving to and from the bustling port. Camels in their loping gait, with Syrians and Arabians swaying at their humps, claimed whatever bit of road they wanted as they brought spices, metals, ivory, and silk for trade. Donkeys, asses, and oxen slumped under the produce and fruits of local traders. Wagons dusted the powdery road as others hauled lumber and stone for building. It was as though Jesus, with one turn in the road, left the simple landscape of the closed Jewish world of Nazareth and entered another and very alien modern world of commerce. The pace was faster, the tongues far more than Hebrew and Aramaic. In the distance he could see the rooftops and the upper stories of buildings in downtown Sepphoris, gleaming in their white plaster and polished marble.

Huts, hovels, and roadside markets began cluttering the roadside, announcing that a city of 8,000, not a village, was close at hand. At the northwest side of Sepphoris Jesus came upon a wealthy section separated by planted sycamore and palms with colonnades bordering the sides, giving a Roman splendor to the road. Small villas were set back amid gardens with thick groves of trees and ornate landscaping, affording them a sort of seclusion. Away from the road and up the hillsides were larger villas, located there to be removed from the everyday activities and to have a view of the city. The wealthy lived on the northwest side because the wind blew from there and the common saying was that 'we don't want to be downwind of the riffraff.' It was also the home of many wealthy Jews.

In this section, Jesus found the apartment building as he had been directed. It was four stories tall and built of limestone and brick with a terra cotta roof. The bottom floor was fronted by a small pond. A stout Roman stood outside a main door that seemed to lead up to the other floors. Animal skins or wooden shutters filled the windows. As Jesus approached the building, a scrawny woman hung out of her fifth floor window and poured what looked to be human waste out onto the ground below. It narrowly missed the Roman whose toga was slightly splattered as the waste hit the flagstone that formed a patio to the main entrance. He jumped, then ran away from the building fearing another bucketful, and began angrily searching the windows

161

to see where the excrement had come from. But the woman had quickly ducked back inside.

"Jew barbarians!" he screamed up at the building. He had been talking to a stout man holding sheets of papyrus. These were construction drawings for renovating the building.

Jesus walked up to them, waiting for the man to quit hurling invectives at the perpetrator. "I have been told there is work here for an arch builder or stone man," he said in Greek.

The Roman had very curly hair, so black it had to have been dyed. His face was round, fleshy, and contorted in anger. "Another Jew?!' he barked at Jesus.

"One of the faith," Jesus responded calmly.

"And which part of the cursed faith are you?" he snarled.

A smile swept the face of Jesus, caused as much by the ill temper of the man and what had hit him from the window, as the question he asked. "One faithful to the Word, I would hope."

The man seemed annoyed, "No, no, I mean are you one that can deal with people other than Jews? Some of you people can't, you know. We have no time for religious fanatics. The owner is a Jew who doesn't let his religion get in his way. Can you do that?"

"My faith is in the way of all that I do, but The Father created all people and His Kingdom is open to all, so I, too, find peace with all men."

The Roman didn't know whether to run Jesus off or to keep questioning him. He was just another Jew, a group the Roman thought to be simple-minded and self-centered, but this one had an intriguing way about him; he had a composure that eased the Roman's anger.

"The owner comes tomorrow. Back down the road is an inn. I doubt you have the coins to stay there, but it may be safer than just sleeping by the road. Come in the afternoon. We will have final approvals then, and we will get you and the other workers started." He turned back to the stout man, ignoring any response Jesus might have, but then found it difficult to concentrate on the floor plans and looked back at Jesus who was adjusting his baggage straps to relieve the pressure they were putting on his shoulders.

"What exactly do you do?" he asked, though in a sense he had no interest in Jesus or what he did, but he just impulsively felt the need to keep talking to him.

"I can do walls, doors, windows, and any arch work. I can also do balconies. I work in stone and wood and copper. I can build with or without plans."

The Roman felt compelled to continue the conversation, but didn't know what else to ask, nor could he understand why he was asking this stranger anything. He flicked his hand at Jesus to go, and said simply, "Tomorrow at the ninth hour."

Jesus noticed a tall, thin, black-skinned boy in his teens sitting off to one side on the edge of a crumbling fountain. The boy was staring at him with a decidedly sad look on his face. His feet were wrapped in cloth which served as a kind of shoe. He wore a dirty toga cinched in the middle by a belt. Jesus was touched by his forlorn look and walked over to his side.

"My name is Jesus," he spoke in Greek. "I'm from a village near here, and I don't know my way. Could you help?"

The boy looked up, guarded; his eyes unsure; his mouth still in a pout. "Help?"

"The Roman said there was an inn back down the road. Would you know of it?"

Still eying Jesus warily, he answered, "Yes, that's where my master was stabbed," and he looked at the ground, his shoulders slumping.

Jesus put his hand on the boy's shoulder. "Where is your master now?"

The boy pulled back, causing Jesus' hand to slide off. "He's dead. A week now."

"Why was he stabbed?"

"We were staying there a few days waiting for our apartment here to be ready. We were to move in here. But while we slept someone came into our bed and tried to rob us. My master fought, but was stabbed many times. We were made to leave by the innkeeper who was angry because the master had bled all over the place where we slept. We stayed in an orchard behind the inn for two days until he finally died."

"So you were a slave?"

"I suppose I still am." The boy then asked, "Are you a Jew?"

"Yes, how do you know?"

"You speak Greek, just as the Jews from Galilee, who speak Aramaic and speak Greek."

Jesus looked puzzled, "How would you know that?" he laughed.

163

"My master bought grain from Jewish farmers and sold it in Jerusalem. We went into the countryside many times and knew many Jews. My master told the farmers that he was a Jew so they would deal with him, but he wasn't really."

Jesus began addressing him in Aramaic.

The conversation had relaxed the boy, who stretched his long thin legs out. His skin was the color of dark chocolate; his lips thick and a mix of blue and soft reds. His nose was broad and his hair very short and curly; his eyes were a brilliant brown peering over full cheeks and from under a heavy dark brow. He was very much of African descent.

"How did you become a slave?"

"I am from land on the Upper Nile. It was very isolated, but my father was a priest and a man learned in many religions who moved there from Egypt to be near his original people. He insisted that I learn Greek so I might later deal with the Romans. My village was overrun by Arabian slave traders who beat us and tied us up and took us to a slave market where I was bought by master Benai'ah. He was a trader and in Egypt looking for cotton and grains he could buy and ship to Rome."

"Where will the darkness find you tonight?" Jesus asked sympathetically.

"Looking for food." He was ashamed, "I am the son of a village leader, and in this strange land I must steal to eat. Without my master I don't know where to turn."

"Is his family in Jerusalem?"

"Yes, but if I go and tell them he died, they will say I am now their slave. I want so badly to return to my village, but I don't know where it is from here." Tears washed his eyes and fell in long drops to the stone terrace.

Jesus could feel his throat welling up in sadness for the boy's plight. "Come with me," he said. "I will give you food, and we will rest together tonight near this inn. But I think you must travel back to your master's family and tell them of his death. You are too young to be alone. If they would be good masters, then serve them until they will free you. Then you can return to your village. I will tell you the way to the Holy City. You can survive off the food left for the poor in orchards along the way."

Smiling broadly and wiping tears with his fingers the boy said, "I have heard of your one God and know the Jews fear him greatly, but you must know Him in a different way, or you would not speak to an African and one who worships what you would call pagan gods."

Jesus laughed, "My Father is a loving Shepherd. He would shine his eyes upon you if you would open your heart to His love."

They started down the road, and the boy looked up at Jesus, "Love?"

"Yahweh is a loving Father. He dwells in the soul of all of His children, asking that they serve only Him."

"I worshiped many gods in Egypt, but none like this one. Is his name 'Father'?"

"We are not allowed to say His name or to draw an image of Him. He is the Lord of all the heavens and earth. His power is more than His children can know."

The boy was struck by the joy in Jesus' face as he talked and was thankful that they had met.

"Tell me your name," Jesus said.

"My Nubian name is Mactar. The master gave me the Hebrew name of Josiah, because he wanted the Jews to feel free to speak to me as we did business with the rurals. You know, many will not speak to those that don't believe in the one you call Father."

"You had a very cunning master. If you don't mind, I will call you by your Hebrew name. The journey to the Kingdom is different for all. The message I would give to those who will listen is that The Father knows all his lambs do not follow him at the same time and at the same pace, and that none can ever be perfect in His eyes. That's why He is so forgiving."

"This no-name you say is your father, and now mine—since he is a god, does that mean we are the sons of a god?"

"Yes, we are the sons of the heavenly Father as well as our earthly fathers."

All of this was somewhat confusing to the boy, but he stepped with a certain new pride at the thought that this wise man had told him he was kin to a god. He liked that thought and his step showed it. There was a comfort in this stranger who had walked into his life, by the caring that he showed when no one else did.

"We will find a place for the night near the inn, for staying outside sounds safer than having a room," Jesus said.

"My master and I found the countryside to be very dangerous when we would ride out to buy grains. I would say that few of your people understand this Father you speak of. They work hard and obey your strange laws, but fear Him greatly, but I don't know if they love Him."

"Perhaps one will come who will teach them to do that," Jesus said as much to himself as to the boy.

The winter rains had ended weeks earlier, and the incessant traffic made the road hard and dusty. It painted the feet and legs of the carpenter and the boy in its powdery clouds as they moved toward a safe haven for the coming night.

CHAPTER 7

Azari'ah, the son of Dan, had awakened from a dream filled with the screams of his father. It was a dream with no sights, only screams pealing out of a terrifying void. Sweat had matted his black hair in ringlets across his brow. His heart pounded against his chest as his mind tried to escape the horror of his father's crucifixion and his anguish at thrusting his spear into his father's heaving chest. He greeted the day wanting to kill a Roman.

Smoke wafted up through one of the last of Galilee's remaining forests, a land which had been covered with a variety of trees, long ago stripped in the flat areas between the hills. But the hills remained thickly covered in oaks, sycamore, pine, and heavy underbrush.

This stand near the Roman road between Sepphoris and Caesarea had been left because it was rocky and ravined in too many places to be friendly to the plow. A Jewish band of fourteen men periodically met here at a small, stone house in a hidden rock-strewn ravine. They wanted to make a passionate statement that paying tribute to the Roman Emperor on coins with his face was a form of worship to Caesar and an affront to the commandment against graven images. They were fearsome and filled with the certitude of the zealot.

Kokhba Zakkai rose from his sleeping mat next to Azari'ah and kneeled in prayer. He asked God for the strength to fulfill His desire that Israel be made whole, that it be the great nation it was when David ruled. He always said this prayer before he prepared his bronze-tipped arrows for a Roman breast.

After his short prayer he looked down at the boy Azari'ah. "Why do you sweat so?" he asked. "Was the night too hot for your blood?"

"I dreamt of my father," the boy answered in a troubled voice as he lay on his mat.

Kokhba reached down and touched the boy's arm. "Today, if The Holy One guides us, we will avenge the cruelty on Dan. He was a powerful warrior for The Holy One, and you should be filled with joy that you are the son of such a man. Your father believed that the Jews must defend this precious land against the pagans and begin the fight that will bring The Holy One to rule. The One waits to see if His chosen people deserve a Messiah."

The boy sat up. The others in the one room house had already risen and were outside cooking breakfast. The walls were exposed stone. The room had several benches and only one window over which a deerskin was tacked. The floor was dirt, hard-packed, and cool. Embers barely glowed in a depression in the room's center. Mats and blankets lay in disarray over the floor. The men had been using the secluded house as a hideout. They had recently made several attacks on Roman guards traveling between cities. Many had been killed in ambush, then stripped of their clothing and tied to their horses and left to wander the roads until a passing gentile saw the chance to have a new horse.

Azari'ah was fourteen and slightly built. He had worked on his father's small farm and olive orchard since he was eight. He had been devoted to his father, thinking he was one of Yahweh's warriors; a Jew firm in the faith and anxious to fight for it. The family never had much other than their faith; it had consumed his father and had led him to kill a large Jewish landowner for having dealt with gentiles. For that he had been crucified outside Capernaum as an example.

The boy stood looking Kokhba squarely in the eye. "Do you know who killed my father?" His young face, in the shadowing of the half dark room, appeared much older.

"The Roman jackals, of course," Kokhba said as he began rolling up his mat and robes.

"No," Azari'ah said solemnly. "I did."

Kokhba looked dumbfounded. "I saw Dan on the cross myself. You had nothing to do with it."

"I rode by in the night and threw a spear into his chest. I saw his face fall in death. I heard his last sigh."

Kokhba began to weep, and his tears turned into a moaning, and he tore at his shirt, ripping it away and screaming in a terrible agony. The boy stepped back, fearing he was about to be attacked. The other men came running into the room, knives drawn.

"They have brought the darkness even to our children," he wailed.

The men looked from their leader to the boy standing against a wall appearing wide-eyed and scared. "What is it? What has happened?" they asked.

Kokhba turned to them in anguish, "The Romans insult our race by hanging our best on trees. The act is so horrible, the suffering is so unacceptable to a loved one, that they…this boy killed his own father to stop his screams. And now the boy hears the screams of Dan from the dead echoing in his dreams. The Romans now have the sons killing the fathers."

Azari'ah began trembling and fell to his knees crying hysterically, "Forgive me, forgive me!"

Kokhba went to him and pulling the boy up, wrapped his arms around his shaking figure, and consoled, "You must dedicate your life to the memory of your father. You were caught in an evil web spun by the infidels, and you must repent to the Eternal by helping us drive the pagans into the sea."

The boy collected himself enough to sob, "I have killed my father." He repeated this over and over until Kokhba pushed him back, and grabbing both shoulders, shook the boy hard. "Stop this! It is the devil loosed by the Romans that made you commit the act. Join with us to stop these devils by driving the Romans from our land. It would be your father's wish."

The boy nodded his head, sobbing, and said, "Yes…for my father."

Locals had supplied them with a full breakfast. Support for the band was very strong in the area. They had met here a week ago to rob wealthy gentiles and kill any Jews they caught with them. They would share what they stole with the destitute of the area, and for that they were given the staunch support of the poorest Jews. They were farmer-bandits trying to convince, through their daring, that others should join them in asking Yahweh to bring a Messiah.

Little was said as they ate. They were too stunned by Azari'ah's revelation. His father had been their leader for years. It was unthinkable that the son could kill the father even as he hung dying on a tree, but they agreed with Kokhba that their beloved land was now loosed with devils, and the boy had been under the control of an Angel of Darkness. This realization infused them with a grim determination to seek out Roman soldiers that day and kill them. They were armed with bows and arrows, long, curving Arabian knives, and spears they had taken from soldiers they had killed.

After eating, they nailed the door to the house shut. It was hidden in a thicket and under a large rock overhang. The woods were thick all around the house, and there was no path that led from it to the nearby main road. It was the third hour when they broke camp. The sun was chasing the dark out of the woods. They moved in silence through the morning beneath the trees. Dressed in short tunics and slip-over shirts, they were shadowy figures crossing light shafts on a mission to revere the Word of their God. And it would be a deadly reverence.

The baths of Caesarea towered above the city's main square; an area of shops, cafes, and bordellos. Owners of the bordellos were fixtures of the baths freely roaming among the men and telling of the latest 'loveliest woman in all of Palestine' who had joined their business. Herod had been especially pleased with the design of these public baths, an essential part of any Roman city's culture. He had constructed his private baths at the nearby palace, but enjoyed mixing with his subjects here as well. It was three stories high, and appeared to soar even larger with an enormous atrium spanning the three different baths: lukewarm, hot, and cold. The plumbing that ran the place was an engineering marvel with its furnaces, terra cotta pipes, and underground sewage system. An ornate, marble facing welcomed all of the city's citizens, but the poor were generally out scrambling for survival, so most of the men who came on a daily basis were middle-to-upper class. The enormous Jewish population of the city would come, but they would sit in towels and short robes, as they found the nakedness of the Romans to be disgusting. Nevertheless, if they wished to be a part of the social scene and the business networking it created, they had to frequent the baths. Many, however, were too devout and thought the baths another example of pagan debauchery. Rows of luxury shops and arcades with cafes and open markets faced the baths on either side of the street. The whole area was alive with citizens of all backgrounds. The baths were the city's center.

Nearing the beautifully arched entrance, Paulius whispered to his bearer, "Announce us loudly."

The slave, a tall German, shouted in Greek, "All be aware of the arrival of the honored lawyer Paulius and his guests among the most honored from Italia, the victorious military and business man Cassius Orelius, and the well-known painter for the Emperor Julian Lycanius."

Dozens of well-heeled citizens standing outside the baths gave interested and envious looks at the trio now climbing off their litters and bowing subtly to those bowing at them. "Speak only to those I speak to." Paulius said out of the side of his mouth as they approached the entrance. "As you know, there are many who would climb to our level, who would catch my eye, shake my hand, be seen having a word with me."

As the patrons to the baths bowed to Paulius they greeted, "A good bath to you," and "your humble servant." Paulius said the same in his boisterous voice.

One Hernon said effusively, "The new decorations are wonderful. Your name will always be synonymous with the new atrium ceiling. When we look up, we will think 'Paulius'," he laughed heartily. A friend next to him smiled slyly, "There has been much conjecture over your generosity."

"Fifty thousand sesterces," he said with a nonchalant look.

There was an audible gasp. That was a substantial gift to make to the city, especially since Paulius was not running for an office. It was a show of his force and his masculinity, both crucial to maintaining power in the rarefied air in which he traveled.

Several attendants greeted them in the vaulted entrance area, but Paulius came prepared carrying towels, perfumes, anointing oils, stirgles and sponges, so his slaves waved them off with diffidence.

There was an order to bathing. It could start with reading—a time of reflection and intellectual stimulation—then going through a series of rooms with baths of different temperatures. The baths were large, very shallow pools. Only a meter deep, they were not for swimming but for languishing in and sitting on the edge of. Theft was common, so one had to watch their clothing and towels which were placed on stone shelves above the bath walls. Marble benches were attached to the walls for sitting and visiting. Adjacent to the baths was a long peristyle courtyard, called the palaestra, or play area. Here one would work out: lifting weights, running, boxing, wrestling, doing acrobatics and exercises. It was done in the nude, wearing only a small cap. Jews found naked men running around exercising to be repugnant, and refused to be seen there. Many simply walked along the edge among the colonnades and idly watched. It was a promenade of the pompous; a place where being seen and admired was the goal of every businessman. Gymnastics had historically been considered an essential element of a healthy Roman's life and learning.

"Let's start with a rub down, then go to the tepidarium. If it pleases you, I like to then savor the heat of the caldarium, then cool down in the frigidarium. I wish no exercise, but you may go outside first."

Julian smiled, "Cassius and I have not exercised together since our days at the gymnasium in Rome. Aristophanes, you know, worried in 'Clouds' that 'young men waste their time chattering in public baths instead of going to the gymnasium.' He felt it was evidence of our decline."

"The decline of Rome!" Cassius scoffed. "An impossible thought. Paulius, many here want to have your ear. I think I'll take my feminine friend, Julian, and go into the palaestra for some running. We'll be back shortly and join you for a massage before our bath."

The slaves gave them wooden clogs to wear. They walked through the ornate rooms with intricate floor mosaics, silver spigots, polished bronze, washing pans, and richly painted alabaster vessels filled with oils and wines. The broad rooms gave a feeling of airiness, of soaring space and sky, because of the vaulted and windowed ceilings. There was a slight echo of conversations because of the cavern-like quality of the rooms, and the clogging of the wooden heels against the tiles was an ever-present background echo.

As they crossed the tepidarium and its wide-tiled decking around the pool, a small man with a pouch and tweezers in his hand asked them, "Masters, with very, very little pain, I can remove those hairs that have been bothering your mistresses."

They punched one another and laughed as they ignored his approach. "Yes, we are back in the baths!" Julian harked. "The hair pullers are here."

They stopped at the steaming caldarium pool and listened for a moment to some minstrels playing. A jester wandered through, fanning the steam, putting on a skit as he walked to the delight of the crowd sitting on the edge of the hot water. In the chill of the air in the frigidarium, vendors were selling sweet cakes, deserts, and wine.

Julian stopped and ran his hand over a intricately placed wall mosaic of an Arabian hunting scene. "Numedian stone," he remarked. "They spared no expense here."

As they stepped outside, the afternoon had a touch of spring to it, and the broad, grassy palaestra playing field was filled with men engaged in all manner of sports. Others simply walked under the colonnades that bordered the area, seeing who was there of any consequence and then spotting one of rank, determining how they might obliquely, and with great deftness, move in for a conversation. Cassius took his toga and undergarments off, laid them on a bench, placed a small white cap on the back of his head and sprinted off across the field. Julian took his clothing off and absent-mindedly walked over to a set of weights. It would be an afternoon of great leisure.

Azari'ah was sent to be the lookout. He ran to the top of a large rock where he lay as flat as he could, watching the road in front of him. He was at the edge of the small forest where they had been hiding. The road in front of him stretched away toward grass covered hills and beyond to Caesarea. He was hungry and scared, but unprepared for the absolute fear he felt when a detachment of Roman soldiers appeared over the hill and came amid a sandy-colored cloud of dust. Their horses seemed impatient in their slow gait; their heads jerked against the bits, and the soldiers appeared, broad-shouldered and thick in the way of Romans to the wide-eyed boy. So fast did he slip off the rock that he skinned his knee. Racing back through the woods, he burst into the thicket next to the road where the men were lying.

They were startled and jumped for their knives as he gasped out of breath, "They come! They come!"

The men moved brush up in front of themselves and slid behind several large trees that crowded the road. Bows were drawn and knives tightly gripped. "Take careful aim, Azari'ah," one who was just behind them whispered to the boy.

The boy's hand was shaking so violently he could hardly get the arrow in the bow string. It kept jerking out as now they could hear the thump of the hooves and the voices of the men. To Azari'ah, they brought back the memory of the gruff dialect of the guard that hanged his father. Sweat rolled off his forehead. He could see them easily now, coming at a walk, spread across the road in no order, talking, gesturing, their red shoulder capes fluttering like flags out behind them in the afternoon breeze. Their horses seemed like barrels—the men so large and looming. His ears rang, and the thick grass seemed to reach up to him as his fingers released an arrow through the trees, and he fell backwards in a faint.

Azari'ah did not see the zealots jump from the thickness of the forest and in unison send their arrows plunging into the chests and heads of the eight man detail. The horses reared and twirled, four of the Romans jumped off and advanced with their short swords and shields. The boy did not see the band attack with a ferocity that sent all four Romans falling back and into their horses, then to the ground where they were stabbed repeatedly as they screamed in fear and pain. And he did not hear the Jews roar in unison to Yahweh that they had avenged the death of Dan, that they were ready for the Lord to send a Messiah—a fiery warrior savior who would turn the Land red with Roman and gentile blood.

Azari'ah came to, feeling dizzy and nauseated, rose to his feet and leaned against a tree. Suddenly his bloodstained arrow with a bit of torn flesh on it was being thrust into his face by a joyous Kokhba. "You were the first to fight, son of Dan!" he was yelling. "Your arrow hit first! It was a shoulder shot to their leader, but it threw them off enough for us to hit them from another angle." He hugged the boy. "You have honored your father and The Holy One!"

The fighters stripped the Romans of their clothing, took their food, tied them over their horses, then slapped the animals so that they galloped down the road toward Sepphoris.

"Tonight we have a banquet," Kokhba announced as he rummaged through the captured saddle bags. Several carriages and a small caravan were seen approaching so they quickly brushed down the road, covering the blood, and melted into the woods as they had come — shadowy figures filled with the lust of their victory and praising their God. Azari'ah took up their rear, feeling guilty that he had not aimed his arrow, but had released it in fainting, and wanting badly now to return to Capernaum and his mother's side.

"Honored one, would you care for the services of a tender young boy, or would a Samarian beauty suit your pleasure? We have some who have barely been touched." A young man with bleached-blond hair and a thin boyish body had sided up to Paulius and his guests as they sat, feet dangling in the water in the tepidarium.

Paulius ignored him for a moment and asked his guests, "Did you get a good tan outside? The sun here, even in winter, is excellent for taking that effeminate pale look away."

Cassius, who still had a light sweat on him from the exercise, answered, "The sun was perfect. But now that I have achieved the bronze coloring of a god, I do need the eyes of a lover to tell me how beautiful it is."

"Man or woman?" Julian asked jokingly.

"Oh, I've never had the pleasure of any spintrias (a vulgar name for a male prostitute), but I," and he turned to the man, "would like to see several of your females. Julian?"

"I am very interested in Egypt. I will be going their shortly. Do you have any women from there?"

174

Paulius chuckled, "Egyptians? Why you have seen my slave Esna. I suppose I could allow you a night with her, but she is high born. Of course we would say a high born Egyptian is only slightly above a barbarian, so she would not have the passion of some others."

Julian thought of his remark to Esna about having her travel to Alexandria with him. If Paulius thought he had some attachment to her, Paulius might accede to Julian's borrowing her for a month.

Julian smiled, "An Egyptian slave for the night. You are too gracious. I'll take her after we dine."

Cassius punched him in the side, "If I know you, you will want to paint her, not bed her."

Paulius looked at the man grinning obsequiously at them, "Perhaps a boy for me, but make sure it is a boy. By the gods I would not be accused of bedding with a man."

Cassius scoffed, "It was good enough for Caesar. You remember the awful rumors of his competing for the royal bed with the queen of Bithynia in Gaul when he conquered it."

"Shameless," scowled Paulius. "Caesar got on top of Gaul; the king Nicomedes got on top of Caesar." He flipped his hand at the procurer without looking up at him. "Go and fetch your selection. We'll be at the Augustan cafe across the street after our bath. Do not bring them inside, nor are you to come inside. We'll see you through the window and make arrangements, if we like what we see. Now be gone."

They walked over to the hot, steaming air of the calderium. "We have both dry and wet steam; if you would like the laconium, you can sweat out all of the sea water you might still have." Paulius slid into the extreme heat of the pool. A mist hung over its shallow waters. There was no swimming here, only luxuriating in the heat.

Julian could feel his skin redden in the heat. His mind wandered as he gazed up at the distant, curving ceiling. He mused, "I can see the symmetry of the heavens joining with the centrality of the Emperor in the design of this place," he said dreamily.

Paulius lay heavily in the steaming shallows and observed with a calm resignation, "You think too deeply, poet. Enjoy the moment, for that, my friend, is all that this life is. This is heaven and this is hell. And beyond it…is a very long sleep."

CHAPTER 8

The hooves pounded on the hard earth with staccato claps of thunder—dull, heavy, rolling beats—that could be felt through the feet as the horses came by. There were twelve Roman guards leading three horses with what appeared to be dead men slung over the backs of the animals. The bodies were partially covered, but a hand that flung outward, a foot in an aimless kick from under the flowing robes, revealed there was death underneath. The detachment reigned in at the two-story stone inn. The dust they had been trailing caught up and swirled about them and clouded the large wooden entrance to the building. Jesus and Josiah were just leaving the road to sit under a palm grove and eat.

They stood several feet from the inn and watched as one guard got off his horse and tacked a piece of papyrus between two of the stones at the front of the building. There was already a large group of people milling around the inn; they backed away from the feared symbol of empire as the centurion turned to them and announced loudly to all that could hear, including a rotund innkeeper, who had emerged to see what the commotion was about.

"All hear, all hear! Know that a handsome reward will be offered by Herod Antipas, as well as the legate of the fort in Caesarea, for anyone who knows of these crimes against the Emperor Tiberius." And he waved his arm toward the wrapped corpses. "We suspect it was the Jew groups that live down the way in the hills, and I would tell those of you who might know of these jackals that there will be great suffering by them and their families when they are found out." His eyes surveyed the crowd, and they shrank back under the withering look as though he could detect who might know of these men simply by the intensity of his gaze.

Climbing on his horse, he motioned for the others to follow and they again began their thunderous thumping on the highway into Sepphoris. Jesus and the young African stood alone, away from the crowd as the guards dug their heels into the horses' sides in an orchestrated display of power. As they sped past the two, Jesus could see the arrogance of the Roman soldiers and felt fearful of their might. Much of his life around Nazareth had been spent out of their sight. There was no reason for them to do more than pass through such an insignificant farming village. But because Nazareth was only four miles from the government center, it was impossible not to know of the Roman presence. It was as prevailing as the hot air that encompassed the area.

The inn was named The Camel and set off the road several yards. Made of brick, it was a circle of stalls opening onto a large courtyard. Each room or stall was big enough for several mats on its straw and dirt floor. The rooms were rarely cleaned and roaches moved in shadowy, erratic swiftness searching for food. Rats were frequent visitors and could be heard foraging about in the night, climbing over bags and sleepers with a daring nonchalance. One generally had to bring their own food which the innkeeper would cook out in the open area for a small fee. He occasionally offered vegetables and fruit. The inn had no way of storing or refrigerating food to feed the hosts of people who passed through. Theft was rampant, and one slept lightly.

Fig and olive orchards surrounded the building on both sides and the rear. A large garden covered a small rise behind the inn, which was worked year round. A big, round cistern on one side captured rain water, and there was a large oil press under a shed.

Jesus sat on a rock outcropping next to several dozen people who could not afford to sleep inside, but wanted the measure of safety offered by throwing one's roll on the ground near a center of activity like the inn. The sun was dropping into early evening. Several cooking fires had started up.

"Do you think Jews killed the soldiers?" Josiah asked as he watched Jesus pull some food from his baggage. The boy had not eaten in two days and was dizzy from hunger. He almost ate the bread out of Jesus' hand as he gave it to him.

"There are some of our faith who believe we are to take a role in driving the evil ones out of our land. They look to a Messiah to come and lead them; a leader from our Father."

"Won't be a Messiah. It'll be the Eternal Himself," a high-pitched voice came from their left. It was a small Jew with a look of privation and malnutrition. His tunic was too large; his skinny legs stuck like stems into badly-worn goat skin boots. His beard was carefully trimmed and as dark brown as his hair, which looked like it had been trimmed in a haphazard way. Bags sagged underneath his large brown eyes,which gave him a startled expression because of his thinly-drawn face. He grinned when they looked at him, revealing teeth that were pointed and yellow. He saw both of them stare at his teeth.

Spreading his gums, he grinned at the two. "Just had them put in. What do you think?"

Jesus and Josiah looked at one another and had a hard time suppressing their laughter.

All Jesus could say was, "The question is not what two dust-covered travelers think, but what your wife thinks."

"Very happy," he nodded. "Think it makes me look like a young man again. Had a fine tooth puller put them in. Came from a large dog near my farm."

"Must have been a good looking dog," Jesus said feigning sincerity.

"The name's Benjamin," he introduced himself. "Have a farm west of here." He sat on the ground next to a cart which he pulled himself. It was filled with covered items.

"I'm Jesus of Nazareth and this is Josiah; he's visiting from Africa."

"Heard of it, but don't know of it." He had borrowed a flame from a nearby fire and was starting his own little fire with some brush and grass.

They sat in a small crowd, comprised mostly of men who were camping out next to the inn. Several languages could be heard with Greek being the most common. Jesus and the man spoke in Aramaic. There was a thickness to the darkening air; the sun had disappeared and dust from passing wagons curtained the area in a reddish film as it seemed to have caught and held for a moment the dying light.

"Why are you still out on the road?" Jesus asked.

"I came into the city to trade my herbs and dove for lamp oil, salt and sugar. The markets normally close before noon, but today they stayed open later because Antipas was entertaining a large party from Rome. There was much excitement at the stalls, but he ignored those of us from the country and dealt only with the gentiles and their big stalls with their spices from Damascus. So, I was late leaving and would not dream of being on these roads at night."

"So you trade with gentiles?" Jesus asked.

"Not until recently. I worked my farm only to survive, but with so many people moving into these cities, I now grow my crop for trade. It has made our land worth more, but it has also made it a great risk to own land."

Jesus nodded. "Many around Nazareth have lost their land to those who make loans, then take the land. Many now live off the corners of their fields left unharvested for the poor, fields they owned for generations."

"If you are careful and don't over borrow, you can do well." Benjamin thought for a moment, "It is hard not to come under the influence of the Romans and all the traders who come to do business with them. It makes the farmer greedy to grow more to sell more to have more. The devil lives in our indebtedness. It is so easy to get into and so hard to get out of."

"Should we not lend without expecting anything in return? What credit is to you in the eyes of the Kingdom if you always ask for something back when you give?"

The little man looked surprised. "That sounds crazy to me."

Suddenly moved with an eagerness to speak, Jesus said, "Our Laws say that our prophets instruct us in the power of The Holy One. We owe Him life. We owe Him obedience. To be taken into his Kingdom is what we all desire. That must be all that matters to us—to please Him—which means we must overcome our desire to own instead of devoting our lives in service to Him."

Two colorfully-dressed men with turbans strolled out of The Camel's front door, and as they surveyed the highway and its variety of caravans and wanderers, they aimlessly strolled over to the assortment of travelers making little campsites for the evening outside the Camel. The coming night would be warm, and there was little ventilation in the cramped inn. Some would wind up sleeping in its courtyard or out in the heavy grass around the building. One of the men was small of frame and narrow faced, and very dark skin. The other was a Greek, tall and well formed with large facial features. He had an unusual walk, practiced and determined with every step. He wore a tunic of colored stripes and a floppy, strange looking cap. They were talking, and the Greek was gesturing dramatically with his hands. They had stopped near Benjamin and studied his little hand cart and its wrapped contents.

"Do you speak Greek?" The dark man asked.

"Very little," Benjamin answered.

"I do," said Jesus.

"Ah, Jews, and possibly Galilean Jews," the dark man observed to his friend as though they were studying plants.

"Then you would prefer we speak in the tongue of the rurals," the dark man said in Aramaic. "Sorry, but I doubt that I will ever master Hebrew. I am from India, but here, as everywhere I travel, I take a name of the area so it is easy to address me. I have taken the name of Severus. My friend here is a pretender (actor) by the name of

Sidonnius. We met in Tiberias and are traveling together for safety and enlightenment."

Benjamin eyed them warily. He wondered if they were Satan in disguise.

The one called Sidonnius smiled broadly. His features were very pronounced, and his figure very fit. "I know little Aramaic, so I must speak in Greek." He proceeded to do so very slowly. "We overheard you mention a Messiah. While traveling throughout Judea we spoke with those Jews who would speak with us, and many have told of an expected King, a leader who would restore this land to greatness. Who would this be?"

Benjamin answered in Aramaic with great seriousness, "So say the prophets, 'For behold the Lord will come in fire, and his chariots like the storm wind.' It will be a terrible time for all those who resist, who do not accept the Laws. A Messiah like King David will lead us and reign."

The one calling himself Severus quickly translated into Greek, then said, "This seems to be a fearsome god. I am Buddhist and I find the suffering that Jews believe they do is much like my religion where our founder, Gautama Buddha, said that one cannot separate suffering from life. I keep looking for similarities in the different religions, but I have not found one where a leader sent by a god would come and destroy all who don't accept Him. This is a frightening spirit."

The conversation had easily carried to the ears of the several dozen travelers lying about in the grass. Many had gotten up from their mats or robes and ambled over to hear Jesus speaking to Benjamin. There was little else to do as darkness had now descended. Benjamin's fire of twigs and grass gave a soft, flickering light to Jesus' face. He sat slightly elevated above the fire on a low rock wall.

"I say unto you, there is only one Father, and He is a loving Father who created all of the world's children and chose especially those of the nation of Israel. But His heart is open to all. He makes His sun rise on the good and on the evil. He needs no Messiah to claim what is already His, this land. He needs to send no king, no David. The prophets do speak of one who will come in the form of a man. He will speak with the authority of The Father. The Word says the Kingdom is coming, but not in a fire storm. It is our own repentance we must worry over, not whether we will be saved by a heavenly messenger."

Another Jew who had walked over demanded, "You read the Laws to say there will be no Messiah! That the Eternal will not drive the devils back to Italia and restore our nation!? Then what is our belief for? We need a mighty new king to lead us!"

Jesus saw the angry disbelief in the man's face. The fire shadowed all their faces, accentuating the downward cast of their mouths and the crinkling skin around their furrowed brows. To a downtrodden nation, to feel there was to be no fiery expulsion of the oppressors, was unthinkable and unsettling. All awaited a rescue.

Some in the crowd did not know Aramaic and stood simply to enjoy the intensity of a debate. To the lives of the lonely traders, any diversion, especially one that might turn into a fight, was welcomed.

Jesus noticed the large circle of listeners and raised his voice to reach them. The wall on which he was sitting gave him some height so they could see him. He felt confident in the circle and in his ability to form his ideas into a simple presentation. He thought before he spoke and his voice had a reasoned and deliberate tone to it. He did not yell, but there was a force to the way he spoke, an energy and a definite passion that was like watching a great actor. He was a figure who physically appeared to be a lowly traveling worker until he began speaking, then he was transformed into a compelling teacher—magnetic, clear, entertaining—all delivered in the distinctive Aramaic of the northern Galilean hill country.

"I must tell you, a king who is not of The Father would be like the blind leading the blind. They would both fall into a pit. The prophets say that the Father will send a servant, and many will be astonished at him, so shall he startle many nations, for that which has not been told them they shall see, and that which they have not heard they shall understand."

A thickly-built man wearing a cap stepped from the crowd and asked suspiciously, "Who are you to say these things; to say a servant comes, but not a king, no fiery war that restores our nation? Who is your teacher?"

Jesus looked across the fire at the man's glowering countenance. "I am one who has prayed to The Father for an understanding of His Word. I am one who reads the scriptures, who has listened to our priests in the Temple, to our Pharisees in the villages, to the Community of Bathers, and I have considered all these things. What I speak of is what I understand. The word I say is the Word I hear."

The man stepped next to the fire. He was short in statue and bald with a trimmed black beard and mustache. His face was jowly in the cheeks. His nose was thick and slightly twisted, as though it had been broken. His eyes seemed slightly bloodshot. He had a slur to his voice and swayed as if he had been drinking.

He looked Jesus up and down. "You look like an artisan or a traveling worker. You say you were at the Temple; were you taught there in a school?"

"As it is said, 'Hearken to me, you who pursue deliverance, you who seek The Father, look to the rock from which you were hewn.' The Temple is a sacred place to the Nation, but I take these words to mean that that all of the children can go directly to The Father, to the rock, to know Him," Jesus responded.

The man stepped over the small fire and up to the rock glaring at Jesus. His face glistened with sweat and his breath reeked of vomit and wine. Jesus slid off the rock and stood facing the man, which angered the drunk even more.

"Look at you, plow man! You speak against the Temple and with no authority! What kind of Jew would you be?"

"I would not speak against the Temple," Jesus corrected. "I am a Jew, a simple servant, who knows that the Nation is as lost as it was in the wilderness and it needs..." The man then took a wild swing, missing his face but landing a solid punch to Jesus' left shoulder, spinning him back hard against the wall.

The man yelled in a fury, "You would insult our priests with your ravings! You have had no teaching. You're an impostor, another one of the road walking devils who would confuse; a would be prophet with no claim to authority beyond his own rantings!"

The crowd pressed closer, eager to see a fight, but Jesus straightened himself and turned his other shoulder to the man. His face showed a disarming calm in spite of his racing heart and clinched fists, but he felt a power in refusing to give in to the man's temper. It fortified him, freed him from the moment in a wonderful exhilaration. He was beyond the shouts, free of his normal passion and desire to climb on the wave of anger.

Seeing that Jesus was not going to strike back, the man yelled, "You're also a coward! You turn the other shoulder. You are no more than a woman. I won't dirty my hands with the likes of you!"

"It is not in striking back that we please The One, but I say to you be merciful as He is merciful. Turn the other cheek to those who would strike you. Anger is the land where the Evil One reigns. And don't judge so you won't be judged. For the standard you use will be the standard used against you." There was a mesmerizing quality to Jesus' voice, so utterly calm in the face of the man's intense anger.

The man spat on the ground, realizing he had been bested by this man. There was something frightful about Jesus' demeanor, something too powerful to continue swinging against, something unknown and unknowable in Jesus' eyes that stared unblinking out of the night. Uttering a string of obscenities, the man pushed and stumbled his way back through the crowd. There was silence for a moment and then murmurings of disappointment that no fight had taken place. Those who could not understand Aramaic filtered away back to their fires. The few farmers began to debate what they had heard. Benjamin approached Jesus with a stunned, awed look. Slowly he sank to his knees directly in front of Jesus, and looking up, said, "Teacher, you have been touched by The Holy One who rules over all. Never have I been so moved. Could it be that He speaks through you?"

Jesus was filled with joy and forgot the pain still radiating from his shoulder. "We are all the son of man, Benjamin. He speaks through us all."

"You must come to our village and teach. You speak for each of us. You say the Maker is more than the leader of a tribe, but One who would worry over each of us as though we were His only child. Your message is a comfort, unlike the threats of the rabbis. They speak of a god of fear and punishment. You speak of a god of love."

"I speak of a way that fulfills the word of Moses, and it is not one of fear or threats," Jesus said simply. "If I show you that way, will you follow?" He was very interested in seeing if someone would actually join a movement he might start.

The man nodded, first hesitating then with assurance, "Yes, I…I think I will, and I will tell others." Then he blurted out, "But I am a Jew of the Torah. Understand, I do not seek another religion."

"And it is not another religion of which I speak, beloved." And having said that, Jesus suddenly felt very tired. He was still hungry, having given the boy most of his food; the boy had sat wide-eyed throughout the whole confrontation. "I must go now," he said to the man with the dog's teeth.

"Go? Shall I follow now?" Benjamin asked.

Jesus smiled a weary smile, "Perhaps soon, but now I need the peace of the orchard and time with The Father."

Severus spoke up, "You speak as one learned, but waste your time with a dog-toothed old man. Why ask this nobody if he would follow you? Why not go to your Temple and speak before the priests? You could speak to thousands there and become rich and powerful. Or perhaps you fear they would scoff at your lowly appearance as one unschooled."

Jesus stared at him impatiently, "In The Father's Kingdom, the least will be first, and the first will be last. The Father cares for the heart of the son of man not the outside, not the thickness of the robe, nor its coloring, or the jewels on one's wrist. It is the meek, the humble, the true of heart that will inherit heaven. Every man is special to the Maker, so I will speak to those who would listen, regardless of who they may be." Jesus turned to go.

"But wait," the Indian Severus said. "You are a curiosity to us. We would like to ask you more questions. We travel to learn."

Anger flashed over Jesus' face with a surprising suddenness and energy. "You learn only what the ignorant know. You learn only with the mind and learn nothing with the heart. Yours is a rocky ground where little truth will ever grow. You will never know more than the smartest man knows, whose knowledge is but a seed against the mighty oak that is our Father." And he disappeared into the darkness that enveloped the thick orchard behind them. The boy started to follow, but Jesus left so quickly and seemed too distant in his weariness. Josiah wanted to hear more; the voice was captivating and the ideas seemed to make more sense than the host of gods the boy had worshiped in Egypt. In the morning, he thought, there would be time to ask questions.

"He reminds me of Gautama," Severus said. "He was also a humble man who was attacked as a false prophet, and in the Dhammapada, the Buddha said 'Happily shall I live without hostility among the hostile.' It is one of our Eternal Laws. There are similarities here. Could it be that we have found another holy one, Sidonius?"

The Greek ran his hands through his blond hair. "You must know the roads are filled with prophets and stargazers. I study them all to add to my theatrics. I have a wonderful act where I have a traveling prophet convince himself he is the son of a god, only to run into that god while on the road. It gets great laughs. Perhaps I will include this one. I'll title it 'The Son', and it will be about a mystic who doesn't know if he's the son of a man or the son of a god. This one's a blessed soul, but one who confuses, even angers others." Sidonius rubbed his chin, pensively running the character through his mind, and asking no one in particular, "Who was this fellow? Did someone get his name? I'm working on a new comedy, and I could include him, though he seemed more sad than funny."

Severus refused to dismiss Jesus quite so easily. "As I have learned about the Jews, I think the fellow a rebel, one who would move his religion in a new direction, and, as you say, he confuses, but some teachers speak with such clarity that no one can understand. In the morning I will question him some more."

Benjamin lay down on a bedroll next to his cart and said, "You will be questioning one very close to Yahweh, I believe. One very, very close. He speaks for the poor man, the forgotten, and, in doing so, he speaks for all men. Aren't the richest of us poor and forgotten in some way?" Benjamin was looking at Severus, but expected no answer. He wrapped himself in a blanket and closed his eyes. Tomorrow, he would tell his neighbors of this man, of this Jew unlike any he had ever heard.

CHAPTER 9

He was up early with his mind groggy and muddled from over-drinking and under sleeping. Cassius leaned heavily against Julian's door, laying his face against its smooth wood, closing his eyes, and knocking for his friend to wake up.

"There are profits to be made, fellow Roman. Be up. I smell the aroma of breakfast." And he stumbled away and into the creeping light of the inner courtyard.

Esna awoke with a startle in the arms of Julian. She had been dreaming of her home, dreaming Julian had given her wings and that the Goddess Isis had blown a magical wind that carried her out over the Great Sea and down over the Egyptian delta, over the sprawling magnificence of Alexandria, and into the loving arms of her family. The rude knock of Cassius had broken the dream as the hands of her father reached out to her, before she could touch the ground of her beloved city, and know the love of her family. She sat up, realizing she was unclothed and in the bed of a Roman she hardly knew.

Julian mumbled and turned on his side still grappling with sleep. She found her under-garments, pulled her day gown over her head and cinched it with a cord. The lingering dream disturbed her as she paused to look long at the man she felt was her only hope for escape. Her father, she sadly believed, had taken the form of a dream and told her that she might try, but she would never reach his arms again. She stood in the growing light of the small room and tears ran down her cheeks as she opened the door, passing a sleepy Cassius to go to the kitchen to start her duties.

Soon the clatter of hooves was heard on the cobblestones outside Paulius' villa as his two guests wandered into the large center room for breakfast. They paused at a fish tank Paulius had built into the wall. It was enormous — so large that he bred fish in it for eating.

"Our guard is here. The legate will have two troops with us. One will stay behind a ways. The road to Sepphoris has seen some trouble by the Jews intent on stirring up their people. Apparently, there is a spot through the woods where ambushes have occurred. We will start through with our guard and the others will ride to our side and through the woods. You brave men don't mind a little excitement, do you?"

Julian reclined on a sofa before the long dining table. Esna entered with the other servants carrying silver trays with pancakes, date syrup, boiled eggs, and yogurt with herbs and cucumbers. Marinated goat cheese was on a small plate and sprinkled with olive oil, cumin seed and coriander leaves.

Paulius knew that Esna had slept with Julian and with a sly grin asked broadly, "Did we all sleep well last night?"

Esna never looked up, but Julian could see her blushing and looking distressed. His heart filled with a strange hurting for her plight, but his upbringing said that she was a slave and he should only feel so much for her, yet…

Cassius drank juice from a goblet and said, "Well, some of us slept alone," and he raised an eyebrow toward Julian. "But if the bandits wish to engage in battle today, it will be my pleasure. I've not felt a sword in hand for several years now. You say these might be Jews?"

Paulius gulped down a pancake as it dripped oils onto his clothing. "Our presence inflames a certain segment of the population. This group stabs their own people if they find them consorting with a Roman, or even one not of their faith." He grinned broadly, revealing the pancake still stuffed in his cheeks. "I, too, feel like shedding some blood. It would be great sport, perhaps even a highlight of your trip."

Cassius dipped into his yogurt and asked with a smirk, "Should Julian ask the slave girl if it would be alright if he wore his sword, or should he tell the bandits he would rather draw their pictures?"

This was met by uproarious laughing by Paulius and Cassius, and then by Julian, who saw he must join in their fun or there would be no end to it.

"I like that," Julian proclaimed. "You all stand back with your swords, and I will calm the savages with my quill and ink. And since the Jew doesn't believe in having his likeness portrayed, they will run for the hills rather than submit to my talents. Why, I could subdue this entire nation by simply threatening to draw their likenesses!"

They all laughed and Paulius called for more pancakes.

Jesus was up before the others. He was hungry and without food since he had shared what the widow had given him with the boy. He threw his heavy robe off and stood in the still air. A gray light preceded the sun in that soft moment when the darkness is wiped away like a smudge being dissolved.

"A bite for a poor man?" said an abrupt voice came from behind him. Jesus turned to see a thin man leaning on a staff with a large bag hanging from his shoulder. He recognized him as one called a Cynic,

187

a gentile, one of the host of philosophers who begged in return for their speeches on how to discover life's Truths.

"You think your philosophies earn you bread, but you leave only food for the mind and not for the soul. To me, you give nothing but take everything," Jesus admonished the man.

Their words awoke those around them, and soon people were stirring all along the road surrounding the inn. Embers were stoked and breakfast fires lighted, but most were eager to run back into the nearby orchard, relieve themselves and be on their way.

Benjamin noticed Jesus looking through his baggage where he found a few almonds. "Let me share some of my meal," he said, pulling Jesus by his hand next to the cart. "And I have enough for your young friend. You say he is from Egypt?"

"Yes, he is a slave whose master was killed in this inn. He must go to the Holy City and tell his master's family, but he wants to return to his homeland."

The farmer mused as he cut up several fruits and divided out small barley cakes. "So much of who we are is because of our time in Egypt. I have always thought of going there and walking in the steps of Moses. Perhaps I will make enough off my farm this spring to do just that." He laughed to himself at the thought of his being able to afford to travel anywhere beyond his once a year pilgrimage to Jerusalem. Egypt seemed like another world.

Jesus looked over at Josiah who was sitting up and looking around in a boyish confusion over why he was awake so early. "Josiah, did you walk in the steps of Moses?" Jesus kidded.

"Moses?" The boy rubbed his head.

"He was an ordinary man whom The Father touched and asked to lead his people out of your country. He doubted his ability to do so. He asked The Father not to make him a leader, but The Father sees strengths in all of us, and He chose this unlikely man." Jesus seemed to delight in telling the story as he chewed slowly on a shallot.

"Does your Father know the gods of Egypt?" Josiah asked as he walked over and was handed a piece of bread with grape jelly spread over it.

"My Father knows the gods of Egypt to be false gods. They exist only in the minds of those who speak of them and are as lifeless as the statues erected to them."

The boy didn't want to disagree with this man who had befriended and now fed him, though he doubted what Jesus said to be true.

His early life had been filled with the endless array of gods and the man-god called Pharaoh that defined the Egyptian culture.

"My father knows of gods few in Egypt have heard of," the boy said. "My father speaks of lands far to the south of Egypt with great mountains and jungles and animal herds as far as the eye sees. He said there was enough ivory to make a man rich forever. That is where he traveled once to see the land of his ancestors. He said there was a place of strange beauty and mystery. He even found the place where the great Nile starts."

"You know where the Nile starts?" It was the eager voice of the Indian. He had come out of the inn ready to study the crowd for any unusual tidbits. The actor accompanied him.

The boy looked up at the turbaned man. "Well, no, not me, but my father does."

"And where would your father live, boy?"

"In a village on the Upper Nile, far from the delta, or he did before slave traders came and captured all of us. I don't know if they caught my father. We ran when they came."

"Just why are you here if your father is in Egypt?"

"I am a slave, but my master was killed. I have followed this Jesus here because of his kindness."

"What if I took you with me to Egypt?" the Indian moved close to Josiah, looking at him intently. "I'll be going to Caesarea in a few days, and we could go together. You could show me your father's village."

Josiah almost broke into tears. "You would do that!" He exclaimed.

"You must first go and tell the family of your master. Tell them that he is dead," Jesus interrupted.

Severus frowned, "But I have been to Jerusalem and don't wish to return. My time is limited. If you wish to return to your homeland, I suggest you forget the man who made you a slave and come with me."

Josiah looked at Jesus then at Severus, confused and anxious. "I…I would like very much to return to my home," he said, but with uncertainty.

"Of course you do," Jesus consoled him, "but your master's family loved him and they will never know what became of him if you don't go and tell them."

"That's nonsense," scoffed Severus. "He made you a slave and took you from your home. You owe his family nothing, but to flee this land and regain your freedom."

189

"The question The Father is asking you, Josiah, is can you forget yourself and what you want and think of the needs of another?"

"The Father, my eye," the booming voice of the actor suddenly interjected. "The roads are filled with oracles, magicians, and sooth-sayers like you. You've all got some mysterious answer to the ills of man. The boy was a slave; can't you understand that? Severus offers him freedom and you ask him to return to his owners and perhaps never see his home again, so it will make this Father, who no one can see, happy."

Jesus looked at the actor with an intensity that startled the man; not a threatening look, but a very knowing gaze. "You of little faith would see the world through a mirror. All you will ever know and serve is the face staring back. We are put here to be servants. You would deny this boy that road. You would tell him to serve only him-self, to be the king of his own little kingdom. I tell you and I tell him that there is a place greater than this — a place where the heart rules that is far more glorious than anything his home in Egypt will ever offer."

The actor, now in some anger, reached down and picked up a handful of dirt. He let it slowly run between his fingers in a dusty stream. "I have seen the dead. This is what they look like after a short time. This is where they, where you and I, will go. None of the gods I know of has ever sent a dead man back, nor have they revealed any kingdom of which you speak. We must drink deeply of this cup called life, for when it is empty, there is nothing left to taste."

There was a moment of silence. They all seemed to weigh what each had said. Jesus then said, "You know neither me nor my Father. I do not speak the empty words of the oracles. If you knew me, you would also know The Father. But you do not have ears to hear."

Severus scratched his chin. "Now that's interesting. That would mean that you and this Father are one, or somehow linked together." He looked at Seconius as though they were observing a new phe-nomenon. His voice was detached, though filled with interest. "I told you yesterday, Seconius, there was something special about this man, though I do question his idea of the boy not grasping my offer for freedom."

He looked at Benjamin who had been listening while he packed up his soup pot and prepared to pull his cart onto the road. "You are a Jew. Is this the talk of a Jew? Or is this man of another religion?"

Benjamin seemed a little hesitant, almost afraid to answer. He was a strict observer of every aspect of the Laws, to the point where he was reluctant to offer an opinion beyond what he knew. He spoke in measured terms. "He is a Jew, yes. He speaks from the prophets but I wish he would come and speak to our Pharisee and the scribes and lawyers of our area. I would like to know what they say." He paused, looking at Jesus, "I do think the Holy One has touched this man, this ordinary man, as He did Moses." Then hedging a little, he said, "But I would like the opinion of the authorities. I do hope that you will teach in our area, Jesus." Picking up the handles to his cart, he said, "I must be off now." And he pulled his cart into the growing traffic, suddenly afraid and uncertain of how to define Jesus.

"I must go, too," Jesus said as he picked up his baggage.

"We're heading that way after we gather our belongings. Boy, do you wish to see your home again, or do you wish to remain a slave in this land?"

Josiah looked at the ground, perplexed. Jesus had given him friend-ship and food, but this stranger offered him freedom. He felt a deep homesickness and a rush of anxiety about being alone in this alien land.

"I want to see my father again," he said quietly.

Jesus put his hand on Josiah's shoulder and smiled, "You have heard the Word; you now know there is One who loves you. If your heart seeks the comfort that only He can offer, then speak to Him and He will listen."

Josiah felt a soothing warmth as he looked into Jesus' eyes. He nodded that he understood.

Jesus shouldered his bags and headed toward Sepphoris.

"Today will be our last chance to kill Romans," Kokhba said as he stirred the embers inside their hideout. "We are late for plowing."

Azari'ah was eating almonds and wanting to return to Capernaum. He was glad this would be the last day. The thought of confronting the Roman guard again terrified him, and he felt ashamed of his fear. Local farmers had come to bring them breakfast and to receive what-ever clothing, accessories, or arms the group would parcel out.

As the zealot band planned their ambush, Nathan, his son, and four centurions approached the wooded area on their way to the apartment building. They had left before dawn. One of the lookouts burst into the hideout and said a small party was approaching and the rest of the road looked empty. The band of fourteen grabbed their weapons and bolted out the door and down the paths only they could see through the woods. Azari'ah wanted desperately to stay behind, but knew he must honor the name of his warrior father. So he scampered, bow in hand, after them.

They hid themselves in the thick growth of brush and trees and behind a scattering of rock and boulders. They could hear the high-pitched laugh of Nathan before they saw the group. The horses whinnied and jangled in their harnesses, their hoof beats clomped louder as they approached. Suddenly the noises stopped, and now they were close enough for the band to see them just down the way. They saw a tall boy dismount and walk into the woods near where Azari'ah lay hiding, though none of the men in the band realized he was there.

Azari'ah saw the boy dismount, cross the road and start to enter the woods where he sat crouched behind several large rocks. His eyes widened, his neck tightened, and he slowly pulled the bow to the front of him and placed an arrow in it. His hand was shaking as it had yesterday. He felt weak and totally confused over what to do. Should he kill the boy? He looked Jewish and said something in Hebrew as a cactus scraped his leg. What was he doing just walking toward him like this? And then as he started to pull down his trousers and relieve himself, he saw Azari'ah. The son of Dan stood and pulled the bow string until it was taut. He had the arrow pointed at Jonas who, startled, fell back against a small tree.

Azari'ah's arm shook violently, sweat beaded across his forehead, and he felt as though he would faint again. He wondered why the others did not attack, but Nathan and the troops had encountered a large camel caravan and had allowed their horses to wander along as they chatted with the Syrian drivers. The band had no choice but to remain hidden. They were not enough to attack so many.

"Aren't you Jewish?" Jonas blurted out in Hebrew, his eyes wide with terror.

Azari'ah felt uncertain about what to say or do, but he answered, "Yes, but not one who betrays the laws by riding with murderers of our people."

"But, but we must. To protect ourselves from..." then he caught himself, realizing he was about to accuse the boy with the arrow pointed at him.

Azari'ah said it for him, "From Jews who would kill Jews?"

Jonas did not know what to say. He heard his father's laugh, now distant, and knew they were moving up the road. He glanced to either side to see if there were a way to escape, but the bow, arched and quivering was only a few feet away.

Azari'ah mustered up a blustery voice full of bravado and feeling triumphant, he lowered the bow. "I don't kill Jews, only Roman centurions. But thank Yahweh you did not find me in a foul mood this morning. Now go! Ride with the murderers!"

Jonas backed away slowly, keeping his eye on the bow, then when he was a few feet away he turned and walked quickly through the remaining trees and out onto the road. His father's group were now some ways off with the caravan, and he gathered the reins of his grazing horse and galloped off exhausted from the scare.

"How long can it take someone to relieve themselves?" his father asked with a laugh.

Jonas said nothing. The words of the boy rang in his ears, and he felt an envy at the adventure this fellow Jewish boy must be having lying in ambushes. He also sensed a discomfort at riding with a Roman guard, an act scorned by most of his faith.

The retinue of Paulius was an hour behind. They spoke of encountering bandits and the tactics of hand to hand fighting: how to thrust and step back and lunge. They told stories of their own experience serving in the Roman army in Gaul and against the barbarians to the North of Italy. It was mandatory for the high born to serve if they hoped to stay in the ranks of the elite.

Just out of sight and to their side, twenty-four horsemen rode into the woods. "Ah, this is exciting!" Paulius boasted. "My hands have not formed on a sword handle in years. Hah! Yes! Let's do some battle here!" he cheered as much to himself as to his friends. They pushed their horses in the spirit of the moment and at the sight of the forest ahead.

From his forward position Azari'ah saw them coming and ran through the woods to the band, whispering loudly, "They come!"

Three of the guards were to the front, followed by Paulius, Julian and Cassius, two slaves, and a single guard to the rear. "This is a rich party. We will provide the poor with much from this group of devils." Kokhba gloated in anticipation.

Emboldened by his stand with Jonas and at not fainting, Azari'ah was eager to actually shoot his arrows at one of the guards, at least

193

from the wood's edge. As the party rode up, several arrows were released into their ranks. One hit the lead guard squarely on his helmet, knocking his head sharply to one side, but causing the arrow to glance off. A second arrow hit the man in the shoulder driving deep into him and piercing his heart. He slumped forward without a sound over his horse's neck. The band ran screaming like enraged animals at the Romans, whose horses were twirling in fright and kicking the dry dirt and dust in a angry cloud, crashing into one another and making it difficult for a defense to be mounted. Paulius gained quick control of his animal and spurred it forward into the charging Jews. Leaning down and bellowing at one Jew, he sliced his face almost in two with a mighty swing of his sword. Cassius had jumped from his horse, as had Julian, and they stood next to two soldiers in a traditional Roman formation like an armed wall.

Azari'ah never saw the sword coming at him. So caught up in the excitement of the attack and preparing to fire his arrow at Julian, he never heard the Roman guard moving out of the woods to surprise the attacking Jews from behind. The sword, swung from a horse, hit Azari'ah's raised bow first, easily cutting it in two, and that was enough to deflect it so the edge did not hit the boy in the head, but its broad side did. It knocked him sprawling into the road and left a gash across his cheekbone. His face was quickly covered in blood so the soldier assumed he had killed the boy and moved on to join the rest of the fight.

The killing did not take long. Caught between a fierce defense by Paulius' group and the troops pouring out of the woods, the Jews were hacked and stabbed unmercifully. Cassius ran one Jew through the back who was turning to see what the noise was behind them. Julian held back, seeing no point in killing the trapped bandits. Paulius thrust his short spear into one who had dropped to his knees with a wound. Only Kokhba escaped. He jumped on the horse of the first soldier killed and raced up the highway and into the woods. Several horsemen pursued him for a minute, but saw it futile to chase him in woods with which they were not familiar.

Five of the Jews surrendered and were severely beaten by the soldiers before being tied up. Those who were killed were tied to trees next to the road, so that all who passed could see them. Azari'ah was thought dead. He was being dragged by the feet to be tied to a tree when he moaned.

"This one lives!" A soldier shouted to his commander.

The leader walked over, looked down at the dusty, bloody boy and groused, "They even have their children out killing now. He will look good hanging from a tree. Tie him and throw him over my horse."

Dazed and terrified as he looked at the blood all over his shirt, Azari'ah felt the burn of the dirt and blood in the gash and stumbled against the horse. His hands were tied so tightly that he quickly lost feeling in them. Then he was rudely pitched over the big animal's rump so that his head hung over the other side. Azari'ah spoke mainly Aramaic and understood little of the Greek conversations going on around him.

Paulius was feeling lusty. He pranced around the dead, cleaning the tips of his sword and spear with fervor. "It does a man good to join in battle. It's good for the heart."

Cassius also felt good about having killed one. "What great sport, Paulius! Better to be in the fight than merely watching it as we did yesterday. Wonderful entertainment!"

Paulius was pleased that his client had such a thrilling adventure and would be the first to spread the news of the fight when they returned to Caesarea. Having killed a few outlaws would be good for business.

CHAPTER 10

There were already a number of workers sitting on the ground outside the apartment building when Jesus walked up. Three were Jews, the others Samaritans and Syrians. They had been hired by a short man with a thick neck and full lips. He held rolls of papyrus under his arms and was discussing something with the building manager whom Jesus had seen the day before. Jesus walked up to the workers and said in Aramaic, "The Eternal has blessed this day."

The Jews nodded and said, "So be it." The other workers did not understand Aramaic, so they ignored him, except to notice his unusual face and gentle nature.

Jesus and the workers sat in idle conversation about the building and the work each would be doing until one remarked, "We angered many in our village by coming here to work. They say it makes us unclean to work alongside gentiles. They don't weaken my faith; they strengthen it."

One of the Jews was a well-groomed man of medium height with the large arms of one who works with metal. An apron and metal-working tools were secured in a leather bag at his feet. He stood away from the other two Jews and his face seemed to puff with resentment. Jesus noticed this and said to the man, "You are from Jerusalem, are you not?"

The man looked up in surprise. "Are you some magician?" he growled.

"No, you just have the look of the pious. And now that I hear you speak, your tongue is from the Holy City. Welcome to Galilee."

"Galilee is not where I wish to be welcomed. It is a place of brigands, of thieves and those who know little about the Law and its observance."

Jesus moved closer to him. "I see you are of the guild of coppermakers. Your work must be one of the reasons the Temple is so magnificent."

The man was silent for a moment not knowing whether to overcome his disgust for Galileans in general, or to respond to this one who was showing some civility. He finally glanced at Jesus and answered, "The great works are finished there. Many skilled craftsmen now walk the countryside looking for work."

"Then this building will be blessed by your skills and the strength of your faith."

196

The man seemed a little puzzled at why Jesus was being so friendly, but he relaxed a little. "Your tongue is of Galilee, but your words carry more wisdom than I expected here."

"You will find the faith very strong here," Jesus smiled, "though in different ways than down in Judea."

The man scoffed, "The hills of the south may be parched, but the Word flowers there with a brilliance that will never be known in this land."

Jesus knew it was pointless to debate the issue. Galileans were looked down on as uncouth, undisciplined, hot tempered and loose in their faith. It was a prejudice generally ignored by the amiable Jews of the rich farmland known as Galilee.

"Are you a teacher?" one of the other men asked.

"I wish to be." It was the first time Jesus had admitted this to anyone and he felt a sense of pride after having said it.

"Then why are you working here and not at the Temple, or a School of the Books?"

Jesus lay his tools on the ground. "I will go there when I am ready, but for now I must work to help my family."

The coppersmith smiled and said sardonically, "The Father is great, especially on a full stomach. Those things we will not give up are our idols. If you cannot give up work to be a teacher, then you worship work before all else."

Jesus blushed and laughed in self-deprecation. The man was exactly right. How easy it was to make an excuse, he thought.

Jesus thought for a moment, then said to him, "You are right; we should not be anxious about our life, about what we eat, or about what we wear. For life is more than food, and the body more than clothing. Doesn't The Father feed the sparrows? Hasn't He clothed the lilies with a beauty that Solomon in all his glory could not attain? If we seek The Father's Kingdom, all things shall be ours."

The two Jews sat listening with great interest. Both were stone masons, avowed in their faith and dedicated to the scriptures.

"You are a teacher!" one exclaimed. "You must come to our village and say these things in our assembly."

The other, a swarthy man with a heavy, black beard and thick, short hair, said, "If you believe what you have just said, then I ask again, why are you here in this pagan capital and not before your own people teaching?"

The question went unanswered as the pounding of hooves and the jangle of bridles and leather announced the arrival of Nathan, Jonas, and their personal staff. "Ah, Decimus and Terence," Nathan greeted the architect and the Roman who managed the apartments.

Decimus walked up to Nathan who was astride his horse and said, "We owe considerable favor to your coming to meet with us."

Nathan dismounted slowly, tired from the ride. He stretched before returning the greeting. "No, you favor me by agreeing to use your renowned talent to help repair this old building. I have an interested buyer behind me. I would urge you to tell him of the splendid new designs you have for making this a place the high born would seek out."

Terence clasped Nathan's arm in greeting. He had managed the building for several years for Nathan, and though he roundly hated Jews, he did not consider Nathan a Jew and had a good relationship with him. Nathan just had more personality and was more open and approachable, Terence felt. He did not seem so caught up in his faith to the exclusion of all else.

Terence said with a big smile, "I hear that you want to make this one of the great buildings in Sepphoris. That is a delight after dealing with the rabble that live like rats here now. There are profits to be had, but not from the low class we have."

Nathan nodded. "But let's hear no more of that today. We have a Roman behind us who is interested in buying. I want you to speak more of the location we have near the villas yonder and of how you could keep the place rented when it is repaired."

"And this would not be a lie," Terence said. "I know many in Sepphoris. I can advertise the place at the baths."

Nathan gazed around at the workers reclining on marble benches and in the grass along the front of the building. "So what do you know of these men?" he asked.

Decimus said, "We've got some excellent metalworkers I've used before. They will be good for putting in the new balconies and the iron work I'm suggesting for the front. Over there are plaster men for the walls, tile men for the floor mosaics I showed you earlier, and a number of stone masons. There." He pointed at the Jews talking to Jesus. "I was told they are excellent at stone and woodwork. The one better dressed worked on Herod's temple and is very talented with copper. I have a magnificent fountain drawn here as a center point to the front, and I believe the tall one is a good all-around artisan. I don't know his work; he was recommended. I'll try him on the fountain."

Nathan's eyes lingered on the relaxed figure of Jesus. "Hmm... unusual looking," he mumbled.

Taking the plans from his architect, Nathan suggested, "Why not get them to work, while we go over the details. I want the place busy while the prospective buyer is here. It will take away from the miserable condition I have allowed the place to come to."

"Jonas," Nathan said. "Help out. It will do you good to work with your hands."

Terence smiled inwardly at the suggestion of a man of wealth ordering his son to work with his hands. No Roman of any rank would ever say that to his son. 'Work with your hands!' he thought in disbelief. Even the educated Jews have no self-respect.

It was mid-afternoon before Paulius and his entourage of guards and prisoners turned off the highway and into the lane leading to the building.

Paulius, seeing a possible fee if there were a sale, immediately started appraising the situation for Cassius. "A splendid location. Look at the villas in the hills there. Why you can see the temples of Antipas' palace and the fort over the tree line. And the workers look like bees swarming over the place." He then chuckled, "Nathan wasted no time. Let's go and look at the drawings."

They dismounted and the slaves led their horses to a large shallow cistern filled with water. The commander of the guard said, "I think we'll have some of that water too before going to the city."

Azari'ah's head throbbed painfully from his wound, and breathing was difficult because of the jostling ride and the way he lay across the horse. As the commander pulled his horses by the bridle, the wooden bit rubbed hard against the animal's tongue, and the horse jerked back causing Azari'ah to slide off and land on his back on the ground. The commander did not notice and the boy lay with the breath knocked out of him. One of the guards grabbed him and pushed him toward the cistern and the bowed heads of the drinking horses.

"Go and drink with the other animals," he cursed and pushed the boy sprawling into the water of the large circular clay pond.

Nathan came over and greeted them, "I feel brave today. I only had my son and a few aged guards to protect me. You bring half of the fort."

Paulius laughed heartily. "It was wonderful. We set a trap for bandits, and it worked perfectly. Eight were killed, and we have several prisoners. There lies one in your cistern, a boy, but still a murderer."

Nathan knew of the Jews who ambushed from the woods. He hated what they did, but also felt guilty because he was not a part of their fight. But for the most part, he worried that they would bring the wrath of the Romans down harder on the Jews and threaten what allowances the Emperor granted to them; this was the great fear of the Jewish ruling class and those of wealth and position. Nathan despised the Roman occupation, but a peace had been made with them that allowed the Jews to worship their God and govern their own people to a certain point. It was a delicate balance that depended on the Jewish priesthood maintaining some measure of control over the Jews at large. Pilate and Antipas were both capable of vicious retribution, especially Pilate.

Nathan walked that thin line between being true to his faith while working within the Roman system. His son came over as he was talking to Paulius and tugged at his sleeve.

"Father could I speak with you?"

"Huh?" Nathan saw a look of great concern on Jonas' face. As they stepped aside, they had a clear view of the guards having fun with Azari'ah and the other prisoners. They were shoving them against the flanks of the horses and from one horse to the other, as though they were balls being pitched around. All four prisoners were soon breathless, fell against the animals, then collapsed on the ground. The soldiers dragged them back to the cistern, shoved them over its shallow waters, held their heads under, and finally drowned one of the Jews. Azari'ah was left sputtering and gasping as his head came up, and he called, "Father!" in Hebrew.

The sight angered Nathan. And Paulius, ever aware of his clients, walked over to the commander and said quietly, "Cornelius, I believe my good friend, the legate, would say we should save them for hanging. No one sees their punishment if you kill them all for sport here."

Cornelius, realizing the rank of Paulius in Caesarea, said, "I was just thinking of that myself, honored one." And he ordered the punishment stopped.

Azari'ah was shoved on the grass against a large date palm where he fell, vomiting up water. Paulius saw out of the corner of his eye that Nathan and his son were having an animated conversation and looking at Azari'ah. He edged closer to them as he continued talking to the commander about investment ideas he had that might interest Cornelius when he left the guard. He overheard snatches of Jonas' urgings to his father.

"...Could have killed me...arrow at my heart. Can't...commander...him go?"

Nathan could be heard clearly to the focused ear of the lawyer. "I cannot ask that, my son. The boy might be a Jew, but he is also a bandit. We must live with the Romans. We cannot ask them to free one who would kill them."

Nathan then walked toward the front of the building where the workmen were obviously hard at work bringing the place to a new level of acceptance.

Paulius said, "Commander, this may be a place you would move to when your duties are up. Why don't you give my friend Cassius here your opinions on what improvements you might like?"

Flattered by the attention of one so powerful, Cornelius walked with Cassius and Julian over the lawn and across a stone terrace that ran the length of the front of the building.

Jesus was removing old window frames as the men approached, and he felt the anger of a nation at the swagger of the men as they walked. They had cultivated an air of arrogance to intimidate both Romans of lower rank and those they conquered.

Paulius ambled over to the dejected Jonas who was watching the crumpled figure of Azari'ah a few feet away. Hardly moving his lips, Paulius said, "The boy there will be hung from a tree for his crimes. He will scream when they nail his ankles to the tree, and you can hear it for a mile. After he hangs for a day, if the birds have not plucked out his eyes, a guard will come and club his knees until they are smashed, and he can no longer push himself up. He will scream again, but will soon begin to drown, choking on his own fluids and spitting up blood. It will be horrible for a mere boy to endure. Perhaps you might wish to show him one last act of kindness by loosening his wrists a little."

Jonas' eyes were wide. He swallowed hard at hearing these details about the horror of death by crucifixion, and also, of being challenged to help. His eyes darted to the few remaining guards. Most had gone to the fort. Five remained with the commander, and they strolled along with him thirty feet away to the front of the building. Their horses snapped at the early spring grasses. The animals had moved between the boy and the guard.

"Can we keep a secret?" Paulius asked Jonas.

"A secret?"

Paulius pulled a small dagger from a sheath on his belt, and secretly eased it into Jonas' palm. "Quickly now. Just loosen them a little. We, of course, do not want him to get free, just a little kindness before he dies."

He moved away from Jonas who stood transfixed for a moment, holding the dagger under his tunic, then frightened and shaking, moved behind the feeding horses and the date palm that Azari'ah lay against.

Crouched behind the big trunk of the palm, Jonas peered around to see the guards some distance away, all listening to the architect describe his plans. Looking around the tree, he saw Azari'ah's back to him and the thick ropes tightly tied around his wrists. Reaching around the tree trunk, Jonas cut at the rope, causing the boy to raise his soaked head from the ground and look back to see Jonas working intently on the rope to cut it. Their eyes met, both with the same terror and uncertainty of their meeting in the forest. Jonas sawed frantically at the tough hemp, finally cutting through it. Never saying a word, he pulled his hand back, but not before Azari'ah could reach out and touch it with a finger. Their eyes spoke without words. Both mouths turned up ever so slightly in recognition that both had now given the other life. Turning away, Jonas quickly hid the knife under a rock at the base of the tree, walked through the horses to the lawn, and moved nonchalantly toward the group.

Paulius caught the event out of the corner of his eye while appearing to be intently listening to Decimus and his plans. Through the legs of the horses, he saw Azari'ah scramble to his feet and run for his life down the drive and into the flood of humanity that filled the nearby road. Smiling to himself, he knew Jonas would relate what had happened to his father who, through his admiration, would without ever saying so, sell the building to Cassius at a very favorable price and Paulius would make his usual substantial fees.

"Let me show you exactly where I want these cast-iron balconies located," Nathan said. "We can have flower pots in each and I want a colorful window dressing of marble."

While the group watched, he climbed a ladder to the second story. "Here I want a curved..." and he reached out underneath a window. Suddenly there was a snap and the left hand side of the wooden lad-

202

der split. Nathan grabbed at the window sill, causing him to twist around and fall to the ground back first.

Paulius screamed, "No!" as Nathan hit the fieldstone terrace with a heavy, muffled slap. The flat of his back hit first, then came a sickening pop as his head, wrapped in a shawl, hit the stones. He lay motionless with a trickle of blood seeping out from the back of his head.

They all rushed around him, with Jonas running up and crying hysterically, "Father! Father!"

The commander Cornelius leaned over his still form and said, "I have done some doctoring on the wounded, let me see him." And he yelled Nathan's name, trying to see if he was conscious and turned his head to reveal the cut that now matted his black hair in blood. He felt for a pulse and found none. He held his hand against Nathan's nose and could feel no wind. Nathan's eyes were closed and when Cornelius opened the lids he looked into a vacant stare. Slowly looking up at the men crowded around, he pronounced with ringing finality, "This man is dead."

There was a groan among the men as Jonas broke through them and fell over his father, sobbing and pleading. Then without anyone seeing from where he came, a slender, rather tall man in work clothing appeared next to the fallen figure. Jesus had moved without thinking; an impulsive act propelled not by his own consciousness, but as though a compelling force directed him to this stricken man.

"Who are you?" Paulius demanded of this intruding worker who none of them knew.

"Why I am a servant of The Father," Jesus answered, sounding surprised he had even been asked.

"The what of the what?" demanded Paulius.

Cassius answered, "He said he's one of Nathan's slaves."

Ignoring their confusion, Jesus said, "This is a lamb whom The Father says is still needed by the children of the Nation."

Paulius' face screwed up in confusion at the answer.

Jesus leaned down and gently moved Jonas off his father. Jonas was as surprised as everyone else, yet did not resist.

"He must be a doctor," Julian offered.

"You waste your time," Cornelius said sadly, "I know a dead man when I see one."

Again, with little thought, Jesus placed his right palm flat against Nathan's still chest and pressed down while holding his left hand to the sky. He bowed his head in prayer and said in a firm voice, "Blessed is he who comes in the name of The Father. Blessed is this lamb, Nathan, who walks in Thy great light. If Thou would see fit to raise this man, Father, his days will be spent in walking in Your Name." And pressing very hard Jesus said, his voice trembling but intense, "Rise now, Nathan, for The Father breathes in you."

Jesus stood and the fallen man's eyes fluttered, his chest heaved, and he moaned.

"He lives!" Paulius said in disbelief.

Jonas cried out, "Father, you live!" Several of the men cried out in a kind of anguish and shock. The others buzzed with astonishment, looking down first at Nathan then at Jesus.

The commander Cornelius was visibly shaken. "Never have I seen this. The man was as dead as any fallen soldier. I felt his heart with my own hands, and there was no beat."

Like awakening from a dream, the reality of what he had just done swept over Jesus. He felt an exhilarating sense of acknowledgement. His heart raced with the excitement of a wondrous answer; a life changing purpose had been revealed to him. He felt full and whole and filled with a joy he had been agonizing to understand, but until this moment had only known in glimpses. They were stunned by the utter joy on the face of Jesus; a joy that transcended the moment, that was out of context with the ancient, sagging apartment building, the hot spring day, the clattering and cursing from the nearby highway. Then the shock of what they had seen gave way to a wave of conversations over what it meant. Was this man a god, a devil, or what?

Cassius leaned toward Julian's ear and smirked, "A magician no doubt. Or perhaps one of the gods showing off a little. The man does have a strange look about him as you can see."

Julian had been struck by what he had seen and said, "Or perhaps it was this god of the Jews he was speaking to; this strange god with no name or appearance."

"Oh, come, Julian. You are too much into fantasy," Cassius scoffed.

Paulius raised his brows, glaring at Jesus, "Just where did you come from? Are you a magician?"

"It does not matter where any of us came from other than to know it was The Father who sent all of us, including you. But it does matter where we are going and I say to you who have ears, the Word is among you. The Kingdom awaits those who will love The Holy One with all their heart and soul, who will ask forgiveness for their sins, love thy neighbors, and direct their lives to being good."

"Good?" Paulius scoffed. "You mean we have a god here who concerns himself with ethics and morality? So you are a philosopher, I would say," he corrected Jesus. "In this land ruled by Rome, what is good is decreed by the Emperor as being good."

Jesus looked angrily at the pompous lawyer, "Worship the devil, and you shall know a terrifying wrath."

"Will it be worse than a night of cheap wine?" Paulius laughed in mockery.

Nathan sat up on one elbow. The bleeding had stopped, but his head was hurting badly. "What…what happened?" he asked weakly.

"You were dead, father, and this…this…," his son did not know what to call Jesus.

"I was dead?" he asked, his eyes looking up at his son in confusion.

Cornelius answered. "I have felt for the heartbeat of many fallen soldiers and you were dead." He looked at Jesus and felt he wanted to drop to his knees, or touch his hem, or say something, but he was at a loss, and could only ask, "What are you called?"

"I am the son of man as are you, Cornelius."

"Have we met? How do you know my name?" He was very disturbed and bothered by the fact that this workman knew his name, and he worried if he were a devil, or a god. And it became more and more terrifying to think that he, Cornelius, in all of his power as a commander of a Roman cohort, could be so shaken by this event and this man.

"We will meet in the Kingdom, for the Holy Light has entered you, and The Father will speak through you when the time is right."

Nathan, holding his head in pain, grimaced and asked, "Would you be more than a teacher? No Pharisee can perform such a miracle. Are you the one the prophets spoke of?"

"We are all priests," Jesus was stalling, trying to collect his thoughts; he was thrilled at what apparently he had done and bolstered by what it implied. "Believe in The Father with all your heart and strength, and He will act through any of us."

Jesus found the words flowing out of him in a unplanned rush. He couldn't truly accept that Nathan had actually been dead, nor what had propelled him to suddenly step in and attempt to revive the man. He thought as he talked that something profound was going on within him, and he allowed himself to go with it.

"You must stay," Nathan insisted. "I will give you an apartment here and provide you with food. We could have Jews come from all over to hear you and see you heal."

Paulius whispered to Cassius, "It would be great for business! We could charge extra for those renting here. We could even charge for entering the grounds to see the healer."

Julian had pulled out a small ink bottle and reed and was doing a quick sketch of Jesus, but he could not get his face right, and he kept scratching over one face after another, as he attempted to capture his likeness. Frustrated with that, he wrote down some of the words Jesus had said.

"Cassius, this is truly remarkable," he exclaimed. "We have witnessed a human doing work reserved for the gods. Think of the great story this will make back home."

Cassius had been studying Jesus carefully. He was moved enough by the event to ask, "Which of the gods are you?"

"You fool!" Jesus rebuked him, his eyes flaring. "I look at your pompous face and see all the devils of the earth. You think this life is nothing but a folly, a pointless wandering, that in the end it means nothing but to say you were a good soldier, gave to the community, and were obedient to the Emperor. It is an emptiness that will haunt you forever. You know nothing of the Kingdom and never will!"

Cassius' lip curled in a show of contempt. "You damned barbarian Jew! You do not talk to one of my position like that. I'll have you flogged till there's no skin left on your bones!"

Paulius saw how this could get out of hand with Cassius and Nathan arguing over Jesus, so he stepped in front of Cassius, so close that their faces were almost pressed together. He said with all the force he could command, yet still quietly, "Forget the damned Jew, we've got a deal to make here."

Nathan was sitting up now and said, "Say your name, healer."

The anger fled from his face and Jesus looked down and said, "I am Jesus, son of Joseph from nearby Nazareth."

"Nazareth? Never heard of it. Was your father on the court at the Temple?"

Jesus almost laughed. "No, no, he was but a carpenter, as am I."

Nathan seemed confused. He looked Jesus up and down, and then as though struck by some revelation he exclaimed, "All of this makes sense; Isaiah said that Yahweh would send His arm and He would be a humble man, a sufferer. By the faith, you could easily be that one. My life is honored by your presence."

Jesus looked at him kindly saying, "Nathan, I must end my work here. The Father has spoken through you and told me that I have other work to do." Touching Nathan on the shoulder in a goodbye, he edged his way through the soldiers to his tools and baggage.

Nathan grabbed his son's arm, saying urgently, "Go and ask if he would come to our home in Caesarea. Tell him he can teach from our home. Go! Hurry!"

Jesus approached the Jewish workers who were standing in awe. One of them said, "Master, you are close to The Holy One. This was a true miracle. Many can heal and others tell of the future through the stars, but no one brings the dead to life. You are truly holy." They knelt before him touching his legs.

Jesus felt gratified, but a little embarrassed at this worshipful attention, and suddenly exhausted. "It is our Father who is holy, beloved. Kneel before Him alone and all of the love of the Kingdom will be yours."

Jonas ran up. "My father asks that you come to our home and teach there. We have many rooms. You could stay with us."

"The Heavenly Father used your father as a vessel from which to pour out His message to me, and I owe Nathan gratitude. Tell him I will come and visit, but first I want to teach across Galilee from many tables and fields."

Jesus walked away, filled with an unrestrained joy, a thrill surpassing any emotion he had ever known. This was a sign, he was sure. He quickly ran over the scene in his mind. 'I prayed, I believed, I touched him.' But doubt also shadowed his elation. 'Was Nathan really dead?' The Jewish workers and soldiers watched in some confusion. They half expected one who had performed such an act to do something else; they wanted more, but all they saw was a man with tears running down his cheeks as he passed them.

One of the guards scoffed, "He cries. Looks like he's a weak god, if he is one at all."

Jesus felt radiant and silently walked toward the horses to head down the drive to the road. He was propelled by an inner voice to leave, to go, to start the mission. Julian walked away from his friends and caught up with Jesus.

He felt like a schoolboy trying to get the attention of his teacher. "I have written your words. I will study them later to understand their meaning. Did your invisible god give you this power to raise the dead?"

Jesus looked at him in sympathy, "Julian, you are of a kind heart, but you worship at the altar of your own mind. Before you study the earth and its people, study the Commandments. The Heavenly Father gave you a mind to know of His love first and then all of the wonders of His earth will unfold. Until and unless you realize this, your wanderings here will have been for nothing. The truths you seek are not in distant lands. They are as close as your own heart." Jesus looked into Julian's eyes and the artist was swept with emotion. He was transfixed by the stare and was overwhelmed with an urgency to ask more questions, to probe and discover what was going on here. Just who was this man: a miracle worker, a magician, or a god?

"Where do you go now?" he asked, too struck to say anything of substance.

"Near Jericho where a very holy one speaks of the Coming. The word here is that the fire that will consume the wicked is starting soon on the Jordan. I shall go see the one who makes this claim."

Shifting his bags, Jesus then said, "Open your heart to the joy, Julian."

"To the joy?" Julian asked in a mumble, as though the word was foreign. He felt the firm hand of Cassius on his shoulder.

Cassius spoke loudly, covering an unsettling anxiety he felt as he looked at Jesus. "Well, Julian, we've had our entertainment by the magician, let's get about making some money here."

Julian felt frozen and did not move.

Jesus pulled himself to his full height. He was as tall as Cassius, but not as thickly built; still, he was impressive in the straightness of his stance. There was a definite bearing about his build, though it was more lean and sparse than bulky, more sinewy than muscular, but thickened hands and bulging forearms spoke of years of wielding a hammer and carrying building stone.

"Money is for today, Cassius," Jesus said. "The Kingdom is forever."

Cassius laughed nervously, "Good, then Julian can make money and worship his gods today, then worship your invisible god and his invisible kingdom..." he stopped in some confusion. "Forever? What is forever but the void of death?" It was a concept that made no sense to the Roman who believed that death was a peaceful state of nothingness.

"The Father's Kingdom is not of this world, and it is eternal, but you cannot be received into it if you worship other gods." Jesus' voice was firm, but assuring.

Cassius scoffed, "Oh, now the God that is feared, though He can't be seen, is also selfish and jealous and demands His worshippers pay homage only to Him! I sense there is a host of gods surrounding us now, all laughing heartily at this comedy. It's too bad they can't see your god, or they would all thrash Him mightily for being so impudent."

Jesus smiled and kept a steady gaze into Cassius' eyes who saw it as an insult coming from one he perceived as a magician at best, and a low life rural at worst.

Cassius subconsciously placed his hand on the short sword latched to his belt. He wanted to strike this man down and to run from him. He was becoming convinced that the carpenter must be a devil who was trying to play tricks with his mind. There was something magnetic about the certitude, fearlessness and subdued gentleness that he had never encountered, and he felt anxious, even fearful. Cassius' life had been sheltered within the privileged elite where gaining power and status, and constantly exhibiting one's masculinity was the ideal to which all men aspired. He had never felt this way confronting a man before, and being confused over who this man was and being angry at his own ineptness, he tugged at Julian's inanimate arm.

"Tell him you'll draw his picture if he doesn't leave, Julian," He teased in a voice that sounded like a scared boy trying to bluff his way out of an overwhelming presence.

Julian said nothing, staring all the while with a dumb struck look at Jesus.

Jesus pressed his lips together in an acknowledging smile, and raised his hand to both men. "May the Righteous One enter both of you and give you peace." With that he turned slowly and walked down the short flagstone paved drive to the busy highway.

Cassius felt a relief and tapped his sword, "He's lucky he left. I was about to rend his ignorant heart with steel," he sneered.

Julian strained to see Jesus as he walked into the traffic of wagons, people, and rolling clouds of dust that hung like a perpetual curtain from the constant stamping of camels, donkeys, and humans.

Cassius stepped in front of Julian's dazed look and said with some concern, "Dear friend, I fear this magician has cast a spell on you. Nathan was never dead. He had the breath knocked from him. This was no miracle, no act of the gods." He clasped Julian's arms and squeezed them. "We have lingered here too long. Paulius must wonder what we are about. Ah, Nathan is now standing. Let's join them."

Finally, Julian nodded as though he had returned from some distant thought and with his composure returning, he smiled with some bravado and said, "Of course. Let's join them. There's money to be made and frescoes to be drawn."

Cassius breathed a sigh of relief, but only after subtly averting his eyes toward the highway until he could no longer see the thin figure of the most troubling man he had ever met.

CHAPTER 11

Galilee was a garden in the early spring. The dark earth of its fields yielded miles of grains, corn, and an almost endless variety of fruits and vegetables. Its soft hills gave way to broad flat valleys where the march of civilizations had filled the ground with layers of lifetimes. Plows constantly smashed through old pots, snagged on pillars of lost temples, and opened the sunken tombs of generations of the forgotten. It was a land where the dead guided the living. There was a permanence to it, an anchoring effect, a fusion where the lines between past and present were so blurred they often seemed like one. The words of the prophets permeated conversations as naturally as though the prophets were neighbors, or could be found still teaching in the Temple. To dig up the past in a field was to affirm it, and to reaffirm the Truths of the ancients about wars, warriors, and the power of the One God.

Jesus took his time walking back toward Capernaum, enjoying the early blooms, feeling the sun's warmth, and praising The Father to any and all who would listen. But he was not entirely at peace within himself. His message of servitude and renewal of faith was scoffed at by as many as it amazed and enthralled. The question, the ultimate question by those who doubted was by what authority Jesus made his claims. But he arrived in Capernaum, emboldened with the surety that his message was the truth. He thrilled to its simplicity, and worked on phrases and stories as he walked to make it reflect more the life of the Jewish peasant, and to give it a memorable uniqueness. He determined that he would follow an old custom of speaking in parables. It was a method of presentation and teaching for which he found he had a natural talent.

Because he realized how easily he could be misunderstood, and how easily many could reject what he said, Jesus concluded that he would only be successful if his message was directed toward those who truly wanted to hear and discover. Parables were the layered message with which to do that. Those who passed him on the road saw a man absorbed in his thoughts, talking to himself at times, stopping to study a flower, or watch the darting swirls of a swallow. One of the endless philosophers, they thought, or perhaps a man mad in the head, a wandering dreamer.

Jesus did not miss a chance to stop and talk with those working the fields, listening to their worries and hearing of their hopes for the

211

new growing season. Their prayers were for rain at the right time and for relief from the cycle of debt. But most simply wished for survival and enough extra denari to pay for the coming Passover in Jerusalem.

It was late afternoon when he entered Capernaum. He walked straight down to the quay to see if Simon and Andrew were in from fishing. They could be seen out on the waters pulling in nets. He recognized Simon, even at a distance, because of his burly size, and the faint semblance of his gruff voice cursing the fish as he hauled them in. The docks were small but busy, with fishermen and those who would buy their catch. There was loud dickering, the smell of fish, boats battering against the stone slips that jutted out into the lake, and men draping their dripping nets over racks to dry during the night.

"Jesus!" a voice called out. It was James, the son of Zebe-dee. He and his brother and father were spreading their nets on racks along the shoreline.

Jesus smiled and waved as he walked off the quay and along the shore to the men. "You work too hard; you should have been a plow maker." Jesus grinned as he watched them sorting out the heavy netting. "I saw a little, hammer a little, and…"

"Yes, and you make very little," the short, wiry James joked. They had met a year earlier while Jesus worked on several new houses in Capernaum. A casual conversation had led to many long talks between Jesus and the two brothers about their faith and the state of the people. The brothers were angry at the Romans, and angry at the compromising Sadducee priests and their wealth at the Temple. All looked for a Messiah.

"We've not seen you in a while," said John, also small-of-frame and statue, but possessed of large arms and thick hands.

"I have had much work, but I have also been thinking and praying," Jesus said as he sat on the grassy slope of the little bank that led from the water to the waterfront street of the village. He watched as they sorted through the tangle of nets. He was tired and hungry from his walk. They had two goat skin containers from which they were sipping date wine.

"You look weary," the older Zebe-dee observed. "Have some wine. It's not the best, but it will rest you after a long day."

He accepted and took a long drink. "I have missed our discussions," Jesus said as he wiped his lips with the back of his hand. "The countryside is alive with talk as we have had."

"Oh, we hear it at the docks all the time," James offered with some anger in his voice. "The common Israelite works himself to death, while our leaders enrich themselves with our taxes and sacrifices. How else could they wear the robes and jewelry they do?"

"We know the Romans to be devils and they act it. But our own, they have become like Romans in their grab for treasure. We don't know who to throw out first," John said.

The father, a tall, angular man with a white beard and mustache said, "You say that you have thought and prayed. I remember when we spoke last, I was impressed with your words. Have you any new thoughts on the prophecies?"

"I have found that many of our people have the faith the size of this grain of sand. They long for The Father to come and relieve them of their poverty, their sickness, their desire to have what the priests have, to rid our Nation of the evil that is Rome, the false gods of the Greeks. They talk of a Messiah, of a new King David, of signs that will say Yahweh is coming. Many are like the wanderers who live off the corner of the field. They expect the owner to do all the work. And I mean our priests when I say that."

James finished repairing a portion of the netting and walked over and sat next to Jesus. His hair was very thick and curly. He was clean-shaven; his skin a light, olive tint. He was in his twenty-seventh year, but the incessant sun had wrinkled him so that he looked older. His eyes came to anger easily. "You say that we should rise up ourselves? That we should go against our own leaders, or that we should drive the Romans out?"

"That's what I say!" John said firmly as he joined them on the bank. "Our land is defiled by our leaders as much as the devils from Greece and Italia. Greek is now the language of our land. Profit is the goal of the day. Gods of every description line our roadways in their little temples erected by anyone with the money to do so. But I find that many around the sea here are more determined than ever to keep their covenant with Yahweh. And many would join in arms against the Romans if a leader could be found. We might even get the community of bathers that dwell in our villages to join us." He had lowered his voice so his words would not go beyond their reclining forms.

"Hello there!" It was the unmistakable booming voice of Simon. He and his brother had brought their boat into dock and were lifting baskets of fish out on the dock. While Andrew and two other men dealt with several buyers, Simon ambled off the docks with a man as

213

thin as the reeds growing in the sea's shallows. He wore a bleached white robe that stopped at his knees. His hair and beard were carefully trimmed. Jesus noticed how unusually clean the man's fingernails were compared to most working men's. They came over to the grassy area; Simon reached down, grabbed the wine skin in his great hand, then turned it up.

James smiled with a look of chagrin, "I'm glad he doesn't drink water. Every cistern in Galilee would be empty."

John smirked, "This man needs his own grape orchard." He pointed with his finger to the man with Simon, "Jesus, this is Izaius. He fishes with this lion-throated blasphemer. He has vowed to convert Simon to the community of the poor where he will: move to Qumran, take a vow of celibacy, stop swearing, and bathe constantly."

Izaius roared in laughter, knowing Simon as he did. Izaius had a dark beard and his face was small and very tanned. His coloring stood dramatically against the white of his clothing. The others had more soiled and stained dress. "I would have better fortune in driving out the Romans than making this fish-breathed wine lover walk the straight path, especially if it included keeping his eyes off fancy women." He was looking at Simon now sprawled out on the cool grass bank.

Simon burped loudly and grinned broadly as if to insult their remarks about his appetites. "Well, Jesus, it is good to see you back so soon, but you sit in very rough company here. These might be men of the dagger who will poke an unfaithful Jew quicker than they will slice up a sleeping Roman guard."

Zebe-dee left the netting, picked up another goat skin and walked over to them. He stood very erect. He was fifty-five and quite strong in his shoulders from years of hauling in nets laden with frantic fish. "Simon, your mind is getting as large as your arms. You know my two rogue sons well. They would hold the laws in one hand and a sword in the other and rally all the other hot heads in a suicidal fight against Jews and Romans alike, against all who did not agree with their interpretation." He said this with the sarcasm of a father who enjoys kidding his children, but does so with a grain of truth in his humor.

Simon looked at Jesus who was staring serenely across the flat surface of the lake. It was as though the waters were lazing in the late afternoon, knowing the day's efforts were ended. Jesus had removed the covering on his head and his hair was matted down where the covering had pressed against it.

"I have thought much of your words, Jesus. I wish you would say more to our friends here," Simon said.

Jesus paused for a moment as though it were taking an effort to come out of the dreamy look he had while gazing at the sea. He then spoke with a calm conviction. "The Nation is badly split, as we were just saying. We are lambs wandering in search of a shepherd, even though The Holy One, whose path that we should follow, is very clear in His instructions. He asks that we prepare now for His coming. We will not be restored as a nation until we come together as a nation in repentance for the sins we commit daily. I travel the land; I see the poverty, but it is as much a poverty of the spirit as it is of treasure. We do not prepare our hearts and minds for the coming Kingdom as much as we worry about the robes we desire, the new oxen we want, the taxes we must pay to Pilate and Antipas, or the correct way to observe our endless laws."

Simon responded initially with some annoyance, "But of course we want better robes and, no, we don't want to give our meager coins to the devil Antipas." He missed Jesus' point. "Yes, I agree we are badly split as a people. So we need a leader. We need a Messiah who will unite the people. Then we can drive out the Romans."

Izaius spoke up as he sat with his arms folded on his knees. "As you know, we in the community believe there will be two Messiahs, and we are convinced that the Coming is near. The Teacher of Righteousness was told by The Holy One years ago what we in the Community must do to prepare for it; that is to prepare to fight alongside the angels. It will be very bloody and terrifying, and unfortunately, most of the children of Israel will perish."

Jesus seemed engrossed in his own thoughts and as he continued to stare out across the softening colors of dusk painting the waters in pinks and purples from the setting sun, he said in a distant voice, "The Kingdom comes and the Nation is not ready. They must hear the Word. They must prepare for the Coming. It is close, I tell you; it may even be about us now."

The four men looked at him in some astonishment. James asked, "Do you say the End of Days is here and now? Oh, that would be the greatest joy we could know; that the heavens are about to open and The Holy One is coming with all of His vengeance."

"I tell you that it is so," Jesus looked at each of them with a steady eye.

They didn't know how to take it. It was a bold, possibly blasphemous statement, and one that momentarily stopped the conversation as each man studied the carpenter. For anyone to interpret a scripture by saying, 'I' and not 'so say the prophets' was dangerous. They looked over his face, especially his eyes with their intensity and assuredness. His brows were thick and black, forming a dark line under which his brown eyes glistened. They looked for something special about his clothing, even his worn bags, his dusty boots, but to all appearances he seemed as they did except for his facial features: a landscape of contrasts, as Rebekah had thought, but riveting in its configuration.

James, after a long pause, asked, "You say so, but who told you?"

Jesus said with the utmost confidence, "The Holy One told me."

There was an audible gasp. Izaius, whose strict and highly disciplined sect of the faith was convinced the end was near, was not surprised that Jesus had stated it was coming, but like the rest was surprised to hear Jesus say he had been told directly by the Lord. He looked around suspiciously to see if anyone on the street just above them was listening.

"You say Yahweh speaks directly to you?" He asked.

Jesus' face had a serenity about it that none of the men had seen in their previous meetings with him. "Why should it be surprising that The Father speaks to me. Does He not speak to you? I say His breath is in all of us; His Word is in the fields and on the waters of this sea. He is around us and with us now. He speaks to us and through us, each and everyone."

Simon became excited as he had in his last encounter with Jesus, saying, "He said these things to me in my home, and I was greatly surprised. I think he is a new teacher, possibly even a prophet. He looks as one who owns little."

"I find myself seeking out the truly poor, the destitute, the lepers, and those mad in their minds. It is said that we must stand at the right hand of the poor, and we will receive a reward from Him who stands at the right hand of The Holy One. Does it not insult the poor to stand before them in fine linens and jewels?"

Simon offered a whimpering request, "But couldn't you dress up a little — look a little more like a teacher instead of just a...laborer?"

"Did The Holy One dress Adam? He wore only The One's love and it was enough."

Simon chuckled mischievously, "Well, Jesus, you could teach naked. That would sure get the attention of the women!"

While the others grinned, Izaius looked very serious. It was obvious he was provoked in his thoughts by what Jesus just said. "I disagree, or I should say, the Community of which I belong disagrees, that lepers, the blind, and the mad have a place in the coming Kingdom. But I like your idea of our people returning to the simplicity of the First Man. I do like that," he repeated.

"Are we not all teachers and priests? Weren't we given a special place in the eyes of The Father? Though He dwells in the Holy City, He also dwells in every heart, but it is up to you to give that heart to Him. It is up to you to knock at His door." Jesus looked over the men then around the banks and said with great earnestness, "I can feel His Presence over all of us at this moment. Unseen, but I can see Him in the beauty of each of you."

Simon felt uncomfortable at the mystical nature of Jesus, but at the same time was riveted by it. "We're good sons of Abraham," Simon blurted out. "The Holy One should be here."

James asked, "But, Jesus, you say it is not enough to be a good observer of the Law?"

"Works alone are not enough. Being a son of Abraham is not enough. You must give all of yourself, be willing to give up all that you own and love, then the Kingdom will be yours."

Simon was interested in the opinion of Jesus about the End of Days. "So the Father has told you, and you actually heard this, that The End was coming?"

"No one can say the exact hour or day, but it is close at hand. It is the past. It is now, and in the future, and we, as a Nation, must come together under His banner."

Zebe-dee had been listening to the dialogue. "I have often wondered what the Messiah will look like," he mused. "It is said that one like the son of man (in human form) will come clothed in a long robe and a golden girdle around his breast, and descend on a white cloud with a golden crown on his head. Have you thought of these things, Jesus?"

Jesus was sitting with his legs crossed. His back was very straight. "We worry too much over what the messenger will look like," Jesus said. "Other scriptures say he will be an ordinary man. Zechariah even says he will be pierced and the people will mourn for him. I see a messenger who will be sent to suffer for the sins of the Nation and may be killed. The power of his message will be more than many want to hear."

Zebe-dee sat upright, almost screaming, "No! No! The Son of The Holy One could never be killed by man. He comes himself to kill and to rule. He would be invincible!"

The others were startled as much by the older man's outburst as they were by Jesus' statement. Their eyes darted to Jesus.

He looked removed from them. His face had a radiance that was a curiosity in its absoluteness. None of the men could remember seeing someone look like that.

As he looked directly at Zebe-dee, Jesus' eyes misted with tears, and he responded almost in a whisper, "the son of man will be a messenger who will teach the Nation how to become one with The Father. Why would The Father send His own Arm to kill the children?" Jesus asked rhetorically. "He wants all to enter His door."

"All?" Simon asked as though the thought was incomprehensible.

"Did The Father not make all of the peoples?" Jesus asked with a logic that broke beyond customary Jewish thinking.

James looked at Jesus in a questioning way. "We heard from a horseman that a wealthy Jew from Caesarea fell from a ladder and was pronounced dead outside of Sepphoris. A carpenter there, a woodworker from Nazareth, placed his hands on the man and he came back to life. They say it was a miracle. Was that man you?"

Jesus looked reluctant to speak, paused, then answered, "The Father works through us all. His signs are everywhere." Then feeling humbled by the implications of the question and uncertain of himself, Jesus said humbly, "Some said the man was not really dead."

"So it was you who did this?" Izaius asked with great interest and excitement.

"I was there, but The Father works through each of us if we have enough faith. I would not speak of it again." Jesus dismissed the event with an embarrassed shrug.

"I don't think people return from the dead. He must have been knocked out," Zebe-dee said as he shook his head in doubt.

"You are truly a new teacher, and maybe a miracle worker," Simon exclaimed to Jesus, ignoring the request to forget the event. "You should tell others what you tell us. Perhaps you will find that many want to follow you. We could have an army before you know it," he said eagerly.

"Simon, I don't seek armies to change this world. Change can come only when all of the children of Israel change. Then our Nation will be restored," and he pointed his finger at them for emphasis, "but only when we are born anew, born of water and of the spirit."

Simon's eyes blazed. "A holy army! He's right, you know!" he exclaimed and looked at the others. "We can only restore our Nation if we all come together under one banner, the banner of Yahweh. We're too split today. We have no common cause. We can't even agree on our own religion. Don't you see?"

James, John, and their father nodded vigorously.

Izaius looked contemplative, studying Jesus. "The Community of the Poor would agree with much of what you say, but we are very strict about who we would accept in our community. No lepers, sinners, fornicators, blind, or crippled. Would you include them in your army?"

Jesus stood and shouldered his bags. He felt they had again missed his point. "Would you limit the power of The Father to accept who He wishes? There are many doors to His mansion. But it will be His choice to say who enters. Ours is not to judge for Him." He looked down at them sitting attentively on the grass. "I will go and pray that if a few of us come together it will show the way for others to come and join."

John caught the idea saying, "We could call ourselves 'The Way.'" He looked at the others for approval. They all nodded thoughtfully and agreed 'The Way' sounded good.

"I am going to the Community at Qumran and then to hear the Baptizer. I would hear for myself how both of these might help bring the Nation together. When I return, I might seek each of you. We will see then what you truly want to fish for."

He smiled at each of them, touching each shoulder before walking down the shoreline toward the west. When he passed the dock and the city, they saw him in the distance kneel in prayer along the shore. They had been silent the whole time he was walking, and then Simon said, "The Holy One has come to this man unlike any I have ever seen. He has changed even in the past few days. Could he be more...than a teacher? There are many miracle workers, you know, whom The Holy One works through. But this one is unusual, different from other healers I have heard."

Izaius said, "I am traveling to Qumran tonight. I will tell the Guardian that this man comes and that he speaks of the Coming and of raising an army, as do we."

John mused, "I thought he said he wasn't seeking an army, but if he is, I wish that he had more…" he stumbled for words, "spears, swords; we will need weapons to fight with. If he is going to start an uprising to throw out the evil ones, he will need more than words. I will tell our friends to tell their friends we have found one who will raise an army."

"Well, if he really did bring a man back from the dead, I would say he has the powers to slay the Romans by himself," James said. "Do you think he did that? Could the man have been truly dead? I've never heard of such a thing."

"I've never heard a man such as him," Simon felt a growing confidence, a commitment to the figure still kneeling on the shore in the orange wash of the falling sun.

CHAPTER 12

Jesus filled the doorway of his mother's one room house. She was placing thick boards over the shallow pit which held her cooking fire. The floor was made of flagstone. She looked up in surprise. "I didn't think you would be back so soon," Mary said as she positioned the boards so the embers could not touch them and set the house ablaze during the night.

He grinned and handed her two coins. "I've taken a vow of poverty, and I was getting too rich."

"Ha!" she laughed abruptly. "Poverty should come easily to you."

"I remember when you and your father had all that building work at Bethsaida," she said as she admired his tall, straight frame. He was built so much like his father, she thought. He had Joseph's very brown piercing eyes and the reddish-brown hair of his grandfather Jacob. "We bought a second plowing ox with the earnings. But your father gave most of the money to those in need around Nazareth." She looked wistfully over Jesus' shoulder as though she were looking at her husband.

"It gave him the greatest pleasure to give to those in the Community of the Poor living in Nazareth. He believed they were the purist of the sons of man, but he was not willing to give us up and move to Jerusalem and live with them. He was a holy man. His pleasure was in giving. He was truly a servant." She looked away as the memories swept over her.

"Mother, I want to follow more in the steps of The Father." Jesus pulled off an over wrap and sat on a small, cushioned stool next to an oil-burning hand lamp. The room was warm, and the light of several lamps gave it a pleasant softness.

She looked back at Jesus and said, "Well, I would hope that you would son. You and Joseph were very close, and I know his death hurt you deeply."

Jesus hesitated a moment, realizing she had misunderstood him. "No, I mean I wish to come closer to the heavenly Father."

She absentmindedly reached into a large clay jar for several barley cakes. From another jar she pulled out a handful of raisins and put them on a plate with the barley cakes and handed it to him. She poured some goat's milk from a skin into a cup and gave him that. Earlier, she had parched some grain in her iron skillet and mixed it with salt. Going to a long shelf bowing heavily in the middle with the weight of an endless array of bowls and pots, she gave him a portion of the parched grain.

He looked at the food placed on the table, then looked at her with a sense of gratitude. "Mother, you have been the center of our family for many years now. It has been of great comfort to me knowing that I could always come to you for love and," he waved his hand over the food, "to share in anything that you have. But my life has changed, and I will be taking a path that leads away from my work and possibly from my family."

She was confused and wiped her hands nervously on her apron. "What do you say?" Her voice was urgent; the words came out in a cry. "Would you move to another land?"

"No, I would become a teacher. It will take me away from here for long periods. It will require that I give all of my heart and soul to walk in the Word."

She sat next to him at his feet. Her eyes were perplexed and anxious. "I don't understand. If you wish to teach the scriptures, you would need to get more schooling, and that is for the young in the School of Books."

"My father called me to the faith as a youngster as did the traveling Pharisee who set up school in Nazareth. A boy could have had no better teachers. But I am now called by the heavenly Father, and it is a more urgent call. It demands that I carry a message that says the prophecies are now to be fulfilled — that I go to the sons of man and tell them that we must be born anew. But it is not a story of wrath or fear; it is a glorious promise of joy, of forgiveness, of hope. It is a story that says we are all connected to one another by the gift of life and of love."

His intensity and conviction seemed to pull him away from her; she could feel it, like a rending, a separation that filled her with the loss a mother feels when a child, regardless of his age, leaves. There was heavy finality about his words and the way he was saying them. She had lost him, and she was confused and a little disturbed over the way he was talking.

"I am overjoyed, son, that The Holy One has touched you, but what is this talk of being reborn? I've not heard any scribes or Pharisees speak of it."

"Our own people argue endlessly over the Laws. Many of our leaders enrich themselves because of their knowledge of the Laws. Satan influences the interpretations to divide or enslave us. Instead, we need to join as one in the Word, but first we must individually seek that more perfect time of Adam, when man was as one with The Creator. I will tell this to those who have ears. Many will be angered, but a few will enter through the narrow gate I describe." He look burdened and sad. "Few will understand, Mother."

"Shouldn't you testify in the names of the prophets from whom you speak?" Mary looked perplexed.

"I have been criticized for not starting every sentence with, 'and so say the prophets,' but this is my way of saying what I believe. I know that my words ride on the breath of the Almighty."

"Son!" She gasped, bringing her hand to her mouth. "Are you saying...who do you think you are?"

"I am a lamb of the Shepherd, a child of The Holy Father, as are you and all of Israel. The Father speaks to each of us, but few listen, because few are willing to do what is clearly written in the scriptures. But The Father speaks to me clearly about these sayings, so I have no need to start every sentence by saying from what authority I speak."

She stood and paced the little room, fidgeting with jars along the shelves, her mind racing between joy and concern, confusion and relief that this son was so much like his father, but fearful that he was going too far in his beliefs. The thought even crossed her mind for an instant that her son might be a heretic; one blinded by his pursuit of the correctness of the scriptures as only he saw them. She didn't want to lose this beloved boy to the extremes that were familiar to all who walked the roads. The road teachers who ranted with the abrasiveness of squawking crows were either stoned or dismissed as crazy.

"You must be careful, son. You must be very careful in how you, a builder, interpret the scriptures. Many have been killed for going too far. You must not sound as though The Holy One spoke directly to you, or the knife men will stab you, or the religious leaders will have your body broken with stones." There was almost a terror in her eyes.

"But where would you speak? And to whom?" She pressed him.

"I will speak to all who will listen wherever they are — in the fields, at tables, or in houses of assembly."

"If you feel The Holy One so strongly, why not go to Jerusalem and speak on the Temple steps as you did as a child?"

He shook his head. His eyes narrowed and seemed to draw back under his thick brows. "A child can be a wonderment; a man can be a threat. Much of what I now believe is critical of the way the Temple is being abused. To go there with my message would be seen as blasphemy or sedition, and I would be stoned."

He felt her concern, and it hurt his heart to see her almost paralyzed with fear for him. And then he stood and came to her with a look she had never known. It was a stunning radiance that shook her and brought tears running out over her cheeks, sweeping her doubts before them.

"Something has happened to you," she whispered in the wonder of his face, now in a peace that was transforming in its gentleness.

He placed his hands lightly on her shoulders. "There has been and always will be a holiness about you, Mother." His eyes also filled with tears. "You will hear me speak words you have never known me to speak. Know that I do it in honor of the love that The Father gives to me; the kind of forgiving and unrestrained love that you have always shown to us."

He hugged her again, and they both cried softly in the joy and in the sadness of the realization that their lives were about to be forever changed.

He stepped back, wiping the streak of a tear from her cheek, then wiped his own cheeks and said, "I leave for Jericho. I would go and learn from my cousin, John. He is called the Baptizer; some say he may even be a prophet. He's down on the edge of the wilderness. I hope to find my place there, perhaps to teach with him. I hear he also speaks of the Coming and of repentance."

"Oh, Elizabeth. I've not thought of her in years. She was much older than I, and then they went into the wilderness to be closer to where Moses brought our Nation. I can remember visiting them once; they were very poor, but stronger in their faith than anyone I've ever known other than your father. They had John late in life. When they died, he lived on the Dead Sea at the Community of the Poor."

She then took his hands and squeezed them, "Oh, but please don't leave tonight!" she beseeched him. "The roads are far too dangerous. Stay the night. I will fix you pancakes from wheat flour in the morning," she begged, trying to tempt him with his favorite food.

He grinned broadly, "Mother, you know all my weaknesses, but where I go now I must say 'no' more than I say 'yes'. I must be willing to give up all that I have and cherish if I am to be an example to others."

Her face furrowed with worry and uncertainty. "Well, here, you must take food." And she began stuffing his bag with dried fruits, smoked fish, and several boiled eggs.

He put his hand on hers. "That is more than enough, Mother. The Father will provide for me. I must believe that."

"You're not going to live with the Bathers at the Dead Sea?" she asked worriedly.

"I want to visit Qumran. I would ask if they would open their camp to all of our faith and join the rest of the Nation in preparing for the Coming. But I fear they believe that only they are the keeper of the Word, and they don't allow the unclean. I see a Kingdom more open than that, so I doubt my visit will gain much."

"Well, they are good men, very strong in their faith, but I am gladdened that you will not go there to live," she smiled. "They have very strict rules about talking at table and The Holy One knows few who love to talk at the table more than you."

He laughed. "You know me too well."

She watched him put his clothing bag and food pouch over his shoulders. He placed his tool bag in a corner, and stood looking at it for a moment as though he were parting with an old friend, a defining possession that anchored his life and its worth. She walked up to him and touched his cheek.

"My son, I want tell you something I have not spoken of since you were a child. To hear you speak, as you now do, I know that The Holiest has truly entered your life, and I rejoice in this."

Her eyes misted over as she spoke. "Just before your father and I were to marry, I had a strong, vivid dream where an angel came into my room and said that a special child, a messenger, had been placed in my body by the Holiest One. It was so overwhelming that I was convinced that it had not been a dream. When I told Joseph, he looked quite startled, saying that he, too, had had the same dream. We were both frightened and overjoyed. We told our family members, but some were angered. One even told her friends that I had lain with a Roman soldier, that we were trying to make an excuse for my being with child. Your father was very angry about someone saying I was not pure. He could have left me for we were not yet married."

Jesus could feel the pain and hurt that she still harbored over the gossip, and motioned for them sit on nearby cushions. He reached out and cupped his hand against her cheek. A tear flowed from her eye and rested against his hand as her eyes lingered on his.

225

"We were on the highway when I felt the first pains of your birth," she continued. "Joseph was looking for work. We came upon an inn late at night and were refused a space. The innkeeper told us we could sleep with the animals of the travelers. We had no choice but to find a place among the camels and sheep. Almost before I could lie down, you were born. My cries stirred the animals. I can still hear their mewings and snorts, and the pricking of the straw on which I lay. A mysterious woman brought water from a cistern for the animals and she helped your father as you arrived. She washed you and wrapped you in strips of cotton cloth she tore from one of her own robes. Your father later said the woman was an angel, a part of this act of the Holy One. She never said a word and disappeared as quickly as she appeared. Joseph took you outside and held you up to the heavens and gave thanks. As he did, he was struck by an almost overpowering light. It was a star, but much, much brighter than any star ever before seen in these parts. Joseph and I talked about it being an announcement of the coming of the Kingdom, and of how our child would be from the root of David—the promised Messiah who would proclaim the arrival of the Lord.

"And then another strange thing happened. During the night three men in exquisite dress arrived on camels. They wore great hats of silk and bright colors and their finely-woven robes glistened in the night light. Their perfumes smelled of exotic, distant lands and they spoke with great wisdom. They were traveling through and heard that a special child, one who would announce the Coming, was to be born soon. As I lay and listened in amazement, they opened bags and gave you precious gifts, saying you must be the special one because of the intense light in the sky. No one in the inn woke. No one saw this but us. We told few and showed the gifts to even fewer. They would have thought we had stolen them. We were too too poor for these things. Unless we had had a stronger sign, your father would have been stoned if he had spoken of this night."

Mary continued, "As the years passed I said little about this. Now I hear you saying things that make me wonder; these words you speak, are they the sign? Would you, my Jesus, be that Arm of the Lord?" Her eyes looked at Jesus in awe at the thought and in fright that she might offend her God at even thinking such a thought, if it were not true.

But his eyes answered her with complete assurance. They gazed with a knowledge beyond her comprehension; his eyes were so mystical and mystifying that Mary felt her frame shake as though a chilling wind had rushed through the tiny room. Regaining her composure, she said, "I do wish when you return from your travel, you might teach in the meeting house in Nazareth. That would be an honor to Joseph who spoke there often."

He stood at the door, looked long at her small, tear-streaked face, and with a proud smile answered, "In his honor I will speak."

The door scraped against the hard stone floor of the house, and he disappeared into the darkness. She would know little sleep that night as she prayed for her son's protection and God's forgiveness if she had doubted His intentions. And she questioned prayerfully if that long ago dream and that distant shining star had indeed been a message; a promise of glory and redemption that her first son would now fulfill.

It would take four days to walk from Capernaum, down the length of the Sea of Galilee, to the Dead Sea called Lake Asphaltitis by the Romans. The lush garden fertility of northern Galilee was a stark contrast to the sudden and surprising emptiness of Judea. The landscape of few countries changed so rapidly in such a short space. Spring arrived early in Galilee, welcomed by a fecundity of wildflowers and greening fields.

Tiberias, only eight and a half miles south of Capernaum, was the new gleaming wonder of Galilee; the all-white city on the sea, built as a statement to the power and presence of Rome. Tiberias was a rather narrow city that ran along the Galilean waters now called the Sea of Tiberius by the Romans. It looked to all eyes like a Roman city complete with: a well-planned grid of streets, colonnaded walkways, parks and plazas, underground sewers, a profusion of statuaries and temples, a magnificent public bath, an amphitheater, and a large plaza around some hot springs called Hammath-Tiberias. All citizens relaxed in its hot waters though it had a rather repugnant odor.

Lording above it, on a flattened mount overlooking the city, was the sprawling palace of fifty-year-old tetrarch, Herod Antipas. He was a pudgy man of medium height, with heavily-scented hair, and the rather dark skin of his father. He had been granted a governorship of the Galilee area by the Emperor Augustus to honor a request in his father's will. Galilee was more like a princedom which Antipas was allowed great leeway in governing, unlike Judea, which Pilate, as a Roman officer, ruled strictly as a Roman province. Antipas' main tasks were to continually send monetary tributes to Rome and to keep peace in the land.

He did both, in part by allowing the Jewish council, the Sanhedrin, a good deal of latitude in governing the Jews. He ruled at the whim of the Emperor Tiberius, and Antipas lived in paranoid fear that the mercurial man would find him in disfavor. He constantly spread gossip about Pilate, about the ruling Sanhedrin members, and about officials from the other provinces. He seemed to bore easily and appeared to have little to do other than entertain himself. His two favorite pastimes were inviting Roman friends to visit him, and taking his entourage and sailing to Rome to attend one of its many festivals. Luxurious living was his life. Serving the citizens of Galilee was the least of his worries.

Antipas' brutality was well-known, but the Jews were not as concerned about that as they were his taxes. Tiberias had been built through an oppressive taxation that had left many farmers bankrupt. Lying about what one owned became an accepted part of the Jewish culture in order to avoid paying the excessive tributes.

Jesus walked along the wall of the marble and limestone city. It was easy to see why a poor Israelite would be tempted to leave the hard scrabble life of the farm for the opportunities of this market center. How easily we are tempted, he thought, but he also felt a sense of comfort in having removed this desire to own and to possess from his mind. It gave him a freedom he had never known and a focus on what he truly wanted to do now with his life.

Jesus' thoughts were suddenly interrupted by the thunder of hooves and the clatter of bridle, saddle, and weaponry as a detail of soldiers and official-looking Romans almost ran over him as it swept unconcerned over the stone paved highway leading into the city proper. Brushed by one of the horses, Jesus was spun off the road, but regained his footing long enough to recognize the fleeting profiles of Julian and Cassius as they disappeared within the city gates.

Jesus looked at several other travelers who dove for the side of the road to avoid the Romans, and they all shook their fists and cursed at the Roman arrogance. This was one of the many dangers of road travel, as the Roman soldiers delighted in pressing their power on the locals by thundering among them and scattering them like chickens.

Paulius led the group through the city gates. He turned in his saddle with a wide grin. "Didn't I tell you? Magnificent isn't it?"

They had visited Sepphoris after Cassius agreed to buy the apartments from Nathan. Sepphoris had been sacked by rebellious Galileans after Herod's death and partially rebuilt by his son as a splendid copy of Rome set in the heart of Galilee. But Tiberias was even more stunning, an ideal of the perfect Roman urban area. Not satisfied with his work at Sepphoris, the tetrarch Antipas recently moved his capital to this western shore of the Sea of Galilee. Here he had built a gleaming city of marble. Because it was built over an old Jewish cemetery, initially no one would move there, so he ordered hundreds of people to leave their homes for his new city. Now it was a siren call to the impoverished of the area to come and make their life in a Greek-speaking, Roman-worshiping metropolis.

Paulius' entourage was in too much of a hurry to enjoy the sights on this trip. They had gained an appointment with Antipas at his palace, then they were scheduled to ride out to the farm on which Cassius was foreclosing. They had to be there before dark. It was now a little after midday.

"Ah hah, look there," Paulius pointed with pleasure as they clattered down the stone streets. Lording over the city and the sea, up on a sharply rising hill, was Antipas' palace.

Julian was thrilled. "Wondrous," he gushed. "What a grand statement of the magnificence of the empire. We must return here so I can sketch this scene. Our friends will find great amusement in this."

"I might want you to put this scene on a wall at the apartment building," Cassius offered, as they spurred their horses up the steep road that led to the palace.

Paulius said, "I must warn you that Antipas' appetite for women has him in some difficulty. He recently married his half-brother's wife, Herodias, while still married to the daughter of the nearby Nabatean leader Aretas IV. The daughter heard of her impending divorce and slipped away to her father in humiliation. I hear old Aretas IV has drawn together an army and might attack. This has Antipas nearly desperate with fear that the local Jews will use the moment to start an uprising. He's very wary about anyone stirring up the people just now."

Cassius laughed cynically. "That supports what I heard of him. He has all of his father's energy to build, but little of his abilities to rule."

They rode up to the top of the mount and into a spectacular palace compound of statue-rimmed pools, floors of intricately prepared mosaics or colored marbles, porticoes and colonnades, and a two-story palace with many large windows and an atrium roof. Their horses were taken by palace aids, and they were led by two large guards through a courtyard to a pool overlooking the brilliant blue of the sea. The entire place seemed to sparkle in the bright sun and the natural gleam of its architecture. Antipas was reclining on his left elbow on a trichlenia, a low divan, surrounded by servants. Silver bowls of pistachios, melon slices, and apricots covered a low table in front of him. Glass bottles of wine were arrayed next to the bowls. A young boy was putting oil on the legs of the man who would be king to protect him from sunburn.

"Ah, Romans!" Antipas heralded across the small clear pool waters. "Welcome to the most beautiful view in the empire. Next to the Emperor's gardens, of course."

As they walked around the pool, Paulius said out of the side of his mouth, "Count the times he will kiss the backside of Tiberius before we leave."

Paulius was his usual effusive self, praising the carefully tanned Antipas for the healthy glow of his skin, the unsurpassed beauty of the new city, and the view. Antipas was not born a Roman, but a Jew, and the Romans would not speak to him, even in the cordiality of the moment, with the relaxed familiarity with which they would speak to other Romans of their rank. They maintained a slight distance; they were born to the Roman culture of masculinity, and it emanated subtly from their every move and inflection.

"Most honored tetrarch," Paulius bowed, please accept my humble present in honor of your recent fiftieth birthday."

It was a small, highly-polished wooden box inlaid with jewels that contained an assortment of fragrant spices.

"Oh, you are too obedient," Antipas gushed as he turned the box in his hand and took a long delicious smell from its contents.

"I wish you could have been at the party. We held it at the Jericho palace. Many friends from Rome came down. I know the entire Senate and our Emperor would have come if the business of the empire had not kept them away."

Paulius nudged Cassius in the side.

Then a look of sadness passed over Antipas' face and he remarked as he looked out at the sea, "I will also accept this as a remembrance of my father who died this month thirty-three years ago. A monument of a man," Antipas whispered sadly.

Born in Judea, Antipas had been sent to Rome for his education and was well known there. His father had willed a portion of Palestine to him, but he had not been allowed by Rome to call himself a king, a oversight that continually galled his new wife Herodias. Antipas enjoyed his little empire; it was more a social affair for him. It allowed him to put on endless parties for his friends in Rome who would travel down for hunts and banquets. And he would go at the hint of an invitation to anyone's festival party in Italy. In fact, to those who observed, it seemed he was out of the country as much as he was there.

"So, Julian," the pudgy and obviously aging tetrarch asked after introductions had been made and drinks offered, "you would sketch my palace and put it in the great villas of Rome?" He seemed to forever be begging for a compliment.

Julian turned to look out at the panoramic view of the city below and the sea stretching over to the far mountains. It was a study in the varying intensities of the color blue from the deep clarity of the vast sky to the darker hue of that color in the sea, all set against the earth tones of barren hills of limestone; punctuated here and there by clumps of trees.

Bottles of perfumes were hanging in jeweled containers everywhere. Scents wafted about in their various subtleties. "This is magnificent, tetrarch. You have a fine sense of lines, placement, and colors. I would like to come back in a few days and sketch this creation. I do believe many in the Senate may wish this to grace their dining area."

"Oh, you are too gracious!" Antipas said gleefully. "What an honor for my palace to be witnessed by the powerful as they dine. Perhaps you could consider showing your drawings to the Emperor even."

Paulius winked at Cassius over Antipas' obsequiousness, as Julian answered that he would be glad to show off his drawings of this palace to the elite of Rome.

"I'm on my way to the countryside to foreclose on an estate to which my father loaned money," Cassius said as they munched on cinnamon-dusted cheese, various thin cakes, honey, and yogurt sesame sauce. Servants stood with towels for the men to wipe their hands. The master servant held a dark bottle of wine before Antipas

231

for his approval before opening it. A small Greek man passed a silver platter, bowing as each guest took from the tray.

Letting Cassius' words hang for a moment, Antipas carefully examined a tag attached by wax to the end of the bottle. "Ah, Falernian vintage from Campagna," he exulted. "We may be on the outer edges of the civilized world, but good wine does find its way to us."

Antipas had a servant, a young boy, hold a mirror to his face so he could study his hair. It had obviously been died black. Pleased, he brushed the mirror away and responded, "I keep the Jews generally quiet. That is the one charge, next to taxes of course, that Tiberius asks of me. Keep them quiet. Keep the treasury full."

"So you don't think we will need more than the five guards we have with us?" Cassius asked.

"To drive one of these miserable families off their farm? No. Five should show them we will stand for no trouble. We have good relations with their forever whining leaders at the Temple, but they properly fear my authority. They know I will stand for no insurrection."

Antipas whispered to one of the master servants to go and fetch gifts for his guests. It was Antipas' custom to stock all manner of gold bracelets and other items so that he could provide gifts to guests whose favor he especially wanted to curry.

"I have many eyes throughout Galilee." He snickered, "My father would sneak about the streets and cafes in disguises and do his own spying on his subjects. How clever! I'm carefully watching one potential trouble maker south of here, a lunatic called John the Baptizer. He keeps yelling like a bleating goat about the end of the world! How insane! I think an announcement of that importance should be reserved for the Emperor!" He ended the sentence with a loud laugh, and they all chuckled at the thought of a deranged man in the desert knowing when the world might end. "On the one hand, I must admit to being intrigued by his sayings. He is a Jew. On the other hand he insults my personal life, and I will have none of that. I may have to do battle with Aretas, and I do not need a fanatic starting an insurrection against me as I prepare for war."

Paulius faked a moan, "Unfortunately, all of the religions and philosophies have their fanatics. But the peace that Rome brings to a land must always be protected from the crazed."

The edges of the pool were decorated with statues to various gods, but prominently displayed at the end facing the sea was an amphora balanced on a small pedestal. It was the traditional long clay wine container of the times. Cassius thought it odd a wine container be placed in such an obvious position.

"Honored one, why would a wine jar be displayed with your statues of gods?"

Antipas responded with his shrill laugh, "Ah, it is a tribute to my father. It was wine he ordered now fifty years ago from the estate of Laenius. He so adored Philonian wine, and I keep it to honor his love of Bacchus and the good life."

Cassius strolled over to admire the old container, and as he noticed the Latin inscription on a faded wax stamp attached to its neck, he read — unintentionally — out loud, "for Herod, a King and a Jew."

Antipas, only a few steps away on his divan, heard the mumble and with some concern said, "Father considered himself very much a Jew. It was obviously so or he would not have built the great Temple in Jerusalem and made sure the Sanhedrin had the right priests ruling there. And his powers were almost absolute. But it was a constant tension he endured…how to be a Jew and be a friend of Caesar's at the same time." With a childish giggle, he mused, "I don't have that as a worry. My friendship with Tiberius and his being divine is alright with me. Now this doesn't mean that I forsake the god of my father. Can't we have a god on the earth and one of the heavens?" he smiled mischievously at them. Then holding his hand to his mouth in a mock confidence, he kidded, "But don't tell my subjects that!"

Paulius patronized the tetrarch, "I have always heard that you have a high place in the Emperor's palace. Perhaps it is because you are loyal to him and not just to this invisible god."

"Oh, I was born a Jew," Antipas felt he needed to correct any misunderstanding," and I honor the Temple. But I was also born to a giant of the times, a heroic ruler who transformed this land of tribes and little structure, to a wealthy trading partner, a jewel within the empire's crown. So it is my job to maintain the stability that my father created while allowing the Jews their laws as long as they do not threaten the laws of the empire. It is a challenge similar to my father's."

For the next hour they snacked, discussed events in Rome, and toured the palace. They met his bejeweled wife Herodias, a woman Paulius already knew to be flagrantly ambitious for her reluctant husband. In a whispered aside she told Paulius to mention to his Roman friends that they would be respecting the memory of Herod to also bestow kingship upon his son. Paulius said it would be his duty to do so, and then rolled his eyes as he turned from her.

As they stood, Antipas gathered a long towel about his sweating body and said, "Julian, I would be honored if you would return tomorrow and spend the night here. I can see the gods smiling as you please us with your artistic genius. Cassius, if you run into trouble today, you know my guard is at your assistance. And honored Paulius, I hope you will remember me at the baths in Caesarea. I will be traveling there soon on the way to a banquet in Greece. I will bring you a gift from there if I can find something that suits one of your rank."

He then gave each of them a gold amulet, inlaid with precious stones. They concurred, as they rode down the hill, that he was a simpering little ruler, but very accomplished at simpering.

Jesus passed behind the city walls on a path that avoided the stone paved road that was the official Roman highway to the south.

The lower end of Tiberias was entered through two enormous round towers that were part of its gate. He stopped and shook his head at the effort they represented and of how the Romans saw architecture as statement. Size was a key ingredient. The bigger and more ostentatious the better. At the gates several tax collectors had created a jam of caravans as they demanded that each entering bundle and box be opened for inspection. The collector would not allow a single piece of merchandise to enter the city without being appropriately weighed and having duties paid for it.

It was mid-afternoon when Jesus came upon a field of young barley and corn. A fine home sat back from the road in a grove of fig and olive trees, shaded by taller sycamores and oaks. It was made of stone, but unlike most homes in the area, its roof was terra cotta and looked Roman. Off to the left against a slight hill rose the columned entrance to the family tombs. The front of the tomb had been covered in stucco and almost glowed in its whiteness.

At the tomb several people appeared to be arguing, their arms flailed around, and one beat himself on his chest. Jesus could hear their voices sailing out over the long field, but could not understand their words. He sat on a small pile of stones in the shade of a tree, pulled out some figs, and munched slowly on them as he watched. Soon one of the men shook his fists at the other, an older man, and abruptly walked with an angry gait away from the tomb and house toward Jesus. He did not see Jesus sitting in the shade of the tree and walked up muttering to himself before being startled by the figure he almost stumbled into.

Jesus stood quickly and smiled, a fig in one hand, and his goat skin with a few tired sips of watered-down date wine in the other.

"Is our property a rest stop for every wandering beggar?" the young man asked indignantly.

Realizing his tone of voice told as much about being startled as being mad, Jesus responded, "I would not be a beggar, beloved, but only one admiring these fields and home, and enjoying the shade of your tree."

"Admire them while you can, traveler, they won't be ours much longer." Sweat beaded his olive complexion. His hair was black, wiry, long, and tied back in a small bun. He wore no beard. His eyes were sunken underneath his brows in a way that gave them a penetrating glare.

"Why would you sell such prized land?" Jesus asked.

The question set the young man off again. "Sell!" he almost shouted. "It is being taken in foreclosure by a Roman. They come today, and generations of Zabeths will be desecrated by the new pagan owners."

"I'm truly sorry, but this has been happening all over our land. Did you find you had to borrow from a Roman?" Jesus asked.

The man looked agitated. "Our family was split when my father decided to do business with a wealthy pagan lender from Rome. I begged him not to even speak with this Satan. But my father wanted to leave a big inheritance for us. The Roman told father if he would grow extra wheat he would buy it at a high price. But so many other farmers planted wheat that the prices dropped, then the rains did not come before the harvest, and we lost our money. So we can't pay back the loan." The young man sat down dejectedly at the base of the tree.

Jesus knelt next to him and began a short, inaudible prayer. The man looked up to see Jesus' brows furrowed and jaw clinched in an obvious intense display of concentrated prayer. When Jesus finished, the man asked, "Are you a scribe? You don't look like a priest."

Jesus looked up with all the tension gone and his face a study in perfect calm. "I am Jesus." He stopped for a second and then said, "And I am a teacher of the Word." He liked the phrase and the mystical 'word', and felt great contentment at having moved away from introducing himself as a carpenter from an unmapped village.

"I am Mikias. I…I did not mean to insult you, but I am very angry at my father, and…"

Jesus shook his head in understanding. "The angels of anger shadow my heart also. And when I get angry, I am saddened at myself for allowing the evil one to control me." He chuckled and touched Mikias' arm. "I feel anger when I feel anger. I get more angry at myself than the reason for my madness."

For the first time Mikias seemed to calm down, but the heat of his words turned to a morose helplessness. "We were just arguing there," his head nodded toward the tomb, "about whether or not to sell the family tomb to raise money to pay off the debt. My father refused to do so, saying it would insult our family name. He would rather lose his heritage than sell it. I suffer also at the thought of selling the tomb, but if we don't, we lose everything."

Jesus sat next to him. "I would ask what if you knew that the end of man was to be here and now? What if you knew The Holiest One was coming to take all of those who loved and obeyed Him into His Kingdom? Would you still worry over that house and these fields?"

Mikias looked quizzically at him. "But I would want them in the restored Nation. When The Holy One comes, won't He drive the Romans out and rule our land as its King? Would I not still need my house?"

"Mikias, the Kingdom is not of this world. It is a place too perfect, too filled with love for us to imagine. Your house, your fields, the tomb there, none are of any importance in The Father's land. You will have no need of this." Jesus swept his hand toward the farm.

A look of suspicion rode over Mikias' features. "You say you are a teacher. Did you study under the priests at the Temple. Are you a scholar in the Temple?"

Jesus felt frustration building within him. How would he ever get beyond this endless question of his authority? He had found when questioned that if he answered with another question, he avoided confrontation and made his point at the same time.

"Mikias let me ask you…in your prayer time and study of the scriptures, have you ever felt the presence of The Father?"

Mikias looked a little embarrassed. He almost stuttered, "Why, yes, of course."

"And so have I and so have all those who are faithful. So you know that The Father speaks to you."

It was hot even in the shade, and Mikias wiped his brow, "In the scriptures, The Holy One speaks to all of us, teacher."

"And so has He spoken to me. His Word has come to me with the fierceness of a winter storm and the gentleness of grass rustling in a spring field. And His voice has freed me from my desires to own linen robes, to have a villa in Jerusalem, or even to have the love of a woman."

"Are you one of the Pious Ones who has been purified at Qumran?"

Jesus had Mikias in a steady gaze throughout the conversation, inviting the young Jew to reveal himself to this man who was willing to make his own self vulnerable. It was suddenly as though they had known one another forever.

"No, I am a member of none of the sects or fraternities. I read the scriptures in my own way. Through them, I now know that The Father gives us a great freedom to know Him."

"Freedom?" Mikias interrupted.

"He says that our lives must be centered on love; love for Him first, then love for one another. This frees us from our possessions. Too many of our people love their fields and oxen and perfumes so much that there is no room left. The Father has released us to live the love he extends to us. It is beyond your beautiful home and these fertile fields and that great tomb. It is a love that connects all of us, not to possessions, but to one another. He gives life and His love to all of us to share. He clothes the lilies and the grass and feeds the sparrow. Don't you think he cares even more for His children and will care for you, also? I will care for you, Mikias, if you come to my door." Jesus closed with such a sweetness that Mikias sat back hard against the trunk of the sycamore, as though the words were so overwhelmingly powerful they pushed his body down.

Jesus continued, "I would tell you that you need not argue with your father over this land. Give it to the Romans, then you will have freed yourself from an exile. Your love of possessions has driven you from The Holy One as surely as if you had been driven out of Israel. You see, the true promised land is as close as your own heart, but for many it is a journey too difficult to make."

Mikias stood slowly and looked longingly out over the fields. "But it is so much of our life. It is our heritage. Our dead ancestors lie in their ossuaries awaiting the Coming. The fields are the richest in the area. The home is the envy of all who see it." His voice pleaded as though his beseeching would place a protective hand over the sprawling farm.

Jesus reached down and ran his fingers through the dark-recently plowed soil. It felt cool, finely mixed; its richness was evident to the touch.

"I know why you love this earth so much, Mikias." Jesus let the soil sift through his hands. "It is your food, your work, your wealth. Your ancestors devoted their lives to working this ground. It is who you think you are, but this is how Satan works."

Mikias started wondering why this calming man was here. It seemed so odd that in the middle of a family crisis he had just appeared. He was now more curious than ever as to who this dusty man really was. There was a strength in his peaceful nature.

"But what has happened," Jesus continued, "is that you have created a circle of gods on this land. It is not your land, but The Father's. That knowledge is as old as our faith. But your heart weeps at losing this land because it has become more important to you than glorifying The Father who created the land. Where is your faith, Mikias!" Jesus admonished him.

Mikias stood frozen in confusion about the suddenness of this encounter, his heartbreak over losing his home, and his guilt over the truth of Jesus' words.

"Your father made an honest contract, and it worked in the favor of the Roman. Did The Father use poor weather to see how your family would act in the face of troubles? Is he testing you? I don't know, but my heart tells me that He will take care of you. If you go to Him now and ask forgiveness for having betrayed His glory for your own glory, He will welcome you to the coming Kingdom. This loss will be your greater gain if only you will free yourself from the devils who live in this soil in numbers as great as the plants."

Mikias looked at Jesus in reverence, "You are from Him, aren't you?"

"Yes," answered Jesus with a certitude that convinced both himself and Mikias.

Mikias fell stricken to his knees in the shadow of the tree and asked if Jesus would have mercy on his soul.

Without thinking, Jesus said, "I forgive you, Mikias." And it felt right to him, but at the same time he felt a burden so powerful that his shoulders slumped under its reality. What he said was blasphemy, and he would be stoned if others heard it. But then again, it did feel so right.

Their solitude was shattered by the familiar sound of pounding hooves. Looking down the road, he saw Julian and Cassius and their guard leading a dust swirl toward the farm. They ignored the wagon path that led across the side of the field to the house, and instead, swerved by the tree and tore at a gallop, clods flying, across the foot-high green of the young barley shoots. It was typically Roman to display power at all times, especially during an entrance.

As they thundered past the tree, Julian noticed a man kneeling in front of a familiar figure, but only after they past did it dawn on him who it was. "It's him!" he yelled, twisting back in the saddle.

Cassius, riding next to him yelled back, "What? It's who?"

Turning back in his saddle, feeling like he was being carried along by the momentum of their group, Julian answered, "That is the one. The man who saved Nathan."

"What?!" Cassius exclaimed. "How did he get here? Maybe he'll turn the dirt into money and save the farm," Cassius laughed heartily as they pulled up, among much dust and flying debris as the horses were reined in hard, their coats awash in the lather of their heat, mouths twisting and opening against the pain of the bits.

Julian dismounted and looked across the long field to see Jesus and Mikias walking slowly toward the house. His heart quickened to the point that he felt dizzy. He followed along dumbly behind Cassius and the Roman guard as they knocked loudly on the large wooden door to the house. The door opened slowly, and a proud-looking, white-haired man with a long, crooked nose stood before them.

Cassius drew himself to his full height and asked officially, "Would you be Zeb-thalim, the owner? The man whose sign is on this document?" He held out a small scroll. Cassius spoke in Greek, of which Zeb-thalim knew, but not fluently. He called for one of his sons to come and translate the Greek into Aramaic.

The document was written in Latin, and Zeb-thalim could not read it, but he recognized his sign scrawled in Hebrew. He nodded with a steely look in his eyes and answered, "Yes."

"Then are you prepared to pay the interest tendered by my father on this loan?" Cassius' voice boomed as though he were addressing an audience.

"We needed rain to bring in the fullness of the crop, but it did not come." It did not answer the question, but it was all he could say.

The wailing of a woman could be heard from inside the house, then the crying of several men. The son, who was translating, could hardly repeat the words he was sobbing so heavily.

"It says nothing in the contract here about rain. You signed it. You agreed to it, so by the authority given in this contract and backed by the laws of the empire I hereby take this property as full payment for the debt owed."

As the words were translated by the son, the wailing and moaning intensified from within the house.

"As you can see by the fields, we are expecting a good harvest. It will be in shortly." Zeb-thalim was trying to negotiate, "We will be able to pay you what is owed and more."

A sneer lifted one edge of Cassius' mouth. "This all is very simple. You signed a contract that said you would forfeit this farm if you didn't pay on this day. The contract does not say, 'wait and see if the weather or the locust or the gods allow for a further harvest.' The laws do not bend. That is the strength of the empire." He paused for effect. "My father is a compassionate man, and we will need someone to continue working the farm. You may stay as a tenant if you wish. You can build a house for yourself in the fields."

Looking pleased with himself, he turned to Julian, Paulius, and the guard, as though he sought their applause for his first foreclosure. As he did, a maddening scream was heard as a man exploded from the darkened inside of the house and flung himself into Cassius. The force sent the Roman flying back into the guard as they fell in a tangle of bodies and limbs. The youngest son, a burly short man, was yelling and flailing at Cassius' face. He sat astride the surprised Roman, splattering blood with every blow to Cassius' nose and severely bruising his cheeks. A guard, who had been holding the horses, rushed up and, in a long swift step, kicked Zeb-thalim's son squarely on the temple and sent him flying off Cassius and into an unconscious heap on the ground.

The entire family rushed to attend to the son but were met by the five guards with swords drawn and shields up. Cassius was helped up by Julian. Blood ran freely from his lips, and he stumbled momentarily, stunned by the attack and the growing pain in his ribs and head. Julian led him staggering and confused toward a well at one side of the house.

All seven family members stomped the ground, tore at their clothing, and cried to God to save their farm. Mikias ran up behind the soldiers and leaned over his brother to discover his eyes in a blank stare toward the endless horizon of death. The kick had crushed one side of his skull and instantly killed him. Mikias fell, sobbing over the lifeless form, and the guards, thinking they were about to be attacked from the rear, turned in a crouch, with their swords extended.

What had caught their eye was Jesus standing alone some distance away in the field. He enjoined them in Greek, "He means no harm. He only mourns for his brother."

The guards, seeing no threat, stepped back and allowed the family to rush in a sobbing circle around the body. Mikias stood with tears running down his cheeks, his face flushed in a twisted pain. He sobbed loudly, looking at Jesus. Mikias in his grief was struck by the solitary figure of Jesus standing motionless—so contained and calm, so statuesque in the budding green of the field. Jesus raised his hand as though he were going to wave or stop some unseen force, but stopped halfway, unfurled his fingers, and stood frozen and somehow majestic.

Jesus was thirty feet away and spoke in a clear, soothing voice, "Rejoice, Mikias, he is with The Father. Cry in joy for one who gave his life to protect this place of faith from the pagans."

"You were sent to be here now, weren't you?" Mikias sobbed as he walked into the field and bowed on his knees before Jesus.

Other members of the family in their wailing noticed their brother kneeling before the straight figure.

Zeb-thalim stood slowly, looking confused as tears rolled down his face. Then shocked that his son would kneel before any man, yelled, "Son, what is this blasphemy? What man do you dare kneel before?"

"The Holy One knew this was going to happen, and He sent His messenger to be with me," Mikias stood calmly in a sudden serenity that seemed to remove him from the screeching of his mother and sisters.

The old man sputtered, "Messenger! This looks like a plow maker. Have you lost your senses, son?"

Mikias smiled gently at his father and said, "He comes as Isaiah said he would, Father; one who has no beauty that we should desire, but one sent as a righteous teacher."

Zeb-thalim walked out to them and looked hard at Jesus, studying his face with an undeniable doubt and growing anger. "Show me a sign, or I'll throw the first stone at you!" demanded the father.

Jesus said firmly, "I am not here to perform tricks, Zeb-thalim. You can find those from the magicians. My words travel on the breath of The Eternal, as could yours, if you would only put Him first even above this land. Then ask and you shall receive all that you require."

"You infidel!" Zeb-thalim screamed and ran off to the edge of the field. He returned with a large stone which he held threateningly above his head. The guards laughed and asked if the miracle worker would dissolve the stone.

Mikias stood between Jesus and Zeb-thalim. "Don't you see? We have placed our hearts more in this place than in our faith. We fight each other over how to save it; we spend our days in endless toil trying to grow more and earn more, and look where it has gotten us: a dead brother, a lost home, and you and I fighting at our ancestors' tombs."

Zeb-thalim spoke with great authority to his son, his voice quivering in a barely controlled fury. Sweat covered his brow and blood was smeared over his cheeks from having pressed his face against his son's crushed skull.

"Our family is of the root of Abraham. And we are known by all for our good works. We leave more harvest at the corners of our fields for the passing poor than any neighbor. Don't you tell me this family has not kept the faith!"

"Satan can live in the places we love," Jesus said. "He can make your love for them so great that there is no love left for The Father. What has a man profited, Zeb-thalim, if he gains a large treasure yet loses his own soul?"

"Who are you to come on our land as we are being chased off?" The old man tried to push his way around Mikias as he clutched the stone. "You must be Satan himself to taunt a holy family!"

Seeing he was only making the situation worse, Jesus stepped back in sadness, feeling a sense of despair over the hostility his words could generate. "I am sorry this has happened. I will pray that The Father blesses this family and shows you how sorrow can be a journey to joy."

"Get out, Satan!" The old man screamed and threw the stone past his son's grappling hands. It brushed against Jesus' leg leaving a reddened whelp. Jesus felt the impact and the immediate sting of scrapped skin. He walked with a hobble across the field and toward the road.

Julian had watched from the well as Mikias saw Jesus standing serenely alone in the field, removed from the commotion of the wailing family. And then when Mikias went out and knelt, Julian, almost moved to tears, was swept by emotions he had never felt in his life.

Cassius leaned against the well, his face stinging, after he splashed water on it to wash away the blood. He regained his composure and said bitterly, "Let's kill the whole damn family." And he walked toward the guard at the front of the house and told them the family would have to leave before the sun set or they would be summarily speared for trespassing.

Julian hardly noticed his friend walk away, so focused was he on the retreating figure of Jesus. Drawn by a force he could not fathom, he climbed on his horse and trotted it along the path from the house and toward the tree at the road's edge where Jesus stood adjusting the shoulder strap of his baggage. Julian reined his horse and got off. He felt timid and uncertain, almost foolish for having followed this man.

"Hello, Julian," Jesus looked up with a loving smile.

Julian looked at the ground then at the almond shape of Jesus' deep brown eyes. "I have thought much of you, since the miracle. I have thought much of your words and have them written down. I tried to draw you, but couldn't, and I can draw anything. It is my talent."

"This face?" Jesus laughed in embarrassment.

Julian was very anxious and nervous and not interested in joking.

"I, uh, wanted to ask you what is demanded for one to enter this Kingdom you speak of?"

Jesus put his hand on Julian's shoulder, and Julian could feel the heat from his hand. "Our faith has ten commandments, but the most important is to accept The Father as the only heavenly spirit and love Him with all your heart and mind and soul."

"So to worship this god as the only God…I might could do that. What else?"

Jesus looked at the handsome face, the bracelets and rings, and fine linen Julian wore. "You would have to give up all your possessions and follow me. This fine horse, your jewelry," Jesus paused, "even your drawing reeds. You could never draw another face or you would defile The Holy One."

Julian looked startled. "Not do figures! That is my life."

"To enter the Kingdom you would have to be willing to give up your life." Jesus was carefully studying the artist's face as it fell into a dark despair.

"Give up my way of earning a living?" His voice sounded weak.

"Give up even your wife and children," Jesus said unyielding.

243

Julian looked shocked. "My wife?!" And he slumped against his horse, dejected.

Tears filled Julian's eyes. "I want to follow you, teacher. I believe that you are a special messenger from your God. I have never felt this way about a perfect stranger, about our neighborhood gods, or about almost anything. I am a seeker of the truth, and I believe there is a unique truth in what you say about our world. It is so simple it is hard to fathom. It is...like looking into the sea from above. My eyes try to penetrate the surface, seeing vaguely the world beneath the water; a world of light and strange shimmering forms, but I...I can't seem to bring it into focus right now. My heart aches to follow you and learn more and know more of this joy about which you speak, but..." He searched for words. "But to give up all that I hold dear, to have faith in a god I cannot see, I..."

Julian took the reins of his horse and collected himself enough to say, "My heart is filled with the love of which you speak. Perhaps after I have drawn more frescoes and discovered much of this world, then I will return." Julian looked at Jesus with a pleading look, trying to muster some confidence. "I'll be back when I am an older man, perhaps just before I die. I'll seek you out. I'll be ready for your Kingdom and its Truths then."

Julian slowly turned his horse back toward the farm and moved across the field and away from the thin, shaded figure. Jesus was shaking his head in the sad knowledge that they would never meet again, that Julian would never knock, and the door would never open.

Like all travelers, Jesus had to be careful as he walked along the thick rushes of woods and brush that course the banks of the Jordan River. There was a tropical feel about the bottom land. Wild boar and hyena lurked about, and an occasional lion threatened the solitary traveler. A greater threat were the bandits who made the dense, jungle-like river area their home.

On the second day he passed a man who had trapped the highly-prized honey badger and was trading its skin, valued for its water-proofing, to a caravan of Syrians heading to Tiberias. The Syrians gave the trapper some rare myrrh they had gotten from Arabs in Jericho. The trapper had also caught three gazelles in nets, and after much wrangling and cursing, the Syrians took the skinned animals, giving him several small jars of pepper which they had gotten in the stone city of Petra.

Jesus saw the low, purplish-white flowers of marjoram sprinkling the sandy roadsides like snow, and savored the sweet smelling blooms of the gnarled and thorny acacia tree. He had made tables out of its beautiful orange-grained wood. Almond trees had just bloomed and spring barley harvests awaited.

He smelled the fragrant gum of the towering cedar and sat on a high hill in the shade of a great oak. And as he made his way over rocky ground, he watched in amusement as families of the rat-like hyrax scampered to the safety of their warrens. Trumpeting clouds of white storks loped in lazy-winged swoops across the sky on the third day of his journey, as they migrated north out of Africa. Jesus walked with a jaunty step, his mind clear and set. He prayed often, sometimes while walking, other times lying flat on the ground far off the road away from all eyes. He reveled in this isolation and focus. His prayers were long and conversational, but always humbling and solicitous. And he constantly practiced his delivery, his message—using the land and its life to form stories—observing, listening to conversations along the road as well as along the edges of fields and orchards where workers gathered and ate their lunch. He never missed an opportunity to break bread and talk, and all the while he listened and observed and wove words into short stories that captured his message. To help him remember and practice his new message, he wrote these thoughts on papyrus strips.

The further south Jesus walked, the more desolate the land became. The hills, though not high, became more jagged and steep; the sand-colored dusty ground crumbled under foot. The Jordan was a different river in different parts of Israel. Here it moved quickly and was a deep, murky brown color. On the eastern side of the river the land rose up like the lumpish walls of a furrow with the Jordan being the point where some great plow might have sliced the earth. The barren orangish-tan colored hills escaped into the utter desolation of the area called Perea and on into Arabia. The land had a vague color to it; muted as a corpse. It appeared a hellish place; waterless, with little plant life, but home to high-stepping lizards and an occasional striped hyena.

Jesus smelled Jericho before he saw it. Its balsam trees released their fragrance to the winds and announced that this ancient oasis city was near. Herod had built his winter palace in Jericho, favoring the mild, dry air while it snowed in Jerusalem only fifteen miles to the East. He had also built parks, colonnaded roads, broad avenues, and an amphitheater. Like all of his works, he went for the splendid, and out of this flat and barren earth he had recreated a bit of Rome and Greece. Soon after Herod died, a slave had burned his palace, but his son Arche-laus had rebuilt it in even more marvelous fashion. Jesus saw in its grand stone work all that was wrong with the Roman culture. It was controlling in its scope and grandiosity. Every pillar, marble statue, and ornate facade represented the power of the empire. It was architecture as statement, and it worked. Enormous wealth and power were reflected in the cultivated parks and paved streets, pools, fountains, mosaics, brass, gold and silver leaf accents; it stood in overwhelming contrast to the dowdy and dull defensive architecture of the Jews, whose squat and unadorned buildings were extensions of the earth's stone and mud.

The springs offered the dusty traveler a refreshing respite, and Jesus tarried at the clear waters, drinking and talking with those who gathered there. When asked by one woman where he was heading, he told her Qumran, and the woman said it was only seven miles south, but that he should enjoy a night in Jericho before going. Qumran, she confided, was said to be very harsh. A man standing nearby offered that the religious community members, however you called them, walked in the stubbornness of their heart, and he admired them for their devotion. They were honest, honorable, but wrong, he ventured.

It was late afternoon when Jesus approached Qumran. Located on a sandstone bluff surrounded by corroded hills that resembled melted wax—obviously ancient, worn, and easily eroded by the rare winter rains that stormed through the riverbeds which, when dry, were like sandy highways to nowhere. The Dead Sea spreads broad and intensely blue below the bluffs. The stone building was originally a small fortress and trade stop-over, then deserted. It proved the perfect place for the ascetic group of Jews who were convinced that the faith had been corrupted by Herod, and that the Temple and its Herod-appointed priests no longer represented the Word. They were called by several names — the Community, The Bathers, The Poor, The Sons of Light — and they also had several thousand followers who chose not to live an ascetic life of denial and celibacy. They lived in villages of Palestine in what they called camps. Many of the celibates lived in Jerusalem. This complex was one of several outposts where those who broke the strict Temple Scroll rules came to be purified. It was also a place for being initiated into the order. They lived devot-

246

edly by the Books of Moses and by their own complex rules. They were very much Jewish, but very different at the same time.

Their code of conduct, called the Temple Rules, commanded, for instance, that no male member have sexual relations within the walls of Jerusalem. If they did, they must come to Qumran for several days of repentance, where they would bathe frequently and have their garments cleaned. Cleanliness was almost an obsession with the group, and large cisterns of water and walk-in pools were much in evidence. In addition, a number of men lived there as permanent cooks and as leaders in the repentance and initiation ceremonies. They also had a scriptorium filled with the writings of the Jewish faith, its scriptures, and the interpretations of Judaism by the sect. Many of the scrolls used in Jerusalem were brought there for copying. The tedious act of copying was considered God's work, and a form of redemption.

Jesus arrived as the men were coming in from working their small corn patches and vegetable gardens. Much of their food had to be brought in from more fertile areas. They had constructed a remarkably effective water collection system which was now full from the winter rains. Great open cisterns sat filled under a clear sky. As Jesus approached the stone walls of the single community, a man in a white, short, tunic-like robe walked up to him. He carried a hoe and was perspiring in the late-day heat.

"Peace to you, traveler," the man said.

"I am a weary traveler," Jesus said. "Would there be water and food for one who has come far to see you?"

"You would be of the faith? I know your words to be from the Galilee."

"Yes, the Galilee. One who has had those of this community visit my father's house. Now I am one who comes to pray and talk with you."

The man had a stern look on his thin, tanned face. His hair was cut short and he was clean shaven. "I am Honi. I have recently given my land and my palm trees to this Yahad (community). I am here to learn the ways. Will you be a member?"

Jesus pressed his lips together in a kind of smile and answered obliquely, "I am searching for my place, but I don't know that it is here."

Jesus didn't notice the usual trash, broken furniture, and scavenging dogs around the outbuildings as one would see around many Palestinian communities. An aqueduct from the hills above the plateau brought rainwater and emptied it into a large decantation pool, where it was purified. From there it drained into seven cisterns which distributed it through the building. It was an impressive water system.

Jesus appreciated the ingeniousness of the system and said, "We should send your stone masons throughout the Judea. You could turn all of the land into a garden."

The man smiled and agreed, "When I first came to this desolate spot, I thought no man could live here, but it has been transformed into an oasis. It has allowed us to have a place for purification away from the corruption of the Temple leaders. It is a perfect place for initiating those who would enter The Community. And those who sin can come here and repent. We have many cisterns for purification of the body and clothing here. One can achieve a fullness of the spirit in living as Moses did in the wilderness. We are the purest of the Jews. part of the We and we alone will claim Jerusalem when the mighty hand of God comes down. Would you be a soldier in the coming battle?"

Jesus smiled. "A soldier? My sword is my words. I will defeat the dark ones, but it will not be through swords, but through love."

The man looked quizzically, "Through love?"

Jesus smiled inwardly. He had come to enjoy the predictable response to his mention of the word 'love', as though it were a word of another language.

To one side of the complex were hundreds of graves marked by small stone piles. "How many people live here?" Jesus asked. "It doesn't look large enough here for so many graves."

"Oh, these are graves of both celibate members and the families of members who live throughout Israel. They wished to be buried close to the wilderness. It is predicted that the great war between the Prince of Light and the Prince of Darkness will start here."

They walked alongside the main building which consisted of two wings. Part of the place had been extended to two stories, and there appeared to be a watch tower which had been built a century earlier when the place was a fort. Made of thick stones covered in white stucco, the rambling building stood solid and stark against the beige drabness of the area. There was a simplicity about the place. It was neat, groomed, and efficient.

"I will take you to the Guardian, Esav." They walked alongside the building as other men came in from the gardens and the oil presses.

They all stopped at a small walled area with steps that descended into a bath. Some distance from this main building, Jesus could see several outbuildings and what appeared to be women and children, but he saw only men here at the building as they entered through an outer gate, passed through one courtyard, then into another. A thick wooden door at the base of the two-story, stone tower led them into the semi-darkness of a large entryway. Honi asked Jesus to wait there. Jesus noticed how plain the white walls were and how moldings and other interior decorations (normal found in wealthy Jewish homes) were missing.

"You would be the stone worker from Nazareth. I am Esav." The silence had been interrupted by the entrance of a lithe figure, a spare man of calm appearance, but very self-assured and controlling. He was the leader of the faith, called the Guardian. He wore the white-bleached robe apparently common to all who lived in this place.

"I am Jesus. My father was a friend of members of this community when I was growing up. There was a camp of your faith in our village; a very devout family."

"We have those who wish to live a life as close to the Lord as is possible, and those who feel the need for a wife, children, and commerce. There are several thousand of us, but no more than fifty ever live here. Izaius of Capernaum arrived yesterday and told me of your coming. He said that you said the Kingdom was close at hand. He thought you were celibate and cared little for belongings. He thought you might wish to join our community. He startled us by saying you had brought a man back from the dead."

Jesus could feel Esav's eyes searching over him, studying his reactions, assaying, analyzing; it was easy to see why he was the high priest, the one they called the Guardian. "Those who walk close to the Word are capable of many works. I have failed many times in my walk, but I feel The Father has now provided a clear light for me," Jesus said responding in an indirect way.

Esav was fascinated by the softness, almost child-like quality, of Jesus' voice, a voice at odds with the complexity of his face. "We welcome those of pure heart who would join in preparation for the Coming. We welcome those who believe that we alone represent the true intentions of the Lord."

Jesus knew how exclusionary the Community was, and he tested Esav in that regard to see if there were any flexibility. "I read the prophets to say that the Kingdom is open to all that are pure of heart.

249

It will be interesting to see how many Nations are accepted at the End of Days."

Esav's eyebrow arched slightly, as though he were about to rebuke that statement and its implications. The Rules of the Community, a detailed set of rules that guided their daily lives, stated that only those aligned with the Community would enter heaven. But he calmly said, "Come. You must be in need of bread."

They started down a narrow winding hallway. "We may both be walking the same straight path. If your wish is to be a loving servant of the Lord, you will find great comfort here. We prepare ourselves for His coming with a devotion and obedience that I think is similar to what I have heard of your life."

Jesus smiled, "Those who have known me for my life probably see me as a dreamer, one who works with his hands, but spends most of his time on the hills near our village deep in thought or reading."

"Oh, you read?" Esav responded with a touch of surprise and admiration. "It is rare that one who works with his hands can do so."

Jesus didn't respond but followed Esav's guiding hand as they walked up some stairs and entered a door to the left which led into a large room where men were working on a brick and stucco table and also on a number of odd-looking desks. The desks were made of stone and plastered over then set on pedestals made of reeds. Those writing on these desks sat on wooden boards almost on the ground. It was an uncomfortable way for the writers to sit, as they had to lean up and over the desk tops.

"This is our scriptorium," the Guardian said. "We preserve the scriptures, for the Coming will be a time of fire and death and disruption. Our scrolls may be the only evidence of the Rules, as told by the Teacher of Righteousness, and of the scriptures, after the terrible wrath. We have plans to hide them in the nearby caves if we see that the fires would destroy our building here. Our brothers in Jerusalem also plan to hide their scrolls in our caves. As you can see, it can be painful to write for a long time, but it is in service and for redemption that these scribes work." Elongated scroll jars with bowl-shaped lids stood in each corner.

Eight men sat at the long table. Animal skins and papyrus sheets were used to write on. The skins had been scrapped and stretched tightly. The ink consisted of charcoal and gum and was kept in long, cylindrical bronze ink wells. The table had holes filled with water so that the scribe could wash his fingers before writing a reference to

God, which was written with the initials YHWH. Scrolls wrapped in protective linen protruded along shelves across one wall. None of the scribes spoke; the only noise was the scratching sound of their quills writing on the skins and on the flattened papyrus plant.

As they stepped out of the room Jesus said,"I know that you have preserved the scriptures and made them available across Judea. Your camps in every village have copies of them. But many of the common people still can not read Hebrew or any writings," Jesus said.

"Our writings reflect the teachings of the Teacher of Righteousness. They contain not only the Books of Moses in a very accurate form, but our own rules and disciplines. Our scrolls have been purchased by those of the faith from Egypt and Ethiopia to Damascus and far above. Since our rules do not allow us to take the skin of animals killed outside Jerusalem into the Holy City, we copy and keep our scrolls out here. In doing so, we earn our place with the Lord through our obedience in preserving His Books. It is a very difficult discipline to copy as much as we do." The man spoke in a measured way.

Returning to the first floor, they walked past a large storeroom filled with bags of grain and enormous storage jars and into the kitchen. Two cooks looked up at them in silence. They were making bread in a large clay oven. A hive dripping with honey lay in a clay pot, and grape juice was being poured in a number of clay cups. Smooth, hard-fired pink earthenware held flour for bread making.

Walking into a small bedroom with a table and chair, Esav said, "We live humbly. We live poorly. We share all we have. We are scrupulous in our honesty. This is a place of peace, contentment, and purification. We seek to come as close to living out the Law as is possible. Living in this barren place is so refreshing to the soul. We have no temptations here. It is a very disciplined life which is necessary if one is to come close to the Truth. This is where many of our Community come when they have sinned in Jerusalem. This is where we await the coming of the two Messiahs. We attempt to be perfect men. And at the end, we will return to reclaim Jerusalem."

Jesus said, "You have come to a holy place to live your faith. This is near where Moses viewed the promised land, where The Father said 'I will give it unto thy seed.' I too enjoy its isolation. There is a purity, an unadorned truth about the wilderness. I, too, am attempting to come as close as possible to the first man, to be at that time when there was no ownership, no priests between man and the Kingdom, no womanly beauty to attract the eye…nothing but a straight way to The Father."

Esav smiled knowingly. "Now you're going to say, 'but I am of the flesh.'"

Jesus nodded and responded, "I would overcome the flesh. I would become the Spirit." His eyes blazed as though he were in another place, far removed from the heat of the room and the prying queries of the Guardian.

Esav quoted one of his group's manuals, "The nature of all the children of men is ruled jointly by the angel of light and the angel of darkness, and during their lives all men experience a portion of each angel's divisions and walk in the ways of each one."

Jesus looked at him as they remained standing in the center of the small, bare bedroom. "I am trying to walk only in the Light. I am, as you say, of the flesh and of the Light and the Dark. But I am moving quickly now away from the Dark."

Encouraged by what he had just heard, the Guardian asked, "I would ask you to clarify something straight away. Izairus, who said you were coming, said there was a strength in you that frightened him. You spoke with a certainty about the Kingdom in a way he had not heard. He said you were from the line of David. I saw you coming from my window across the emptiness by the sea. I shuddered as I watched you approach. Why would I feel that way? Are you more than you appear to be? Are you of the flesh, or do you tempt me with your words to be appear to be of the flesh?"

Jesus smiled faintly and said, "You honor me with these words from your lips, but your heart is far from me. I say that we are a tribe divided unto itself, and I would join us together under the banner of The Father. You would keep out the lame and the sinner and those poor in spirit. I say ours is a Master who forgives all. This separates me from you. Man is not and will never be perfect. I say there are many doors; you say there is but one, and your door allows in only a handful. You prepare for war. I prepare for peace."

They stood in the small room staring at one another until the Guardian sighed deeply and his words flowed in resignation and disappointment. "I thought when Izairus told me of you, and when I saw you so solitary, yet so grand, against the desolation of the salt flats by the sea, I thought for a moment, I wondered if you could be the Prince of Light, the Messiah from the House of David — the one we await. But the one who comes to lead us would not admonish our beliefs. You would have this band of the pure ready for your leadership. You would have your army, and we would follow you in battle against the wicked ones. But I can only think that you are no more than I see here; a lone Jew on your own quest and not the one we seek."

"I am, as you say, a lowly servant, one voice crying alone," Jesus said softly. "We share our faith in the same Father, and I agree not all who pray His name shall enter the Kingdom. I had come thinking I would learn more of your road to heaven, but if what I have heard of your rules and interpretations from your members in Galilee is true, then I cannot walk in your way. May your ears be open to The Father's voice of love and forgiveness."

"You waste your time and mine, traveler. And your message, if it is that of love, is weak and will find only the beggars, the disfigured and the lonely." Esav rebuked Jesus with a controlled disdain. The dialogue had turned from one of query and testing to a realization that the meeting was pointless.

"I will pray for you and your community," Jesus said, as he turned to leave. "I go to one near the wilderness who is said to be as firm in his belief as are you."

Esav was curious. "And who might that be? It's not a prophet is it?"

"It is one called John the Baptizer. He is a distant cousin of mine. I've not seen him in years, but I hear he is speaking a powerful message of the coming Glory."

Esav smiled knowingly. "I might have known, but I didn't realize he was kin to you. Speaking out must run in your family. John was raised here for a part of his life after his parents died nearby. He is filled with the fire of The Holy One, but he left our community because he was convinced the Kingdom is open to all who will repent. He would include whores, lepers, the blind, anyone and everyone. His is not a message for the pure."

Jesus knew of the Community's disdain for the afflicted and now felt naive for having ever having come here.

They walked back through the kitchen. Esav stopped at the long cutting table where the men were stacking the bread for the evening meal. He handed Jesus a large flat piece saying, "You are closer to us than you are to the Pharisees and certainly to the Sadducees. We wish to be as one with the Lord. We are the purest of the Jews. Think of us and come back if you wish to prepare for the coming triumphant End of Days." Esav attempted to be conciliatory.

Jesus nodded, and they returned to the entry way. "I thank you for this bread. Listen for my message. It will prepare you for the coming peace."

Esav smiled and shook his head as he opened the door for Jesus and watched him leave through the large courtyard and disappear out the compound's gate. Jesus stepped into the shadows of the ending day. The path led down to the vast emptiness of the Dead Sea salt flats and the sea itself. He walked away frustrated by the harsh views of these Jews who would be so virtuous that they would abandon their people and their cities to live so alone and aloof. As he walked and chewed on the bread, he prayed for some guidance on how he could ever bring the Jews together. Perhaps the answer would be found in the camp of his cousin.

The sky quickly emptied of light, and a deep black swept in, releasing a brilliant field of stars like a great hand scattering seed. The darkness ushered in an immediate chill in the air. Jesus would sleep wrapped in his robe out on the flats. He would draw his strength from the awesome wonder of the spreading heavens and the utter solitude of the wilderness where Moses had ended his ministry and started a nation. There was a great clearing and focus that came to his mind in the night, alone in a wilderness of little sight or sound. In this utter naturalness, void of possessions and people, he found revelation, strength, and purpose. He felt God here with a force that was almost overwhelming, as real as the lost legions of hills and the endless span of the cloudless sky. There was vision in this void.

CHAPTER 13

"He that hath two coats, let him impart to him that hath none, and he that hath food let him do likewise," the voice rang clear and unobstructed.

Jesus could hear the shouting voice as he came over a rise in the road and down a slight incline, to flat ground next to the narrow muddy waters of the Jordan. He looked out over a large crowd that sat listening to a man in clothing cut from the skin of a camel. A thick leather belt cinched his waist. His hair was black and tangled, his face weathered, though he did not appear to be very old. He was sinewy in build; muscles showed under his sunburned skin. His voice was urgent and carried easily to the back of the crowd of several hundred. There appeared to be a great campsite there with goat-skin tents and cooking fires spread along the river bank.

"The sin of this land starts with Herod Antipas, the ruler who defied all the laws of marriage by disowning his wife and marrying the wife of his brother-in-law. This is the same jackal who strips our people of their earnings so he can build marble monuments to Greece and Rome. He builds Tiberias and Sepphoris with the strength of our backs, and our so-called leaders in Jerusalem raise not one voice against him. Why? Because they, too, are living off our backs. They tax your wages, take your sacrifices, build luxurious villas, dye their robes blue, eat whole cows, and scent their homes with balsam. Our land is alive with sin, and you must get in line to admit that you also are sinning!"

He stood at the edge of the Jordan; muddy, shallow, and narrow at that point, almost more of a stream than a river. It was a sing-song voice, high, but not shrill, with a distinct rhythmic cadence that inspired and caught the listener in its message. He was always earnest and intense, and sometimes angry and threatening. There was a definite fierceness about him.

A small man dressed in a short, dirty robe was hopping about, his hands waving in the air at the back of the standing throng. His teeth were the yellow of squash and jagged like a canine's. His beard was long and unkempt. His eyes were crazed and rolling about as he shouted "Amen!" repeatedly. He almost danced into Jesus, not seeing his approaching figure. The man looked up at him and with saliva splattering from his mouth exclaimed, "There's a fire here on the Jordan! Go into the waters or be burned by the avenging angels."

255

Jesus was stopped by the man's smell and his leering, deranged look, then silently reached out and lay a hand on the man's shoulder. The man whimpered like a cuddled puppy and suddenly stood quiet and dazed. Jesus nodded at him and moved into the crowd.

Then he stopped, almost stunned, when he heard John admonish, "Think not to say within yourselves, 'we have Abraham as our father', for I say unto you that God is as able to accept any human in His Kingdom as He is to raise up children out of stones." His voice then raised in a warning and his wiry arm stabbed the air, "Do not lean on your birth as a child of Abraham, for that is an excuse, a weak staff that unto itself will not bring you into the arms of the Lord!"

Chills rolled across Jesus' skin. This is the place, he thought. These are the words I have said, and now this prophet repeats them. His face broke into a broad smile as he moved up the rise from the river to get a better view.

He stopped under the shade of a large sycamore. It was one of the few trees of any size in the area except along the river's bank. Small bushes and plants grew in profusion at the water's edge, thirsting in this low, arid place for any moisture they could plead out of the sandy soil.

A man in striped head wear and a tunic of fine weave remarked, "That's the trouble with the damnable sons of Abraham; they think they and they alone can enter the Kingdom. I would like to worship their god, but this man and others say there is no place for me."

Jesus stepped next to the man and said, "The Holy One selects who enters, not man. If your heart accepts the One Father with all your strength, then you would be first, and those who brag that they are of the root of Abraham, they will be last."

The man looked a little startled. He and his friend appeared to be Palestinians and well-off, according to the dyes on their robes and their high hats of swirling cloth. Gold bracelets squeezed up their forearms. They had little figures hanging from their necks of the Egyptian god Ammon and the Roman god Apollo. They smelled strongly of perfumes. "Are you one of the Baptizer's group?"

"I am from the Galilee. I have come to hear his words." Jesus looked out over the crowd. "I see many have come."

"The Galilee!" The shorter of the two scoffed. "Did anything good ever come out of that place other than rogues and bandits? You run there when you've got something to run from."

Jesus smiled at him. "Many of the sons of man in the Galilee question some of our priests and the way they abuse the Temple, so we are said not to be firm in our faith. But it is a holy land where the desire to restore our Nation and free it from the wicked ones runs very strong."

The smaller man said sarcastically, "That means drive out the Romans."

Jesus said, "It means we wish to fulfill our covenant with The Holy One in the land He promised to us. That is hard to do when our people can be hanged from trees for wanting to rule this land that belongs to us by divine proclamation."

The taller man, who had a short, black beard and was balding, said, "I am Reuben of Jerusalem. I have worshiped many of the gods, have watched healers, been confounded by magicians, startled by miracle workers, read the future by astrologers, and listened to philosophers in my search for the answers to life. And then I heard in the marketplace of this man who says the end is near. But he says that his god will swallow up death, that we do not have to be just asleep for eternity, that our soul can live in some sort of paradise. Many have been struck by his warning and are very afraid. Rumors about him have people concerned all over Judea. That's why there are hundreds here daily. My life is empty, and I fear my death. I traveled here to see if his words were true and how I might get ready for this end. Now I find out this conquering god is only for the so-called Chosen Few. I am a gentile. If he comes, I will be destroyed. It is very terrifying." He shook; he was highly agitated, and his face was covered in sweat.

Jesus faced Reuben, put his left hand on his quivering shoulder, and said firmly, "Do not fear this day of the Coming. Rejoice and know that the Holy Spirit is listening for those who call. His house is large, and there is room for you if you seek it. Ours is a loving Father who asks only that we give our heart and soul to that love. You and all of mankind are welcome in His house. "

The man's lips, pursed and thick, began to quiver. He could feel a heat coming from the hand of Jesus whose voice seemed to have a quality of the wind; a stirring, erie movement of words. Reuben fell to his knees, confused and weeping. His friend looked around to see if others were looking, then cautiously moved to kneel also. The wailing of Reuben at the feet of Jesus caused those at the back of the crowd to stir, mumble, and turn to see what was happening.

Jesus put his hands on both men's heads and said so that only those nearby could hear, "Blessed are the poor in spirit, for theirs is the kingdom of heaven. Blessed are they who hunger and thirst after righteousness, for they shall be filled. He that seeks shall find, and to him that knocks the door shall be opened."

"Though I am a gentile, I can still go to this Kingdom?" The man asked in a cry.

A large number of people at the back of the crowd who were sitting close to the tree, heard the wailing and quietly shifted their bodies around to watch and listen to the disturbance. The Baptizer continued to speak loudly and forcefully, almost in a shout, admonishing, threatening, and shaking his thick fists in the hot air. He also noticed as he spoke, the tall figure on the rise under the sycamore. He saw the two men kneeling and saw some of the crowd, some of his crowd, turn and listen. He kept teaching, but he was disturbed by the reaction of the people to the man under the tree.

Jesus placed his hand on the man's shoulder and said, "The Holy One says, 'Look to Me, and be saved, all you ends of the earth…to Me every knee shall bow, every tongue shall take an oath.' That means, as it says, that you too have a place in heaven."

"What else must I do, teacher?" the man asked anxiously.

"Do as the Baptizer says. Repent, admit your sins. Profess your belief in the One Creator. Tell Him you will give up all your wealth, even your family and your very life if He asks it." Jesus lifted up the jeweled amulet the man wore around his neck and said softly, "Lay not up for yourselves treasures upon earth, where moth and rust corrupt them, but lay up your treasures in heaven where no thief can steal them."

Reuben's friend looked up confused. "Do we stay in our bodies and walk around here, or do we go to some place beyond the sun?"

"You will have no need for your body. You will go in spirit, but you will be recognized. It will be a joy unlike anything you can imagine; a love beyond any you have known." Jesus looked at them reassuringly, and Reuben put his arms around Jesus' legs and rejoiced.

Looking up at Jesus, Reuben was dumbstruck by the mesmerizing gaze that left him almost paralyzed. "You must be from this Creator, or how could you know this?" he asked. "You must be some kind of holy messenger. Are you the Messiah we hear of that will save the Jews?"

A buzz started among those at the back of the crowd now watching and listening. Pieces of the exchange between Jesus and the man had been picked up against the drumbeat of the Baptizer's shouting. The word 'Messiah' surged through the crowd.

Jesus could feel the pressure building inside him as dozens in the crowd rose and started coming toward him. He urged Reuben to stand now, as he felt some uncertainty, even uneasiness over the unexpected conversation and now this reaction. Jesus had never had a nonbeliever fall at his feet like this. It was both fulfilling and disconcerting, because as the crowd turned to see what was going on, he was confronted with seizing this moment to proclaim more of his thoughts, and to assert himself as a true teacher directed by The Father, or to move away quickly and think about where he wanted to go with this success. He walked away. His confidence in his faith and in his teachings were at a high point. Now there were too many people to ignore who had heard his thoughts and who were touched by his words. But to have the crowd turn toward him and, in effect, for him to start competing with John the Baptist in the middle of his teaching was unthinkable. He had come to be a part of John's ministry, even a disciple, not to compete with it. So, with his thoughts in conflict over the emergence of a simultaneously electrifying, but absolutely humbling feeling, Jesus found it easier to move away from events and to rethink what was happening to him.

As he started to walk away, Reuben had a desperate look in his eye and beseeched, "Where do you go, master? You're not leaving are you?"

"No, Reuben, I will not leave you. I will never leave you as The Father has guided me to speak with you. But I'm suddenly weak and need to speak with Him, to pray." And having said those words, he shook his head as he turned in wonderment and confusion about why he had said them and from where the words had come. His words seemed to originateo outside himself.

An older woman from the crowd, sheepish and not knowing who this man was, but having heard enough of the conversation to be intrigued, said, "Pray with us, master. Lead us in a psalm. With your voice, you must be a beautiful singer of the scriptures."

Jesus felt uncomfortable. He looked down the slope to the banks of the Jordan where John's voice boomed out, and saw John looking his way. "Forgive me, beloved, I believe The Father would rather we not make prayer a show, but use prayer as a time to be alone with Him."

"You do?" she reacted with some surprise. "But our priests pray loud and long. When they pray in the marketplace, they stop and bend over in front of as many people as they can."

His eyes narrowed in obvious anger, "The priests are hypocrites. They are like the actors in the amphitheater at Tiberias. They love the costumes of their offices, the jewelry, and the expensive dyes with which they color their clothing. They prance as though life were a stage. They love the crowds, not to mention your taxes and sacrifices. No, the Holy Spirit loves you alone, without the trappings or the incantations of others. You can speak directly to The Holy One. He is as open to your words as much as He is to any priest's."

There was an audible gasp from the people now standing around Jesus and the two men. "Do you say we do not need the Temple?" a man asked cautiously.

"The Temple is a sacred place that all Jews should honor. But I say that The Father is all around us, not just in one holy place. Would we restrict one so powerful, and say He could only be found at one place? No man can tell The Father where He must be!"

The faces of the crowd looked perplexed as they considered Jesus' words. One person finally agreed, "You speak well. Yahweh made the world and is of the whole world. He can be right next to us, even be one of us."

There was general agreement, and another listener asked, "Are you a Pharisee or a Sadducee? Are you one of John's disciples? We have not seen you before."

Jesus smiled, answering, "I come as do you, to hear his teaching. And, yes, I am a Jew, but not one of those who love greetings in the marketplace and front row seats at the assemblies. They would wash the outside of their cup and forget the inside. But it is the inside that must be cleaned first, as must each of our hearts."

Reuben said, "Perhaps you are more a Jew than they. You do not tell us who you truly are. John needs to hear you. I like what you say better. You have given me hope. John scares me."

"John is a holy man," Jesus said. "He speaks with a courage that is rare among Jews, but now I must go speak to The Father; forgive my leaving." He ducked behind the tree and walked off toward a rocky bluff that rose among the barren hills bordering the river.

A man dressed in the clothing of success had been listening and asked, "Did you get his name? Does someone know who this man is?"

The woman who had spoken first said, "I know you to be a scribe; you should have had your quill and ink and taken down what he said. The man, whoever he is, said things that many will like to hear. I think he is a special messenger."

Someone next to her, warned, "But many others would not like to hear it, and would stone one who speaks such."

The group slowly dispersed toward their tents and campfires, spreading the word of how this man with the touch of his hand had converted a pagan to the faith. John finished and was surrounded by dozens who were asking him questions. As he answered them, his eye caught the man who had been under the sycamore and was now climbing one of the bluffs in the distance, solitary and slow moving against the eroded waste of the rocks and crumbling edges of the limestone hills. John wondered who this was and what he had said to attract part of his crowd. And why was the man walking away toward the desolation of the wilderness? Seeing one who had been near the stranger, John excused himself from those questioning and praising him and strode over to a goat skin tent on the edge of the Jordan.

"Daughter," he asked the woman named Beth, who had first spoken to Jesus. "Who was the one you spoke with 'neath the tree?"

She was fanning the embers of a little campfire and looked up, "Master, I was going to come and tell you of this man. He looks…I don't know, different, and he said words that will excite many and anger others. I think he must be a new teacher, one that will have the priests looking for stones. I heard the word 'Messiah' and I rushed to hear him. He didn't look like one, but there is something different about him. He is also very holy, I think."

"Did you ask his name?" John asked.

"He didn't give it, master. He went off to the wilderness saying he had to pray, saying he could speak directly to The Holy One."

"He did say that?" John looked hard at the slopes, but could no longer see the figure. His mind raced with the possibilities of who this might be? "If you see him again, would you tell him I would like to see him?" John requested.

Suddenly John was almost bumped off his feet by two large, thick-necked men in embroidered shirts and fine robes with blue stripes. They excused themselves for having brushed against him, but John, who was relatively short and wiry, could tell by the smug look on their faces that they were trying to intimidate him.

The largest one, a balding man with a thick, black beard said, "We are attendants to the chief priest, we are scribes; the other six are Sadducees and Pharisees on the Temple court. We have come from Jerusalem to see how much of the scriptures you really know."

"You have not come to hear me," John rebuked them, standing his ground and putting his hands defiantly on his hips. "You have come to hear the words of Hosea and Elijah."

A smaller, older, and round-bodied man wearing linen robes stepped between them as though they were in his way. "I am Malak'ah, a member of the Sanhedrin. I hear blasphemies of the Temple in your rantings. What do you say?"

John smiled knowingly; his wild, unkempt appearance was in stark contrast to their immaculate dress. "The prophets say the Kingdom is near. They say one will come from the wilderness, an arm of the Lord. Do you not say these things in the Temple? I am but a voice crying out in the wilderness retelling the words of the prophets."

The priest sneered, looking John up and down. "You are not trained in the scriptures. Why, you probably can't even read. Who is a wild man dressed worse than a street beggar to say the end is here? And where is the Messiah you speak of—are you him?" They all laughed as they surveyed his wiry, ragged figure.

John lashed out, leaning toward them as though he would strike them. "Vipers! Devils who live in villas and drink fine wines and wear linens, you will be the first in hell!"

The two big men gripped their fists. The priest's face puffed out in a reddened rush of anger, his black eyes protruding as he grabbed the arms of the scribes either for support or because he didn't know what else to do. This filthy man insulting him was too nasty to touch, he thought.

"Blasphemer!" He spat out. "You dirty little rock roach! You keep cursing the Temple and you will be picking stones from your filthy mouth!"

John regained his composure as if to ignore the fulminations of the priest. "A stone will not stop the word of The Holy One. I am but a messenger. Another will come who is closer to our Father than I or you robed wonders. And he comes soon. You generation of vipers who glory in the Temple, gorging yourselves on the sacrifices of the poor, I warn you to flee from the wrath to come!"

Another priest with them stepped forward, warning, "Your foolish words about Herod Antipas could get all of us in trouble. A sane man doesn't criticize the tetrarch about his marriages."

"By your silence you allow the scoundrel Antipas, a man who drains our people dry with his taxes, to live in a way that insults our Lord. You are so afraid of his taking away your power at the Temple that you sell your souls to this devil."

A crowd now surrounded them, cheering at the courage and rebelliousness of John.

The priests, not wanting to push the confrontation any further, shouted, "We are listening to you. Be very careful of your words. You are warned!" And they turned, with the two scribes, scowling, and pushed their way through the crowd toward their horses.

When they had walked beyond the area of tents, Malak'ah told the group, "This man is very dangerous. He stirs the ignorant to insurrection. We'll report this to the high priest. His words about Antipas will anger the high priest and Antipas. It could cause the tetrarch to look with disfavor on all of us. I may ride to his palace and tell him of this wild man, so we will be cleared of any association with him. This baptizer may be a Jew, but he's not our kind of Jew."

The crowd cheered and crowded around John, who announced that he would be baptizing at dusk, but he needed to rest now. He and several men left the area together for a campsite in a grove of trees. It was mid afternoon, and the sky was unmarked by clouds. The intense sun bleached the blue coloring from the sky and heated the shore area so that everyone sought the shade of a tree, bush, or the reeds at the river's edge. There they had to keep a wary eye out for crocodiles, snakes, and the ever-present scorpions. Hundred of people were scattered over several acres of river shore. It was a disorganized scene; a tent here, a bedroll there, all located on a sandy banked area with no grass where only the hardiest of brush and trees could grow. Some had come from nearby Bethany for the day, or from across the river from Jericho. Dozens had traveled the few miles down from Jerusalem. Some called the deep and twisted route The Valley of the Shadow of Death as it narrowed and inclined steeply through the rugged hills. This place of shadows and turns was a hideout for road bandits, and it was smarter to travel in groups for protection.

There was a faint wind shuffling the heated air along the bluff where Jesus knelt. The ground was covered with small pebbles. He could feel them dig into his knees, so he got up, lay a small wrap down, then knelt on it. He was excited and deeply moved by the events at the river. He prayed with his hands turned palms up and his eyes looking into the pearl blue of the sun-hazed sky.

"My Holy Father, who is in heaven, hallowed be Thy name. You reign over your children in ways that we cannot know. But we see your glory in the fields, your love in the face of a child, your forgiveness as we fall so short of what you would have us to be. I ask you this day, Father, to guide me, to give words to my lips, courage to my heart, wisdom to my mind, as I would be Your messenger. I am so weak, and you are so strong. I fall short of the mark when the people now come and ask of me who You are, and what Your Kingdom has for them. It saddens me deeply when I can't find the right words, the right sayings, to make them understand. But they look at my clothing and at me, and they do not see one worthy of saying what I say. They expect a Messiah who rides on a fiery cloud, leading an army of angels, and they see only me, a plow maker. They desire thunder and trumpets, and it is only my voice. Should I have a finer robe, Father? Should I seek out bracelets and a tall hat?

I believe I am close to truly knowing You. I now know that I am here for a special reason, and forgive me, Father, if I be vain, but when the man knelt before me today, I knew that Your hand was upon me, and my heart overflowed with the wonder of that moment. You have ways of showing Your hand in our lives, Father, and I thank You for taking away many of my doubts about my purpose here. We are a torn Nation. You have shown me that the Nation must come together under you. You have put the words on my lips that have moved some people to look to me and not just at me. I now believe that I might be the one to lead our Nation, but it is a terrifying thought, Father—to be seen as Your messenger; to be seen as one, even, and I say this with great reluctance, seen as one in the company of Moses. You have guided me to this place of John the Baptizer. You have told him also of Your Coming. But have You told him of who I am? Is he an Elijah? Is that why he is here in the wilderness to announce, not just Your Coming, but Your messenger? I wonder these things, Father. I wonder, as only You know. I will see what John says that You want me to hear. I thank You for Your guidance, Father. I believe I am closer to learning of my mission for Your glory. But Father, You know the weaknesses I feel, the uncertainties, so I humbly ask for the strength of Your mighty hand. All that I do is for Your glory. I pray in Your Holy Name, amen and amen."

264

He rose and looked out over the serene barrenness of the hills. There was no sound except for the crunch of his leather soles against the loose sand and rock when he moved. As he enjoyed the wild freedom he found in the singularity of the place, his mind poured its thoughts out into the great emptiness; he felt renewed and refreshed. It was late in the afternoon, and he was very hungry. His mouth was parched. His goat skin had long ago been drained of water. So he started down the escarpment, half-sliding on the pebbles, until he found a vague trail that led back to the Jordan, and he prayed for answers to end this agonizing torment of who he really was.

"I tell you it is not enough to be a descendant of Abraham," John's voice thundered along the river bank as he stood knee deep in the shallows. "Don't just think because you are of the root, don't just think because you do good works that you will be chosen at the Coming. And it will be a terrible time. The axe will be laid unto the root of the trees; therefore, every tree which bringeth not forth good fruit is hewn down and cast into the fire!"

An older woman stepped off the shallow sandy bank and into the water, looking as though she were in a trance. Tears wrote trails down the dust of her cheeks. "Will you be hewn down, daughter? Have you transgressed against the divine commands? Will you be cast in the burning fires?" John was fairly shouting at the terrified woman. His voice easily rang out over the muddy waters of the Jordan. He drew the woman to his side and placed his arm on her back.

She weeped, "Yes."

"Do you now beg The Father for forgiveness? Do you accept Him as the One Creator?"

"I do, yes, I do," she began to cry out loud, then wailed in a high-pitched moan, unable to speak anymore. It was a song that gripped the crowded banks. A true terror began to infiltrate their souls, and many cried out in desperation, and others took up the woman's sorrowful wail. The entire area became a song of anguish and remorse over lives foolishly spent; a high-pitched keening of the soul.

John seized the moment. "Yea, beloved, you have avoided the fiery cloud," he shouted. "You stand ready to be reborn, to be renewed, to come as a child, innocent of all sins. You stand ready to cross out of the wilderness into the promised land. I humbly ask that The Holy One accept your admission and forgive you."

The Jordan was waist deep where John held her trembling arm a moment, then dunked her under and as quickly pulled her up. She started sputtering and crying and praising the heavens. The bank was lined with people waiting their turn. Their emotions turned from curiosity to elation—each singing, shouting, howling, even repeating a favorite scripture; someone shook and tapped a cymbal, another played a flute. There was a rhythm along the sandy bank—a loose, but discernible rhythm, a kind of chant—a growing, unbounded joy. The more he baptized, the more the emotionalism grew and the more they shook and jerked, each in their own way to their own beat, until the bank convulsed with shouts and weeping and hands wringing to the sky, and mud-caked feet stamping on the dry sand.

Jesus stood some distance away, smiling broadly; elated and touched by the cries of joy. He happened to be standing next to a small tent and noticed a woman sitting at the front of a tent, disconsolate and oblivious to the events a few feet away. Her name was Dinah from Hebron, some miles below Jerusalem. Her husband danced on the bank. She felt very ill and distraught by the events and sat gripping her knees with her arms, and rocking in the way the depressed can.

"Daughter," he leaned down to her, "why would a flower so beautiful hide in the darkness of a tent?"

She said nothing and continued rocking to an unheard rhythm.

"Would you have a drink of water for a traveler?" he persisted.

She glanced up; her head had been resting on her knees as she watched her husband stamping his feet and wailing scripture in a sing-song fashion. Reaching into the tent she pulled out a bloated goat skin container and handed it to Jesus without saying a word.

Jesus poured a little in his container and smiled at her. "Your kindness to a stranger shows the loving light in your heart."

She looked up at him again, this time with more interest, but still morose.

"The Father brings great joy to the people." he said.

The rest of the camp had been watching the shoreline in curiosity. One by one they started leaving their shade and eagerly walked to the shore, soon to be seen swaying, then singing their own song, or lining up to go into the river. It became a crush of people along the bank, and dust hung in the air, stirred by their stamping and sliding and hopping about, each in their own way.

"You look weary," he said.

She looked out at the commotion and said in a low voice, "My family did not want me to come here. They say this baptizer defames the Temple and that this gathering is dangerous. The people here might get stirred up and rise against the Temple."

Jesus sat next to her. "These are all good Jews, as is John. He says no more than the prophets; that we must once again come out of the wilderness as a people, as we did with Moses. John is fulfilling the prophecy and trying to tell our Nation that each of us on our own must come to The Father. We can not rely on our Jewishness alone."

She glanced at him again, still a little annoyed at his earlier questions, but caught by the soothing nature of his voice and the peaceful look of his face, unusual as it was; handsome even, no, perhaps ugly, but certainly different. His smiling eyes crinkled in a boyish way that was disarming and infectious, so she began talking to him.

"But the priests and the teachers in Jerusalem are talking about this John, and spreading the word that he is a troublemaker, that he is a threat to the Temple, that he is a devil, that no teacher looks like a wild man as he does. He has no robes."

Jesus laughed out loud, "Well, he could use a new robe, but he is clean. He spends half his time in the river."

She gave a begrudging smile and wondered who this man was. "You have drunk my water and spoken to me, but I do not know your name."

"I am Jesus, from the village of Nazareth."

"Nazareth?" She looked puzzled. "What land is that in?"

He smiled, acknowledging to himself how insignificant his little village was. "It is in Galilee near Sepphoris. I have traveled to hear this man, who is my cousin, though I've not seen him in years. I have come to see if he has a message for me."

"A message?"

"Yes, I believe The Father has sent me to hear this man's words. Otherwise, why would I be sitting in this wilderness without food or water watching a man cleansing people in the Jordan?" He was trying to joke with her, to ease her mind.

She looked despondent and gazed down at her sandals. "I came because my husband made me. Our Lord rests in our glorious Temple, not on this scorpion-infested beach."

Then she felt Jesus' fingers touch her shoulder, like a feather, barely there, but then like something much firmer; a force that seemed to penetrate her. "Daughter, the Holy Spirit lives in only one place that

267

is important to you, and that is your heart. That is the one Temple you must visit. And He has brought you here for me to tell you this."

She stood up confused, angry, uncertain, curious. "Who do you think you are?" She demanded with some annoyance. "Are you from the Temple; a scribe, a teacher? How can any man say they speak for the Lord and not be stoned to death?"

A number of people were aroused by her loud words, and they rose from their tents and bedrolls and strolled over to listen.

Jesus felt a moment of doubt as he caught sight of so many moving toward them. He looked up, praying to himself, 'Father, I beg that You give me the strength to say the right words in the face of this doubt.'

He then moved closer to her. She was short and pretty; a young woman of eighteen, with black ringlets hanging to her rounded cheeks. She was perfumed and had an auburn-colored makeup over her face. Tiny rings swayed from her earlobes and one from her nose. An amulet filled with perfume dangled from a long necklace. Her eyes were deep brown and shiny with tears.

"It is not me you must believe, daughter; I am but a woodworker, but I ask that you believe the Word of our Father as he spoke through the prophets. I simply say what the prophets said." Jesus felt he was backing off from his earlier conviction that he could say he was a direct messenger of God. He worried that she would not believe him if he said the truth as he felt it. And then he felt a sense of shame that he was not telling the truth, so pulling himself up to his full height, he said, "We are all priests. Because I tell you of the Word as I understand it does not mean that I blaspheme the Holy One. I say the words that my heart places on my lips. I say the words that the scriptures place in my mind and that my eyes show me daily. I say the words that The Holiest One breathes into me. The story of The Father is not just bound in the scrolls at the Temple, they are tales told in the heart. The Truth is not a song of the synagogue. It is a song of your soul."

"You're the one at the tree," a man said. "I believe you were sent here to this baptizing place for a purpose. You give answers to questions I have long had. You are a teacher. You should be with John."

The woman looked embarrassed saying, "Forgive me, master. I have been heavy with worry about coming here. But I see that you are a gentle man who would comfort me. I am drawn to your words, though I do not know who you are. I feel great relief, and I praise the words you speak."

"Any words from my lips are words of The Father. I speak as He directs me, and I would say the same to you." She suddenly felt compelled to stretch her arms upward and stand for a girlish moment on her toes then did a turn as though she would break into a dance. She seemed to those watching to change dramatically.

A young man who had been listening went running toward the crowd on the bank yelling, "I've seen the sign! He comes!" And a surge of people moved around him to learn more.

The gathering around the tent murmured about what Jesus had said and the girl's reaction—so sudden—to the power of his words. Several split off to tell others on the bank, many of whom were followers of John. Those they told turned from the baptizing and ran toward the tent where Jesus had spoken, but he was gone. They found the young woman weeping with joy and praising the man whose name she couldn't remember. He seemed to have disappeared in the crush of people around the tent. Everyone was questioning those who had heard Jesus about what he had said. The girl repeated it as best she could, and they all nodded that this was a new teacher. John's helpers went back to the river, and when he had finished baptizing for the day, they told him of a man who had soothed the troubled heart of a distraught woman, a man many there seemed to be talking about.

"Was he tall with reddish hair and a Galilean accent?" John asked as water dripped from his camel skin mantel.

"Yes," one said. "And earlier I had seen him at that tree over there with a gentile who was so struck by his words that he knelt and cried. This is a powerful teacher. We must find him." They then returned to John's campsite. The evening was starting to set in, and cooking fires were lighting up. Many gathered together and spoke of John and how they had repented and were now ready for the Coming. A few spoke of the new teacher and wondered who he was. Some worried over the priest and his anger and what he would do. All felt that something very special was going on along this desolate river bank.

As they approached the tents of his campsite, John paused. Standing next to his fire and watching him and his disciples approach was the man they had just discussed. He wore no cap or dress on his head and in the fleeing light of the day, his long hair caught the angling rays of a setting sun, bringing out a reddish tint to its underlying dark brown coloring. His face was sunburned from the day's glare because he had no oils to put on for protection. There was something about his appearance that struck the group as they approached. He was speaking to a slightly-built young man, one of John's group named Nathaniel.

"You live in the next village from me," Nathaniel said in a friendly tone. "I'm from Cana and must be leaving soon for a wedding my cousin is having. It promises to be very large."

"Then the father better be pressing many grapes now. The wine can flow for days." They both laughed, acknowledging the drawn out festivities a Jewish wedding could entail.

"I have heard much about your teaching today," the Baptizer said as he walked up and put his hands on Jesus' arms in a welcome. "Many here speak of you. I heard one say he saw a sign in the effect you had on a woman."

Jesus looked directly at him and, ignoring his welcome, asked with great gravity, "Are you Elijah come back to life?"

John shook his ragged head; his hair was uncut and uncombed, with a film of dust clinging to its swirls. "No, no. But I do speak from his sayings. I am a child of the wilderness; my beloved father and mother lived here. I have always felt the Nation must be born again on this spot where the Israelites entered so many years ago. I would have the people come out of exile once again, by crossing the Jordan and being cleansed of their sins in its sacred waters. I say, they must be born again."

"You don't remember," Jesus said changing the subject for a moment. "We are of the same root. I am Jesus from Nazareth. My mother is Mary, your mother's cousin."

John grinned broadly and looked hard at Jesus, trying to see some family resemblance. "I do remember mother's cousin, Mary," he said, "but only vaguely. You and I may have played together, but I must tell you I remember little—as we were so young."

John motioned to a mat in front of his tent, "It is good to have family here, so come, you must sup with us and tell us of your teachings. You seemed to have caused a stir in the crowds." He raised a shaggy eyebrow and said smiling, "From the crowd I saw drawn to you, perhaps I should come out of the river and listen to you."

Some sat down on the bare ground and others on several small rugs. A woman passed around a bowl filled with dates and radishes. Jesus took several and said, "No, I have traveled to hear you, to see if there was a sign in what you say that I might follow."

270

John was listening for a hint of why this man was here and who he really was. At the back of his mind was the possibility that Jesus was the promised One; there was something so profoundly different, almost disturbing about his demeanor; a mixture of gentleness and deep conviction, his voice, his face, the way he stood and presented himself.

"Perhaps you are a sign to me. Would that be possible?" John asked cautiously.

"I go where The Father tells me to go. If I am a sign to you or to anyone, it is at His bidding, but then this is true for all who believe in His Holiness. We are all His messengers." Jesus did not feel moved to say that he was thinking God had singled him out, but he felt the urge growing to do just that.

"From where have you traveled?" one of the men asked.

"I am from the village of Nazareth. It is just below Sepphoris. My father was a carpenter and a very holy man. I did not want to forsake the trade of my father, so I, too, am a builder, but I have found that we cannot serve two masters. So I very recently stopped making arches and doors. My work is now whatever The Father would have me do."

"Are you a member of the community at Qumran?" another asked. "They have given up all they own and expect to be fed by the kindness of others if they travel."

"No, but I was just there. John, they told me that you had been raised there after the death of your parents. They were sorry that you had chosen to leave. But they will not yield from their strict ways and their anger at the priests at the Temple. I come to do as you do, to ask that our people forget this world and think of the one coming. And I say salvation is open to all, and that includes the lepers, gentiles, and tax collectors. The Community of Bathers does not agree. They go against the written word by excluding so many of our people. The Holy Place is a mansion of many rooms."

"The Community is too narrow with its rules and disciplines. I tired of it. What we speak here is very simple." John paused, then looking into Jesus' eyes, said, "The Holy One has filled you with a rare and open love. There are few whose heart is open to all such as yours is. There are almost none who can understand the terrible days that are coming. The Father will chop them down as easily as I take an axe to a fig tree. I started alone in this wilderness, a single voice." He motioned at the great encampment spreading around them like a

271

small tent city. "Now thousands have come from all over our land. The word is out that the end is near, and the people are filled with terror at the coming wrath. The prophecies are about to be fulfilled."

Nathaniel put down a plate of dried fish and said, "John says it cost too much money to get to heaven the way the priests control everything. His message says we don't have to pay tribute to the Temple. We can go straightaway to The Father. It has great appeal to the poor, but it angers the religious leaders. They fear he goes around their power."

"Our land is overrun with hatred and argument," Jesus said. He felt he wasn't making his point with the thin-figured John. "The wicked ones from Italia have poisoned our land with their commerce and greed. But our people also argue among themselves over the meaning of the Books of Moses. The Laws have become almost their own god. The people need to be united under the one great message of The Father, which is a message of love; love of Him and love of one's neighbor. It is a message that knows no sex, no wealth, no ownership, not even family. It is man as was the First Man; at one with The Maker."

John eyed the figure sitting next to him. He was taken with his look and his voice and the way he had appeared in the camp and how people had instantly been moved by his presence. The thought crossed his mind that this man might not be a man, but he was not yet sure. John was content to preach to Jews. He wondered why Jesus kept speaking of bringing gentiles and pagans into the Kingdom.

"Do you agree then that the Kingdom is coming and that we must repent?" John asked.

"I still wonder if you are not Elijah, and only appear to be my cousin. But whether you are the prophet, or a new prophet, you have made this ground holy. Yes, I believe this is the time of fulfillment of the Books. I see it approaching in the air, as one sees a cloud rise out of the west and knows a storm approaches, or feels the wind blow from the south and knows there will be heat. So why don't we recognize a coming God?"

"I am only John and one who has studied the prophets, but I am not a prophet." John had been told before that he was Elijah reincarnated.

A tall, thick-chested man to their left was rubbing oil on welts from bee stings he received while gathering honey for the group. He offered in a deep voice, "John believes that The End will be announced in the form of a man who will teach and lead our people; one from the line of David, a new king, a savior, a Messiah."

Another spoke up. "And this Messiah on the terrible day of atonement will restore Israel to its greatness, and God will reign over the faithful in Jerusalem."

John and the others nodded and watched Jesus' reaction.

Jesus spoke with great certainty and authority. "So says Isaiah, that this Arm of The Father shall be revealed as a man of sorrows, one who will bear the grief of the whole Nation of Israel; one The Father will be pleased in blessing. This righteous servant shall bear the sins of the world. He will also give his life for the Nation and return to life on the third day. I don't know that it will be a king we receive. It might just be a man." He paused, then said, very carefully, "One like you or I."

"You think the Messiah will be killed? Many would consider this blasphemy!" John seemed taken aback. Then he caught himself because he was fearful of this man. He continued looking for a sign that would reveal who he truly was, so he continued to probe. "I know the scripture you speak of well," John said. "But you say it in a way that shows you truly understand. Does the coming of this Messiah, or this man, mean something special to you?"

Jesus didn't answer directly, "It means that a Son will be sent among us, not one that would be noticed for who He is; a root out of dry ground. It means He will be asked to endure great suffering; He will be reviled and persecuted. But it will be as an act of love, for The Holy One will have sent this Arm as a sign to the children, that by His grace death can be conquered. This Son will die that we may be reborn in the Spirit."

John sat silently. He had never heard anyone give this interpretation. He poked at the embers in front of him with a pine twig, looking at the embers, then cutting his eyes over to this unique figure. He thought it safe to pursue the subject again. "Die for our sins, huh? The Father would send a Messiah, His own Arm, to lead the End of Days and He would allow this messenger to be killed?"

The group surrounding them numbered several dozen of John's followers, all leaning in to hear the exchange, for they thought something very special was occurring here. There was much mumbling and whispering at John's question.

"So say the prophets," Jesus answered calmly. "But this will mean The Father does not attempt to change our Nation by sending armies, but by sending a single messenger who will be as every man and who will suffer greatly and take on our sins and die for us. He would die so that the nations would be saved. This will be a prophet like Moses, and one sent directly from The Father."

John's mouth parted and almost fell open. He leaned forward and placed his palms flat on the ground as though he would fall over if he did not receive some kind of support. The others gasped and moaned their surprise and anguish over hearing such a revelation.

John was clearly uncertain about Jesus' real identity, so he finally responded in disbelief, mixed with reverence. "I have heard no one say the Messiah is coming to die. I hear all say he is coming to carry out our Lord's message that the end is here and each man must save his own soul. And the Messiah will come as a champion, a holy warrior brandishing sword and riding waves of fire." John visibly shook at the thought of the horrors he predicted.

Jesus' face had a wondrous calm that drew the men to him. He was almost hypnotic in his appeal. "The Father has freed each of the children of Israel with this new covenant of which you teach. The joy in it is that it frees the people from thinking that the priests and the Temple must be the center of their faith. It promises eternal happiness, if only we will accept that we alone, on our own, can enter the Kingdom. It is a message of freedom and salvation. We are judged on our own, and not along with the rest of humanity."

John interrupted in surprise, "New covenant?!"

"As I have said," Jesus repeated with some frustration, "his Son will bring a new covenant of love. The Father will reveal his love for our people by bringing His Son to show by example how we should live. The prophets say He will allow His Son to die for our wrongs. Death will be forever defeated when the Son returns to life. For this great act, the new covenant asks that we center our lives around glorifying The Father and loving our neighbor."

"I would hope this Messiah will gather the people in an army, if he does nothing else," John groused, impatient with any answer that did not include the generally accepted thought that a part of God's salvation plan was to drive out the Romans.

Several of John's disciples had slid around closer to Jesus and were listening raptly to his words. "I try and understand you, teacher," Nathaniel stated. He looked intently at Jesus who was sitting relaxed with his legs bent out in front of him and leaning slightly on his right arm. "But we have always been taught to fear the Ancient of Days.

This reading you have where you emphasize love…it is different from the Baptizer's message."

"Not so much," Jesus disagreed.

"Do you believe, along with John, that we must all repent through baptizing?"

"The Son of man must be born anew. It can come as a part of being cleansed with water, but it must come first through a cleansing of the soul. We must go as innocent as children to heaven's gate, and to do that we must be born again."

"Children?" The group murmured and conjectured over what that meant. Children were loved, to be sure, but children were of little consequence when engaged in theological discussions. They failed to understand what he meant.

"But you also say that the Messiah, the messenger, will die in the battle with Satan."

Jesus' expression passed from a placid look, to an obvious sadness. "In the great tragedy of that moment, when The Son dies, all of mankind will be offered salvation forever. It is our Father's way of showing that He will sacrifice for us, if we will sacrifice for Him. And it shows us that He so loves us that He would sacrifice His own Son." Jesus raised a finger to make a point. "Dearly beloved, The Father knows that man is weak; that he covets possessions, another's oxen, his home, his silver goblets. And He will acknowledge this with the death of the one He sends. The Father will sacrifice His Son for you. Then by His grace will He accept those who have the ears to hear and those who will knock at His door."

There was much conversation, confusion, arguing and groans of surprise, concern, and fear; a gamut of emotions surged over the gathering.

Jesus stood and said matter of factly, "Few will like the messenger or the message. Fewer will enter the gates, for mankind has become accustomed to having possessions. He wants to take them with him into the next world, for they have become his true god. It is not an easy path. It demands denial and discipline, and we are but of the flesh and want the easy way."

John squinted at Jesus. "I am finishing my work here and will soon be going into Samaria at Salim near Tel Balata. I will be looking for a disciple to go to Judea and baptize. Would you be a follower?"

"I am here to learn of the way for me," Jesus answered obliquely. He then stood as though he were about to leave. "I do know I will try and come as close as a human can to the One. Perhaps then you would be a follower of me." A slight smile crept over Jesus' mouth.

Seeing that Jesus was about to leave, John almost pleaded with him to stay, "Would you leave? You have no tent. Would you share in one of ours? Here, have some goat's milk, locusts, and honey."

"I would take some of your sup if you could spare it. I need prayer, and I will find a tree or cave that The Father has prepared for me."

John told one of several women who was cooking over a fire to give Jesus some of their food which consisted of bread baked on a rock, fried fish that had been caught earlier in the day, and locusts that were ground, fried, and mixed with spices.

"Will you come back tomorrow?" John asked.

"Yes," Jesus answered. "I wish that you baptize me, also."

John seemed uncertain of what to say. He stammered, "Oh, so you want to repent, or…"

"There is only one who is perfect. All others must try, and every day ask His forgiveness, because mankind can not be perfect." Jesus looked long at John then said gently, "You, John, as holy as you are, are still less than the least who is in heaven. I would not say you are not holy, only that you are of the seed of mankind and it is a flawed seed." He took food from the women and filled his skin container with milk. He looked at John saying, "The Spirit is at work here. I know why I came." Looking at John, he asked with a face so serene that John trembled.

"Beloved, do you know why I came?" Jesus asked. John stood as though he were frozen. His disciples sat wide-eyed, waiting for the fiercely opinionated baptizer to respond. After a long moment, when all appeared unable to speak, John answered weakly, "I think so, Master."

Jesus nodded knowingly as the two of them were now, independently, beginning to grasp what had been the unknowable, the supreme secret of the Jewish faith — who would be the Arm of God, the Savior. Jesus looked deep into John's eyes, and the baptizer shook in a terrible fear of what the coming end was to bring — the indescribable wrath of an angry God. But then, tears welled in his eyes in relief and joy that he, John, might indeed be the one who announced the Son, and that the prayers of a nation were about to be answered. Jesus touched several on the shoulder with his fingertips. Nathaniel almost fainted. He, too, was convinced that this was the one, The Son, but so captivated was he in the enormity of the moment that all he could do was reach up and touch the fingers that were searing his soul with the possibility that this was the hand of God.

Suddenly, and out of context with the moment, Jesus laughed, and his sudden laughter surprised himself and the rest of the group. Caught up in its joy and celebration, they all, like giddy, foolish children sharing some imaginary joke, began laughing, not uproariously, but happy, out of relief, in acknowledgment that each felt this man might be the one John had proclaimed, and he was no Angel of Wrath, no splendid warrior, but a wonderfully human, human being. All, however, were shadowed by doubts, so the laughter was short-lived, and they settled into a quiet conjecture over what would happen next; what great sign would be forthcoming, if indeed this were the Arm. They longed for a sign.

Feeling as though the burden of the last several years had been lifted off him, Jesus walked away with a spring in his step and disappeared in the evening light among the reeds along the river bank.

The woman who handed Jesus the food asked, "Baptizer, was that the man who the gentile knelt before and who drove the devils from the woman in the tent?"

"Huh? Oh…yes," John mumbled as he continued to stare at the reeds, at the sky and around the camp as he searched for any clue indicating what was happening here, or, John wondered, did he want so strongly for this to be the Messiah that he had fallen under the intensity of this man.

As his disciples chatted about Jesus and his words, John clinched his teeth from a tension rising within. He went from being convinced who Jesus was, to being troubled over this cousin he hardly knew. He was not what John had expected. This notion of the Messiah dying for man was novel and disturbing, and yet so well explained by Jesus that it was believable. His mission over the past months had been to announce the coming Kingdom and the One who would proclaim that Kingdom. Daily, for almost a year, he preached he had watched for a sign. He had searched the heavens at night looking at the stars for a special alignment, listening to the winds to hear a trumpet or a clash of angels in armor. And now this most unassuming of messengers, a common man like Moses and young David had simply walked up, and John had the growing feeling that this man could be the Messiah arriving gently at first, but sure to raise the people with the power of his presence and the unassailable clarity of his words — that they make ready for the glory of God's Coming.

CHAPTER 14

The morning saw more people arriving. Almost all were walking, but those of wealth rode donkeys and the truly well-off rode horses. The camp now spread far from the eastern side of the narrow river, and on the Jerusalem side, also. Several hundred were there now, and emotions were high. Most came from the nearby area. Many were there out of sheer terror that the end of the world was at hand, that this fierce man was pronouncing it and saying those who had not repented would be burned to death. Many in their hearts did not know whether he was right or not, but no one saw the harm in coming out and saying they were sorry. The End of Days was accepted as a fact, and a Messiah was thought to be a necessary part of that ushering in of the restoration of Israel. Rumors of the Baptizer's warnings had swept over Palestine, and few, if they could make their way, saw any reason not to be safe and come out to be cleansed.

Jesus had slept in a shallow recession against a cliff, almost a cave that gave some cover. He awoke hungry. In the distance the smoke from the camp swirled up in thin gray clouds in a breezy air. A bank of early fog hung over the Jordan Valley, and as the sun rose, its light was caught in the fog and exploded into a brilliant diffusion of light, as though the rising sun had been captured in the valley's mist. He looked at the fiery glow of the fog and became convinced that God was in the valley. He stood, stretched, and began to pray.

"The Holiest, I honor Thy name this morn. I praise You for giving me the words to tell of Your glory yesterday. You have directed me to a man who has dedicated his life to Your Coming. He says he is here to announce Your messenger. Would that be me, Father? Is that who I am? As I said Your words yesterday, the gentile fell to his knees and the distraught woman was made happy. But many travel the roads and speak in the assemblies, and people are healed. Am I one of them, destined to travel the roads, or am I more? My body is full of Thy love. My thoughts are consumed in this love and the need to teach it. Your servant asks that You guide him this day. If it be Your Will, I ask that you reveal your plan for me. Reveal to me who I am. I, your servant, ask in Your Holy Name. Amen and amen."

John and several of his disciples were up early, eating breakfast, when they saw him coming through the blast of light in the fog, almost a mirage, an apparition out of the heavy thicket of reeds that rushed at the precious waters of the Jordan. Several doves were flushed out in front of him as though announcing his arrival. Foliage followed the winding coils of the turgid waters like the skin of a snake, for only feet beyond the river's banks was the dry harshness, the pale crumble of sand and pebbles of the river's basin. The river provided the signature of life in the Moab wilderness, sustaining only that which rooted close by its side.

The sight of his coming out of the cloud was stunning, and John was speechless. He tried to say something to one at his side, but could say nothing, and those with him saw the stunned look, and all of them felt a great apprehension.

Dinah saw him also and felt the scene, the drama of the light, to be a sign, and she called out, "Master! Over here!" She leaned down into the tent where her husband was repairing his boot. "Akiba, the one I told you of, is back. Come out and meet him, " she said excitedly.

Her husband was a short man of very brown skin. He wore a turban headdress and a thin robe that hung loosely over him like a long night shirt. His face was rugged and accentuated by prominent cheekbones and a long, hooked nose. He looked to be a mixture of many of the tribes and peoples of the southern part of Palestine, called Idumea, an intensely hot and barren waste of a place on the way to Egypt.

"The One has blessed us with another day to rejoice in His glory," Jesus greeted the woman as he approached her tent. He had combed his hair on the way to the camp and had borrowed a few drops of oil to put on his skin for protection against the sun.

"You would honor us by sharing our breakfast," she said.

Her husband emerged from the tent, eyed Jesus up and down and said, "Dinah has done little since last evening except speak of you. My gratitude to you for calming her worries. She has been very distraught over our being here. Would you honor my table?" He motioned to a woven mat lying to one side of their cooking fire.

Akiba said a short prayer while the three stood, sprinkled water over his fingers and along the outside of his cup, and the men sat. Dinah served them barley cakes with honey someone had found in a nearby tree, pan-roasted chick peas, figs and raisins. It was all Jesus could do to eat with some decorum. He thought of roast lamb as he munched on the crunchy peas. He was weak from hunger and ate eagerly.

"Dinah tells me about your coming to our tent, that you are a new teacher, maybe even a healer. She said you drove the wicked spirits from her." Akiba remarked.

"I now go where our Father guides me. I have given up all my possessions and my work as a carpenter to tell the words The Father places on my lips. If wicked spirits were driven from her, it was by His power. I was simply a messenger." Jesus felt completely comfortable edging closer to a direct connection with God. Gone were the uncertainties that had plagued him; he knew if he did not attempt to establish some authority behind his sayings, he would forever be questioned. He also knew that now in the early stages of his ministry that he was open to attack by those who did not know him. He needed the word of others to give him credibility. He wondered if he should be a disciple of John.

Akiba was curious as to just who the stranger was. "Are you one of the Pious Ones from Qumran?"

"No. Though they are holy men, they would cast out those not perfect in their eyes. It is not ours to judge."

A thin man with a raspy voice and a long beard asked, "Should they not want to keep sinners out of their community? We all try to avoid gentiles and pagans. And shouldn't they be preparing for the End of Days when the Messiah will come to slay the sinners?"

"To answer your first question, beloved, judge not that ye may be judged. Whosoever enters the Kingdom is not the decision of any man, but the provenance of the Father. To judge is to mock The Father's role. Who are we to limit Him?"

"To answer your second question, I say the Kingdom is here now, and it is also in a future day that no man can know. But while we wait for the final days, I say we must prepare our souls for the Kingdom that is here now. There is enough to worry about today. Tomorrow will take care of itself."

"Amen," several murmured as a crowd gathered around the tent.

"See, husband," Dinah exclaimed. "This is a true teacher. He is one of those with special connections to The Holy, blessed be His Name."

"Would you be a disciple of the Baptizer?" A woman asked.

"I am a disciple of The Father, though His Spirit rests on the shoulders of John. If The Father commands that I follow John, then I will."

Akiba said with certainty, "John is the Elijah of our time. The Father has spoken to him and told him the end is now. I believe him and though we risk the curses of the priests, I know this man tells the truth."

"Among them who are born of women, there are none greater than John. Yet even the least in heaven are greater than he." Jesus said to their surprise.

An audible gasp went around the group as they repeated what Jesus had said.

Akiba seemed angered by that assertion. "Do you with the one hand praise the Baptizer and with the other smite him? Is John not good?"

The crowd tensed and looked at Jesus. He put his brass plate down and, unperturbed by Akiba's reaction, said, "Why call him good? There is none good but one, and that is The Father."

Akiba looked confused. "John says if we renounce our sins, then we are seen as good in the eyes of the Lord, and we will be accepted into the new kingdom. Do you say we are not good enough if we renounce our sins?"

"I say that no man can ever be as good as The Father is good. The children are all sinners before The Father. He accepts us as sinners, but sorrows deeply when we dishonor His name. But don't worry; so say Isaiah, that The Father will send one among us who will bear our griefs and sorrows and who will bear the sins of all of man. So do not worry whether John is good... know that The Spirit speaks through him. Worry only over your own soul and know that The Father loves you and glories in your efforts to please Him."

"Husband, this teacher is different from any we have heard," she said, earnestly hoping her Akiba would agree. "I am glad now that we came. He gives me hope."

Akiba had a scowl set on his face which hid the uncertainty he felt about this man and what he had said of John.

"Wife, I will say who is this family's teacher," he said gruffly.

She bowed her head and looked hurt.

Jesus said, "The Truth will split wife from husband, child from mother. Some will be as stony ground, others as fertile ground, and the seed will perish on the one and bear fruit on the other."

"You speak in parables, teacher," Akiba said.

"Often a treasure will not be found if laid out in plain view, but those who would see its riches know they must dig and look for it. Those who have ears will easily hear and know."

A woman shouted, "Praise the Word! This master speaks words no man could say unless said on the breath of The Holy."

Many joined in praising Jesus as one who was especially close to God, while Akiba and others felt their allegiance to John had been challenged. Several in the crowd said they were going to tell John of Jesus and that he should take him on as a main disciple.

"Akiba, I do not speak against the Baptizer. He is a very holy man, and one that I will learn from. I agree with him in that the children of Israel must admit their sins and make a new covenant with The Father. I also agree that the End of Days is near and that all people must prepare themselves."

Jesus stood. "I go now to fulfill my Father's wishes, and I thank you for your breakfast."

Akiba felt somewhat placated, and in his mind Jesus had apologized for intimating that John was not as perfect as Akiba had pictured him to be. Akiba's wife put down a skillet and walked behind Jesus along with a number of others. Akiba called for her to come back, but she ignored his call.

John was in the Jordan praying silently. The banks were starting to fill with people who had finished their breakfast and were ready to be cleansed. There was a great turnover in the camp as people would come first to see what it was all about; then, if so moved, be baptized, stay for another day reveling in the celebrations, then leave. Many had come from Jericho a few miles away. This was a removed and remote spot for many in Palestine. Few could stay too long because of their farms or work, and the fact that they would quickly run out of food.

The spirituality of the camp—its sporadic and discordant music, clapping, praises, individual singing of scriptures, and rhythmic swayings and stompings—all gave the sprawling site a festival atmosphere. People traded foods, spices, jewelry, and wine, and brought water from the big springs at Jericho—the enterprising found a little marketplace springing up amid the religious fervor.

The entrance of several more priests from Jerusalem caught the attention of many and gave concern to some. The priests ignored the people as they brought their horses to a rest under a pine tree grove just downstream from where John welcomed the first repenters into the cool waters and the muddy bottom which oozed about their toes.

The three priests and four aides were easily recognized from the rest of the crowd, first by their horses, then by the colorful stripes of their shirts and robes with blue fringes, and by their turbans. Each wore the ever-present "tephillin," the tiny boxes containing four passages of scripture. They were strapped to their foreheads and their left forearms. They also had a very direct, almost confrontational way they walked and brushed by people. They were not there to be converted.

A man from John's immediate camp saw them and left the baptizing area to greet them.

"I am Eli, a disciple of John. We are fulfilling the words of the prophets here, and we invite you to prepare for the Coming."

A priest, as wide as he was tall, scowled as he looked over Eli's shoulder and into the nearby river at the disheveled figure pouring water over crying converts. "We don't need to prepare for anything," he grumped. "We are prepared. But the man in the river there had best prepare for the coming of Antipas' guard."

Eli blurted in surprise, "A guard? Why would they come here?"

"Apparently, cursing the Temple was not enough; this baptizer had to stir up insurrection by criticizing the recent marriage of Antipas. We hear he could be imprisoned if he continues in this way. We know of others who will have him stoned if he doesn't stop this rebelliousness." It was a subtle threat that the Sadducees on the Jewish Court would organize a mob to take action against John.

A tall, thin, very-tanned, almost swarthy-looking man with a bulbous nose, reddened on the end, stepped forward. He spoke in a careful voice in direct contrast to his associate. "We want no harm to come to anyone of the faith, but this baptizer causes concern to the high priest and his council. We believe he advocates that the priests, the Temple, even the sacrifices be ignored; that people simply come to him and repent and the Kingdom will be theirs. We also come to warn him of the anger of Antipas. You can understand how we must maintain good relations with the authorities. We know that the tetrarch is already greatly distressed over John's accusing him of not acting in a moral manner." The man nodded as though he wanted John's disciple to say he agreed.

Eli had been with John for most of his ministry, now in its sixth month. He was fiercely devoted to John and the totality of his commitment. He was convinced that John was the prophet Elijah reborn; a messenger coming out of the wilderness to proclaim the Coming of God and possibly even the Messiah.

Eli reacted angrily. "Do you not even see what is happening here! This is holy ground. This is where Elijah was taken into heaven on a pillar of fire, possibly even where our ancestors crossed into the promised land. This is the fulfillment of the prophets. This is where the Messiah is being announced and the End of Days will begin. The heavens could split open on this very spot and armies of angels descend. Are you blind to to all of this?" He was leaning into them, his fists tight, his neck straining with protruding blood vessels.

The round priest was unimpressed. "The only thing that's going to split open here is the bushy head of that wild man in the river. He speaks blasphemy against the Temple. He speaks without proper authority, and he may cause insurrection against the Romans."

Exasperated, Eli waved his hand in invitation toward the river. "Come hear his words. He simply warns of the Coming and asks that all confess their sins before His wrath descends. That is neither blasphemy, nor insult. Come, I invite you. Stand on the banks and watch the Holy Spirit move through the people. The Baptizer does what you do in the Temple; he urges our people to live by the Commandments. There is no insurrection here."

The group brushed by Eli as though he were beneath their talking to any further, and they moved to the edge of the crowd. The entourage smiled and nodded and blessed those who turned and acknowledged them, but they did not go into the crowd. The priests were uneasy about this emotional following; fearful that it might turn violent.

Out of a clear sky clouds suddenly formed and rolled low to the ground; smudges of gray, undefined rolls and streamers of a churning storm seemed to appear out of nowhere. There was an ominous, threatening look about them. The heavy overcast drew all color from the land. The beiges and pastels of the wilderness area wore a sameness, a prosaic wash of muted color under the dark cover. But the mood of the crowd started to come out of its morning doldrums as tambourines and flutes gave voice, each to its own maker's movement. With the music, disjointed as it was, chants and songs and praises, wails, flutes, tambourines, drums, ram's horns, all punctuated the early still, gaining momentum and voice, and then carrying the people in the power of the songs to sway gently at first, then with more and more fervor until the bank was alive with gyrating, stomping believers. Dust quickly enveloped them as they careened into one another, laughing and clapping and crying in a growing delirium. One scrawny old man, caught in the fervor, careened out of control into the priests, knocking the round one off the bank and with an enormous, spreading splash, into the waters of the Jordan.

He flapped around like a speared fish, trying to regain his balance before finally rising in a rush of water, sputtering and wiping his face and looking horrified at his soaked robes. The tephillin that had stuck out from his forehead had been knocked down over his nose. The crowd roared in laughter. Humiliated and furious, he was hauled up on the shallow bank.

"Blasphemers!" He shrieked. "This preacher is going to get a stone against his head before the week is over, and I'm picking out the first one!"

His entourage patted at the priest's drenched robes and didn't notice the solitary figure standing alone in the water several feet from John. Most entering the water came through a receiving line of attendants on the bank who released them one at a time to step into the shallow water and be received by other attendants who stood around John. There was some organization to the whole affair, though it was still very informal.

Jesus had not gone through the line, but had appeared out of one end of the crowd on the bank and stepped into the water on his own. Barefoot, he could feel the chill of the stream and the softness of the muddy bottom. He wore only a loin cloth.

Jesus' solitary figure caught John's eye as a young girl professed her sins and prepared to be sprinkled. After releasing the girl, John held his hand out to his attendants to hold up on sending the next person. He felt intimidated by Jesus' sudden appearance; he had felt that way from the first time he had seen him, a disturbing, uncertain feeling that was almost frightening. There seemed to be no other sounds or sights—no crowded banks, or stomping, screaming converts; only the singular aloneness of Jesus coming slowly toward him like an apparition; a dream in slow motion, strangely disturbing and profound.

"There comes one mightier than me," John said to the handlers standing next to him. He was short of breath, and the words barely emerged. "The latchet of whose shoes I am not worthy to unloose: he shall baptize you with the Holy Ghost and with fire."

"Master." A young man who was assisting John leaned into him, almost whispering, "Are you saying that this is the One who will lead us?"

Ignoring the question, because he didn't know the answer, John asked, in a tremulous voice, "Why do you come?"

"We all must answer," Jesus said simply. "We must show that there is only one Perfect. We all must be born again as a child."

"Don't I need to be baptized of thee? Why do you come to me?" John was testing the stranger who he thought was here for a special reason. John sensed that Jesus had singled himself out in subtle, but powerful ways. His mind reeled; he was dizzy and nauseous. There was an aspect going on here that was terrifying, but if Jesus was the Messiah, where were the armies of angels, the blasts of horns, the pillars of fire? John needed more of a sign.

"Do I not stand before you of the flesh? Do I not have the same temptations, pains, sufferings and joys as do you? Am I not fully a man? Suffer it to be so now; for thus it becomes us to fulfill all righteousness." Jesus felt John's uncertainty, as they were almost debating the Truth of this moment: this moment that both had agonized over for years — the epic event that would change all of history. John was moving cautiously, but feeling that he was riding a mighty wave that no force could now stop. His ministry, his belief that he was the announcer appeared to be true, and its profundity shook his entire being. For an instant he wanted to run from the river, and then Jesus touched his arm and said with a look of irrefutable grace and conviction, "Do not fear that which you cannot know. The Father knows and that is enough. Do this now in His name."

John felt tense, excited, confused, wary, exhilarated. He caught himself glancing down at his bared chest to see if his racing heart could be seen pounding against the skin. His breath was coming in short, shallow gasps. He feared he would faint. Emotions ran rampant over him as he slowly placed his hand on the head of Jesus, and looking at the absolute serenity of his face, John's hand shook, not knowing what would happen next. As he pushed against the thickness of Jesus' hair, he wondered if he could be announcing the end of the earth as they knew it, the incomprehensible beginning of the coming of heaven to earth; the terrifying, monumental anger of God, the ear-shattering blast of horn and hoof as ten thousand angels rode out of a cloud of fire and brimstone to turn the earth to rivers of blood. John gasped audibly as Jesus' long hair went under the muddy surface, his hand paused in a moment of near paralysis that this in fact might be God's Arm he was holding under the water. At that moment, as he could feel Jesus pushing against his hand and rising from the water, John reeled in abject terror as the river was filled with shafts of light and a commotion from the nearby reeds as a single dove flew out and almost collided with the two men as it flew over. The heavy cloud cover had parted just above them and for a fleeting moment the intensity of the sun burned against John's face. 'Oh, Beloved Holy Spirit, surely this is the Son!' his mind screamed, but though his lips were moving, no sound came and only he knew that his ability to think straight had almost collapsed under the weight of the thought.

From somewhere — was it the bank or out of the sky — it seemed to have no source; a voice was heard to boom, "This is my beloved Son. In him I am well pleased!"

Jesus rose, water cascading off his shoulders, the sun blinding his sight, the dove fluttering in a strange turn over them. Did one actually land on his shoulder? Jesus then cried aloud in unrestrained joy, "He that knows me, knows The Father!"

John stood frozen, not knowing what would happen next. He tried to identify where the voice had come from, but couldn't. His heart pounded out of control. Sweat ran freely down his face. He jerked his head back and forth like someone about to be attacked, but from which quarter he didn't know. He looked up; the hole in the dark churn of clouds held and the sun beaconed on their spot only. Jesus was next to him weeping and looking into his eyes. John held his breath, thinking he would hear a shattering trumpet, the deafening voices of angels heralding the Coming, fire streaming from the low roll of the clouds, and perhaps a vision of God Himself. His head jerked around again to survey the emptiness of the hills, then down the river. He didn't know if he were about to be plucked up, stormed over by the heavenly legions, or if even the river itself would be turned into a boiling cauldron. Frightened, he looked back for Jesus only to see that he had left the water and was walking east toward the desolate hills of the great Moab wilderness.

"Behold, is this the Lamb of God?" John asked after Jesus' retreating figure. He said it loud enough for Jesus to hear, but Jesus didn't turn.

Two of John's disciples started to run after Jesus through the shallow water, taking high steps to clear their knees, yelling, "Messiah! Messiah!" But he kept walking, and upon clearing the shallow bank they slowed in their pursuit and stopped, seeming uncertain as to what to do next. Both were afraid to come to close to Jesus.

"Did you see the light!" an excited attendant was yelling in John's ear. "I saw the sign; He is the One, the Son!"

Another shouted, "He goes to gather His armies in the desert." And overcome with joy, the attendants went high-stepping through the water toward the shore yelling, "We saw the sign; He is come, He is come!"

The crowd who had been singing and stamping and, for the most part, had not witnessed the baptism, began stampeding into the water, all trying to be baptized at once before The End caught them unrepented. They drove their knees against the shallow water in frantic splashes, their arms flailing and pumping trying to gain them more speed as each tried to reach John first.

Jesus walked away stunned, terrified, overjoyed, exhilarated; a raging rush of feelings and fears and joys. He was half following the scriptures in going into the wilderness to be tested, and half delirious from the experience of the baptism. Drawn by a force he couldn't fathom clearly, Jesus moved quickly away from the growing melee at the river. He climbed the escarpment that stands a quarter mile from the Jordan and then on back into the forbidding emptiness of the treeless wastes of low hills where life is occasional in the lazy soar of a vulture, or the skitterish run of a scorpion. The silence is palpable, as real and deafening in its own way as thunder. It absorbs one's mind, freeing, liberating; bringing a singularity of focus. To some it is a terrifying geography; a void the mind can fill with delirium; it screams at one from a world of vague form and little color. Jesus had always found great solace in stillness and remote places, and he moved without thought, and without his food pack, into the emptiness.

The supreme joy of the baptism gave way to an almost paralyzing fear that he was indeed The Chosen One. Walking, stumbling on the loose earth and soon out of sight of the river, he fell down the sudden slope of a dry stream bed and against the rocky outcropping at its bottom. The barest trickle of water seeped from it, and he lay his face against its coolness and let it run over his dry lips. Feeling sick and dizzy, he began to pray.

"Holy Father, who dwells in that most sacred of places, I beg of You to strengthen me. You filled my heart with unimagined joy when the voice rang out that I was Your Beloved Son, and the heavens opened with Your light and You came to me as a dove. I knew there were to be no armies, no fires burning the earth. I now know for certain that Yours is to be a peaceful Coming, as gentle as the flutter of a dove's wings. But, Father, almost at the same time that I feel the joy, a moment later I then feel too weak to fulfill the words of Isaiah, too weak to bear the burden of the sins of man, too frightened to go to my death for others. Father, if I am the Arm You have selected, I am a weak one. I have yearned recently for the love of Rebekah, to hold her in my arms, to gaze forever into the beauty of her face. I have thought of the treasures I could have living with her father and the easiness of that life, or working for the Jew Nathan, or the power the Community could give me to lead them. I am too much human, Father, and the burden I feel You are placing upon me brings with it great sadness and loneliness. To honor Your Kingdom and Your love I must forsake all others and all things. Many don't believe me; they question who I am and by what authority such a poor man speaks. Why did You select me, Father? I am just a man who works with his hands. If you have chosen me, I must endure insult and outrage, perhaps even stoning. Can any man bear so much? And I am but a man, aren't I? You place words on my lips; You give power to my hands, but though I am filled with You, I am still a man aren't I, Father?"

The morning cloud cover had relented under the overbearing sun and had dissipated into a deep blue and empty sky. And as sudden as the vanishing clouds, the feeling of his humanness subsided, and Jesus was overwhelmed with a closeness to God that for a moment made him feel as though he could actually fly up and over the land; it was an exhilaration beyond any he had known, soaring in its freedom, and all encompassing. He held his arms straight out as though they were wings and twisted and turned his body and ran up and over the hill as though he were flying. And as he ran and flapped his arms, he laughed with the hysteria of the truly free; those few who have slipped across the boundaries of reason into a mystical land of absolute spirituality. He stopped and held his head up, trying to peer into the depths of the sky, seeking to see the face of God.

Summoning his courage, he breathed deeply and asked in a clear but beseeching voice "I beg do not be angry with this soul, Father, but I must ask of You if I could be the pillar of cloud, the Arm?"

There was pause. Jesus' eyes warily searched the emptiness about him. Then his eyes flooded with tears, he held his hands toward the sky palms open, and cried into the void, "Could I be of one with You? Could I be as the First Man? Tempt me, Holy One. Test my strengths to turn away from the Angel of Darkness. If I am truly at one with You I will know, and I will come out of this wilderness fearless of the stone and the harsh word."

He stopped in the sandy bottom of a wadi, an ancient and empty stream bed. He anguished and cried aloud, and it echoed against the walls of the canyoned river bed in a reverberating chorus of despair and doubt. He climbed, scratching and scrambling for a foothold in the loose, rocky dirt, up the side of the wall of the ravine until he stood again at the top of the rise.

Lifting his face toward the sky, he shouted into the silence. "They won't listen to me, Father, if I do not speak with Your authority. The roads are filled with those who say they are Your messengers. Oracles and healers fill the land. But now I feel I am one with You. I am of You. You showed Your face at the Jordan, and it was as fierce as the light through the clouds and as gentle as the dove that came to my shoulder. You were the light, and You were the dove, Father. And those are my directions. So simple, so clear. I will be the light and the way, and it will be done with a ministry of love." He laughed in joy, "And I heard the voice at the Jordan say that you were pleased. Pleased!" He shouted the word again and again. He yelled until he was growing hoarse, "It is me, Father! I am You and You are me! I am the Arm and the fiery cloud. I am the Son! I am the Son of the Light! It is not an army You send, but me, an army of one."

A lone figure against the vast, dry emptiness of the wilderness, Jesus lay exhausted. His body ached from the convulsive sobbing of despair and then of the joyous screams from the dawning realization of his mission. Emotions washed over him like an errant tide, uncertain from moment to moment, which way the shore. He knew before he could return that he must be further tested. He could not go back now until there were no questions left, no doubts, no more trying out parables on friends. No hesitations about speaking directly from the authority of The Father. This return must be in the triumphant certitude that his was a holy mission directed by God; a magnificently singular mission where all would know that his words came on the breath of the one he called The Father. It must be a path from which he would never waver; a path that could lead to his death.

The sun blistered the blue out of the morning sky, bleaching it almost white as Jesus sought out a shaded overhang and fell onto the dirt in a deep and dreamless sleep.

At the Jordan, John continued to baptize, but without fervor. His eyes kept returning to the eastern wilderness and its lifeless march of rock strewn hills. He was becoming convinced that this Jesus was not a man, but the living promise of the prophecies fulfilled, and that he had gone off to summon God's armies. They were gathering out there in the wild and the waste in a place of desolation only the devil could survive in, or Satan's worst enemies, the Angels of Light. The banks of the Jordan clanged and rang with the discordant instruments and singing of the masses all clamoring to get into the waters. News that a voice had announced that the startling figure who left the water had indeed been the Messiah had them praising the Lord, begging and weeping and hugging one another out of stark terror that they would not be allowed to repent before the end came scorching out of the eastern desert.

As John dunked another terrified believer into the muddy waters, he waited for the ear-shattering wail of the winged legions, the tongues of flame, and astride a mighty horse, the crowned and blinding figure of God's Arm in the form of Jesus the Christ sword in hand and poised for destruction of the unrepented. As he stood in the tepid waters, John's breaths were short and quick, his eyes flared toward the wilderness, and his heart pounded to a rhythm guided by the hope that God's Glory was now descending on the shoulders of this compelling man who called himself Jesus, the son of a carpenter from a Galilean village named Nazareth.